THOMAS CREEPER AND THE PURPLE CORPSE

J.R. Potter

with illustrations and lyrics by the author

Black Rose Writing | Texas

Cover illustration by Honie Beam, 202X, licensed exclusively by The Bright Agency: www.thebrightagency.com

The author grants the final approval for this literary material.

First printing

ISBN: 978-1-68513-213-2
PUBLISHED BY BLACK ROSE WRITING
www.blackrosewriting.com

Printed in the United States of America
Suggested Retail Price (SRP) $23.95

Thomas Creeper and the Purple Corpse is printed in Garamond

*As a planet-friendly publisher, Black Rose Writing does its best to eliminate unnecessary waste to reduce paper usage and energy costs, while never compromising the reading experience. As a result, the final word count vs. page count may not meet common expectations.

For Amy, who never doubted the magic in all of this even when I did.

And for all my great teachers and mentors through the years. Your kindness, wisdom, and *generosity of spirit* have inspired me to cultivate virtue like a vineyard in my soul.

Thomas Creeper and the Purple Corpse

"Seeing is the hardest and most helpful part. The truth, even when it hurts, has a healing in it, better than fiction or fantasy."

–Thomas Lynch, *Bodies in Motion and at Rest*

"Your composure is so brittle
And you hold yourself so well
Inside you cling to pieces
Of a broken carousel

Tonight these streets are heaving
With young hearts on the chase
We'll have this place on lockdown
It's here for you to taste . . ."

–Sam Fender, "You're Not the Only One"

The Morning Mooring
$2.50
GLOOMSBURY TEENS UNEARTH WONDERS!
Marvale Quarry Site of Discovery
Are Today's Teens Out of Control?
RESURGAM
JP 23
S.I.F.

Prologue

"I Want to Show You..."

He could sense the figure's presence before the sound of footsteps.

Ever since Eddie had awakened in the dank underground room reeking of rot and brine, all days and nights had formed an unbroken circle. Only the horrifying ritual—if that was what it could be called—separated any passage of time.

It always began the same way: the sense of someone else in the room, watching from some dark, invulnerable corner, muffling their breath; then came the crunch of footsteps, crossing the piles of broken things obscured by the darkness; finally, right when Eddie feared his heart might burst from terror—the bright orange spurt of a match—revealing the palest hand, a claw of black and splintered fingernails.

In the radius of that match-light that gave little warmth the mask would appear, floating forward, the silver turning a wavy amber. As the mask drew closer, Eddie could see the blank bar of a mouth, neither smiling nor frowning, cut into the bright metal. Only the eyes—wet, twinkling—peering out from two moon-slivered slats, revealed a curiosity almost feral.

"Tomorrow, Eddie Jones," the throaty voice would whisper, the cruel black eyes never blinking. "Tomorrow."

Before he could scream, or even move—his body had been tied to the chair with a greasy black rope thick as his wrist, the chair bolted to the floor—there would come the prick in his arm, like the sting of a yellow jacket, followed by the sickening slump out of consciousness.

My name is Eddie Jones, he would repeat over and over, whenever he woke to find himself still alive. Whatever he'd been drugged with made his thoughts stretch until they felt thin and diluted, like drops of ink in a giant glass of water. He had to get it right. He had to remember what to say to the police when they found him.

My name is Eddie Jones. I live in apartment 3C at Tide's End Apartments on Weiland Avenue. I'm a line cook at Sappy's Diner. My name is Eddie Jones . . .

But this time, waking from inner to outer darkness, he heard another voice crying out behind the damp walls:

Por favor! Ayúdame! Tienes que sacarme de aquí! Por favor!

Invisible gears. Churning in the reverberating chasm above his head. And the scream behind the walls dying to an inaudible nothing. Hours—*days?*—passing. The gears again, this time as loud as the churn of his empty stomach.

Then, all at once, the ceiling was on fire.

A piercing halo of light—a chandelier—ringed with candles, lowering down, illuminating the slick walls covered with mold and furry-looking moss. The light coming closer, blinding him like the sun, but not warm like the sun, not enough to stop the chattering of his teeth.

The chandelier stopping . . . a few feet from his head. The searing wax splattering down, scalding his forehead and eyebrows. His eyes adjusting, away from the pain of the light and the wax, to the ground, to the piles and piles of white things splattered with dark liquid. *Not bones! Shells! A mountain of shells spilling all around him.*

"Y-y-you don't have to do this! I can get you money! Please! I-I'll get you anything! Anything you want!"

A thin rod, poking out of the darkness, dripping with something.

A paintbrush.

And the cruel voice, no longer a whisper:

"Today, Eddie Jones! I want to show you my kingdom . . . my kingdom of forever!"

Part One:
Burning Shells

Chapter One
The Exploding Mailbox & An Occurrence on the Crosstown Bus

Thirteen-year-old Thomas Creeper dragged his fingers across the window of the Gloomsbury-Hampswich crosstown bus, tracing the beaded tracks of rain until they disappeared behind the rubber seals of the window frame. It was an ordinarily rainy day in Gloomsbury, Massachusetts, in the beginning of September, the time of year when you are either filled with schoolboy or schoolgirl promise at the possibility of a new year . . . or depressed at the slipping away of summer's bountiful buffet of freedom.

For mortician's apprentice and recently turned homeschool student Thomas Creeper, the first week of September arrived like a fresh corpse without any plastic sheet covering its face to brace the shock of its mortal wounds. It was pale, cold, devoid of all life. Thomas had become well-acquainted with the feeling, especially since Jeni Myers had left town.

He could still feel Jeni's letter balled up inside the sweaty inner pocket of his rain jacket. He'd read the letter three times that morning, but for some reason, he couldn't bring himself to throw it away.

At the beginning of summer, Thomas and Jeni had done the impossible: they thwarted the plans of an undead cult called the Sieve who'd haunted Gloomsbury for over a century, preying on its citizens from the shadows like mercurial wraiths. In the process the two friends had become each other's backbone and shield, a rock star team, and perhaps something more . . .

During Fourth of July fireworks at Town Beach, Thomas and Jeni had snuck off and found a secluded picnic table overlooking the shore. Since Gloomsbury didn't have a grand community center that wasn't falling down, or a park that wasn't infested with deadly sinkholes, Town Beach served as the meeting place for all special events.

Fortunately, the picnic table Thomas and Jeni had chosen didn't have many nasty, thigh-piercing splinters on it, a real rarity in Gloomsbury. After peeling away a few needle-sized gougers, and laying down a heavy wool blanket, they climbed on top. Trembling with awe, they watched as a barrage of rockets lit up Gloomsbury Bay, sending showering pops and fizzles all the way to Dyre Dunes, and out past the marshlands of swaying cattails that skirted Gloomsbury's vast shoreline.

At the grand finale Jeni leaned in, nestling her head in the crook of Thomas's neck. When she looked up again, in the explosion of green and purple light, Thomas saw a look that said maybe their decision to remain a "friend team"—as they'd christened their special relationship at the start of summer—wasn't the final word on the mysterious electricity that seemed to pull them closer and closer together.

But as the last rockets fizzled out over Gloomsbury Bay, Jeni looked away. Before Thomas could say anything, Jeni started harping over the latest act of destruction caused by her pyrotechnically-obsessed younger brother Arnold.

"He's really crossed the line this time, Thomas," Jeni moaned. "I mean . . . planting Jumping Jacks on my birthday cake instead of candles? I thought *that* was the limit." Jeni collapsed her face into her hands and made a sharp inhaling sound like she'd huffed a bunch of Vicks VapoRub. "Nope. Turns out he was just warming up."

While Jeni described in detail what the full payload of ten M-80s taped to the inside of a mailbox sounds like when it goes off at seven in the morning ("I almost swallowed my toothbrush, Thomas!"), Thomas peered down at the beach. He made sure he kept nodding his head so Jeni thought he was hanging on every word of her story, although disaster stories involving Arnold Myers were really nothing new.

A blinding beam of horizontal light had gone up across the shoreline. Thomas traced the light's source back to a pair of police patrol cars lined up along the boardwalk. Both cars had their high beams switched on, an attempt perhaps to keep people from getting tripped up in the beds of slimy kelp that washed ashore, or falling face-first into one of Gloomsbury's legendary Portuguese Man-o-Wars, what would mean a guaranteed ticket to the emergency room.

Thomas squinted his eyes. He could actually see Arnold Myers in the distance.

Arnold was standing down by the fireworks' launch pad on Gloomsbury Pier, as close to "the action" as the town Fire Marshal would allow. He sported his favorite glow-in-the-dark jacket, the one with the flames rippling up the back (what had caught Thomas's attention in the first place). The jacket was a gift from Captain Sparky's Firework Bonanza to all its VIP customers. For a few seconds Thomas watched Arnold stomp his feet and flap his arms up and down like an angry, glow-in-the-dark ostrich. He was arguing with someone, but whoever he was arguing with kept pointing back to the boardwalk. *Probably trying to tell them how to do their job*, thought Thomas, smirking a little.

" . . . and I can't believe my parents didn't even ground him either," Jeni continued, choking a corner of the wool blanket as if it were her little brother's neck. "It's totally unfair, Thomas. I miss *one* stupid Sunday family meal and the world's practically over. Arnold blows up the mailbox. Not to mention everything *inside* the mailbox . . ."

Thomas kept nodding. But he wasn't listening. Not really.

He was too busy watching a pair of men the size of football linebackers lift Arnold Myers up and deposit him—kicking and flailing—into a jumble of broken buoys and fishing nets. Had Thomas been paying attention, however, he might have heard something from Jeni's story, something that could have saved him a lot of heartache in the future. *Jeni was waiting to hear back about some big news*, news her pyromaniac brother may have turned to smoke and ash by blowing up the family's mailbox. If only Thomas had been paying attention.

The next six weeks slipped by in a miserable haze of lessons in the Preparing Room at Creeper & Sons Funeral Home, brightened here and there by short adventures with Jeni—trips to the library to see their favorite librarian, Ms. Katz, who they called Ms. K for short, and acrobatic walks along Shellburne Road's winding flood walls.

Though Thomas and Jeni had become local celebrities at the beginning of summer after discovering the bones of Thomas's ancestor Elijah Creeper the First and his reluctant co-conspirator James Hieronymus Sneed, any positive news in Gloomsbury didn't last long. The big feature on Thomas and Jeni that graced the cover of *The Morning Mooring*, the town's newspaper, was soon bundled up for kindling, or set down for dogs with leaky bladders to soil. Sometime around the beginning of August, a sapping mist blew in from the sea fed by Mad Marge, the horrible weather system that circled Gloomsbury. A sluggish torpor set into everyone's bones, eroding any happy thoughts or memories.

Then, in the last week of August, Jeni dropped the bombshell on Thomas.

They were scarfing down pizza at their favorite spot, Sal's Pizzeria, one of the few restaurants in Gloomsbury that didn't give you intestinal fireworks after eating. Jeni made use of the pause in conversation while they waited for Sal's sister Romana to bring the check.

Flashing her trademark Jeni Myers sarcastic smile, Jeni leaned across the table and broke the big news: she'd been selected from a list of over five thousand applicants to attend a prestigious U-16 soccer program in Germany. As it turned out, Jeni had been right; Arnold *had* blown up all the mail, including her acceptance letter to the program. Thankfully, the US coordinator had followed up two weeks later in an e-mail. Jeni would be leaving in a few days.

Thomas hadn't been paying close attention up to that point, having asked Jeni to join him at Sal's with the intent on asking her about "the look" from Fourth of July. When Jeni got to the critical part—how she would be gone for all of freshman year—Thomas bolted straight up in his seat.

"I-I don't get it," he stammered as a tidal wave of anger broke over him. He snatched a piece of crust from his plate and stabbed it at Jeni's face like a dagger. "How could you do this to me, Jen? You're going to leave me here with . . . with just my mom and my dad? And uncle Jed? How can you even say you're my friend?"

"Don't you see what a big deal this is for me, Thomas?" Jeni shot back. "Why are you being such a jerk? *You're* the one who's not being a friend."

When Thomas didn't offer any attempt at an apology, Jeni reached over and ripped the crust out of his hand. She dunked it down into Thomas's Pepsi, splattering soda all over his glasses. Even in all his rage, staring through corn syrup-slickened glasses, Thomas could see tears welling in Jeni's eyes. *Tears in his best friend's eyes.* He had gone too far.

He reached out for Jeni's hand . . . but Jeni slipped away, shouting, "Don't, Thomas!" She stormed out of the restaurant. The welcome bell on the door rattled so hard it jerked loose and clattered to the floor. All eyes turned to Thomas who sunk back into his booth, and hoped to keep sinking, until he was as tiny and insignificant as a flake of red pepper. If he were that small, he wouldn't feel any pain. He wouldn't feel anything at all.

A day later, Jeni sent Thomas an e-mail asking him to come with her to the airport the following morning. But Thomas, still raw from the whole incident at Sal's, never wrote back.

The letter postmarked from Germany arrived one week later.

The letter . . .

Thomas stared out the window of the Gloomsbury-Hampswich crosstown bus. He scowled at a passing billboard for Coconut Resorts showing a man and a woman with sun-bronzed skin cradling each other beneath a palm tree with the sun sinking in the background. Even stupid advertisements made him think of Jeni. *We've got a lot to see out in the world, Thomas,* Jeni had written in her letter. *I think we owe it to ourselves to go experience new things.* The real dagger words in the letter had been scribbled out. But it didn't take a budding detective and forensic wizard like Thomas Creeper to decipher them.

To go experience new things and meet new people.

There were only two other riders on the Gloomsbury-Hampswich crosstown bus that afternoon—only two *living* riders, that is.

To add to Thomas's extensive list of woes—he was the son and heir to a small town funeral business run by his rigid and cantankerous father, Elijah Creeper the Fifth; he was painfully tall, a lanky *lurch-a-saurus* who kids around town called "Creepy Thomas" when they were feeling nice—Thomas could also see the dead everywhere he went. Ever since solving the mystery of his great aunt Silvie's death earlier that summer, ghosts seemed to come out of the woodwork to accost Thomas who they considered a "Fixer," a solver of mysteries unresolved at the time of a person's death, or worse . . . their murder.

The only problem, as the ghost of his great aunt Silvie explained, was that in order to fix a ghost's unresolved case, Thomas needed to possess their "Artifact of Unlocking." An Artifact could be the missing revolver thrown into the ocean after their murder, or the loose nails from a faulty roof beam that shut off their lights forever.

Once an Artifact was recovered, a displeased ghost could then talk and indicate what the Fixer needed to do to help them find peace in the afterlife. But not possessing any of these items at present, Thomas was accompanied daily by ghosts who couldn't speak, but leered back at him with yawning mouths and writhing, apoplectic fingers. They knew neither day or night and respected no boundaries of privacy. A headless ghost dressed in a pinstripe suit had even slid under the stalls at the public restroom at Town Beach to seek out Thomas's services.

Thankfully, Thomas counted only two ghosts on the bus that afternoon: a child with sandy-blonde hair and half her face rotted away; and a soldier in faded blue military fatigues with sunken eyes who tried to get Thomas's attention, but every time he waved, he clutched his hand back to his neck, blood squirting out between his gloved fingers. It was horror outside or *inside* the bus, however Thomas looked—dumb advertisements for a life he would never have, or miserable reminders of the life he could not possibly extricate himself from without becoming a ghost himself . . . and even then there was no guarantee.

He resolved to keep his eyes shut. There was still a good ten minutes before they reached the museum. In the darkness behind his eyes he would be safe, he told himself. But as his horrible luck would have it, his peace of mind didn't last long.

"So you're the new Fixer, huh?"

Seated across from Thomas, next to a snoring older man with his head bowed into his lap, Thomas locked eyes with the slightly blue, slightly glowing face of a ghost, a woman.

She looked frozen somewhere in her late twenties, though being sunken-eyed and quite dead, it made it hard to accurately pinpoint her age. She sported a bob, a kind of short-cropped hairstyle that was fashionable back in the "roaring" years of the 1920s. As for her clothes, that was even more curious. She wore a high-waisted silver dress that seemed to Thomas as if it were made entirely out of shimmering fish scales. There were only two problems with the picture, however:

First, a large blood-stained unicorn head was thrust up through the center of the woman's stomach.

Secondly, and more importantly, ghosts couldn't talk, not without their Artifacts.

The ghost leaned in. The chill of the grave wafted off her body, enveloping Thomas. He lowered his head and gripped the hard plastic seat underneath him until his knuckles turned white.

"I'm Trixie," said the ghost, flashing Thomas a mischievous grin. It reminded Thomas of a painting of a fox he'd seen once on a restaurant wall. "You probably wanna know why I can talk, huh?"

Thomas made no move to answer. But, yes, he wanted to know that one major fact that was throwing everything he knew about being a Fixer—and it wasn't much—into total chaos.

"You won't have to search hard for it, my Artifact, if that's what's got you in such a tizzy," said Trixie. "I think it's why I still got the gift of gab. Carry it around with me wherever I go. Give ya a hint." The fox grin widened. "It's somewhere around . . ." Trixie made a slow, circular motion around her stomach. "Kind of in the vicinity of . . ."

"OKAY! ENOUGH!"

Thomas slouched down a few inches in his seat. In the rearview mirror he could see the bus driver, a burly man, barely squeezed into his uniform, staring back at him with both of his bushy eyebrows raised. Thomas cleared his throat nervously. Once he was sure the bus driver's eyes were fixed firmly back on the road, he whispered out of the corner of his mouth:

"It's the unicorn head coming out of your chest."

"Bingo, bango! They said you were good at your job. Now it'll just take a few minutes. We gotta get back to G-town. You see there was this merry-go-round . . . stupid name when you think about what happened to me . . . more like *impale-ya-round*, huh? Well, anyway, there's this deadbeat named Jefferson. Real *sonofa*—uh . . . swindler, I mean. He shoved me into this mythical freak-face 'cause I wouldn't . . . well, that's none of your business—"

"Sorry," said Thomas, cutting in. "I can't help you."

"You're joking, right?" A spasm passed over Trixie Wheelwright's undead face. It looked like she might have an aneurysm if she wasn't already a ghost. "You know how long it's been since we had a Fixer in Gloomsbury?"

The bus rattled to a halt. Thomas could see the verdigris copper roof of the H.F. Alderfer Museum of Antiquities up ahead. Spiked wrought-iron gates circled the museum's grounds, and large purple flags majestic as sails fluttered outside the entrance announcing the latest exhibition—*Wonder before the Fall: Roman Antiquities from Republic to Empire.* Thomas snatched his backpack and leapt up from his seat, ignoring the gurgle of blood coming from the neck of the soldier ghost that exploded over two old ladies with identically sour-looking faces. Thankfully, the blood was invisible to them. Thomas made his way to the bus door, but as he stepped down onto the curb, he found himself face to face once again with a bloody unicorn head.

"Forty-seven," said Trixie. "Yep! I did the math. It's been forty-seven years since we had a Fixer. I'll make you a deal, Terrence—"

"Thomas."

"Thought I got it wrong. You can't trust those Death Gypsies in Gloomsbury Cemetery. Can you believe they don't even care if anyone finds their Artifacts? All they want to do is sing about horses and caravans and sh . . . er . . . stuff. Anyway, point is, you help me, I help you. Whaddaya say? Help you run through your other cases lickety-split?"

"I don't *have* any other cases. Wait, you can talk to other ghosts? How can you—"

Thomas looked up. The burly bus driver was glaring back at him from his seat with wide, incredulous eyes. Thomas faked a little laugh and shrugged his shoulders. The driver shook his head, muttering something under his breath about "the kid's on drugs," before jerking the bus's accordion doors shut with a loud *TH-WHACK.*

"Thanks for that, by the way," said Thomas, touching his nose to make sure it hadn't been pinched off by the door. "Now even the bus driver thinks I'm a psycho."

"You still haven't answered me, bub." Trixie took out a nail file from a pocket in her dress and proceeded to file her gray nails. "We got a deal or not?"

Thomas walked straight through Trixie. The nerve-numbing chill that had become all too familiar rushed through him. It was like standing in the eye of some Arctic ice storm. He shook off the chill and padded his way up the cobblestone path to the museum's gates, keeping his head down as he went, chin to chest, trying his best to ignore the ghost's shouts behind him.

"Fine! No sweat! I'll just be standing here with a freakin' unicorn head coming out of my stomach! No big deal!"

• • •

It took Thomas only a few seconds inside the museum to reconfirm how much he hated the town of Hampswich.

He hated Hampswich in a completely different way than he hated Gloomsbury with its few days of sunlight a year, and its scores of sluggish citizens deprived of nourishing Vitamin D, each one clinging to their sinking homes and teetering stilt-shacks like human barnacles in what seemed like a death wish to outlast the town's incredible inclemency.

No, Thomas Creeper hated Hampswich for the exact opposite reason.

Because everyone and everything in Hampswich was so obnoxiously cheery.

Even the rain seemed to have picked sides between Gloomsbury and Hampswich, dying to a refreshing sprinkle the moment they crossed over the Rhode Island State Line. Standing in the middle of the museum's rotunda-shaped entrance hall, Thomas could see—*feel*—warm sunlight radiating down through stained glass windows that looked like they belonged in some medieval French cathedral. Had he been anywhere in Gloomsbury, even at the slightest rumor of a sun sighting, he would have heard cars crashing into each other or grinding to halts in the middle of intersections. He would have turned to find some mother of four, emerging from her minivan, forgetting the yogurt plastered to the back window, her jaw open wide like a Neanderthal beholding the gift of fire for the first time. But no one seemed to pay the sunshine any mind in Hampswich.

And that was because they were all so full of sunshine themselves.

Even the ghosts—and Thomas counted at least six as he walked in—seemed perfectly at ease, no one posturing with writhing fingers or wailing mouths. If there was some great resolution they were seeking to their purgatorial existence, they didn't seem in any particular hurry to resolve it.

"Welcome, handsome!" a dulcet voice like a clarinet intoned from across the gleaming foyer.

At first, Thomas was confused. No one had ever used those exact words to describe *him* before. He'd been called a rash of other names—Corpse Boy, Zombie Prick, Lurch Jr.—but nothing ever kind or even remotely complimentary.

He squinted his eyes, searching the room until he noticed a woman waving back at him from behind a large, ornately-carved desk. Cautiously, still expecting an ambush, he approached the desk. A sign written in flowery penmanship had been attached to the desk's front panel. Thomas mouthed the words silently to himself.

Information . . . and Inspiration!

"And how are we on this glorious day?"

The woman behind the desk leaned in closer. She was an exuberant redhead with flushed cheeks. A pair of half-moon-shaped reading glasses sat propped up on her long, swan-like nose. With every word she seemed to beam the full force of her joy down upon Thomas.

"Might I interest you in an audio tour of the latest exhibition narrated by Hampswich's own master thespian, Reginald Merriweather Foster? Or perhaps an information brochure? They really are quite edifying."

Thomas grumbled something approximating "thank you" and took the brochure from the woman's gloved fingers, handling the neatly folded pages as if carrying a death note dipped in anthrax. Retreating a few steps from the information desk, he stopped. He peered back over his shoulder. It was at that moment he beheld a sight as disturbing as seeing a disemboweled poltergeist silently clutching their entrails.

The woman at the desk was still smiling back at him.

She gave Thomas a final wave before going back to staring at the door as if counting down the seconds until the next museumgoer strode in. Thomas shook his head and followed a small tour group under a marble archway into a room bristling with light.

Had he stumbled into an alternate universe? It was like nothing he'd seen before, in real life or in the movies. In the center of the large atrium stood a massive fountain trumpeting plumes of bright water. Arrayed around the fountain were sweet-smelling flowers of all shapes and colors. Two long rows of Corinthian columns stretched the length of the room, narrowing to a point at the far end where a small stage rose with a white grand piano glistening like an opened seashell.

Seated at the piano was a thin grasshopper of a man wearing a white tuxedo with tails. As he fluttered his fingers up and down the keyboard, the notes seemed to echo the soft splashes coming from the fountain. Thomas peered up at the ceiling, his mouth widening with wonder. A dome of amber-colored glass stretched between the columns like a balloon that had been convinced to settle. Through the glass panes soft light the color of honey fell on the room and the faces of the museumgoers who chatted quietly amongst themselves, or reclined in white wicker chairs with glasses of iced tea or sparkling water from the small café. It all made you catch your breath. But for Thomas it also rankled the feeling he already felt for Hampswich because he knew—beyond any shadow of doubt—that no one could truly appreciate such lightness and beauty unless they had grown up in a place so ugly, so starkly contrasted to Hampswich as Gloomsbury Township.

As for the exhibit itself, no expense had been spared. There was an entire room full of Roman coins suspended behind glass panels. The glass bubbled up over each coin, magnifying the faces of the Roman emperors, making them pop out and hold your gaze as if they were alive. The assignment Thomas had been given by his mother, a former teacher at Gloomsbury High, was to sketch three coins from three different eras in Rome's history from republic to empire. He would then have to note the distinguishing features that placed the coins in their respective eras—which emperor's face was on the front, and what was the intended effect of how each Roman ruler was portrayed.

Thomas had read about how the emperor Hadrian had worn a beard, what many historians believe was a reflection of the emperor's love of Greece and its famous philosophers who all sported thick beards. Sure enough, Thomas found a coin from the 2nd century C.E. depicting the bearded emperor Hadrian. Unlike other Roman rulers, Hadrian had been well-liked during his lifetime. Thomas had read all about the treacherous and illicit life of the emperor Nero, how he had his own mother murdered and had even used taxes from the Roman people to pay for his "tour" of Greece where he presented himself as the world's greatest musician. Now *that* was a true villain, thought Thomas. Sketching Nero's coin, with his slightly sneering mouth and troll-like nose, it wasn't hard for him to imagine that this was a person rumored to have set fire to his own kingdom . . . and then sat quietly strumming his lyre as everything burned to ashes.

Perhaps the most famous object on loan to the museum for the exhibition was the *Lupa Capitolina*, the Capitoline Wolf, an Etruscan bronze statue of the wolf that allegedly suckled the two children of Mars, Romulus and Remus, after they were pushed down the Tiber River, washing up on the future site of Rome.

Thomas's mother had seen the picture of the statue in an article in *The Morning Mooring*, what had started Thomas's homeschooling assignment in the first place. For the second part of his assignment Thomas was asked to try to draw conclusions about the Etruscans as a people after studying the Capitoline Wolf. Gazing at the statue placed on a large marble dais in the center of the room, Thomas twiddled his pencil back and forth between his pointer and middle finger. He scratched the back of his neck. *What was he supposed to make of the statue?* That the Etruscans were really into myths, especially ones involving wolves that didn't mind being milked?

"The tots were added later. Much later, in fact," a voice like dry newspaper crackled behind Thomas's left ear.

Thomas whirled around. Standing behind him, leaning on a slender cane, was a grizzled old man in a night-blue suit. He had a face like something left at the end of a fruit and nut bowl, with sagging, red-veined cheeks and thin lips that curled away to drooping lines on either side of his chin like a ventriloquist's doll. Boxy tinted glasses circled his balding head, hiding his eyes. Pinned to his left breast pocket was a bright red button with the word GUIDE in bold letters. The old man stepped forward, tapping his cane in front of him as he hunched and hunkered along.

"I'm wondering . . . hmmm . . . yes, yes," he rasped, leaning on his cane and inhaling deeply. "You have the faintest smell of formaldehyde combined with salt air. Unless you are a taxidermist—which we haven't had around here for years—it means you are one of eight people."

Thomas shook his head. "I-I'm sorry?"

"There are two funeral homes in the surrounding area," said the old man, tapping his cane against the marble floor. "The Creepers in Gloomsbury and the Chesters here in Hampswich. Unless you are the daughter Margaret Chester, who has recently and rather miraculously experienced a lowering in her pre-pubescent voice, you must be Thomas Creeper, the boy who found the bones of James Sneed and your ancestor, Elijah Creeper."

Thomas's pulse quickened a few beats.

"How . . . how did you know all that?"

The old man let out a hoarse chuckle.

"I wasn't a tour guide my whole life, my boy. Nor was I born blind. In fact, I have the peculiar skill of being able to recall much of this world before my untimely accident. To *visualize* everything, if you like." The old man tapped the side of his wrinkled skull with a finger. "Right here in this fossilized globe. Which is why I repeat to you that the statue in front of you is a *pastiche*."

"A pa—what?"

"A piecemeal. A *mélange* of different periods. The two suckling, murderous runts were added later in the Renaissance. An attempt to humanize the story, perhaps? Not a very charming one. Brother kills brother to plant his flag into a molehill? But, there you go. The birth of Rome!"

"Who are you?" Thomas blurted out and immediately felt embarrassed. "I'm sorry, I meant—"

"Why don't we say this," said the old man, sliding a hand into his jacket pocket. "If you can solve the riddle of who *I* am, just as I solved the riddle of who *you* are, Thomas Creeper, then maybe I'll teach you what I know: to see beyond the obvious, into a realm where the fragments of truth may be gathered and illuminated like wondrous fireflies!"

With these last words the old man's smile upturned a little. Thomas felt a shiver go through him. It wasn't the bone-chill of a ghost, more like the thrill of hearing something uttered at the start of a horror film that promised lots of unexpected plot twists and heaps of gore.

The old man removed his hand from the folds of his pocket. When the hand came forward again, there was something fanned between the wrinkled fingers.

A small white card.

"To become a detective, Thomas Creeper—and that's what led you to those skeletons, is it not?—one must possess a sincere love for puzzles, puzzles the rest of the world has neither the skill, nor should we say the *intestinal fortitude* to stomach."

Thomas bit his lip. He considered the card. *What was the harm?* Sure, the old man was a bit of a wacko. But he was right. Thomas did love puzzles. And whoever the old man was, he was obviously very good at "visualizing" things because he was able to figure out who Thomas was in less than thirty seconds without being able to actually see him. Plus, even if he was one of the criminals who popped up on the morning news with the dark-rimmed eyes and stubbly cheeks, it wasn't like he was going to be able to surprise Thomas from the bushes. His blindness was still an irrefutable fact, whatever his peculiar talent for "visualizing" things might be.

Thomas reached out his hand. As his fingers closed over the card, he recoiled and jumped back.

Poking up from the old man's sleeve came a little pink nose.

The whiskered nose wrinkled, sniffing the air expectantly.

"My apologies," sighed the old man. "That's Ipso. Can't leave home without him, I'm afraid. His brother Facto, on the other hand, can't be bothered to roll over unless there's food involved. They're trained Icelandic rats. A wonderful diversion for an old coot like myself."

The small black rat took one last peek at the outside word before disappearing back into the safety of the sleeve.

Thomas took the card from the old man's hand and held it up to his glasses. In the center of the card was a delicate pen and ink drawing of a shell wreathed with flames.

Above the flaming shell was a set of embossed initials done in heavy letterpress:

B.A.C.S.

Thomas turned the card over. There was nothing on the back, no other information, no address or telephone number, only the shell and the four initials. Before he could open his mouth to ask what he was supposed to make of the nondescript card, a woman wearing a floppy raincoat and a plastic rain veil ran over to them, shouting and waving a large map over her head. She sounded terribly distressed, like someone about to miss their connecting flight at an airport they'd never visited before.

"Pardon me! Pardon me!" the woman squawked. "Would you be able to direct me to the death mask of Ful . . . Ful . . ." The woman shook her head, stumbling over the words. "Fulvius Marcius Cinta? Is that right?"

"One of my favorites," exclaimed the old man. "The last captured twitchings of a gladiator who enjoyed having the fingerbones of his victims whittled down and turned into cutlery."

The woman gasped and held a gloved hand to her throat.

"I'm being dramatic, of course," said the old man, letting out another hearty chuckle. "They never proved that. But I did. That's neither here nor there, however. This way to the death mask!"

The old man turned away. After a couple clicks of his cane down the hallway, he stopped. Turning his head back around in Thomas's direction, he smiled strangely and made a slight bow. Then, straightening up and turning around, he resumed his tapping march towards the death mask, the woman in the rain veil trailing close behind.

Thomas stood dumbstruck, watching the old man go. Holding the card up to his face, he wondered:

Who in the world had he just met?

Chapter Two
"Open Me"

Thomas stepped down off the bus onto the rain-swept cobblestones, clanging reminders they'd arrived back in the Land of Pale Flesh and Sorrow—Gloomsbury Township.

Thankfully, the bus driver had been switched for the return trip, so there was no replay of the awkward curbside drama regarding Thomas's perceived insanity or drug use.

An even greater coup was that no other undead passengers had crossed Thomas's field of vision the whole return trip. If they were there, Thomas didn't see them, for his eyes had been glued to the white card clenched tightly in his hand. His mind swam with the blind tour guide's offer. *If you can solve the riddle of who I am, just as I solved the riddle of who you are, Thomas Creeper, then maybe I'll teach you what I know . . .*

The bus roared away, spitting noxious fumes that wafted up, merging with the foggy night air. Thomas coughed into his sleeve and crossed over Weiland Avenue, the main thoroughfare in Old Town, Gloomsbury. He made a sharp right turn onto Thirty-Third Street, pausing beneath the checkered black-and-white awning of Gloomsbury Treats. For a few chilly moments he watched his breath materialize and dematerialize in front of his nose. Sinking temperatures had settled in about town, although it wouldn't be officially autumn for a few more weeks. To make matters worse, the rain that had winnowed to a fine mist in Hampswich had switched back to fat, globby drops upon the return to Gloomsbury. Thomas listened to the raindrops pelting the awning above his head while he cleared his lenses with his thumb. Setting the glasses back on his pinched, very un-Romanesque nose, he mustered his courage and resumed his miserable march back to the funeral home.

He hadn't gone more than a few paces, however, when through the soupy gloom he spied a most welcomed sight.

"You're up early!"

Bounding out of the fog and rain, sprung a massive dog, a wolfhound. The wolfhound rushed to Thomas's side and circled for a few moments, prancing on its hind legs and wagging its tail like the propeller on a prop plane. There were a couple strange things about the dog, though only Thomas could see them. For starters, the dog glowed a queasy, unnaturally green hue; secondly, there were several bullet holes across the dog's side where eerie ectoplasmic light shone through.

"Hiya, Finn," said Thomas, flashing a rare smile. He made a scratching motion around the ghost-dog's ears. If anyone peeking out their upstairs window were to look out at that exact moment, it would have looked like Thomas was tickling the air. The scratching routine was a habit Thomas had fallen into, and though he never felt any real fur—only a slight prickly numbness at the tips of his fingers—his supernatural companion seemed to relish the attention all the same.

Fingal, whose name Thomas had shortened to Finn, had been a parting gift from Thomas's great aunt Silvie, right before she "transmigrated" out of her painful existence into what Thomas could only assume was a good afterlife by the last look she gave him, a look of total release and relaxation.

Because no one except Thomas could see Finn, the dog was the epitome of a constant companion. He would sit in the spare chair at the dentist's office while Thomas got a tooth pulled, or lay at Thomas's feet while Thomas's father flew into another impromptu lecture about the "disgraced state of funerary science" ever since that "firebrand tart Jessica Mitford wrote that trash heap of a book *The American Way of Death*" (Mr. Creeper was famously cantankerous).

Finn was a great friend, and, perhaps more than ever since Jeni had left for Germany, a friend was what Thomas Creeper needed the most.

And so, haunted boy and haunting beast made their way up Thirty-Third onto Thayer, Thomas's street. Hitting the corner, Finn let out a low growl, arching his shoulders into attack position. Thomas was about to tell Finn to knock it off, when out of the corner of his eye he spied the glow of something leaning against the post office box. Seeing the shimmering dress and the tip of a unicorn horn, Thomas didn't stop walking or bother to look up.

"Leave me alone."

"Well, you're making me want to with the way you're acting. Do you know there's another Fixer in Gloomsbury? Yep. Heard about him today over in Hampswich. He's a little older than you. Doesn't seem to mind taking on new cases, either."

Thomas stopped dead in his tracks. *Another Fixer?* A weird sensation—not necessarily fear, not necessarily jealousy—flooded through him. Having no poker face, as Jeni constantly reminded him, he realized he hadn't hidden his emotions from Trixie. Even with his glasses starting to blur over again from all the rain and fog, he could see the fox grin leering back at him.

"Oh yeah," Trixie beamed, strutting forward, her pale baby's bottom chin raised in victory. "And I bet he's a lot nicer."

"Great. Go bother him."

Trixie frowned. Her reverse psychology tactics weren't working. "Listen, Creeper." She sucked in an exasperated breath and ran to catch up with Thomas. As she came closer, Finn let out another throaty growl. Trixie jumped back a few feet. "Hey, what's with the pooch? Your sidekick or somethin'?"

"He's my great aunt Silvie's dog," said Thomas. "She's a ghost. I mean, she *was* a ghost. She gave Finn to me after I—"

"SO YOU DID HELP HER!" Trixie clapped a hand over her frost-blue lips. "I knew it. So you only help fix ghosts in your own family, is that it?"

Thomas had reached his boiling point. He had tried being polite . . . He had tried shaking off Trixie like a bloodsucking mosquito . . . He had tried everything, everything but to tell her to get lost. The hour for pleasantries was over.

"Listen! I told you already!" he barked, waving his hands up and down like a conductor with irritable bowel syndrome. "I can't help you! I'm not your Fixer! And you can tell that to every freakin' ghost you know! I'm not here to . . . to fix all your crappy lives!"

His temples pounded. He could feel his heart lodged somewhere up near his throat. And he knew who he sounded like. An image of his father scowling with his gold-rimmed glasses flashed in Thomas's brain. *He needed Jeni.* He needed her to tell him to "Chill out, professor." One hopeful look from Jeni Myers could make the invisible straightjacket of fear and anxiety Thomas felt tightening around him loosen its stranglehold.

"Hold on, Creeper."

Trixie reached out for Thomas's shoulder—the motion went right through the arm, of course. Thomas winced from the death-chill. When he opened his eyes again, he could see the fox grin had vanished. A depressed look fell over Trixie's undead face.

"I was lying what I said about that guy Jefferson."

Trixie turned away. She stared off into the misting street. "You know that deadbeat I told you about? He's not a deadbeat at all, Thomas. He was my fiancé, and he didn't . . . you know . . . kill me. It was an accident. We were going too fast, holding hands between our two horses. But then the merry-go-round—*God,* I hate that name—well, it tipped over and everything crashed. Jefferson tried to hold onto me . . . but I went flying into the next horse . . ."

Trixie pointed down at the blood-stained unicorn head.

"This sharp little monster. Next thing I know the cheesy wind-up music is starting to fade . . . and I'm looking up at Jefferson standing over me screaming for somebody to get a doctor. I don't think he ever forgave himself, even though it was the carnival's fault. Somebody forgot to check the bolts or something. Could've happened to anyone, I guess. I was hoping since . . . well, I didn't want to say anything before . . . but I saw you reading that letter and crying that maybe—"

"You what?" Thomas leapt back. His fingers balled into fists. "You were stalking me?"

Trixie shrugged. "C'mon, Creeper. What do you think we ghosts do?"

"GET AWAY FROM ME!" Thomas stabbed a finger at Trixie's pale face. "STAY AWAY FROM ME AND STAY AWAY FROM MY HOUSE!"

"Wait! Hold on!"

Trixie watched him go. She shook her head and let out a big sigh, which only made a few spurts of blood gurgle up from the wound in her chest, further staining her pretty party dress.

"I was trying to say," she whispered. "That you of all people should understand, Thomas Creeper. Because you've been in love too."

• • •

Thomas let his book bag slide off his fingers onto the dusty carpet of the funeral home foyer. He stared in horror at the monstrosity hanging on the coat rack in front of his face. It was frilled and fringy. And it was lime-green.

It was a lime-green tuxedo.

"Bet it fits like a glove," a voice cackled from the Viewing Room. "Got the mothballs out of it and everything, Tommy Boy."

Thomas's eyes narrowed. Seated with his back to the door on a maroon couch in the Viewing Room was a person who could make Thomas's fists clench without uttering a single word. And because this person was family, and not just family—but part of the family *business*—it was impossible to go more than a few days without running into him. Jedidiah Creeper, Thomas's uncle, who everyone called Jed, was the reason why people shouted "Uncle!" whenever they were pinned to the carpet, or when the fine hairs on their forearms got pinched.

What Uncle Jed lacked in Thomas's father's acidic temperament, he made up for in poking fun at people whenever he could. He wore a half-mask over his face like the Phantom of the Opera to cover up scars from a napalm explosion during the Vietnam War. And it was this half-masked face that Thomas had come to loathe since his earliest days, days full of fun games for children like "Bloody Knuckles" and "I Bet You Can't Flush the Whole Roll Down the Toilet."

Thomas stared back at the lime-green monstrosity on the rack. A dry cleaning tag was clipped to one of the jacket's lapels. "What is it, Jed?" Thomas called over his shoulder. "Why does she have it out?"

Jed snickered, but gave no answer. Instead, he swiveled back to his portable radio broadcasting the latest shady, off-track betting race from Long Island. He was following the progress of "Bixby," the greyhound he owned with his duplicitous associate, a man named Green, who rolled up to the funeral home once a month in a whale-sized white Cadillac with red wall tires to give Jed his "take" from the winnings. Thomas never knew if Green was the man's first or last name, only that he smoked disgusting cigars that further stunk up the musty, old funeral home. Jed would then promptly spend his take from Bixby's earnings within a day or two, which would have him knocking, sure as clockwork, on Thomas's father's door for yet another family loan.

"There you are, sweetie. How was the museum?"

Adele Creeper, Thomas's mother, made tiny bird-like steps across the dim foyer. A pair of oversized oven mitts covered her bony hands, and her rapidly graying hair was tied up in a bun that further pulled back the skin on her gaunt face.

The first impression one might have of Thomas's mother was probably "sandwich," in that she needed to eat one.

While Mrs. Creeper labored day in and day out to keep her son and husband vitally nourished so they could perform their important tasks around the funeral home, she often forgot to do the same for herself. She was a relentless *giver*, pure of heart, sound of mind. If it could be said that Thomas's father had no heart at all, Thomas's mother's heart was so big it probably took up the entire circumference of her frail, bird-like chest.

"Did you see the Capitoline Wolf and the twins? Was there a huge line?"

"Yes," Thomas sighed out of one corner of his mouth. He was still eying the lime-green tuxedo as if it were a deadly boa constrictor ready to suffocate him. The gaze did not escape his mother.

"Ah! What a relic for Thomas Creeper, famous relic hunter."

Jed snickered from the Viewing Room.

Thomas gritted his teeth.

"I . . . already . . . *have* . . . a tuxedo . . . Mom."

"Oh, this isn't for funerals, sweetie," Mrs. Creeper beamed. "It's a Dancer Plus."

"Yeah, Tommy Boy! A Dancer Plus!" the Viewing Room mimicked back.

Mrs. Creeper's face darkened for a moment, though her smile never slipped. "It used to belong to your father's cousin. You remember Cousin Morrie, don't you?"

"GOOD OLD SLOBBERING COUSIN MORRIE!"

"Ignore him," said Mrs. Creeper. She raised her voice and shouted back at the Viewing Room so the whole house could hear. "HE'S OBVIOUSLY ALREADY IN HIS CUPS!"

To this insult—like all insults that retained a grain of truth to them—Jedidiah Creeper said nothing.

Mrs. Creeper turned back to the tuxedo. Her expression now changed to a look of pure adoration, her green eyes glowing almost as bright as the fabric hanging in front of her.

"This particular model is called a *Bravado*. They were all the rage back in the 50s. Cousin Morrie, before he went—"

"CANS LIKE A SHOWGIRL!"

"BEFORE HE STARTED HAVING WEIGHT PROBLEMS!" Mrs. Creeper shouted back. "He was quite a slender Casanova like you, Thomas. I already matched it with your work tuxedo. A perfect fit."

"Fit? Fit for what?"

"For your ballroom dancing class tomorrow, sweetie. I thought . . . well . . . since your friend Jeni left town . . . you might want to . . . you know . . . get out and spend a little time with other people . . . people your own age."

Thomas glanced over at the Viewing Room. He could no longer see the banded backside of his uncle's head because it was buried deep in his lap, bowled over from laughter.

Shaking his head, muttering under his breath, Thomas pushed past his mother while Uncle Jed roared louder than the cheers coming from his radio. Mrs. Creeper watched her son for a few moments before looking down with a confused expression, realizing for the first time that her hands were still gloved in oven mitts.

Thomas snatched a chicken leg off a casserole plate on the kitchen counter. He began gnawing viciously at the leg, as if intent on murdering the already dead chicken. It hadn't been the best day. Far from it. If Uncle Jed was here and not throwing back drinks at the Longshoreman's Pub, it could only mean one thing:

They had a delivery.

Thomas's "night class," as his father now referred to his training, was back in session.

The last session had been a five-hour exploration through the art of "detecting and concealing the persistent and concomitant effects of disease in necrotic tissue." While Thomas was still not allowed by state regulations to perform any major embalming himself without a license, there was no regulation against him *observing* his father perform such squeamish and stomach-curdling tasks.

A firm believer in on-the-job training and an absolute despiser of "this world of endless waivers and red tape," Mr. Creeper often fudged the rules to save the final, more cosmetic—though no less ghastly—steps of preparing a corpse for his son and sole apprentice. These final steps could include such lovely procedures as toenail filing and "cottoning down the corpse"—a procedure where cotton balls are placed in the lining of the cheeks to give the appearance of good health. Thomas could only imagine what tonight's class would yield.

Thomas tossed the cleaned chicken bone in the trash and washed his hands in the sink. In the closet in the hallway he found his medical smock, newly washed and reeking of its usual blend of bleach mixed with formaldehyde. Sighing with every fiber of his being, he fit his arms into the starchy sleeves. From a cardboard box on a shelf in the closet he removed a pair of vinyl gloves and a medical mask. Behind him he could hear his mother and Uncle Jed continuing their argument—Jed accusing Mrs. Creeper of poisoning him with food that made him "lose an hour of his day every morning in the bathroom," and Thomas's mother inquiring whether the loss was not in fact related to the "boilermakers he drank like they were going out of style at Sappy's Diner, combined with a diet consisting of all things fried." Thomas ignored the sound of something being slammed in the Viewing Room and walked over to the Preparing Room door.

He put on his gloves and mask and took a deep breath. Once he felt ready—and he was never ready to set eyes on a corpse—he turned the cold brass knob and opened the door, leaving behind one strange space of the house for a far stranger one.

Inside he found his father bent over a long metal table called the cooling board, already at work on the first stage of embalming—arterial embalming. At the click of the door, Mr. Creeper turned his head a few inches, nodding slightly, before turning back to his meticulous handiwork.

"Who is it?" Thomas asked in a feeble voice.

A stark beam of cold white light shone down on the cooling board, illuminating the silvery gleam of the mortician's tools. In the beam's glow Thomas saw an old woman laying on her back, mostly covered by a medical sheet—mostly. Thomas's father had already repositioned the corpse back into normal repose, though the look of terror plastered across the old woman's face was not so easily replaced. It was a face Thomas recognized in a heartbeat, a face that was often just a set of narrowed eyes and a hawkish nose, peering out at him from between parted blinds while the sound of a dozen hair dryers roared behind the glass.

It was Debbie "Bunny" Earnshaw, owner of Shampoo n' Shears, Gloomsbury's only ladies salon.

Thomas made a hesitant step towards the cooling board. "What happened?" he whispered.

"I was hoping *you* could tell me that, Elijah Thomas."

Mr. Creeper stepped away from the cooling board. With a swoop of his arm, he brandished a large, empty syringe. Thomas shuddered. He hated "pop quiz time." He wondered why the room was called the Preparing Room since his father rarely ever gave him any warning before launching into a merciless round of questions ("Elijah Thomas, if the intestine has been ruptured by the bullet, how do you propose preventing excess fluid from leaking?"; "Thomas, if the eyeball is missing, do you sew up the ocular cavity immediately or inquire from the family about a prosthetic facsimile?"). If it was a normal everyday problem, Thomas could soundboard the issue with Jeni. But Jeni was gone. In the Preparing Room it was always a question of death, not life.

Thomas swallowed hard into his chest. He could taste the remains of the chicken leg fighting its way back up. He moved closer, examining the corpse for clues. He reached out with a trembling hand and turned one cold palm over, then the next. Hands were often the best indicators of trauma, he knew. Falling victims or victims of violent attacks usually held out their hands to ward off the blow. But there was nothing indicating a fall or attack on Mrs. Earnshaw's hands. He could hear his father's wheezy, nostril-heavy breathing behind him, another caustic lecture already simmering on his lips. *Thomas, the body at death tells us everything. It's a biological mirror, reflecting all cause and effect, don't you see?*

He was supposed to see . . . but he didn't.

He chewed the side of his lip. There was one secret skill he could count on, one last resort in these tense situations that could save him from a tongue-lashing by Elijah Creeper the Fifth.

He could see the dead.

And he most certainly could see Mrs. Earnshaw.

Her ghost had appeared through the tiles in the wall the moment Thomas touched her frigid hands. She was watching Thomas with a terrified look, hovering in the shadows beneath the framed copy of the Funeral Service Oath. Thomas knew the Oath by heart. He and his late brother David had been forced to repeat it, line by line, word for word, as soon as they could form sentences.

I do solemnly swear by that which I hold most sacred;
That I shall be loyal to the Funeral Service Profession,
And just and generous to its members;
That I shall not let the constant relationship
And familiarity with death give me cause
To yield to carelessness or to violate
My obligation to society or to the dignity
Of my profession . . .

There was a sharp *whack* of metal on metal.

Thomas snapped back to reality. He didn't need to look up to know that it was his father calling time on the pop quiz with a whack of his gold-rimmed glasses.

He stared down at the cooling board. A purplish-brown bruise ran the length from Mrs. Earnshaw's neck all the way down to her right clavicle. He peered back at her ghost, ignoring his father's reddening face, his claw-like hands already raised as if to say, "Well! Out with it!" *No bruises on her hands*, Thomas mused, glancing back and forth from Mrs. Earnshaw's corpse to her ghost who was now clutching the back of her neck with Pepto Bismol-pink painted fingernails. The clues crystallized in Thomas's brain and not a second too soon. *No bruises on her hands . . . because she fell backwards.*

"She fell," said Thomas weakly. "Backwards . . . I think."

"You think?" Mr. Creeper shot back, though Thomas could tell by the sound of his voice that he was smiling behind his mask.

"No," said Thomas with a little more confidence. "I know."

A bony hand clapped against Thomas's back.

"Well done, sir!" exclaimed Mr. Creeper. "Well done, indeed! Of course, you missed several other clues. Obvious ones, really. The elbows, for example. Did you not see the stitching? Oh, well. All's the same. Well done, Elijah Thomas."

Thomas turned to go.

"Not so fast," said Mr. Creeper, shaking a large syringe in the air. "Grab your pen and notebook. I will make use of your keen eye in logging Stage Two."

Thomas hated—no, *reviled* was the right word—Stage Two, the aspiration and preservation of the body's many inner cavities. The remains of the chicken leg started to come back up in his throat. He fought it back down . . . barely.

Mr. Creeper held up his gloved hands. "Well? Shall we begin? Unless you'd like to spend the entire night yawning over the cooling board, hmmm?"

Thomas walked over to the sink, ignoring Mrs. Earnshaw gaping at him from the corner like a fish out of water. He found his clipboard and removed the pen from the clip.

"First order of business," Mr. Creeper began. He paused and made a swift nod with his chin to Thomas.

"First order of business," Thomas repeated back in a monotone voice sapped of all earthly joy.

"To commence aspiration, insert trocar into first site of removal, beginning with the abdomen . . ."

• • •

Around eleven-thirty that night, after recording every disturbing detail of Stage Two, Thomas was dismissed. Trudging up the creaking steps to his bedroom, he felt like a prisoner of war who'd been finally set free, but only after having to bury all of his companions.

It was a lousy life. The brief warming period he'd experienced with his father at the beginning of summer after Thomas and Jeni had recovered the two skeletons of Elijah Creeper the First and James Hieronymus Sneed had cooled along with the sinking temperatures.

A recent complaint on the funeral home lodged by the Fipps family, cousins to the Creepers' ancestral enemies the Sneeds, had snowballed into a lawsuit that made Thomas's father's brief season of kindness and congeniality a thing of the past. Old habits die hard. And in a cursed funeral home like Creeper & Sons, in a cursed town like Gloomsbury, Massachusetts, they die the hardest deaths.

Thomas collapsed into his springy desk chair. One of the only positives that hadn't disappeared with the return of his father's corrosive mood was that Mr. Creeper had given Thomas the funeral home's old business computer after upgrading to a new laptop.

At first, Mr. Creeper had believed he'd swindled the Best Buy salesman because of a misquote uncovered between the computer's online price and the price posted in the store. Karma, however, can often be instant as the late great John Lennon once sang. Not really understanding how to operate his new laptop that included a fancy touch screen that could be detached as a tablet, Mr. Creeper felt outsmarted, and thus, all the more swindled.

Thomas clicked the mouse. The old desktop computer blinked on. He hadn't closed out his e-mail from his last session, which he always tried to do in the event one of his parents snuck into his room to snoop around. Not surprisingly, there was no new message from Jeni in his inbox. Thomas couldn't blame her. After all, he'd ignored her request to come to the airport. And her letter spelled everything out in black and white.

Thomas scrolled down through the screen, checking off the spam mail, deleting the offers for muscle-enhancing Power Milk and a request for a twelve-million-dollar money transfer from a Nigerian prince who somehow knew Thomas by name. At the last unread message, he stopped.

The words "Open Me" shone in the subject line.

What was more curious—what had stopped Thomas from dumping the e-mail immediately into the trash folder—was the sender's name.

Fulvius Marcius Cinta.

Thomas scrunched up his face. *Where had he heard that name before?*

He sank back into his desk chair and searched his memory. He pushed aside the recent images of gurgling trocars and tear-stained letters that haunted his conscious thoughts (and probably his unconscious ones too, if he was to be honest).

He closed his eyes and relaxed his shoulders. Ever since he'd formed the Bond, the powerful human-to-ghost connection with his great Aunt Silvie, he could feel a change rustling within him. It was . . . what was it like? *Like leaves upturning right before a storm.* That was the best way he could describe it. He could access things differently now than when his powers first revealed themselves at the beginning of summer, as if his selective photographic memory was somehow getting a super boost from—who could say? It was a mystery, perhaps the greatest mystery he'd yet to unravel. He tried to settle his nerves. That was the way to call the powers into motion. He closed his eyes. He breathed in and out several times. *Nothing.* He stretched his neck and inhaled and exhaled another deep breath. *Still nothing.*

Then, little by little, in the shuttered darkness behind his eyelids something peculiar started to happen.

The darkness receded. Now Thomas could feel light bursting all around him—flashing and pulsing around his neck and ears, warming him down to his core. Beneath the cocoon of light he could feel cool marble running under the soles of his feet. Inside his mind's eye an image blurred and crystallized into view: *a long marble hallway filled with circles of sparkling glass.* A hazy figure staggered into the light, their shadow darkening the glass circles as they passed. Thomas watched the figure move, closer and closer, though their face remained hidden, covered by a wide collar and . . .

A plastic rain veil.

Thomas's eyes flashed open. *The lady at the museum!* She'd asked the tour guide where she could find the death mask of a gladiator . . . a gladiator named Fulvius Marcius Cinta. A weird mood stole over Thomas as he reached forward with his trembling finger and clicked on the message.

A new window flashed open on the computer screen. Inside the window was a blank gray frame with an icon of a camera in the center. Thomas clicked on the camera and a video began buffering. It took a few moments because of the house's slow Wi-Fi, but soon the video started to play. At first, all Thomas saw was impenetrable blackness. Nothing moved, not the slightest stir. Then, from somewhere deep in the void, a voice cried out:

Down here! Please! Help me! Somebody help me!

Thomas's shoulders stiffened. A grinding sound like some great rusty machine winding up drowned out the wailing, helpless voice. A ring of light moved past the camera's eye—a chandelier—filled with flickering candles. The chandelier went *down, down, down*, until suddenly it stopped. In one of the gaps between the chandelier's arms Thomas could see a face.

The face of a man staring up at him, screaming.

Chapter Three

Butterflies & Strange Flotsam

The next morning Thomas awoke twisted in his own bedsheets. Whatever his dreams had been, they must have been nightmares, for when he opened his eyes, he found his sheets tangled around both fists. He had a faint memory of some helpless voice screaming back at him from the bottom of a dark, dank well. And chains—chains and gears all slithering and clanging around.

He snatched his glasses off the chest of drawers next to his bed and peered across the room. On his desk his computer screen flickered white light. The video was still frozen on the monitor, the screaming man's face staring back at Thomas, contorted in a look of pure terror.

He slid out of bed and barefooted his way over the cold floorboards to his desk. Trying his best not to look at the man on the screen, he punched the power button. The monitor zapped out. Chewing the side of his lip, he began pacing back and forth across the dusty bedroom floor. *What should he do?* He knew the right thing was to call the police, let them see the evidence of the crime. *Was it a crime?* Surely, no one could be so deranged to stage something *that* horrible. Going to the police meant involving Sheriff Korvin, someone Thomas didn't exactly have a perfect record with.

Thomas's heart thumped wildly against his ribs. He covered his face with his hands. He wanted to block out everything—the video, the lawsuit, his father back to his old, malevolent ways; his mother wasting away again, not eating and not talking about David's death. It all circled his head like a murder of ravenous crows, each one pecking at him, never letting up.

The sound of a car horn blaring outside broke through the tumult of Thomas's brain. As if reeling from one nightmare to the next, he remembered what day it was. *Saturday! The ballroom dancing class!* And the horror didn't end there.

Uncle Jed was supposed to drive him.

Flying down the rickety steps to the foyer, ready to unload on whatever poor soul crossed his path, he stopped short at the last step.

There it was, draped across the banister, already out of its dry-cleaning bag, ready to shock the world.

The lime-green tuxedo.

"Hurry! You're gonna be late!"

Like some Class-A poltergeist, Mrs. Creeper appeared out of a patch of shadows. She thrust the tuxedo into Thomas's arms. Thomas made the mistake of inhaling. Immediately, he started gagging and choking on dry-cleaning fumes mixed with years and years of mothball stench.

"Go change in the Study while your father's out! Hurry up, Elijah Thomas!"

Though Thomas's mother looked like the wind might blow her over at any moment, with the right determination, she was a force to be reckoned with. Thomas felt two small hands as sturdy as meat hooks propel him through the opened door to the Funeral Director's Study.

"No ifs, ands, or buts," Mrs. Creeper added, jerking the door shut. "That's a use of the Oxford Comma in a series, by the way.

We'll talk about that at your next lesson. Now get dressed before Jed has the whole neighborhood up in arms from all his honking."

Thomas stood speechless for a few moments, gripping the lime-green *Bravado.* Above him, on the wood-paneled walls of the Study, he could feel the pitiless stares of his ancestors—the Elijahs—glowering down from their portraits. Cursing all Fate, Family, and Circumstance, Thomas began fitting his legs and arms into the tuxedo like a starched straight-jacket. The cleaners had done nothing to defuse the disgusting mothball smell. *How long would his dance partner last with her arms wrapped around a mothballed stink bomb?*

Surfacing back into the hallway a minute later, he arrived just in time to hear another stream of ear-splitting honks coming from the street.

"One of these days," seethed Mrs. Creeper, straightening Thomas's bowtie. "I'm going to slip something into his coffee. That's foreshadowing, by the way."

"No, Mom," said Thomas glumly. "That's murder."

Mrs. Creeper smiled: a brief rush of color, flooding her pale face. Planting a kiss on Thomas's cheek, she grabbed him by the wrist and dragged him out the open doorway seeping with the smell of damp earth and rotting wood.

"Make new friends!"

The door slammed, knocking a cup's worth of cold rain off the eaves and down onto Thomas's forehead. Wiping the splatter from his glasses, he sighed into his mothballed collar.

It was going to be a miserable mess of a day.

• • •

Before being taken over by Edgemont Brindle and his dance partner Fiona Marsh in the mid-1990s, the building housing Brindle & Marsh Ballroom Academy had served as Gloomsbury's only working slaughterhouse.

After surviving the climb up the steep gravel driveway overgrown with man-sized cattails and poisonous scabber weed, new students walking into Brindle & Marsh would find themselves assaulted by a total sonic blitz from waltzes like Strauss's "Blue Danube" and Brahms's *Liebeslieder*, cranked to ear-splitting decibels. Once death by classical music had been ruled out, a pervasive stench would waft up out of nowhere, curling in through the nostrils, forcing out all thoughts but one:

Run away.

Many believed the stench that got whipped up and churned by every cha-cha and promenade was the ghost of pounds and pounds of ground beef. Others maintained that it was Madame Marsh's potent perfume that skunked about her sumptuous frame, joining and marrying with the plumes of smoke from the lipstick-stained cigarette that always dangled precariously between her pointer and middle finger. Her eyes were wild with delight today, her bright pink wig shaking like a poodle caught in a ceiling fan.

"You are all iridescent butterflies! Flutter, flutter, my darlings! Shake out your wings in the morning sun—*ACK*! *ACK*!"

Thomas watched out of the corner of his eye as Madame Marsh collapsed onto her stool positioned in the middle of her rickety stage overlooking the ballroom. The elderly dance teacher flew into a coughing fit—her fifth Thomas counted since he'd been dropped off at the dance studio. Unable to shake off the phlegmy fit, Madame Marsh now tried a more direct approach:

Beating her chest with her microphone.

The feedback was tremendous. Thomas covered his ears. Perhaps the greatest miracle that morning was that through all her hacking and spasming, Madame Marsh's cigarette never slipped once. This proved a blessing for everyone. The faded sashes and banners pinned to the dance instructor's wobbly stage, heralding victories from dance competitions over fifty years ago, were all most likely highly flammable.

Holding onto his dance partner—a girl who'd introduced herself at the start of class as Daphne Muldroon before letting out the world's longest gasp as she took in the full impact of Thomas's lime-green *Bravado*—Thomas tried to maintain his focus, but he knew he was about one more wrong step away from getting elbowed in the stomach.

Of the four couples paired that afternoon, Thomas and Daphne were clearly the worst. Mr. Brindle, a rectangularly-jawed man in his early sixties with bleached teeth and a fondness for clothes the color of smoked salmon, had placed the names of all the female dancers inside his greasy fedora. When it came Thomas's turn to choose a partner from the hat, his fingers kept sticking to all the scraps of paper due to the residue left by layers of hair pomade the dance teacher slathered over his scalp every morning. Had anyone made a close inspection, however, they would have noticed that Edgemont Brindle had about as much hair as a newborn baby.

While Madame Marsh barked the directions for the class's next lesson—the box step, the secret ingredient to any proper waltz—Thomas quickly realized that cruel Fate had meddled in the sorting of the pairs.

The three other couples were far quicker learners than Thomas and Daphne, or at least they were better paired *physically*. Thomas was already pushing six feet, while Daphne was small and frail. She wore a scrunchy lilac dress that clashed painfully (and rather audibly) with Thomas's vintage *Bravado*. Her bulging, terror-stricken eyes seemed to widen with every misstep by Thomas, which happened about every other three. For every step Thomas made as the waltz's lead, Daphne was supposed to do the opposite—move backwards in counter-motion. But because of their incredible physical mismatch, their box step was more like a circular stumble.

"Ouch! Stop stepping on me," Daphne hissed through clenched teeth. "You're horrible at this."

"Sorry," said Thomas, cursing and backing into another couple and breaking up what looked like a romantic moment. The girl's partner glared at Thomas, looking like he might draw blood. Thomas forced a fake chuckle, and spun Daphne away.

"I couldn't sleep last night," Thomas continued, leaning closer to Daphne's ear. "I was . . ." He stopped himself. He knew that however much Daphne hated his dancing, she was probably even less likely to believe his story about receiving the horrifying e-mail with the video of the screaming man. After all, she didn't exactly exude sympathy.

"Sick . . . all night," Thomas wheezed after Daphne elbowed him in the tender part of his thigh. "You know . . . praying to the porcelain goddess? Hehe?"

Daphne cast Thomas a terrified look like his hair had just caught fire. Thomas grimaced. He didn't know why another one of Uncle Jed's sayings had popped into his brain. He made a mental note to do a better job of tuning out his uncle who his mother had once called "an embarrassment to embarrassment."

The overhead music clicked off, or rather the needle on the record that had been playing *Vienna to Havana: A Treasury of Dance from Waltz to Tango* skidded off its last track.

Madame Marsh collapsed onto her stool and flung a sopping rag over her forehead. Though her face remained hidden by the rag, she seemed mesmerized by some fond memory from the past—waving her cigarette in the air like a conductor's baton, following the bars of music only she seemed to hear in her head. There was a long, awkward silence. The four couples looked at each other, wondering what to do. Thomas wiped his palms against his pant legs. Daphne focused her froggy eyes on a spot high up in the ceiling.

Suddenly, over Daphne's shoulder, Thomas saw it and gasped.

A phantom hand, gloved in white, was slowly emerging out of a poster on the far wall.

The gloved hand appeared under a particularly sensitive spot in the spread-eagle leap by the famous ballet dancer Mikhail Baryshnikov. As the hand reached forward, it became an arm—an arm wrapped in black and white pinstripe cloth. Thomas slapped his hand over his mouth.

"*Oh god*," said Daphne, backing up a few feet. "You're not gonna like . . . barf on me . . . are you?"

As a full body emerged from the poster—minus the head, for it was curiously missing—Thomas recognized who it belonged to.

Thomas called him "the banker" because he'd never seen anyone else wear pinstripe suits except for the executives at Gloomsbury Mutual who handled all the loans for the funeral home. He was also the same ghost who'd slid under the bathroom stall to accost Thomas at Town Beach. He was slim and short and relatively normal-looking . . . until your eyes came to the starched white collar where a piece of bloody vertebra peeked out like something a dog might want to gnaw.

As Mr. Brindle stepped forward and opened his mouth, the headless banker-ghost passed through him like a supernatural breeze, causing the dance teacher to hiccup loudly. When Mr. Brindle noticed the entire room staring back at him, he flashed a bleached smile, and in a voice grasping for an authentic English accent (but failing to obtain it) exclaimed:

"Let us take a brief reprieve, shall we? I've prepared an afternoon tea of finger sandwiches and kale tea. Perfect for digestion. Remember, healthy digestion means healthy movement . . . inside and out!"

Thomas wondered if he really was going to be sick.

The headless banker-ghost stopped in front of Daphne Muldroon who was standing with her arms crossed, looking about as happy as someone awaiting a root canal. As the pinstriped ghost floated forward—forward and *through* Daphne—she made a squiggly motion with her hips as if someone had dumped a glass of ice water down her back. Catching sight of the impromptu hip-squiggle, Mr. Brindle clapped his hands.

"Very good, Daphne. The Havanese Rhumba! Now let me show you. It goes like this. A one and a two and a three . . ."

Thomas took advantage of the momentary distraction to leave both the headless banker-ghost and his miserable partner in the dust.

Ducking his head behind an air shaft, he followed the rest of the pairs through a door that led out to a small antechamber off the side of the slaughterhouse turned ballroom. As he passed through the door, he could hear Daphne's protests echo through the drafty ballroom.

"I'm serious, Mr. Brindle. I just got chilled. You want me to do what? Imagine my spine's been removed?"

In the next room the students found a small buffet set out for them on a table covered with a yellow tablecloth, or mostly yellow from all the stains. Thomas peered around the freezing room. From the looks of it, he figured the boxcar-shaped room with dented metal walls must have been the slaughterhouse's meat cooler long ago. A few rusted meat hooks still hung in the rafters, though they no longer held dripping porterhouses or ham hocks, but dangling ribbons of flypaper filled with dozens of dead flies.

About as unappetizing as the flypaper was the food itself. Thomas soon discovered that by "finger sandwiches" Mr. Brindle hadn't meant little cucumber or pâté morsels with the crusts cut off, but fish sticks gobbed in tartar sauce that was already starting to turn an unnatural shade of green.

Thomas set down his plate feeling a queasy gurgle erupt in his throat. He was about to reach for a packet of crackers—there was no way he was going near the kale tea that smelled like boiled socks—when his hand glanced off a pale arm that happened to be reaching down at the same exact moment.

"*Zut alors!*" a heavily-accented voice called out. "*Zat* is the second time you *bumpered* me!"

Thomas blinked his eyes. Standing in front of him was a tall girl, almost as tall as Thomas himself, though not nearly as spindly and pale. She wore a bright yellow dress with the hem designed to mimic an upside down flower, petals and all. She had dark brown hair, with bangs and feathery swoops at her temples that curled about her small ears that looked slightly pointed like an elf's. Her black eyebrows narrowed to sharp slivers, but the way her lips seemed forced down in a scowl of mock outrage—combined with the twinkle of delight in her eyes—suggested that the girl was holding back a wave of laughter.

"I-I'm sorry," Thomas stammered, blushing a little. He scrunched up his face, trying to recall the girl's strange accusation. "What did I do to you . . . exactly?"

"You *bumpered* me!" the girl repeated, pointing a finger painted with a purplish-black lacquer at Thomas's face. There was a moment of confusion where it seemed anything could happen. Then the girl's expression changed completely. She let out a spritely laugh and covered her mouth.

"How do you say it?" said the girl, snapping her fingers several times. "It is not *bumpered?*"

Now Thomas remembered. She was the girl he'd backed into on the dance floor. *Backed his bony butt right into her.* He felt his stomach lurch. He wanted to run out of the room and hide behind some rotting hedge.

"We say bumped," he said in a weak, quavering voice.

"*Mon Dieu*," said the girl. "My mother will be angered with me for not listening to my tutor—"

"Angry," said Thomas, though he was speaking to himself. The girl had been pulled away by her partner—the same boy who'd glared at Thomas on the dance floor.

He was what Uncle Jed would call "built like a brick (something with an expletive) house."

His neck formed a broad square in the center of his muscular shoulders, and there was a piece of his lip missing like a little divot. Instead of making him look strange or abnormal, the divot only made him look more tough.

As the older boy pulled his dance partner in the yellow dress back to the circle of other couples, he let go of her hand. Then, still keeping his eyes deadlocked on Thomas, he went over to the wall. Thomas did his best not to look like he was watching the boy's every movement. Unwrapping a packet of crackers from the table, he started chewing nervously. Out of the corner of his eye he could see the older boy sneering at him—a sneer full of unhealthy, strawberry jam-colored gums. Slowly, making sure Thomas could see him, the brickhouse boy reached up to a posterboard and pulled off a thumb tack from a flyer. Thomas winced, choking on dry cracker crumbs. With a shaking hand, he reached down and ladled some ice water into a dirty rocks glass and took a deep swig. When he looked up again the older boy was still scowling back at him from across the room. Thomas understood the thumb tack's warning:

Keep your distance.

"Now what are you doing? You're *so* weird."

Thomas turned to see Daphne Muldroon peering up at him with bulging, unblinking eyes.

Thomas choked on cracker dust.

A gloved hand had appeared, poking out of the center of Daphne's chest. Daphne wiggled violently as the death-chill flooded through her. Choking, unable to contain his shock any longer, Thomas spit out a mouthful of cracker and ice water mash all over Daphne's face.

The afternoon didn't get much better from there.

• • •

Not waiting around to suffer any more ridicule, as soon as class was over Thomas slipped out the back door.

Carefully, he footed his way down through a slippery tangle of sand and scabber weed, following the distant roar of the ocean which would act as his compass to get home. The beach would take him back to Old Town, and from there he could walk the rest of the way to Creeper & Sons. He was glad he'd had the foresight to tell Jed he wanted to walk home from dance class. A bit of salt air and time alone to walk off the after-shocks of the miserable afternoon was just what he needed.

He looked down at one of his jacket sleeves. A splotch of brown discolored the garish green fabric.

Blood.

For the last lesson—the foxtrot—Thomas had been switched to a new partner, Gabriella Marsh, Madame Marsh's own niece, after Daphne never resurfaced from trying to clean herself up in the bathroom. Thomas was thankful for that little act of mercy.

He wasn't sure if he could look Daphne Muldroon in the eye again. At least being homeschooled there was no chance he'd run into her in the hallways at school.

Gabriella turned out to be an extremely gifted dancer and a better match physically for Thomas's height. Hearing about the vomiting incident, however, she kept straining her head a foot away from Thomas like a car whiplash victim. As Madame Marsh barked out instructions for the promenade, the final step in the foxtrot, disaster struck.

Thomas made two short steps towards Gabriella, but on the penultimate move—the crucial *side-step*—he came too close once again to the tall girl in the yellow dress with the thick accent (French, Thomas was certain of it now) and her brickhouse partner.

Thomas felt the tack go through his sleeve, a sharp jab like a wasp's stinger. Because of the deafening music no one heard Thomas cry out. On the next turn the older boy leaned in, flashing his disgusting gums and snarling in Thomas's ear:

"That's for you, Creeper! We're gonna drain you! You and your whole family! You messed up! No one messes with the Fipps family!"

It all made sense now.

The lawsuit. The whole reason why the funeral home was in turmoil.

Thomas knew only bits and pieces of what he'd overheard eavesdropping on his parents' arguments behind the door of the Funeral Director's Study. Something about a faulty casket, one of Creeper & Sons' more expensive models, a Thermolux Repositor.

The Fipps family usually hired Chester Family Funeral Home in Hampswich, but August had been an unnaturally bad month for deaths in the area, so they'd been forced to acquire the services of Creeper & Sons. Apparently, the family had found the casket of the widow Eleanor Fipps tilted vertically all the way up in the dirt the day after the funeral.

With the widow's hand hanging out.

A wealthy relative of the Fipps had gifted the Thermolux for Eleanor's funeral, while the rest of her family had purchased the grave plot. The only problem was that Eleanor Fipps's plot sat on the edge of Gloomsbury Memorial Cemetery, an area known to house some of the town's most notorious sinkholes.

Thirty years ago a particularly fearsome sinkhole residents dubbed "The Great Evaporator" had swallowed up four tombstones and sunk an entire mausoleum. It didn't matter to the Fipps. When the same thing happened to Eleanor Fipps's grave they blamed Creeper & Sons for everything. The Fipps family didn't have a lot of money, but it didn't matter. They were Sneed cousins. With a Sneed family lawyer on their side, Charlie Fipps's family was gunning to sink Creeper & Sons Funeral Services once and for all.

Thomas continued his gloomy march away from the dance studio. After a few minutes of slogging and sliding down the sandy path, he came to a series of bluffs where the sea grass grew tall and wild. A splintered wire-and-wood fence ran through the grass, but it was stamped down in one section, a victim perhaps of the Nor'easter that had hit Gloomsbury a few years, dumping three feet of snow in a single night. Thomas swung his long legs over the break in the fence and made his way down, parting the long grass with his cold fingers and trying not to fall on his face.

He didn't need to look over his shoulder to know the headless banker-ghost was nearby.

He'd seen the ghost ooze through a water stain in the side of the dance studio at the end of class. In a weird way, Thomas didn't mind the ghost stalking him that much. As long as the Fipps boy from dance class wasn't hunting him, he could deal with ghosts.

A few minutes later, after some more careful slogging, Thomas reached the sandy floor of the beach. To his right, the shoreline rose in a dense maze of barnacled rocks and sea drift—crimson filamentous algae; spiral and bladder wrack; a felty green fungus called dead man's fingers that looked like what popped out of the dirt in zombie movies. Thomas knew that way led to Marvale's kelp forest and nature preserve, as well as the ruins of the old limestone quarry Thomas, Jeni, and the seafaring Mulvaney's Raiders had barely escaped from with their lives intact earlier that summer.

Thomas turned left, heading in the direction of Gloomsbury's Town Beach. In the distance he could see the outcropping of brick buildings rising above the bluffs—St. Mary's by the Sea, the church Thomas's family attended, and the stooped, salt-brined shacks of Old Town, Gloomsbury.

He hadn't made it more than a half dozen steps, however, when a thickly-accented voice called out behind him:

"*Arrêtes!* Slow down, *Monsieur Bumper!*"

Thomas wheeled around. He blinked his eyes. It was the exotic girl from dance class, Charlie Fipps's dance partner! Her bangs were all flipped up from running, and there was a breathless look about her. A navy blue peacoat covered her yellow petal dress with the collar turned up. As she caught up to Thomas, she paused, panting in a Wonder Woman-style stance, her arms making triangles with her hips.

For a few awkward seconds neither one of them said anything. The girl set her jaw in another look of mock outrage. When a strained gasp escaped her lips, they both broke down into a fit of laughter. Even Thomas could feel his lips curling up all the way to the corners of his cold cheeks.

"I am called Marylène," said the girl, extending a hand with purple painted nails. "Don't worry about *Char-lie*. That boy is *fou*. Crazy, you say."

Thomas took Marylène's hand. It felt cool and soft in his.

"I'm Thomas."

"I don't feel like going home," said Marylène, brushing her bangs out of her eyes. "Will you permit me to join your walk?"

Thomas had never received such a formal invitation by a girl before. Formalities and translations aside, he was happy to have some company that wasn't supernatural for a change.

"Sure," said Thomas, still smiling.

They turned and started walking down the shoreline.

As they walked on, every now and then they had to jump back to keep from getting soaked by the pummeling waves. A few times Thomas spied the headless banker-ghost lingering at the edge of his vision. The first time the ghost was standing next to an obelisk of balanced stones some passerby had made; the second time he was peeking—if a headless ghost could indeed peek—out from behind a splintered fishing troller that had nothing left but its rusted hull. Thomas was thankful Marylène was oblivious to the ghost. He did his best, even with his horrible "poker face," not to give any indication he saw anything out of the ordinary. They kept on walking.

As they headed down the beach, Marylène explained in broken English how her family had moved to Marvale from France because of her father's work in biology. Her father was studying a rare phenomenon—migrating "sea fireflies"—that had for no explainable reason begun a journey halfway around the world, spawning and respawning in a brilliant path of light.

"They are *Japany*," said Marylène, shivering and drawing her collar tighter around her neck.

"Japanese," Thomas corrected.

"*Oui, oui, pardon.* Japanese," said Marylène. "But that is not what is so *bizarre*, Thomas. *Mon père* . . . my father . . . he says they are following something. Something big!"

Marylène stopped walking.

"What do you think they're following?" asked Thomas, glancing up and locking eyes with Marylène. When Marylène didn't break the stare, he looked shyly away.

"*Un calamar géant*," said Marylène.

"I'm sorry," said Thomas. "I don't understand."

"*Un calamar*," Marylène repeated, snapping her fingers.

Thomas rolled the word over in his head. "Cal . . . Calamari? You mean like a squid?" Just then a wave crashed too close, soaking Thomas's left shoe. He reached down and pulled off the shoe and shook it a couple of times. "They're following a giant squid?"

"*Mais oui*," said Marylène. "*Zat* is it. A giant squid."

Thomas fit his ankle back into his shoe. He tried to piece together Marylène's strange story. She was right. It was indeed *bizarre*.

"And you say these things following the giant squid . . . they're called sea fireflies?"

Marylène shook her bangs. "Not flies . . . *non, non. Crevettes*."

Marylène looked at Thomas for confirmation, but Thomas shrugged his shoulders. Marylène frowned and bit the side of her lip. Then her face lit up as the translation dawned on her.

"Shrimp! These are shrimp, Thomas . . . But they glow. They glow like magic!"

Thomas had no clue what the girl was talking about. It did sound quite magical, though. *Sea fireflies? A giant squid?* If only Mulvaney's Raiders were still around. They'd know what to do, maybe even be able to help Marylène's father with his research.

They resumed their walk. After a long and thoughtful silence, broken here and there by the crash of the waves, Thomas piped up.

"And your father . . . he thinks these shrimp are coming here? To Gloomsbury?"

Marylène shrugged her shoulders. "*Je ne sais pas.* He has a *dessin* . . . a drawing. In the kitchen. *Les crevettes* . . . the shrimp . . . they are moving fast, Thomas. Maybe they will *bumper* us."

Marylène giggled. Thomas opened his mouth to correct her, but he shut up as soon as he saw Marylène side-eying him with her fine eyebrows arched in a ridiculous expression.

"Yeah," said Thomas, laughing a little. "Maybe they will *bumper* us."

• • •

They walked on through the sinking light that grew fainter and fainter, until even the glare of Thomas's *Bravado* got sucked up and absorbed by the deepening gloom.

Thomas and Marylène chatted about their different but equally strange school lives. Marylène was also studying from home, as it turned out, assisting her father for a few months as part of the biology portion of her baccalaureate exam, or "bac" as she called it.

Thomas told Marylène about the funeral home and his parents' plan for him to take over Creeper & Sons someday after he passed his state licensing exams. As Thomas described the new lawsuit with the Fipps, how the Fipps did something sneaky by switching the grave plot at the last minute and then blaming

Thomas's family when the sinkhole swallowed the casket, Marylène made a sour face.

"I knew it," said Marylène. "*Char-lie* and his family. They are crazy people."

"Yep," sighed Thomas. "Pretty crazy."

They'd come to the spot outside Town Beach where the old carnival midway used to stretch nearly a century ago. Any traces of light Mad Marge had allowed to seep through the gloom were rapidly fading. Standing in front of the ink-black surf, Marylène turned into a rough caricature of a shadow wrapped in a dark peacoat. Thomas could still make out her pale face. For a long time he didn't say anything, just watched Marylène's playful expression while the wind whipped her hair around, and the surf seethed in and out—

The scream from Marylène's lips shook Thomas out of his reverie.

"What? What's wrong?"

"Behind you, Thomas!" Marylène turned her head away, shielding her eyes. "Over there! In the stones!"

At first, Thomas didn't see what Marylène was screaming about. Then, little by little, his eyes adjusted.

He stared down at the jumble of rocks that acted as a flood wall for Town Beach. The rocks were covered with barnacles and festooned with whatever the tide had dragged in: torn fishing nets, unrecycled plastic, and . . .

Thomas choked on salt air.

There was an arm—an arm and a hand—not glowing or translucent like a ghost's hand.

A human hand.

The fingers clawed up from the tangle of seaweed and flotsam, stiff and gnarled, like a twisted branch. Thomas could see the outline of a shoulder, curving out of a bed of kelp. He felt every cell in his body start to panic. His temples pounded with white-hot blood. A voice in his head—*his* voice—screamed for him to run away. But he didn't run.

Instead, like some chemical speeding through every vein in his bloodstream, a weird fascination stole over him. He inched closer to the arm and knelt down. He could hear Marylène taking off down the beach, screaming for help, but the screams sounded far away—as if Marylène was shouting from the waking side of a nightmare.

That's when he saw it.

The strange purple color.

It wasn't the bloated-blue of a drowned body like he'd seen so many times in the Preparing Room. This arm was bright purple, and everything connected to it—everything Thomas could see—was purple too.

Chapter Four
The P.B.O.U.D.

In the drafty hallway of the Gloomsbury Sheriff's Office, Thomas listened to the heated conversation going on behind the window above his head.

He could hear Marylène's voice behind the glass, rising and falling in tremorous pitch as she recounted to Sheriff Korvin the discovery of the body tangled up in the flood wall at Town Beach.

There were long pauses in Marylène's story—either from confusion on the sheriff's part over a word in French, or Marylène's own heavy sobbing.

Thomas felt a terrible pang of sadness for Marylène. Though he was by no means comfortable around dead bodies, they were the daily business of living in a working funeral home. The strange purple corpse tangled up in the sea wall at Town Beach was probably the first dead body Marylène had ever seen.

The conversation had turned into an all-out interrogation. *As if we had anything to do with it!* Thomas wanted to scream up at the window. He found himself thinking back to the beginning of summer when he and Jeni had materialized in the early wisps of morning light, dragging the missing skeletons of Elijah Creeper and James Hieronymus Sneed across Town Beach.

Sheriff Korvin had been the first official to arrive on the beach following Thomas and Jeni's discovery. Thomas hated the visit Korvin had made to Creeper & Sons the next day. He hated his little notepad, the way his darting eyes roved over him suspiciously for forty-five minutes ("So you just barged into the quarry? You didn't think the sign 'No Trespassing' applied to you, eh?").

It didn't help either that the sheriff's son Gary had a famous hatred for Thomas. The last Thomas had heard of Gary he'd been shipped off to a military school in Pennsylvania for "swirling" a fellow student so badly that the poor freshman needed mouth-to-mouth resuscitation. Thomas felt as bad for the swirled boy as he did for whoever had given him toilet water mouth-to-mouth.

Thomas gripped the cold metal of his chair until his knuckles turned an even whiter shade of pale. He wondered if there was some kind of trick going on. It felt like some horrible conspiracy. *Why had they been escorted back to the Sheriff's Office in separate cars? And why had Korvin asked to speak to them one at a time?*

Behind the office window there came a thunderous slam.

"ZAT IS ALL I KNOW, MONSIEUR KORVIN! LAISSEZ-MOI! I WANT TO SPEAK TO MY FATHER!"

"Calm down, Ms. Gaumont. We've already called your father. He's on his way. Now just a few more questions. Calm down . . ."

But it was more than a few questions. The interrogation rattled on for another ten minutes during which Marylène went from inconsolable to outraged. There were several pointed words barked behind the glass—words Thomas could only assume, not knowing French, were nasty swear words. At least the thought of Sheriff Korvin getting chewed out in another language made Thomas feel a little better, though his amusement didn't last long.

A dreadful thought like an Arnold Myers firecracker exploded in his brain:

His parents would have expected him back home hours ago!

Frantically, he scoured the hallway for a telephone. Through an open office door across the hallway he could see one sitting on an empty desk. It was one of the older models, with several fat buttons blinking action on other lines. He could make a quick call, not explain everything, but enough so his parents would call off any search party in progress.

He was about to sneak over to the other room when a figure strode in from the shadows at the far end of the hall and proceeded to seat himself directly across from Thomas.

He was an older boy—sixteen, maybe seventeen, Thomas wagered. A perverse humor surrounded the boy's whole being: his facial features, his body language, the kind of comic impishness you find in daredevils and practical jokers. His hair was long and jet-black, pulled back over his ears, and a peppered ring of stubble circled his slightly sneering mouth. He wore a turtleneck the color of cabernet wine underneath a black leather jacket that reminded Thomas of the bomber jackets worn by fighter pilots in the WWII documentary he'd seen in History class in eighth grade.

And then there were the gloves.

Thomas could never remember seeing any teenager he knew wear leather gloves, let alone *inside* a building. While Thomas tried his best to ignore him, the older boy proceeded to drum his gloved fingers against his pants, looking left and right down the hallway, as if the experience of waiting a measly few seconds was the most boring thing that had ever happened in his entire life. Flashing a smile full of small, ferret-like teeth, the older boy leaned forward, and whispered across the room to Thomas:

"Give you three guesses."

Thomas looked around the room for a few seconds until he realized the older boy was talking to him.

"I *said* I'll give you three guesses."

"What?"

"Three guesses. C'mon. You look like chess club material. It'll be fun."

Now Thomas was certain that whoever the older boy was, he was probably at the police station for doing something criminal.

Thomas sank back in his chair. He tilted his ear up towards the glass. He was trying to hear if Marylène had come up with any swear words to call Korvin in English this time.

There was a sound of crinkling leather from across the room. The older boy shifted in his seat. Out of the corner of his eye, Thomas spied the spine of a book poking out from one of the pockets in the leather jacket. There was a strange pattern running up and down the spine—little silver triangles with silver dots set inside them. A memory started to dislodge from somewhere deep in Thomas's brain. He closed his eyes. Whatever the memory was in the back of his mind it was all fuzzy—like looking through a window thick with frost. *Where had he seen a book like that before?*

"Fine, hoss. Shut me out. You're no fun," the older boy said, shaking his head in exaggerated disgust. "The name's Cyril, by the way. Cyril Barnes. And I'm the other—"

"Look!" Thomas shot back, opening his eyes and whipping his head around. "I don't care who you are! So why don't you—"

But when Thomas heard the word *Fixer* come out of the older boy's mouth, he shut up immediately.

Cyril Barnes leaned back in his seat, flashing his ferret smile.

"Did you say—"

"Yep. I'm the other Fixer."

Thomas felt the weird rush of jealousy mixed with fear, the same unnerving sensation he'd felt when Trixie first told him about the existence of another Fixer in Gloomsbury.

"I'd shake your hand, brother Fixer," said Cyril, "but I've come down with a nasty cold. Don't want you sneezing out your brains all over corpses on my account."

"Why are you here?" Thomas blurted out, ignoring the fact that whoever Cyril Barnes was he seemed to know a lot about Thomas.

Cyril shrugged. "Same as you. Well . . ."

He got up, crossed the room, and sat down next to Thomas. There was a funny cologne smell about him, Thomas now detected. It smelt like someone trying to hide the fact they secretly smoked cigarettes.

"Well, not the *same* as you *exactly*," Cyril continued, not looking at Thomas, but at some invisible point out in front of him. "I had a case that involved a certain Artifact of Unlocking that these porkers were looking for. Thought I'd throw them a bone, you know? Say, you haven't come across a lady named Trixie, have you?"

Thomas cringed at the mention of the insufferable ghost-woman. "Yeah, she said she'd met another . . ."

For some reason he didn't want to say *Fixer*, as if saying the word might make the existence of Fixers, Bonds, and Artifacts all the more real.

"Did she now?" said Cyril, smiling wildly. "Oh, what a peach. I offered to help her, of course, but seems she still has her sights on you, Creeper. Can't say why. I mean with you *begrudgingly* accepting the Bond and all its gifts—"

"Look!" Thomas bolted up in his seat. He was getting tired of people—living or dead—popping into his life whenever they pleased. "What do you want? I'm about to get my ass handed to me in a few moments for something I didn't even do." He was almost frothing at the mouth now, but he didn't care what he said or who he looked like. "And . . . and I'd like to have a little peace and quiet before that happens."

Cyril Barnes closed his eyes and nodded a couple of times. An expression of understanding—or mock understanding, it was hard to say—came over him. Thomas slid back down in his seat and blew a ragged breath out his nostrils like a horse.

Then something utterly bewildering happened.

Thomas watched Cyril's lips flutter as if he was trying to remember something—or the opposite—like he was trying to commit to memory something he'd just learned.

Thomas watched as Cyril swept a gloved finger over the spine of the book hanging out of his pocket. A second later, Cyril's steel-gray eyes were back on him, twinkling with deranged mirth.

"Yeaaaaaaah," said Cyril, letting out an insidious little chuckle. "I wouldn't worry about that. See for yourself."

He made a quick nod at the window with his stubbled chin.

"I'm serious, Creeper. Check it out."

The office room had gone eerily silent. Thomas peered up at the unnecessary ceiling fan hanging in the center of the freezing hallway. The blades had become stuck mid-spin, as if someone had suddenly flicked off the switch. *Had there been some kind of freak power outage?* Even the copier in the corner, which had been pounding out packet after packet of some new brochure, had ground to a halt. The unsettling chill returned once more to Thomas. While Cyril raised his eyebrows up and down looking all impish and demented, Thomas pushed himself up from his chair and peered into the office window.

He could see Marylène.

She was bent over her seat facing the sheriff's desk. She clutched her head in her hands, but her shoulders were stiff. Her hands didn't move . . . Thomas couldn't believe it. *Marylène was frozen!* Feeling his heart quicken a few beats, he looked past

Marylène to Korvin's desk. He gasped. *Korvin was frozen too!* The sheriff was leaning over his desk, waving a long finger at Marylène, but neither the finger nor the sheriff seemed to budge an inch.

Thomas sank back in his chair. He looked around blankly at the air in front of his face, gaping in total amazement.

"Okay, Creeper," said Cyril, cracking his fingers inside his leather gloves. "Here's what's gonna happen. I know your family's in hot water with this whole Fipps thing . . ."

Thomas turned his head slowly, as if shaking himself out of a dream. He opened his mouth to speak, but Cyril shook his head, silencing him with a gloved finger.

"Don't worry about how I know. Just listen. You may recall a certain rumor that Eleanor Fipps's son Gerald may have gotten a little tipsy a year ago and crashed his car into one of the shops in town? Well, good old Gerry fled the scene, of course, and it was a certain special someone by the name of J.W. Sneed who paid off the police to make the whole thing go away. Those new police cruisers you rode around in today? Surprise! That's where the bribe money went. Korvin told everyone it was a sinkhole. What a dirt bag. Anyway, there's a police log of the whole thing in Korvin's bottom drawer. I figure you have about one minute before my little magic trick wears off. Grab the folder in there and you'll have some ammunition against these bastards. Might even make them drop the whole thing . . ." Cyril made a dusting motion with his gloves. "Clean slate, Creeper. Everybody goes back to loving their fences and hating their neighbors . . . you know, the good, old-fashioned New England way."

"You mean blackmail?" whispered Thomas, trying to piece everything together. His brain swam in a noodly sea of confusion. "Wait, why are you helping me?"

Cyril flashed his ferret smile. "Let's just say we Fixers need to look out for each other. We're a dying race, you know. Now, listen. You're gonna need this."

From another pocket in the leather jacket Cyril took out a small box.

"It's called the P.B.O.U.D.," said Cyril, holding the box out in front of Thomas's nose. "It means 'Pill Box of Unknowable Depth'. You open the lid clockwise and whatever you want to stuff into it—big or small, but probably not like a car, haven't tried that yet—it'll get sucked up and stored for later. Just make sure you close it counter-clockwise . . . and have enough room when you open it later if you've got something really big to unload . . ."

There seemed to be a lot of *ands*.

". . . and don't stick a finger in there unless you want to get sucked in yourself. Okay? Got it?"

Cyril slapped the P.B.O.U.D. against Thomas's chest. Thomas wheezed and grabbed hold of the weird object, nearly dropping it to the linoleum floor.

"It's freezing," he mumbled, shifting the pill box back in forth in his hands. "Where'd you find it?"

"We don't have time for story hour, I'm afraid," said Cyril, getting up from his seat. "Now, go. Remember. Bottom drawer. It'll be in a manila envelope. If I did the spell right, the drawer should be unlocked."

"Spell? Should be? Wait! Hold on!"

But Cyril was already muttering something with his eyes closed and his finger on the spine of the book again.

Before Thomas could open his mouth, a wave of magnetism flung him backwards.

Then there was a popping sound—like a million tiny bubbles going off inside his ears. The next thing Thomas knew he was standing inside the office door with Cyril pointing at him from the other side of the glass.

• • •

For a few hair-raising seconds Thomas stood motionless while everything he knew about the world jockeyed for position within his brain. He felt woozy, as if the backwards somersault through office window had brought on a rush of vertigo. But he was alive. At least he thought he was?

He checked his hands. No blood. No snapped bones or severed arteries. The P.B.O.U.D. still rested in the middle of his left palm. The porcelain gleamed beneath the bracing halogen lights. The box had warmed up a little since Thomas had morphed through the glass window, though it still felt as cold as clutching the bottom of an ice cream cup. He glanced from the P.B.O.U.D. to the window. Cyril was glaring back at him, pointing furiously at his wristwatch. Thomas turned slowly around. Marylène was still frozen in her chair the same as before, her head cradled in her hands; Korvin's finger was still raised like a general screaming for his troops to charge. Slowly, carefully, feeling fear overwhelm disbelief and an incredible desire to vomit, Thomas sidled around the desk until he came around to the drawer side. He crouched down. He sucked in a choked breath.

One of Korvin's boots was starting to twitch!

He jerked back up. Now Cyril was jumping up and down behind the window, clutching his temples with his gloved hands. Biting the side of his lip, Thomas crouched back down. He stared under the desk at the toe of the boot in front of him. Now both of the sheriff's boots were starting to move. It got worse.

A low moan—like the beginning of an old siren winding up—sounded across the room, coming from Marylène's direction.

Thomas pulled back the bottom desk drawer. His mouth dropped open, disbelief once again firmly taking hold. There were other manila folders inside the drawer. *Cyril hadn't said anything about other folders!*

Panic like a poisonous drug spread through Thomas's body. Marylène's moan grew louder. He could hear Cyril's muffled voice behind the glass, yelling for him to grab the folder and get out. *But how could he know which one was the right folder?* Making a silent prayer, he reached in and snatched a handful of folders off the top. He slammed the drawer shut right as Sheriff Korvin's leg became unstuck.

Hands shaking, barely holding onto the P.B.O.U.D., Thomas jerked the porcelain lid clockwise. He felt his eyebrows roll all the way up through his scalp as a weird cyclone of wind mixed with turquoise light shot up from the opening in the pill box. Squinting in the blinding turquoise light, Thomas peered down at the pile of folders bunched under his arm. It was crazy. *How could something so small suck up a bunch of folders?*

"Whaaaaaaaaaa . . ."

Thomas looked up to find the sheriff's lips trembling and fighting to form words.

Time was running out.

Thinking another silent prayer, Thomas held the corners of the folders over the swirling opening in the pill box. As soon as the cream-colored edges touched the turquoise light, the folders ripped from Thomas's fingers and began twisting into a tight, cone-shaped bundle. The bundle shrunk and kept shrinking until suddenly it disappeared altogether. Jerking the lid shut, counter-clockwise this time as Cyril had directed, Thomas leapt out from behind the desk.

He landed a split second later right next to Marylène whose moaning had finally ceased as she finally came unfrozen.

Lifting her head from her lap, she stared back at Thomas with watery, red-rimmed eyes filled with confusion. There were words on her lips, but this time it wasn't a question of translation that prevented them from forming.

It was pure and utter befuddlement.

"Creeper!" a deep baritone voice bellowed from across the room.

Thomas looked up to find the Sheriff Korvin glaring back at him with blood-thirsty vengeance. A large vein throbbed in the center of the sheriff's forehead, and beads of sweat trickled down his sideburns. The nasty glare soon dissolved to confusion, however, as the sheriff's eyes focused down on his finger, as if he couldn't remember why he'd raised it in the first place.

"Creeper! I-I thought I told you to wait out in the hallway! I'll deal with you in a moment!"

Thomas folded his arms behind his back, carefully slipping the P.B.O.U.D. into his back pocket.

"I came in to tell you . . ." Thomas began. He looked back and forth from Marylène to the sheriff. They were both staring at him, expecting some kind of explanation. He cocked his head towards the window, looking for Cyril, hoping the older boy had another magic trick up his sleeve that could fix the awkward situation. His jaw dropped open. *Cyril was gone!* Instead, standing where Cyril had been only moments ago was a man in a wooly sweater with wild, feathery hair and slightly pointed ears—ears just like Marylène's.

Marylène had caught sight of the face behind the glass too. She ran to the door.

"Right," said Thomas, taking a deep gulp as he fit the pieces of the lie together. "I wanted to tell you that Marylène's dad is here."

Pausing at the office door, Marylène flashed Sheriff Korvin one last look of pure hatred before running out into the hallway to embrace her father.

Now there was one side effect from the whole freezing incident Thomas—nor Sheriff Korvin himself—had anticipated.

A dark stain had appeared down the front of the sheriff's gray pants.

The stain spread, gushing down one leg, yet there were no overturned coffee mug or glass of water on the desk. Following Thomas's shocked gaze, Sheriff Korvin peered down, his eyes welling with horror. Swiveling around, keeping his back to Thomas, he growled:

"GET OUT OF HERE, CREEPER! I'LL GET YOUR STATEMENT LATER! GET OUUUUUUTTTTTTTT!"

Thomas didn't need to be told a third time.

He scooted out the office door. He caught up with Marylène down the hallway, a few steps from the door that lead out into the parking lot.

"Marylène!"

The hug Marylène threw around Thomas's wiry shoulders was about as expected as Sheriff Korvin wetting himself during the whole magical time-freezing incident.

"Thomas," Marylène whispered, her breath warm against Thomas's ear. "*Zat* was *orr-ible. Orr-ible.*"

"I know," Thomas whispered back.

Marylène let go and wiped a few stray tears from her cheek with the back of her hand.

"Are you going to be okay?" asked Thomas.

Suddenly, the door to the parking lot yanked open.

Marylène's father poked his head into the hallway with a perturbed look on his bearded, backlit face. Marylène and her father exchanged a few hushed words in French while Mr.

Gaumont looked Thomas over—most likely fascinated by Thomas's lime-green *Bravado*. Then, letting out a grunt that couldn't be judged definitively as approval or disapproval, Mr. Gaumont poked his head back out the door. The door clicked shut. They were alone again.

"I don't have a mobile," said Marylène, "but we have a phone at the *facilité*. We are at the Alderfer Foundation in Marvale. You will call me, Thomas, *oui*?"

"Yes," said Thomas, smiling a little. "I mean *oui*. I'll call you."

There was a loud rapping of knuckles on the parking lot door. Marylène smiled back at Thomas. The sorrowful expression on her face shifted for a moment. With a sigh she opened the door and stepped out into the glare of the brightly-lit parking lot.

Thomas turned around to spy one of the police officers whipping past him.

He was a beefy, blockheaded man, the same officer who'd escorted Thomas back from the beach. Flying past Thomas, boot heels reverberating off the dirty cinderblock walls, he screamed:

"D-D-DON'T WORRY, SIR! I'VE GOT MY SPARE! I'M COMING! DON'T WORRY!"

Thomas could see a pair of light gray pants held high above the policeman's head.

It was a strange end to a very strange day.

And it wasn't over yet.

Chapter Five
Contents & Further Discontent

Fifteen minutes later, after a wild sprint through Old Town, Thomas arrived at the rotting sign of Creeper & Sons Funeral Home.

The wind had picked up. Wild gusts ripped through the gnarled oak trees, scattering fall leaves from the branches. The dark cypresses that loomed over the old Victorian funeral home looked like mammoth-sized caterpillars, writhing furiously in the wind.

Hooking his legs through the front gate, Thomas bolted up the flagstones. As his sneakers hit the last step on the porch, a thunderclap burst overhead, splitting the air like a cannon blast. Jumping back at the sound, Thomas snuck under an eave of the porch . . . only to land directly under an overflowing gutter spout. Soaked head to toe, feeling like an unwanted door-to-door salesman, he crept towards the front door and peered in.

Through the smudgy, mold-speckled glass he tried to detect any movement inside. The foyer was dark and still as a tomb. Thomas relaxed his shoulders. Even with all the many unused rooms in the old funeral home, his parents would never buy the story he'd been somewhere inside the house all along. *Unless* . . .

Unless he'd fallen into one of the caskets while cleaning it and the lid had snapped shut!

After all, it had happened before. Cleaning and polishing the caskets were part of Thomas's daily chores. Some of the extra-thick caskets you could climb in, shut the lid, and yell your brains out and barely a squeak would sound on the other side.

Thomas shook his head. It was a hard sell—*too* hard, and he was a poor salesman. Jeni could think fast like that on her feet. Not him. At the slightest hint of fabrication his father would flay him open with a firing line of questions that would expose any poorly-crafted lie. It wasn't worth it.

He waited. Still no movement in the foyer.

Farther down the hallway, nothing flickered the hazy bar of light under the kitchen door that was always a sign someone was moving around inside. He thought about his predicament. He was late—no question about that. But had he done anything wrong?

His parents couldn't be furious with him when they heard about the corpse at Town Beach. And Korvin had . . . what was the word they used in spy novels? *Detained* him. Korvin had kept him at the station without a warrant or any justification for suspicion, what detectives called probable cause.

Thomas felt a bloom of confidence rush through him. He patted the spot where the P.B.O.U.D. sat snug and cold inside the front pocket of his lime-green tuxedo that he prayed the rain had ruined forever. If Cyril's magic pill box worked, and Thomas had snatched the right folder with Gerald Fipps's police report, then he had something that could actually help his parents. No, not just help. His heart sped up.

He could save the family business!

By the end of the night, he'd be a hero, even if that particular word never found its way to Elijah Creeper the Fifth's lips. All he needed to do was find a way to explain how the folder came into his possession in the first place. But not necessarily *his* possession. His eyes gleamed with Jeni Myers-like guile as the beginnings of a hazardous scheme took shape in his mind.

As he turned the door handle and crept into the musty foyer, he found someone who could help him pull off his great scheme, if only Thomas could figure out what was in it for him.

Hearing the sound of the door, a tall and shifty figure emerged from his usual den of heckling and betting in the Viewing Room. Staring up at the half-masked face in front of him, Thomas's confidence in his plan began to evaporate, as a cackling, unnerving voice rang out through the foyer, right after another wild clap of thunder shook the house.

"Hope you like roast beef, Tommy Boy. 'Cause you're about to get roasted."

Daggers of lightning flashed outside the moldy drapes. In the flickering light Jedidiah Creeper cut a fearsome and ridiculous caricature. He was wearing a grease-stained apron over his usual Army jacket filled with patches like "P.O.W." and "I Served, You Didn't!" There was even a patch of a muscular lobster hoisting an AK-47, signifying Jed as a member of the Fraternal Order of Longshoreman, a distinction Thomas was certain Jed had only gained after stealing the patch to get into certain Fraternal bars where his money was still accepted.

"Look, Jed . . ."

Jed flicked on the overhead chandelier. He made a sucking sound with his teeth and gums, relishing the sight of his nephew in his soaked *Bravado*.

"Before you say anything . . ."

Jed slouched back against the doorframe leading into the Viewing Room. Still grinning like a madman, he began wiping off his greasy fingers with a rag. Thomas opened his mouth to plead again, but Jed held up a stained finger and hissed:

"Bup! Bup! It's my turn, Tommy Boy. Take a seat."

Jed hooked a chair around from the Viewing Room and slammed it down in front of Thomas.

"Jed—"

"I SAID SIT DOWN! THEY'RE NOT HERE! THEY'RE OUT LOOKING FOR YOU, YOU PUTZ!"

Thomas was actually shocked. Jed had never yelled at *him* before. Everyone else in the house, sure. But not him.

Thomas sidled over to the chair. As he slumped down, a memory of his fifth birthday came flooding back to him. It was the time Jed had told Thomas's few friends—the few ones who weren't afraid to come to a funeral home for a birthday party—how Jed had watched Viet Cong soldiers take turns pulling out his best friend's fingernails when he and Jed were prisoners of war. *It's not a game of 'pull my finger' you want to play, kiddos!* Jed had whispered into the shocked and terrified faces. *They don't come off like candy wrappers, I can tell you that much!*

Thomas had evaded Sheriff Korvin's interrogation that afternoon. No magic spell, however, would get him out of his uncle's firing squad.

"Now, here I am," Jed purred in a wicked voice, circling Thomas's chair like a hawk, "trying to fix an explosion in the oven so your dear mother can get back to poisoning us, when I hear them going on about you being two hours late from ninny-prancing class. You should've seen your dad, Tommy Boy. I was kind of hoping for a heart attack."

Thomas didn't have time for some ridiculous monologue. He had to get upstairs. He had to find a way to open the P.B.O.U.D. and see if the Fipps folder was inside before his parents came home and his father really *did* have a heart attack.

"Hold on," said Jed, throwing up a greasy hand. "Let me finish. But then I get to thinking. Your little sweetheart, Jessie—"

"Jeni."

"Well, she's not around anymore, is she? So what's a guy with no more friends left in this dumpy sinkhole of a town doing? Don't think you're headed to the library in that get-up."

Thomas glowered up at his weird uncle, but the half-grin peeking through the dirty mask had dissolved.

"This is the part where you spill the beans, kid," said Jed in a voice that had lost any trace of amusement.

Thomas sucked in a deep breath. He couldn't believe it. He was going to have to confide in his uncle, in this horrible specimen of humanity who told twisted stories to children to scar them for the rest of their lives like he was scarred himself, inside and out.

"Okay, fine," said Thomas, standing up from his chair and mustering his courage. "Here's the deal—"

Before Thomas could get a word out, over the howling wind he heard shouting coming from the front yard. He squinted and peered through the opening in the drapes. His breath caught in his throat as his eyes locked on a sight as brutal and as horrifying as anything supernatural he'd witnessed that week:

His father was stomping up the flagstones, his face flush with unbridled rage. Thomas had to act fast.

"I've got something I think that can save us, Jed. The business, I mean."

Jed slouched back against the doorframe. He didn't open his mouth to offer any horrible or sarcastic rebuttal. Instead, he went back to wiping his greasy hands which Thomas took as his way of saying *Okay, I'm listening.*

"I got this folder from Korvin's office."

Thomas could hear his father. He had reached the porch steps. His incensed voice sounded in the spaces between thunder claps.

This is the last time, Adele. I'm sending him away. You hear me! I'll make do on my own.

"The folder says Gerald Fipps was drunk," Thomas continued. "He really did crash into the Tackle Box last year. I have it all upstairs. Can you . . ."

The next words felt as excruciating to say as getting his own fingernails wrenched from their cuticles. Thomas had never asked Jed for anything in his life. If his uncle had done anything for him, it wasn't out of love or kindness. It was because Jed had been forced to do it by Thomas's parents.

"Would you . . ."

An argument on the porch had slowed Elijah Creeper the Fifth's march to the front door. Thomas could hear the bird-like warble of his mother playing counterpoint to his father's symphonic fury.

"Would you *please* cover for me if I give you the folder, Jed? You could say you paid someone you met at Sappy's who works at the Sheriff's Office. Yeah! That's it! You paid them to grab the folder for you."

Thomas smiled. He was thinking pretty fast on his feet, almost as good as Jeni. *Would it work?* Jed looked like he was one step away from opening the door and letting him fry.

"I was at Korvin's office this afternoon. I'm telling you the truth. He wanted to ask me about a body they found down by Town Beach . . ."

Jed's unmasked eye widened with interest.

"Please, Jed. I'll help you with whatever you . . ." Thomas cringed. "Need help with. I just need to go upstairs and—"

Jed sprang to the door and with one swift motion locked it.

"Jed, what are you—"

Jed held a grease-stained finger to his lips. Baffled and speechless, Thomas watched his uncle reach into his apron and start fiddling in one of the inner pockets of his Army jacket.

The doorknob started to turn . . .

Thomas ducked into the shadows of the Viewing Room as the pounding began on the other side of the door, followed by some horrible words, words no human being—young or old—should ever hear.

Open this door or I'm going to get some Novocain and thread and sew your eyelids shut in your sleep!

A few chirpy buttons sounded in the foyer. Hooking his head away from the doorframe, Thomas looked over at Jed. His uncle was cradling his small, outdated flip phone against his scarred ear.

"Green? Yeah. It's me. J-Boy."

Thomas scrunched up his face. *J-Boy? What?*

"Cancel it. Yeah. You heard me. I'll close the deal myself."

Jed flipped the phone shut. In a voice devoid of its usual sarcasm and malice, he turned to Thomas and whispered:

"Alright. I'll cover for you, Tommy Boy. Go do what you gotta do."

Thomas leapt for the stairs. But when he got halfway up the staircase, he turned back.

"Jed, what were you telling Mr. Green to cancel?"

The familiar leering grin returned to the unmasked side of Jed's face. The pounding on the other side of the door grew louder, though it didn't seem to faze Jedidiah Creeper one bit.

"A hit on Gerald Fipps," said Jed nonchalantly. "Green knows a lot of good family men in Atlantic City."

Thomas choked on his own breath, or maybe it was the dust motes he'd kicked up flying up the staircase.

"You were going to have Gerald Fipps . . . *assassinated*?" Thomas whispered back. "By like . . . the mafia?"

Jed shrugged his shoulders, as if what he'd heard wasn't worth getting all worked up about, like the time his prize-winning greyhound Bixby ripped out the throat of one of his fellow competitors . . . a second before he crossed the finish line.

"Family's family, Tommy Boy," said Jed, still flashing his half-masked grin. "Those mafia guys know that better than anybody."

Jed made a shooing motion with a greasy hand.

Slowly, Thomas turned back around. He crept up the final steps in petrified silence. *He couldn't believe it!* His uncle had set in motion a dangerous scheme, a scheme far more dangerous and criminal than the one Thomas had concocted himself. *What would've happened if he hadn't snatched the folder from Korvin's office?* Thomas shuddered to know.

When he reached the dark rectangle of the second floor landing he looked out over the foyer. He watched Jed twist the lock and throw open the door. Spreading his arms wide, in a voice sparkling with sarcasm, he shouted up into the rafters:

"*Buonasera!* Welcome to the Olive Garden! Are you here for the bottomless breadsticks?"

• • •

Thomas shut the door to his bedroom and closed his eyes while a three-part circus broke out downstairs.

He could hear his father shouting, followed by his mother's warbled pleading. *Lower your voice, Elijah! Listen to Jed! He said Thomas is home safe!* Perhaps for the first time in his life, Jed fought to be the only voice of reason in the room. *Now, shut your traps for a second! Tommy Boy got stopped by Korvin! Tommy found a body down by Town Beach walking back from ninny-prancing class. Fine, Adele! Ballroom dancing! Whatever! Korvin kept him in the clink for questioning. Now before you lose your* [expletive] *minds, listen . . .*

But this part—this very crucial part—Thomas couldn't hear. *What lie was Jed spinning?* He cracked the door open a few inches and strained his neck to listen.

Footsteps moved away from the foyer. He heard his father snarl. *I need to get off my feet. Come into the Study.* Then he heard his mother chime in. *I'll go get something heated up.* Soon all Thomas could hear was his father and Jed's muffled voices behind the door of the Funeral Director's Study and the distant clink of plates coming from the kitchen.

Thomas closed his bedroom door. As he turned back around, his eyes locked on a swirling green glow on his bed. Finn, the faithful ghost-dog, was up from his daily slumbers in dimensions unknown to living men—or living dogs—for that matter.

The wolfhound's great tongue, also bathed in bright green ectoplasm, lolled out one side of his mouth as he looked expectantly up at Thomas, ready for a new adventure.

"Not now, Finn," said Thomas, rushing over to his desk and clicking on his desk lamp. The ghost-dog sank back despondently into the folds of the bed. He kept one eye peeled on Thomas in the off-chance something interesting or potentially dangerous called for his protection.

Thomas fished into the pocket of his soaked tuxedo and pulled out the P.B.O.U.D.. He laid the magic pill box on the desk and craned the springy lamp so that the beam of light focused directly down on the pill box's cold, egg-shaped lid.

Thomas squinted his eyes, examining the mysterious box. Yellow and blue flowers circled the lid in a delicate pattern. To anyone who didn't know better, it looked like a regular old antique pill box your grandmother might have.

Where a little gold clasp would have been on the side, like the one Thomas had seen his mother use for her migraine pills, this pill box had no clasp at all. The two halves were ringed with gold.

When Thomas first opened the antique box at Korvin's office, clockwise as Cyril had directed, he'd felt a little resistance, as if the two halves were magnetized in some way, which was strange, though if he was being honest, there was nothing really normal about anything that happened in the past twenty-four hours.

"Okay," Thomas whispered as he scrutinized every detail in the pill box. "But how do I get anything out?"

He lowered his head until his nose was almost touching the lid. When he'd opened the P.B.O.U.D. in Korvin's office nothing had flown out. That couldn't be the way objects came out, only *in*. He put the pill box on its side, searching for writing, for some secret clue he would have missed if he was only looking at the top. Nothing.

He put the P.B.O.U.D. on its back and blinked his eyes a few times. As he removed his hand, a hazy image started to take shape inside the porcelain, like something rising up from the bottom of a glass of milk.

The image crystallized into a face.

A face of a woman, smiling back at him.

Thomas felt the fine hairs on his neck prick up. *The woman moved!* She turned from a side profile to staring directly up at Thomas with dark, enchanting eyes. She had a powdered face with heavily rouged cheeks and a sizeable beauty mark over her top lip like a little shaded-out moon. She wore a periwinkle blue gown with a sumptuous bodice and frilly white sleeves that started below the elbow. As for her hair, she had an explosion of tan curls all meticulously folded in so many intricate layers it must have taken the hairdresser a whole day to pull it off.

Suddenly, the woman raised a small fan over her head and flashed Thomas a coy smile.

Above the tip of the fan words began to materialize.

Thomas mouthed the words in breathless wonder, feeling as if his legs might give out at any second.

Madame Purfoy says:
Tap lid twice to open
Then stand back AT ONCE

The woman gazed up at Thomas. Flashing a little smirk, she raised a thin, penciled eyebrow. When Thomas didn't move, she scrunched up her face and pointed back at the letters with her fan. Thomas turned the pill box over. He was about to tap the lid when he remembered what Cyril had told him. *Make sure you have enough room when you open it later in case you have something huge to unload.* He wasn't unloading anything that big. *But what if something else was stuck inside?*

With a trembling hand, he carried the P.B.O.U.D. over to the center of his bedroom and placed it down on the creaky floorboards. Sensing something out of the ordinary about to happen, Finn cocked his ears from his spot on the bed. Licking his lips, the ghost-dog let out a little expectant bark.

"Yeah, don't get too excited," said Thomas. "I might blow up the house."

Thomas leaned down and made two sharp taps on the pill box's lid. He jumped back. The P.B.O.U.D. started to vibrate. The weird turquoise light prickled around the golden ring, throwing sparks everywhere.

The lid flashed open.

Expanding inside a beam of turquoise light came the bundle of folders from Korvin's office. The folders floated in the air while Thomas fell back against his bed, feeling the death-chill of Finn wafting against his shoulders. As the folders hovered in the electrified air, Thomas could see fragments circling them—dark and rusted bits of metal. Then the light sucked back into the pill box. The lid snapped shut. The folders and rusted fragments clattered to the floor.

Thomas ran over. Finn gusted off the bed in his own ghostly way, following dutifully behind. Thomas knelt down.

In the swirling green glow coming off Finn he surveyed the contents of the P.B.O.U.D.. Beneath another folder marked "First and Second Victims" he could read the name Gerald Fipps written in mechanical penmanship.

Thomas snatched the folder, flapped it open, and pored through the document. His eyes glowed triumphantly in the unnatural light. *It was all there!* Korvin must have kept the report in his desk as "collateral." He remembered the word from a book he read about Cold War spies keeping incriminating photos of other spies in the event a big secret got divulged or they defected to the enemy's side. Thomas glanced past the mechanically handwritten pages describing Gerald Fipps's drunk-driving incident, focusing on a strange metal object lying on the floor, one of the rusted fragments that had tumbled out of the P.B.O.U.D..

Thomas picked up the metal piece and held it under the freezing glow coming off Finn's snout. Finn examined the object with a knowing look. He had no clue what Thomas was investigating, but possessing that wordless understanding that is the hallmark of all great dogs—even undead ones—he knew whatever his master and companion held in his hand must be of some great importance. And indeed it was.

The rusted fragment Thomas held in his hand was shaped like a sliver of moon. But the sliver was broken at the two crests, forming two swoops like a capital cursive *E*. Thomas traced his cold finger around the swoops. *What was it? And what was it doing inside the P.B.O.U.D.?* He didn't have time to speculate. He had to get the evidence down to Jed so Jed could convince Thomas's father not to disown his only surviving son and "sew his eyelids shut" in his sleep.

He flapped Gerald Fipps's folder shut and scrambled to his feet. He ran over to the window and placed the rusted fragment on the ledge so that it wouldn't get sucked up by a vacuum or kicked under his bed. Flinging open his bedroom door, he flew out onto the landing. He whipped down the rickety steps, reaching the door of the Funeral Director's Study right as Jed was backing out.

"Trust me, brother o' mine," Jed called back through the crack of the door, "you'll want to see this. I have it right out here."

Jed swiveled around, knocking into Thomas.

"About time. Is that it?"

"Yep. It's all there. I think we got 'em, Jed."

Jed's eyes sparkled with wicked delight. For a split second it looked like he might reach over and pinch Thomas's cheek, something Thomas was certainly not prepared for.

"I thought I heard you, Thomas."

Mrs. Creeper emerged from the kitchen, oven mitts gloving her hands as usual. Jed took his cue to leave. Flashing Thomas another wicked half-masked grin, he squeezed back through the Funeral Director's Study and shut the door behind him.

"Don't you worry, Thomas," said Mrs. Creeper, having noticed the dark splotches where Thomas's lime-green *Bravado* had been soaked through. "Sally at the Hygienic Hem is an absolute wizard with chemicals. She'll have everything back in working order in time for next weekend. Don't you worry at all."

Thomas sighed, though his mood had brightened considerably, even if there was a chance that the *Bravado* wasn't ruined after all. He could hear Jed jumping up and down and roaring behind the door.

It's a gold mine, Elijah. A trifecta that's gonna hit BIG.

"Come on," said Mrs. Creeper, turning Thomas around by the elbow. "Let's find you some dry clothes and get you something to eat. You can tell me all about your terrible time down at Town Beach. I'm so sorry, Thomas. Why are these things always happening to you?"

Thomas shrugged. "No clue. Unlucky, I guess."

Mrs. Creeper sighed and cast Thomas a loving but worried glance. Shaking her head, she turned back towards the kitchen, Thomas trailing slowly behind her.

"What happened in here?" Thomas asked as soon as his sopping feet hit the tiled floor.

The room was overloaded with dozens of stacked glasses and plates. There was barely any space left at the table.

"Your uncle actually fixed something for once," said Mrs. Creeper, peeling back the tinfoil on a large casserole plate. A smell of overcooked meat and cheese, not entirely unpleasant, filled the room. "The disposal backed up into the dishwasher," Mrs. Creeper continued. "Not sure how that happened."

Thomas was about to say something smart about the messy state of the kitchen, when he realized he'd sound exactly like Jed. His mother didn't need any more flak after all the hours she spent taking care of them and working to keep the funeral home afloat.

"There are fresh clothes in the dryer, sweetie. I'll make a plate for you while you clean up."

Thomas slipped over to the utility room off the side of the kitchen. The room was dark, thankfully, so Thomas had some privacy. He quickly changed in the darkness and soon was back at the table with a slab of pasta, cheese, and sausage, bubbling on a plate in front of him.

While he dug in, his mother peppered him with questions about the body down at Town Beach. Thomas did his best to make sense between steaming bites. With every horrible description his mother seemed to retreat farther and farther back towards the sink, gripping her frail neck as if being choked, her green eyes wide with terror.

When Thomas got to the part about the corpse's body being painted an unnatural purple, Mrs. Creeper let out a gasp and backed straight into a large pewter beer stein teetering precariously on the edge of the sink. The beer stein tumbled to the floor. Luckily, it had been emptied hours ago. The smeared drinking vessel belonged to Jed, and helped him "think clearly" whenever he was working on repairs. Not surprisingly, most repairs never saw completion after Jed's "barley goblet," as he referred to his beloved beer stein, got refilled several times over.

Mrs. Creeper gathered up the beer stein from the floor. Thomas could hear her grumbling under her breath—something about Jed leaving the "wreckage of his life like toys all around the house for someone else to clean up."

Suddenly, the phone hanging on the side of the cupboard rattled in its antique cradle. Mrs. Creeper got up and answered the phone.

"Hello? Oh, what a wonderful surprise."

Thomas listened as his mother's voice changed altogether, sweetening to a tender cadence that told him whoever was on the phone had to be someone special.

"He's right here. I'm looking at him right now. I'm sure he can't wait to catch up with you. Hold on, I'll get him."

Thomas looked up from his half-finished plate. He mouthed the words "Who is it?"

An image of feathery bangs and elf-like ears flashed inside his brain.

"I guess today isn't a total washout," said Mrs. Creeper, thrusting the phone into Thomas's face. "Would you believe it? It's your friend Jeni. All the way from London."

Chapter Six
Total Darkness, Burning Shells

On any other miserable day, under any other miserable circumstance, a call from Jeni would be like a rare sun sighting to Thomas. Any gloomy thoughts circling his world would be instantly cast off; he'd start to breathe free and easy again. But tonight, under very different circumstances, he felt like locking himself in the utility closet and never coming out again.

As Mrs. Creeper handed over the phone and scooted out of the room, she flashed Thomas a very obvious, very embarrassing "let me give you some privacy" look that only made the flush in Thomas's cheeks go even more scarlet. He felt waves of guilt flood over him as he held the handset up to his lips—guilt for snapping at Jeni at Sal's; guilt for being a jerk and not answering Jeni's request to join her at the airport; and a new kind of guilt, which didn't fully make sense to Thomas yet, but was still guilt all the same:

Guilt for having feelings for another girl, a girl he'd only known for a few hours.

"Hello? Thomas? Are you there?"

Thomas opened his mouth to speak . . . but the words wouldn't come out. A wall of guilt held them back. Finally, after hearing a lot of shifting around on the other end of the phone, Thomas forced himself to speak.

"Oh, hey, Jen. I was . . ."

Think, you idiot, think! Say something normal!

". . . getting out of the shower."

The shower? He slapped his forehead so loudly Jeni probably heard it across the Atlantic.

"Oh, sorry. Should I—"

"No, no, no, no," Thomas stammered. "It's fine. How . . . how are you . . . Jenalyn?"

Jenalyn? Really? What are you doing, man?

There was another awkward pause, which Thomas assumed was Jeni processing why he'd used Jeni's full name, the one only her parents called her when she was in trouble.

"Not great to be honest," Jeni continued after an excruciating silence. "I mean . . . the program's out of this world. The other girls are really cool, Thomas. Well, most of them. There's a few snotty ones who act like they're part of the Royal Family. We toured Buckingham Palace today, and I think they got grand delusions . . . I mean delusions of grandeur. You know what I mean."

Buckingham Palace? Thomas felt a pang of jealousy. *Jeni was getting to see the rest of the world. Just like she'd said in her letter.*

"We came over on the train last night to play this British school called Armsley—or Aignsley? I don't know. One of the two. We lost yesterday. But we're back at it bright and early in the morning . . . which is like in four hours, I think."

"Four hours!"

"Yup." Jeni muffled a yawn into the phone. "I don't have my watch on, but I'm pretty sure it's like 3 a.m. here."

"What are you doing calling me?" Thomas palmed his face again. "I mean . . . thanks, Jen. I feel really horrible for going off on you like that at Sal's. I shouldn't have—"

"Chill out, professor," said Jeni. "Don't worry so much. I can't believe I got so ticked off and ditched you like that. We're supposed to split the bill, right? We always go halfsies . . . you know . . . unless I steal Arnold's allowance."

They both giggled. Thomas couldn't believe it. It was if someone had hit the release valve on all the anxiety and guilt churning around inside him. He exhaled sweet relief. *Jeni Myers didn't hate his guts.*

There was another long pause.

"Still there, professor?"

"Yep, still here."

Jeni yawned again, not bothering to muffle it this time. "I wanted to call you . . . well, because I miss you. Miss *hanging out* with you," Jeni added quickly. "But, really, I had to call you because of something I saw tonight."

"Tonight?" asked Thomas. "What did you see? Are you okay—"

"I'm fine. It's *you* I'm worried about, professor."

"Me? Why are you worried about me? I'm fine."

"I'm not so sure."

There was another long pause. *Did Jeni already know about the corpse on Town Beach? Jeni was smart, but she wasn't psychic. How could she know about that?*

"Remember when we got those gifts from Mulvaney's Raiders? Your Ocu-Occu goggles and my moon ring?"

"Yeaaaaah."

"Well, Richie said that the ring could show me things . . . things in the moon."

Jeni cleared her throat. Thomas shifted his weight, wondering what in the world Jeni was going on about.

"Well," Jeni continued in a nervous voice. "I couldn't sleep 'cause I was missing home . . . and you . . . anyway, I got up and stepped out on this balcony outside our hotel room. It's clear here tonight. Not like Gloomsbury, Thomas. I don't know why, but I brought the moon ring with me on the trip. I held it up and . . ."

Jeni's voice faltered. Thomas pressed his ear harder against the speaker. It sounded like Jeni was about to cry.

"That's when I saw it, Thomas . . . for a split second . . . inside the moon."

"Saw what?"

"I saw you, Thomas."

Now Thomas was sure Jeni was crying.

"I saw you in the moon and there was this shadow in front of you . . . only I couldn't see the shadow's face. But they were pushing you, Thomas, and you were falling.

"Falling into total darkness . . ."

• • •

After Jeni shared with Thomas the horrible vision gifted to her by the moon ring, there wasn't much talk about anything else.

They ended the conversation on an ominous cliffhanger—Jeni telling Thomas to "take extra special care, because she wasn't there to watch his back," and Thomas trying to comfort Jeni, which felt misplaced, seeing that he was the one the moon ring revealed to be in danger.

After promising to e-mail Jeni and be better about checking in, he said goodnight, which he realized was almost good morning in England. He hung up the phone. If he was lucky, he could sneak upstairs without having an embarrassing conversation with his mother where she would want to know every little detail about the Jeni situation. After the day Thomas had suffered through, he didn't have any emotional juice left in the tank.

He crept past the door to the Funeral Director's Study. He was thankful he'd left his drenched sneakers in the laundry room, what would certainly have given him away. He was almost in the clear—his foot planted on the first step of the staircase—when his mother emerged from the Viewing Room.

"That was so sweet of your friend to call long distance. How's she doing?"

"Fine, good," said Thomas curtly. "Okay, goodnight." He turned and started up the staircase.

"Wait."

Uh-oh, thought Thomas. *Here we go.*

"I forgot to tell you that you need to hand in your report from the Alderfer Museum visit. When you get the chance. But soon. I have to make sure I'm submitting our work to the District Board on time. I know today was pretty awful for you. Maybe you can type it up over the next few days? And here."

Mrs. Creeper held out a beat-up old paperback and almost dropped it as a sudden eruption sounded behind the Funeral Director's Study. Thomas could hear his father shouting behind the door:

And you don't think that we'll be prosecuted with an even greater penalty when Fipps reveals we've stolen official police documents?

And Jed shouting back:

That's the best part! We make a photocopy. We'll tell Gerry we know who has the original, and if he doesn't want his dirty laundry dumped out all over town, he better cease and desist.

Apparently, Jed hadn't struck gold just yet. Mrs. Creeper cast a dark look down the hall to the Funeral Director's Study.

Thomas took the worn paperback from his mother, turning it over so he could read the cover. It was a copy of Emily Brontë's *Wuthering Heights*. There was a swooped tear at the top of the cover, so all Thomas could read was *uthering Heig*.

"I think you'll like it," said Mrs. Creeper, smiling as if she had unlocked some secret door. For a split second Thomas had a vision of the beloved English teacher at Gloomsbury High his mother once was, before his father got so embroiled with work that he became incapable of handling anything that didn't involve a trocar and formaldehyde.

"You'll hate and love Heathcliff, I think. Not the cartoon cat, I'm afraid. He's one of the central characters in the book. Some people have called him the greatest anti-hero in Western literature."

Suddenly, Thomas had another vision—a vision of his uncle. *Jed certainly fit the bill of "anti-hero," didn't he?* Helping the family business in his own shady way after years and years of villainy.

"Thanks," said Thomas. "I'll work on the report tomorrow."

"When you get a chance. I'm sorry about today. I know you've seen bodies before but . . ." Mrs. Creeper shrugged. A look of love mixed with worry returned to her pale face. "Not like this. Goodnight, sweetie."

"Goodnight."

Thomas turned and trudged up the staircase to his bedroom. Making it to his bed, he collapsed onto the dusty mattress, but sleep wouldn't come. He tried muffling the crack-and-roar of the lightning and thunder with his pillow. The storm was relentless. It seemed like hours later when exhaustion finally took its toll, and he slipped into a dark and dreamless sleep.

Sometime during the subtle softening of gray that heralds dawn in Gloomsbury, Thomas's eyelids flashed open.

The storm had rolled away, leaving only the steady pitter-patter of rain tapping its inscrutable Morse Code against the gutters and windows. Thomas squinted his eyes, peering into the dreary haze seeping in through his window.

A mass of green light swirled in the center of the room.

Without his glasses on, all Thomas could make out was an amorphous green glow. He reached behind him and snatched his glasses off the chest of drawers. Glasses back on, he waited for his eyes to adjust. The green glow sharpened. He could see Finn standing in the middle of the room, stamping his paws on top of something on the floor. Sliding down off the bed, Thomas crossed the clammy floorboards to investigate.

"What's got you up, buddy?"

He crouched down on his knees and pantomimed a scratch over the ghost-dog's ears. Finn gave a short bark that only Thomas could hear and leapt back a few feet.

In the ectoplasmic glow Thomas could see it.

It was one of the folders, the one with "First and Second Victims" written across the cover in Korvin's mechanical handwriting. While Finn shifted his giant tongue back and forth in expectation, Thomas flipped open the water-stained manila cover and gasped.

"No . . ."

It was a series of photographs.

Photographs of dead bodies.

He felt the room wobble as if he was standing in the cargo hold of a listing ship. He held the photographs closer to Finn's unnatural light. There were two bodies—a man with a shaved head and a tattoo on his chest and a woman with smeared lipstick. They were both tangled up in sea-drift. And they both were . . .

Purple.

Thomas fell backwards against his desk. He slid to the floor, gripping the photographs with trembling fingers. He stared blankly at a few dust motes dancing in the weird green light in front of his face. There could be no doubt about it now. Sheriff Korvin was hiding an even bigger secret than Gerry Fipps's drunk-driving accident.

There were other corpses.

Purple corpses, washing up all around Gloomsbury.

None matching those descriptions had come through the funeral home and nothing had been mentioned in the newspapers. *Was Korvin keeping them somewhere else, trying to keep word from spreading around town?* Gloomsbury wasn't prepared to deal with a serial killer, especially not one who dyed their victims purple. It was a media bomb waiting to go off.

For a long time Thomas sat on the floor, holding the horrible photographs while the rain tapped against the windows and gutters and his pulse pounded in his ears. Swallowing deep into his chest, he slid the photographs back into the folder, stood up, and went to his desk and clicked on his desk lamp.

He pulled back the handle on his desk drawer; it gave way with a loud screech. He stared at the door, listening for any movement downstairs. When he was certain no one had heard the screech, he gazed down at the open drawer. The old tour guide's card sat on top of a pile of baseball cards, the illustration of the white shell wreathed with flames still clear in the shadows of the drawer.

It was time. He couldn't handle everything alone.

He needed help.

He picked up the card, drew in a deep breath, and closed his eyes. In the second darkness behind his eyelids he asked the Endless Library once more for help. He knew it was there, lingering outside the blurred edges of his perceptions, never fully out of reach. It was like a good memory, one he could track back to through the fog and confusion of his daily fears and doubts.

He only needed to make himself very still and ask—ask with his whole heart—and he knew an answer would come.

Help me, he implored the Endless Library. *Help me solve this riddle so I can make it all stop.*

He clamped his eyes shut and waited. Nothing happened. No clear page floated up from the depths of his soul, no secret clue appeared like the time the Endless Library had revealed the trick with iodine that proved Thomas's friend Pop Mulvaney had been murdered. Thomas relaxed his breathing. Maybe he was forcing it. He ignored everything in the room—the wind rustling outside, the creak of the house's old floorboards—until all he could hear was the rise and fall of his breath. Still nothing. Dejected, he crept back to his bed and collapsed.

When he eventually managed to fall back to sleep the card was still clenched tight in his right hand. Sometime later that night, in that semi-conscious state between dream and awake, a voice called out to him. It was a soothing voice, like soft music, echoing across a large body of water.

Burning shells, Thomas Creeper. Do you remember the place where the old ones burned shells in Gloomsbury?

"Yes," Thomas mumbled. "Burning . . . shells."

Slowly, feeling without being aware he was feeling, he sensed the presence of bookshelves rising up all around him. The invisible shelves pressed against the four corners of his bed, each shelf laden with innumerable books of all shapes and sizes. As Thomas nodded in his sleep, the bookshelves began to sink back, back into the formless void of dreams.

"I know . . ." he whispered to the void. "I've been there before."

Part Two:

Laurel and Ivy

Chapter Seven

Interception on the Way to the Gold Coast

The next morning, a bleary, gray Sunday with the smell of leaf mold hanging thick in the air, Thomas awoke to an unprecedented scene at Creeper & Sons.

He could hear his parents and Jed downstairs in the kitchen. They were chatting in low, amiable tones. It sounded—and this was the unbelievable part—like they were sharing a pleasant morning meal, something that had never happened in Creeper family history, not even at Christmas, and especially not with Jed who liked to spoil appetites with anecdotes about scavenged food options in P.O.W. camps ("Trust me! You develop a taste for things with lots of legs!").

Even stranger was the sound of Thomas's father's voice. He sounded . . . it wasn't possible.

He sounded relaxed.

And not just relaxed. A boom of laughter sounded from the kitchen.

Elijah Creeper the Fifth sounded happy.

Intrigued, and a little wary of such a cosmic shift, Thomas tiptoed his way down the staircase and across the hallway, making sure he kept out of sight. Slipping into the shadows outside the kitchen door, he cocked his ear to the doorframe and listened. His mother's warble was unmistakable.

"Yes, yes, Elijah, but I don't know. It seems like a gamble even with Jed's 'ace in the hole.' What happens when they go to Korvin, and he realizes what's been taken right out from under him—"

"I said the same thing, Adele," Thomas's father shot back, though without the caustic bite that usually flavored his speech. "But Jed has a good point. Korvin's stuck between a rock and a hard place on this one. He's been caught in a full-scale cover-up. Korvin must have kept the report in the event Gerry's snobby Sneed cousins put the screws to him. I don't want to admit it, but Jed's actually thought this one through for a change."

Thomas poked his face out of the shadows and peered into the kitchen. He covered his mouth. His father reached out a bony hand and . . .

. . . patted Jed on the shoulder.

Thomas wanted to scream. Nothing made sense. Down was up and right was left. The world had spun off its regular axis. They were whirling into total chaos. He debated going back up the stairs and trying it all over again. *Maybe he'd stumbled into one of those Marvel multiverses?* Maybe if he went upstairs and came back down it would all revert back to normal. He dipped his head down and retreated from the doorway.

Creak!

"Thomas? Is that you? Come join us! Jed bought pastries."

Trying his best to hide his shock—*Jed bought pastries? Um, WHAT?*—Thomas slunk into the kitchen. As he inched his way around the kitchen table, Mr. Creeper looked up, a ruddy red tinge brightening his sunken cheeks.

"Didn't I tell you the other day, Elijah Thomas?" Mr. Creeper said, waving a finger over his head as if he were Moses commanding the Red Seas to part. "I told you with you focusing on your training and with everyone *focusing* and *working*"—he stamped the floor with every syllable stress, making the coffee cups rattle and the creamer almost pitch over on its saucer—"Yes! With everyone working towards one unified goal, I knew we'd persevere through this mire of entitlement and sabotage from these country club, lace curtain sons of—"

"Elijah!" Mrs. Creeper inhaled sharply.

Thomas slipped a Danish out of an opened box on the side table. In his peripheral vision he could see Jed radiating perverse joy from across the table. Jed made a couple of nods in Thomas's direction as if to say *Told ya, Tommy Boy. Told ya I'd seal the deal.*

"All I'm saying, Adele," Mr. Creeper continued, "is that we have a chance to make a good push for the new year. Without any of this . . . muck hanging over our heads."

Mr. Creeper collapsed back into his chair. For a second it looked like Thomas's father was going to get all misty-eyed. Thomas, for one, knew he wouldn't know how to deal with that. Seeing his father in good spirits was enough to handle without throwing any gushy emotions on top of it.

It was a good thing Thomas had already concocted another plan to get out of the house as soon as he finished his delicious cherry Danish. When he jolted awake in his bed that morning, he had the tingling sensation someone had slipped him a clue overnight.

Maybe the Endless Library had heard his plea after all and had come to his rescue. And though Thomas wasn't sure whose soothing voice he heard echoing in his ears when his head jerked up from his pillow, he was certain of one thing:

He knew where the old tour guide from the museum lived.

Maybe not the exact house *per se*, but the general vicinity. All that was left was convincing his parents to give him the day off.

Judging by his father's ebullient mood, there was no better time to ask.

Slinking his way over to the sink, Thomas watched his father and Jed fly back into another hushed discussion over Gerry Fipps's fate. They were now grinning and rubbing their hands together like greedy children on Christmas Eve, imagining all the presents stacked up for them beneath the tree.

"We got 'em by the family jewels," hissed Jed. "I'll make photocopies today . . . and then . . . then I'll pay Gerry Fipps a little visit."

Jed tipped his mask and let out a nasty shriek which caused Thomas's mother to momentarily drop the plate she was rinsing. She quickly recovered the plate, but instead of launching into some usual diatribe aimed at her irritating brother-in-law, she sighed and went right back to rinsing.

"Mom," Thomas whispered while Jed overturned a coffee cup at the table and then proceeded to wipe up the spill with the sleeve of his Army jacket.

"Yes, sweetie?"

"I met this guy the other day at the Alderfer. He's a tour guide at the museum. He said he'd be happy to answer any questions for my report on the Capitoline Wolf."

It wasn't exactly a lie. The old man *had* offered to help him, just not with any report.

"Well, look at you," said Mrs. Creeper, slapping a wet rag against the sink. She looked like she might explode with joy—all ninety-two pounds of her. "You're making new friends left and right, Elijah Thomas."

"Yeaaaaaah," wheezed Thomas. "Anyway, I was thinking of interviewing him and maybe going to the library afterwards . . . for, like, you know, secondary material."

"What a brilliant idea." Mrs. Creeper threw a bony hug around her son. Before Thomas could squirm away, he felt the kiss planted on his cheek.

"Ugh! Gross, Mom!"

Mrs. Creeper ignored her son's embarrassment and turned to face the pair of brothers yammering away at the table like two schoolboys.

"Can't tell if this is a good thing, Thomas," Mrs. Creeper whispered out of the side of her mouth. "At least your father seems happy, doesn't he? Can't remember the last time *that* happened."

Thomas and his mother watched the two brothers for a little while longer. They both felt a weighty trepidation building despite the cheers and boost in morale. For his part, Thomas felt complicit in the new Fipps scheme—after all, it had been his idea. A sapping dread spread through him as he watched Jed and his father speculate about would happen once Gerry Fipps was pinned down with the blackmail ("Bet he'll take that crappy Pinto and drive right off Town Pier!" Jed howled. "Yes! Yes!" Thomas's father roared back. "Or . . . maybe they'll finally pack up and head for Hoboken! One can hope, Jedidiah!").

Neither Thomas or his mother knew how long the two brothers' ceasefire would last, nor did they want to think about the very dangerous, very real possibility, nipping at the hopeful mood that had settled in around the funeral home, warming it like an unexpected sun sighting:

What would happen when everything went wrong?

• • •

If you went back into the primordial sea-soup of Gloomsbury's earliest beginnings, way back before any set of human feet first tracked its many miles of sand, stone, and mud, you'd find piles and piles of shells.

Thomas remembered learning way too much about shells one paralyzingly-cold afternoon back in fifth grade, on a class field trip to Town Beach.

The intention of the field trip—as far as anyone could tell—was to teach students about how Gloomsbury's first settlers figured out how to make a kind of improvised cement using ingredients found in abundance all around them: clay, sea grass, and shells.

By burning heaps of shells inside a primitive kiln made out of mud and sea grass, and after a long drawn-out process called "slaking," which sounds about as fun as it sounds, the early settlers struck "gray gold," a pliable lime putty that could be stored and molded to create dwellings. More importantly, the technique could be harnessed to build the sturdy flood walls that held back the ever-shifting, ever-unpredictable swells rolling in from Gloomsbury Bay.

Unfortunately for Thomas, there had been little supervision with the kiln experiment that afternoon in fifth grade. Ms. Brood, who'd filled in last minute for Thomas's teacher, Ms. Hanson, after she called out sick with a terrible case of spine sap,[1] was well into her eighties, and her attention and eyesight seemed to focus solely on the giant cup of Earl Grey tea she stuck her face into morning, noon, and night. Seizing his opportunity, Gary Korvin, Thomas's arch-nemesis, snuck up while Thomas wasn't looking, and

---

[1] "Spine sap," or *aqua spinio malabilious*, as it is known to the medical community, is a kind of feverish malaise peculiar to the Gloomsbury-Marvale region, causing headaches, nausea, and the spine to steadily ooze a viscous fluid that is the opposite of warm.

snapped a small flint lighter behind Thomas's left ear, the kind used to ignite Bunsen burners.[2]

Thomas cried bloody murder. His screams were instantly drowned out by the crashing waves. Gary snuck away, scot-free. In the end, the wind was too wild, the mud and sea grass too wet, and Ms. Brood's attention too misplaced.

Thomas never forgot that afternoon down by Town Beach. It was scarred into his memory, the same way his left earlobe was forever marked by a squiggle of skin that looked like a segment of an earthworm's body when the light catches it . . . another reason why Thomas hated Gary Korvin's guts.

Slipping out of the house after the uncomfortable breakfast scene, Thomas turned right off of Thayer onto Beech. As he crossed over the rain-slickened cobblestones, out of the corner of his eye he spied a familiar but unwelcome sight:

The headless banker-ghost.

He was hanging around a trellis of tangled filth that might have held flowers once. Thomas tucked his head to his chest and sprinted. If he'd been spotted, he could try to shake the ghost off at the next intersection. He hustled down the block, keeping his head low, watching out for "cracking points" in the cement, powder-white fissures of limestone that signaled a deadly sinkhole lurking inches below the surface.

He turned left off Beech onto Shellburne, a road both he and Jeni knew well from their many adventures through town. Shellburne led out to "the Gold Coast," the unofficial name for the two-mile long isthmus of austere cliffs that jutted out over Gloomsbury Bay and housed the mansions of Gloomsbury's elite—families like the Feinhursts and the Pratchetts, famous for

---

[2] A Bunsen burner is a small, gas-powered laboratory device schools have trusted students with over the years, often against their better judgment.

inventing the patented "Pratchett Lobster Knuckler" for efficiently cracking lobster shells. And, of course, Gloomsbury's wealthiest family—the Sneeds, and their sequestered compound, only accessible by gatehouse or boathouse, the mysterious and clandestine world of Ivymount.

Thomas knew every gatehouse on Shellburne, every padlocked fence, every perilous fall from every barnacled jetty down to the shell-strewn beach below. *Shells! It had been right there under his nose all along*. It was even there in the name of the road. If only he hadn't blocked out the memory from the fifth grade field trip. Now Ms. Brood's doddering, croaky voice came back to him:

Years ago, the first Gloomsbury settlers burned shells on the site where Shellburne Road now sits, giving the road its name today . . .

There was even a colossal furnace sunk half-way into the sea, off the side of the east flood wall on Shellburne. Jeni and Thomas had spent one afternoon in late spring counting the cormorants sunning and drying their wings atop the furnace's splattered ruins. Thomas could remember thinking the site looked like an aquatic version of the Tintern Abbey poem by William Wordsworth they'd read in English class that year.

Feeling a bloom of confidence, Thomas continued his sprint, making a beeline for Shellburne's flood walls. With every few steps he glanced back over his shoulder, making sure the headless banker-ghost hadn't caught up. He grinned. *His plan was working!* No sign of the ghost anywhere. He rounded a corner and paused, doubled-over with both hands resting on the lowest tier of a fountain full of muddy rain and teeming with moss.

The two Shellburne flood walls were right up ahead. The walls faced each other, forming the protective barriers around the Gold Coast. Thomas stared back through the rising fog. He was still safe. Gulping a few gasps of salty air, he started heading for one of the flood walls when a familiar voice called out behind his shoulder:

"Listen, Creeper, before you say anything."

Thomas spun around. He could feel rage bubbling up inside him again. He had told her to back off. He had told her to stop stalking him. His gaze rose slowly from the ground to a unicorn-bludgeoned dress.

"This is the last time you'll see me, so don't freak out," said Trixie. "I wanted to tell you that I don't need your help. That Cyril Barnes kid says he'll help me with my problem. You're off the hook. Anyway, he says you don't really accept the gifts of the Bond or whatnot. So, no sweat. And no hard feelings. None at all."

Thomas opened his mouth to let Trixie have it, to really tell her off this time so she never haunted his footsteps ever again, when something completely unpredictable happened.

All of his anger flickered out of him.

It was like someone had shook him like a match, leaving only the useless smoke. As the fog parted along with his anger, Thomas could see Trixie more clearly. Gazing back at her, for the first time Thomas felt sadness for the ghost break over him like a wave. She was leaning against the trunk of a wet tree, filing her nails like she often did. But for some reason today she looked less spunky and a little lost, like someone lingering in a doorway not sure whether they should go in or leave. Thomas's heart sank. *This isn't right. Why do I feel so bad for her?* But he did. He felt absolutely horrible.

"Hey, Trixie."

Hearing the change in Thomas's voice, Trixie straightened up and stopped filing her nails. She hunched her shoulders and leaned in, visibly shaken off her defensive axis.

"What's come over you?"

"Nothing. It's been a weird couple of days."

"That bad, huh?"

"Yep."

"Want to talk about it?"

"Not really."

"Alright if I keep you company, then? Where ya headed?"

Thomas weighed the pros and cons of letting Trixie in on the crazy couple of days since she last stalked him—the weird Fulvius Marcius Cinta e-mail; the lawsuit; the purple corpse washing up on Town Beach; the photographs of other purple corpses in Korvin's folder. He decided to keep everything under wraps for the time being. At least there would be less questions, questions he didn't know how to answer yet.

"I'm looking for this guy from the Alderfer museum," he began hesitantly. "You know . . . that day you followed me on the bus?"

"Followed you? Ha! Don't flatter yourself. I was . . . " Trixie bit her lip and glanced around absently. "Doing research. Yeah, that's right. Heard about a Fixer running around town, and I was following up on that information. Checking my facts is all."

Thomas cast Trixie an incredulous look.

"I said don't flatter yourself." Trixie grimaced and pointed the nail file at Thomas's face. Her dark eyes narrowed. "Creeper! Get down! You *are* being followed!"

Hearing the weird change in Trixie's voice, Thomas crouched down. He huddled against a large urn sculpted into the side of a fountain that no longer trumpeted water but teemed with weeds and gross-smelling moss. At first, he couldn't see what Trixie was all up in arms about. Then, through the fog, came a flurry of pinstriped arms and legs. The headless banker-ghost appeared, creeping towards them, making sharp, insistent steps as if he knew their hiding spot. Then, as quickly as he appeared, he veered away as if drawn like a dog to another scent. He slipped back into the gloom and was gone.

Thomas stood up and dusted some mud off his jeans. "So you can see them? Other ghosts, I mean."

"See them?" said Trixie. "Some even talk. Not like you living people do. We don't need Artifacts, either. Sometimes we can think what we want to say to each other and that's enough. That's called telepathic, right? But all ghosts are different. There are some really scary ones out there who like to scream their brains out. That fella over there? He's different. Doesn't say a word, just does this whole mime thing." Trixie made her face go blank and started gesturing with her arms as if she was stuck behind glass. "Real odd duck. Jerry Feinhurst's his name. Feel bad for the guy, not being able to find his head and all. Anyways, you said you were headed somewhere?"

Thomas retrieved the small business card from his pocket and held it up so Trixie could read it.

Trixie made a sour face.

"What kind of scam is that? Somebody thinks they're such a big deal they don't even put their address or phone number or nothing? Just some lousy initials and . . . what is that? A sketch of a muffin?"

"It's a shell," said Thomas, tracing the image with his finger. "See? Those are flames."

"Right. I knew that. It's all this . . ." Trixie gestured to the swirling fog. Then her eyes lit up. "Wait! That's it! A big fat shell! Same place as the horn man! C'mon, Creeper!"

"Same place as what—"

But Trixie was already tearing off through the fog.

Thomas ran after her, his eyes fixed on Trixie's shimmering party dress. A squeal of tires sounded up ahead. Out of the fog came the buttermilk blur of two large headlights. Thomas threw himself against a prickly hedgerow to let the car pass. The driver must not have noticed him through the gloom, because the car didn't slow down, but kept zooming along until its red taillights disappeared around a bend. Thomas sighted Trixie up beyond a tall hedgerow and took off again.

As the road climbed higher and higher, the flood walls widened, wrapping their stony arms around a set of intimidating Victorian mansions. Here were the homes of Gloomsbury's elite, families like the Pratchetts, steel and iron moguls and creators of the legendary Lobster Knuckler. In the shadow of the Pratchett mansion Trixie came to a halt.

"Up there," said Trixie. "Past those houses. That's where I saw it. There's a shell painted on one of the gates."

"Yeah, so?" said Thomas. "There are probably a lot like that. We're in New England, remember?"

"Not *any* shell, doofus. That's an oyster shell, right? The light wasn't good when you showed it to me. That's why I thought it looked like a muffin. But it's an oyster shell, no doubt about it."

Thomas stared back at Trixie. His horrible poker face didn't hide his astonishment.

"So I know my shells," said Trixie. "Big whoop. It was tough times in G-town when I was your age. We dove for all kinds of grub. Anything you could get your hands on to stay alive. Now if I can only remember where I saw it . . ."

Trixie fluttered her fingers against her pale baby's bottom chin and frowned. Then her eyes lit up. The fox grin flashed again.

"That's it! That one over there! I stopped at the gate when I heard the horn coming from over the hill. You see, Jefferson, my fiancé, he loved that New Orleans sound. He was a real horn nut, Thomas. Trombone was his big love . . . well, you know, after me. Anyway, I was wandering around, thinking about how crappy it is to have this unicorn sticking out of my belly, when I hear someone blowing a horn up there in the middle of the night. Real sweet, Thomas, like good old King Oliver. Like that song 'When You're Smiling'."

Trixie closed her eyes and started to sway. Her blue lips curled to the corners of her pale cheeks as she rocked and swayed in time with what seemed like a lovely memory replaying in her mind. Then, remembering where she was, her eyelids open. She stared sheepishly back at Thomas.

"You don't know what I'm talking about, do you, bub?"

"Nope."

"Well, c'mon. Let's see if anyone's home."

They hurried down the road until they came to another bulge in the flood wall. Out of the gloom another Victorian mansion loomed. This one had a gabled roof just like Thomas's house, though its roof was covered in copper snowguards called snowbirds that gleamed faintly through the fog. A winding stone path led down from the house, terminating in a picket fence with a gate overrun with vines and the white wood stained a moldy gray. As Thomas crept towards the gate, he could hear Trixie's voice calling out behind him.

"See! I told you I'd help you with your other cases. Betcha didn't think you needed a Fixer's assistant, huh?"

Across a large brace panel in the gate Thomas could make out the letters. The paint was chipped away in places, and a few of the letters were covered by vines. He reached down into his pocket and pulled out the business card. Brushing back a few vines with one hand, he could see the image of a giant shell painted into the wood, and beneath the shell, a set of letters. He held the card up to the panel, comparing the image and the letters. Trixie was right. He smiled.

A blast of icy death-chill pressed against his shoulder. He turned to find Trixie standing next to him, smiling her semi-feral grin.

"It's alright, bub," she whispered. "You can thank me later."

• • •

Thomas pushed back the unlatched gate. The old wood gave way with a whine of rusted hinges. Together he and Trixie climbed the steep path of jagged granite flagstones until they reached a small porch framed by two pillars stained and speckled with mold.

The wind hissed and seethed through the gaps in the pillars, rustling a wreath of withered ivy hanging from the front door. A brass door knocker shaped like a large seashell—an oyster shell—gleamed faintly in the shadows cast by the brown and crinkled leaves. The ring on the knocker was polish-worn from all the hands that had made calls on the house through the years.

Thomas reached out his hand, grasping for the ring . . .

NOW IS THE FATEFUL TURN,
THE *READER'S* TURN!

SHOULD POOR THOMAS
FULFILL FATE'S PROMISE?

AND FIND WHAT'S IN STORE
BEHIND THE DOOR?

PERHAPS WE'LL *MIRROR*-SHOW
M A Y H E M ' S M A D O V E R F L O W

SHOULD FECKLESS THOMAS
TURN TAIL . . . AND *GO!*

BUT IF TIME LOVES A HERO,
SET YOUR *FEAR-DOMETERS*
BACK TO ZERO

AND MOVE AHEAD
PAST THIS NEXT PAGE OF DREAD!

Chapter Eight
The Lost Art of *Rottuteningar*

Before Thomas could grab hold of the ring there came a series of sharp *clinks* and *clanks*, followed by several jerking bolt thrusts. Upon the last thrust, the door swung open. No light glimmered in the doorway; indeed, it would have been impossible, for an imposing figure stood blocking all light from seeping out.

A giant woman in a dark wool dress the color of the unlit ocean stood in the doorway. Thomas did not see her face—not yet. His eyes were focused on the feather duster a few inches from his nose. Two gnarled hands clenched the cleaning tool as if brandishing a mighty two-handed broadsword. Thomas's gaze now rose upwards until he reached a stocky block of weathered flesh-scape that bore no curling lines around the eyes from years of smiling. As the old woman's tightly-drawn mouth opened to speak, a froggy, surprisingly deep voice called down to Thomas.

"*Já?* What is it?"

Thomas turned to Trixie for help, but Trixie held both hands over her head as if to say *Got no clue, bub.* The old woman followed Thomas's gaze. Seeing no one else on the porch, she let out a grunt.

"You speak! You speak now!"

The feather duster raised a few inches in warning. Thomas could see the broken places where the feathers were bent or altogether missing. He had the sudden premonition that more than a few cushions had been walloped by the duster in times past.

"I'm Thomas, Thomas Creeper." Thomas fished out the small business card from his pocket and held it up with a trembling hand. "He gave it to me at the museum. He said that if I could figure out who he was, then I should come find him."

The woman stared at the card and then back at Thomas. The contempt and annoyance she exuded from every pore of her being seemed to lessen as some root of understanding took hold, though she didn't take the card. Instead, turning on her heel, she moved away from the door. Light filled the vacated space, revealing a large entrance room with a polished black-and-white checkerboard floor.

"Well?" Thomas heard Trixie sigh behind his ear. "You gonna hang out here all day like the pizza delivery boy waiting for a tip, or you gonna go follow Miss Sunshine inside?"

Muttering low under his breath, Thomas shook his head and stepped inside the foyer.

He shut the door behind him and removed his rain coat and hung it on a brass rack near the door. Turning around slowly, eyes welling with wonder, he surveyed the room and its collection of objects, each one more curious than the next.

In the center of the room sat a large sculpture of a man with antlers and hooves hoisting a bunch of grapes into his mouth and looking rather deranged. Left of the sculpture, positioned between a pair of marble busts of two gloomy men with ornately-carved beards, a wooden pedestal rose like a lectern at a church. A book sat on the pedestal, the cover overlayed in brilliant gold leaf. As for the room itself, it was circular in design. On the left side, a marble staircase ascended to a second floor landing. The right side of the room held a small gallery of paintings with gilded frames illuminated by overhead lamps. From where Thomas stood he couldn't make out what the paintings themselves were about, only rough shapes with thick brush strokes like Van Gogh's "Starry Night" his teacher Ms. Nielson had made them all study in art class.

Not knowing what he should do or where he should go, Thomas waited awkwardly for a few moments, listening to a conversation going on somewhere deeper in the house. A beeping sound separated the two voices, as if whoever was talking was using some kind of intercom.

BEEP! HISSSSS. Eckard?

BEEP! HISSSSS. 10-4. Rolling back. Locks secure around the gym.

On a door at the far side of the foyer, Thomas could make out the shadowed silhouette of the giant woman who had greeted him on the doorstep, still gripping her feather duster. That was the room where the strange conversation seemed to be coming from. Thomas turned to Trixie. He whispered low so he didn't arouse any attention from the other room.

"Don't talk to me now, okay? They can't see or hear you, but that doesn't mean you're not gonna mess this whole thing up for me."

"Mess this up? Why you little . . . Ugh!"

The reaction was just what Thomas was hoping for.

Trixie stormed off, passing through the old woman who had suddenly appeared at the other end of the room. The action caused the old woman to sneeze—violently—something Thomas hadn't anticipated. Not thinking, merely reacting, the old woman covered her face with the feather duster, which only precipitated more sneezing. Sneezing and cursing in a guttural foreign language, she pointed to the doorway where the weird conversation full of beeps and hisses was coming from. Thomas got the message. He picked up his pace and headed for the door.

Before he passed through, however, he stopped. He spied something strange out of the corner of his eye.

It was Trixie.

She didn't look peeved anymore. She was standing inside another room, this one colored by exotic green wallpaper like the skin of some tropical frog. Trixie's mouth was moving, and there was an overjoyed look on her face, a look Thomas had only seen when she'd gone into her weird memory-trance earlier, swaying to the music of King Oliver. Thomas craned his neck. *Who was she talking to?* Thomas remembered Trixie's words earlier, how she'd explained the way some ghosts communicate with each other by merely thinking what they wanted to say. At least from Trixie's overjoyed expression this didn't seem like one of the screamers she'd warned Thomas about. He started to head over to investigate when his sneakers squeaked against the polished marble, giving him away.

"Come in! Come in!" a raspy voice called out behind the doorway. "Don't loiter on the threshold, my young detective. And please, pay no mind to Sigrún. That woman could scare the pants off the devil himself."

Having no other option but to turn back and probably get smacked by a feather duster, Thomas pushed open the door and stepped inside.

If the curiosities of the foyer were intriguing, this side chamber was even more wondrous and peculiar.

In the center of the room were a pair of couches upholstered in dazzling blue and white fabric. Above one couch rose a vast network of swooping, curling plastic tubes like a crazy subway system. A printed sign hung from one of the larger tubes. Thomas squinted his eyes and read the words: *Chunnel to France.* Underneath the letters were a series of raised dots Thomas recognized as braille from the magazines he'd seen at the doctor's office. His curious eyes followed another tube the color of green sea glass. It also had a sign: *Knickerbocker to Myrtle Avenue.* The tube wound and spiraled its way up into a large terrarium-sized chamber that looked like a miniature playground complete with tire swing, monkey bars, and sand box. Thomas covered his mouth with his hand, not just from the pungent animal aroma the many scented candles positioned around the room did little to conceal, but from the sheer amount of time, money, and dedication it must have taken to achieve such a weird playground for the benefit of—

Thomas's foot struck the side of an opened carboard box.

He read the words stamped down the box's side.

Rat Chute Boogie: Master Set.

It all made sense now.

The whole sprawling tube metropolis was for the benefit of rats.

"Quick, Thomas! Come see the latest developments happening in the *völundarhús* box. Ipso's ahead by a good margin, but with the right encouragement I believe our poor boy Facto can regain the lead and secure the cheese."

Mesmerized by the strange tube world, for the first time Thomas noticed a bald head poking up from behind one of the couches.

He made a few hesitant steps forward, stepping over a sign that had fallen to the carpet that read *Minotaur's Labyrinth.* He crept over and sat down on the vacant couch.

Seated across from him, smiling gleefully, was the old tour guide from the Alderfer Museum. Today he wore a colorful suit of weaving blues, oranges, and pinks called a madras with a matching bowtie. The same boxy, tinted glasses covered a large portion of his wrinkled face of which the pitted strawberry of a nose was still the defining feature. The mysterious tour guide sat hunched over a large coffee table, waving his hands like a magician over a lidless wooden box. Thomas watched as the old man reached down and moved his hands around inside the box.

"That's it! Get it, Ipso! Don't burn out so soon! We don't need another case of the tortoise and the hare!"

Intrigued, Thomas leaned over and peered inside.

Inside he discovered an intricate maze of passageways. Two rats—one smallish and black, the other fat and caramel brown—were hard at work, pushing a set of dice through the wooden maze. There were several knicks and dings in the wood floor, which made Thomas think that whatever the strange game was it had been played many times before. In the center of the maze was a chamber where the prize—a wedge of cheese—awaited the victor.

"The game, as I'm sure you're wondering," said the old man, "is called '*Rottuteningar*,' which crudely translated into English means 'Rat Dice.' Allegedly, it was created by Icelandic sailors who got bored out of their gourds while stranded during windless days at sea. One thing every ship seems to have is rats. How the first sailors trained these glorious beasts to go for the cheese is a mystery, one I hope someday to—"

All of a sudden there was a sequence of sharp beeps.

It was the same beeping Thomas had heard from the hallway. The beeps sounded again. He followed the sound back to a small radio with a blinking LED screen resting on a side table next to the old man's couch. There was a crackle of static. A voice sounded in the speaker. Thomas felt his stomach muscles tighten beneath his shirt. He recognized the voice.

Sheriff Korvin.

Don't go blabbing to anyone about the third one, Johnson. I already have Morris and those other jackasses at the Morning Mooring filling up my voicemail and beating on the coroner's door for an interview. Who the hell tipped them off about a third body?

Thomas watched the smile on the old man's face slip a little. Reaching over, he twisted a knob on the radio. The speaker crackled and went silent.

"We'll get to that dark business soon enough, my young friend." The old man leaned back over the coffee table. He placed his wrinkled hands back inside the maze box and felt around, pursing his lips with every touch and tap. He smiled broadly. "Ah! You see! I told you our dear little tortoise, Facto, would come through in the end. He's followed his nose right to the source, just like a good detective, Thomas."

The old man reached down and patted the bumbling brown rat who'd pushed his dice all the way to the central chamber and gained his prize. Thomas smiled as he watched the rat go through the block of cheese like a buzz saw.

"Now, now. No moping, Ipso," the old man chided, lowering his hand so the smaller black rat could climb aboard like a ramp. "Here, Thomas. Take him. Don't worry, he's quite hygienic. You'll find more germs on the Gloomsbury-Hampswich crosstown bus than on these fine gentlemen. They get baths twice a week. Poor Sigrún. May the Vatican grant her sainthood someday. Take him, Thomas. I think he likes you."

Before Thomas could protest the old man handed the small black rat across the coffee table. The creature landed softly into Thomas's outstretched palms, its scratchy feet prickling his skin. The rat stood up and sniffed the air a few times, scanning Thomas with wet, curious eyes. For the first time Thomas noticed a white blaze running down the center of the rat's forehead, along with another interesting feature: a huge chunk was missing from the rat's left ear. As Thomas considered these unique markings, the rat flew up his arm . . . and perched on top of his shoulder!

"What's he doing now, Thomas?"

"He's . . . um, sitting on my shoulder."

The old man clapped his hands. "I knew it! Ipso approves! He's a stern judge of character. You pass the test, Thomas."

Thomas cracked a smile. The rat lowered down and soon seemed as happy as sitting on top of a big block of cheese.

"I-I'm sorry," Thomas said after a long pause. "Please don't take this the wrong way, but—"

"Who am I and why are you here? Fair questions," said the old man, smiling again. He raised a wrinkled pointer finger into the air. "If you will permit our first detective challenge to run a little longer, I'd say that the clues to my identity are hidden somewhere in this room."

Thomas gazed at the rat pipe metropolis. "So you're some kind of . . . um . . . rat specialist . . . guy?"

The old man chuckled. "Hardly! I mean that if a budding detective were to scrutinize the photos *behind* them . . ."

The old man waved a wrinkled hand at a series of photographs hanging on the wall by the door. Thomas hadn't noticed the photographs or the wall, his eyes having been fixed on the weirder, rodent-related objects in the room.

". . . they might arrive at some interesting conclusions."

Thomas pushed himself up from the couch. Ipso didn't seem to mind the change in location. As Thomas stepped over to investigate the photographs, the rat lowered down, jockeying a few seconds before finding his balance. Crossing the room, Thomas caught sight of Trixie through the drapes of a large bay window.

She was standing on a side porch outside talking with someone.

The figure next to Trixie stepped closer and appeared between the drapes. A finger of fear poked Thomas between his shoulder blades. *A ghost!* The ghost standing next to Trixie wore a brown felt hat called a porkpie, tipped back on the crown of his head. His dark skin shone almost blue-black beneath the pale, ethereal glow circling his body. He wore a white shirt with a black bowtie that dangled loose and untied beneath his goateed chin. In his hands he held what looked like a smaller, more compact trumpet, which he seemed to be showing Trixie, turning the instrument around on its side and pointing at its many sparkling valves.

The raspy voice behind Thomas's shoulder startled him.

"Find anything interesting yet?"

Now Trixie was pointing at Thomas, moving her mouth like she was talking a mile a minute. Thomas watched the expression on the other ghost's face morph into a look of wonder. *Better not be telling him I'm a Fixer*, thought Thomas, clenching his fists. He cast Trixie a nasty look and turned back to the wall of photographs.

The first photograph that caught Thomas's eye displayed two figures—two small boys about the same age, clad in matching white shirts and shorts, leaning against a flagpole and looking rather miserable. Behind them a great yard yawned, the grass all finely mowed like the fairway on a golf course. A mansion rose in the background, a fortress of shuttered windows and sloping and falling rooflines. Thomas lifted his hand then stopped and looked back, making sure he hadn't upset Ipso's balance. The rat was quite content. Slowly, Thomas reached out and brushed away a film of dust from the photograph in front of him. There was a small round speck in one of the mansion's windows. He leaned forward.

There was a face in the window.

Even with the poor lighting, Thomas could make out a few distinguishing features: dark hair, pale face, the outline of a dress. *A young girl.* Looking at the girl's half-hidden face, Thomas felt a shiver prickle through him followed by a loneliness he couldn't quite place. *Get a grip, man.* He shook off the weird feeling and shifted his gaze to another photograph.

In this next one Thomas recognized his host, the old tour guide and rat enthusiast, though he looked considerably younger. He didn't have any wrinkles, and instead of his boxy, square-rimmed glasses he sported shades with slightly rounded frames called aviators. He was leaning up against an old police cruiser, wearing a navy blue uniform. A gold star on the left breast pocket glinted faintly in the sepia-toned light.

"You were a policeman?"

No answer came from the couch.

Thomas's gaze wandered down to a small gold plate on the frame. The plate seemed to have eluded the housekeeper's duster. Thomas brushed away a thick film of dust. He shifted his body so the light over his head could catch the lettering.

To Sheriff Byron A.C. Sneed

For Your Great Service to the Town and People of Gloomsbury

"Wait," said Thomas, his voice cracking with fear. "You're a Sneed?"

Thomas turned around. Byron Atticus Courtney Sneed made a small bow from his seat.

"Creepers and Sneeds," Byron rasped, shaking his head and frowning deeply so the lines around his mouth grew even tighter. "It seems that the great story of Gloomsbury demands another chapter from our two families, Thomas Creeper. For good . . . or for ill."

• • •

Thomas stood for a long time as the bewildering particulars of the past few minutes collided like atoms in his brain.

He looked over at the window. Trixie and her new ghost friend were gone. A dry taste filled his mouth. *Was this another Sneed trick? Had the old man lured him here with the point of pulling off some cruel joke at his expense?*

"LUNCH!" a throaty voice bellowed from the hallway.

Thomas jumped back, swinging an elbow and inadvertently knocking one of the picture frames off the wall. Horrified, he watched the frame clatter to the ground, glass shards flying out all over the carpet. At the sound of the crash, Ipso stood up on his hind legs. He made a few sniffs at the air. Turning, he regarded the culprit with wet, curious eyes.

"I'm so sorry," said Thomas, hunching down. "I'll clean it up—"

"Please don't trouble yourself," said Byron. "Too many nasty broken pieces. Sigrún, if you would be so kind to get a broom and dustbin."

Plonking footsteps echoed through the hallway. A closet door was thrust open followed by a curse in the strange, guttural language. Tapping his way around the couch with his cane, Byron made his way over to Thomas. Soon he was smiling his broad smile again, his veiny cheeks flushed with color.

"This way, my friend. Before it gets cold."

"I'm sorry," said Thomas. "I should get back home . . . No, wait. Shoot."

He'd forgotten about the report! He had to get the interview he'd promised his mother if he wanted to keep up the ruse he was on a research assignment.

"What is it, Thomas?" said Byron, pausing and folding his hands over the top of his cane.

"It's just . . . I told my mom. You see, I'm homeschooled and my mom's my teacher and I told her . . . Oh, it's stupid—"

"It can't be stupid if it's causing you this much consternation," said Byron. "Out with it. Facto and I promise to be impartial judges, won't we, Facto?" The old man raised a wrinkled hand and gave a little scruff to the rat on his shoulder who was already busy sniffing at the delicious scents wafting in from across the foyer.

"I told my mom I wanted to interview you for this report about the exhibit at the Alderfer."

"Fantastic," said Byron. "I have an extra tape recorder you can use. We'll get your interview and then get you on your way. How does that sound? Now, if you please . . ." He tilted his bald head at the door. "Sigrún makes a roast duck that would make the dead come back to life." Letting out a hearty chuckle, he turned away. As he clicked his cane out the door and down the marble hallway, Thomas pondered the weight of these words, not feeling particularly good about them.

Soon they were munching on crispy duck served on gleaming silver platters. After serving Thomas and Byron, Sigrún prepared two small plates for Ipso and Facto and set them down on the table. As the rats dug into their meals, Thomas glimpsed a miracle: a smile broke over the brooding housekeeper's face. Catching Thomas looking up at her, Sigrún scowled and spun away, retreating to the pantry where she set about brutalizing vegetables with merciless, guillotine-style chops.

Clicking on Byron's tape recorder, Thomas fired off a few questions he thought would make good material for his report. It soon made sense why Byron was so helpful at the Alderfer. He was no dilettante, but a real scholar of the ancient world. Citing from memory the writing of Rome's foremost historians Livy, Suetonius, and Tacitus, Byron led Thomas on a fascinating virtual journey back to Rome's humble beginnings from republic to imperial powerhouse. Forty minutes flew by as Byron presented highlights from Rome's past: its consolidation of the Mediterranean in the Punic Wars ("You wouldn't want to be standing chewing grapes in Tuscany when Hannibal's elephants came thundering through!"); the ingenious inventions of the engineer Frontinus whose aqueducts allowed millions of gallons of water to be moved across the empire ("You don't want to taste that water when the Tiber overflows, believe me, Thomas!"); and, of course, a brief history of Rome's bronze, silver, and gold coinage. Though she was more than a little annoyed at the request, Sigrún brought a small display case from Byron's study containing a genuine *aureus*, a gold Roman coin, with the face of the emperor Marcus Aurelius, the so-called Philosopher King.

Thomas set down his fork. His plate was nearly empty. The food had been delicious, the duck slathered in a syrupy sauce tasting of fresh oranges. Byron, on the other hand, had barely been able to get a morsel down during his lecture. He beamed a ruddy red, cheek to cheek, though Thomas suspected the second glass of wine Sigrún had poured for him might have had something to do with it.

"Now for the other business at hand," Byron whispered. He reached over and clicked off the tape recorder.

"Oh, sorry," said Thomas.

"Stop apologizing, my young friend. I'd like to keep this part of our discussion 'off the books' as they say. Ipso and Facto won't tell a soul, I promise. From the sound of it, I doubt they'd have much to report."

Thomas looked over at the two rats. They both had rolled over on their backs, their paunch bellies hoisted high in the air. One even seemed to be snoring.

"There's . . . something else," Byron continued in a halting, hesitant voice. All the humor drained from his face. Licking his cracked lips he began again, slowly, anxiously, as if each word were a harmful pill that hurt going down. "It's something our sheriff doesn't understand about all of this . . . dark business."

"Korvin? What do you mean?"

"It's just a hunch. I know that seems like flimsy cause for moving forward, but I can't shake it. Something's been left at each crime scene, something marked upon these poor souls that are washing up around Gloomsbury. I've listened to the chatter with my top secret device over there. Korvin wants the details kept out of the reports. He thinks it will buy him time to solve everything. But he's all thumbs, Thomas. The whole Gloomsbury Sheriff's Office doesn't have a *scintilla* of the detective skill you and I have, or Ipso and Facto for that matter."

Thomas wanted to blurt out everything: the P.B.O.U.D., the reports he and Cyril had smuggled out of Korvin's office, and—most important of all—the email with the terrifying video sent by Fulvius Marcius Cinta. For the time being, however, the missing information in Korvin's reports seemed more important. *What was Korvin trying to cover up?*

"What do you mean something's been marked on these people?" Thomas asked.

Byron shook his head and frowned. "You saw the color on the body down by Town Beach, yes?"

"How did you know about that?" Thomas threw a glance at the small portable radio sitting on the side table. He was pretty sure it was illegal, even if Byron had been Gloomsbury's sheriff long ago. "Right. The radio. Korvin must have said something."

"Yes," said Byron. "I'm sorry you had to see that, Thomas. But it's fate. I'm sure of it. You? Me? Creeper and Sneed? It's all one story, don't you see? The long, dark story of our town. But we'll write a better ending, won't we, Thomas? And it begins with two letters. Whoever is doing this, they're leaving marks on each body. Letters. One on each eyelid."

The dry taste returned to Thomas's mouth. All the syrupy-sweet goodness from the meal evaporated. The dining room warped in and out like a rush of vertigo. He was certain Trixie and the other ghost were back at the window watching them. He turned his head nervously, but all he saw were the drawn drapes with nothing moving behind them.

"*RN*," said Byron. "Those are the letters the killer has inked on the eyelids of these poor souls. Korvin thinks it's someone's initials, someone living here in Gloomsbury, some maniac nurse who's gone off their rocker. RN's the professional designation for resident nurse, as you probably know. At least that's a little more out of the box. I'll give Korvin credit for that. But I have this hunch, Thomas, it's something bigger . . . "

Byron held his knife into the air. His wrinkled hand trembled. "I have this hunch."

Chapter Nine
Flip Carson Stumbles on a Clue

Thomas had been holding all his secret cards close to his chest, waiting to see if he could really trust Byron Sneed. For his part, Byron had shown Thomas all of his cards, his whole deck. Moreover, he had shared vital information with Thomas that no one else in Gloomsbury except Sheriff Korvin and a few of his officers knew. It was time to come clean about the e-mail and the video sent by whoever was masquerading as Fulvius Marcius Cinta.

Thomas described the video to Byron in horrifying detail—the dark pit and the chandelier ringed with candles, the screaming man, everything. When it was all over, Byron sank back into his chair. A troubled look washed over his face. Slowly, as if shaking off some terrible revelation, he straightened up and whispered:

"You do know what this means, don't you, Thomas? The killer or one of their accomplices was at the museum that day. You saw that room. How many people were there?"

Thomas shrugged. "I don't know. Fifty? Sixty people?"

"A good showing for a weekday afternoon," said Byron. "We need ids on all of them, but I can't go marching in and demand to see the museum's security footage. Why would a blind old man ask to see that?" Byron groaned. "No, no, we have to use what we know. And what *do* we know, Thomas?"

"That the killer is interested in ancient stuff . . . like Roman stuff?"

"Right. And not just that. Whoever they are, they're interested in a far more personal subject."

Thomas scrunched up his face. "What?"

"*Us*," said Byron, shaking his head. "They're watching us, Thomas. Playing a game of cat and mouse. I think that video you received is some kind of perverse challenge."

"A challenge?"

"A call to action. I think the killer is running us through a maze of their own making, like the *völundarhús* box over there in my study. We need a way out, Thomas. We need *illumination.* We need to see past these cruel vestiges, these wisps and fragments of terror."

Thomas swallowed hard into his chest. "H-h-how do we do that?"

Byron stood up, scraping the legs of his chair across the floor. The sound roused the two Icelandic rats from their slumber. As if ready to join the conquest of another great game, they stood up on their hind legs and started sniffing the air expectantly.

"We beat Korvin to the punch, that's how. I'll use my secret device to listen in, see what I can find out that Korvin doesn't want us to know. In the meantime, I'm giving you a second assignment in addition to your Roman studies. I want you to explore those two letters. Your agile brain unlocked the final resting place of our two ancestors. I have no doubt it will do the same in this new chapter of evil."

Thomas nodded. Confusion gripped him like some spectral ghoul shaking him by his collar. He didn't know where to start. *Two letters?* He knew a little bit about exponential math theory. It could be a billion permutations, a billion different leads. Suddenly, as if to silence all the panic in his brain, an image flashed inside

Thomas's mind's eye, the image of a smiling woman, wearing tortoise shell glasses and holding a teetering stack of books. *He did know someone who could help them. Why hadn't he thought of her before?*

"Okay," said Thomas. "I have this friend. Ms. Katz. She's a genius. She's Gloomsbury's head librarian. I think she might be able to help."

"And do you trust her, Thomas?"

"Of course. She helped my friend Jeni and me when we needed help with . . ."

He didn't know where Byron stood on the whole issue of ghosts springing back to life. He decided it was probably best to leave out any mention of the undead menace known as Jacob Crowley and his Sieve henchmen.

". . . with another case," Thomas quickly recovered. "The one that led us to finding the Creeper and Sneed bones in the quarry in Marvale."

Byron snatched his cane from the back of another chair. "Excellent! It's settled then. We bring in an ally. I'll have Sigrún drop you off at the library if you like."

An audible groan sounded in the recesses of the house.

"No, that's okay," said Thomas. "I'll walk. I need to think through all of this."

Byron smiled his cracked smile. "Well, then, Detective Creeper, I suggest you keep your wits about you. I'll be in touch soon. Let me show you out."

"No, I'm fine," said Thomas. He'd made a second detection in the room: Trixie and her ghost friend had reappeared. They were now standing on either side of Byron like undead bookends. Thomas had managed to survive the whole afternoon without revealing his big secret—that he could see ghosts. He wasn't going to slip up now.

He turned for the door. As he passed through the doorway, he locked eyes with the old housekeeper. The feather duster was gone, replaced by a large kitchen knife stained blood-red and covered with a mess of seeds. It was an unnerving sight to say the least.

"Thank you for lunch," mumbled Thomas as he squeaked past. He backed his way into the foyer and nearly bumped into the sculpture of the deranged man hoisting the bunch of grapes over his mouth. Grabbing his raincoat from the rack, he threw it on, turned the door handle, and stepped out once more into the whipping wind.

He checked his watch. Still two hours before he was expected back for his night class at the funeral home. His mind swam with questions—questions about purple ink and letters tattooed on dead eyelids. Maybe Ms. Katz could help him unpack some of these riddles. She probably would tell him to go to the police. Even if she couldn't help him, just being around her smiling, thoughtful presence would make him feel better. As this warm thought crossed his mind, he turned to find Trixie emerging from behind one of the porch's stained pillars.

"Holy hell! So that old fruitcake's spending his time eavesdropping on the boys in blue, huh? I guess playing Pinochle and napping just isn't enough for him. "

"Pin—what are you talking about?" Thomas called back over his shoulder, working his way down the winding flagstone path. "Whatever. I gotta get to the library."

"Hold up a sec, will ya?" said Trixie, running after him, drawing her death-chill closer. "Listen to this, Creeper. Gabe says he's figured it all out."

"Gabe? Figured out what?"

"Why we, I mean *we* . . . " Trixie gestured to the other ghost, her new friend from Byron's house. The ghost-musician appeared a few steps behind Trixie and tipped his porkpie hat at Thomas.

"Why we're still here," Trixie sighed. "In G-town—you know, Gloomsbury." She swung around, blocking Thomas's path. "Gabe says it all came to him while he was playing his cornet." She made a nod again at the other ghost who smiled back, raising his gleaming instrument into the air like a trophy. "How aces is that, Thomas?"

"What are you talking about?"

Thomas shook his head. He didn't have time for some long, drawn-out tangent about the inner workings of the supernatural world. He needed to get to the library. He had to find out what the letters meant. He started down the steps again . . . only to walk head-first into what felt like a Sub-Zero cooler.

He jerked back. Trixie's pale face appeared in front of him, her fox grin smiling back at him through tendrils of fog. Something freezing stabbed through Thomas's sternum. He leapt back. The tip of the bloody unicorn coming out of Trixie's dress unskewered itself from Thomas's chest.

"STOP THAT!" Thomas screamed, clutching his chest. "Why do you ghosts always have to do that? Pass through us whenever you feel like it?"

"Well, I wouldn't *have to* if you'd park those black leather Cadillacs for one minute and listen to me."

"Black leather—what the hell are you talking about?"

Trixie placed her hands on her hips. "I'm *trying* to tell you the big news, Thomas. I can't believe you, Mr. Smart-Ass Junior Detective, hadn't figured it out yet. It all makes perfect sense."

"What makes perfect sense?" Thomas stared back up the path to the shadow of the house. He relaxed. Byron and Sigrún weren't peeking through the blinds, watching him scream his lungs out at nothing but empty air. He turned back. Trixie's fox grin stretched to its max.

"That Gabe and I are angels, Thomas. How absolutely aces is that?"

• • •

As Thomas and his two ghost companions cut their way through the soupy gloom on their way out of the Gold Coast, Thomas decided to play Trixie's game.

"Okay, so let me get this straight. If you two *are* angels, then where are your wings, huh? Not to mention I don't remember hearing anything about an angel who flew down from heaven with a unicorn head coming out of their stomach."

"Oh, that's rich," said Trixie. "Sometimes I wonder why the whole Fixer torch got passed to such a dense block of unbelieving cra—"

A squeal of tires cut off Trixie's relentless potty mouth.

A pair of headlights zoomed out of the fog. The driver blared on their horn as the car rocketed past and disappeared back into the gloom. Cursing and muttering, Thomas unstuck his body from the prickly boxwood he'd thrown himself against in a last-ditch effort not to become roadkill. Regaining his footing, brushing dead leaves and cobwebs off his coat, he watched Gabe smile and fit his lips over the mouthpiece of his cornet. The ghost gave a loud shriek, mimicking the sound of the passing car horn before letting out a run of swinging, syncopated notes.

Trixie stopped and smiled back at Thomas. "I'm marooned on this sad island of a world and who shows up? The best damn horn man since old King Oliver."

Gabe tipped his hat again and made a slight bow before letting out another run of dazzling notes. Trixie shifted her gaze back to Thomas. The annoyed look from before returned.

"And I got you. A Fixer who doesn't want to fix even a sad sap like *him*."

Thomas followed the direction of Trixie's pale finger to a sight that made his shoulders stiffen and his hands ball up at his sides.

Jerry Feinhurst, the friendly neighborhood headless banker-ghost, had spotted them once again.

"Nah, that boy's an angel too," Gabe piped up behind Thomas. "Can't find his head is all. But he's a good one, that's for sure."

Thomas watched the headless banker-ghost sidle towards them. Gabe cracked a smile. Raising the cornet to his lips, he blasted another swinging riff. Though the headless ghost of Jerry Feinhurst had been subjected to ear-splitting waltzes at Brindle & Marsh Dance Studio only the day before, that kind of music seemed to have little effect on him. Today, underneath the spell of Gabe's glowing cornet, Headless Jerry swayed and moved his pinstriped legs as if they were as bendable as overcooked spaghetti.

"You see," said Gabe after the last note died. "Everyone says blues—jazz—whatever you want to call that good stew, that it's the devil's music. Makes people crazy. I say, nah, man. How could something so bad make people feel so good?"

For a few mystified moments Thomas watched the three ghosts—angels, whatever they wanted to call themselves. Spying a small stone bench flanked by moldy hydrangeas near the side of the road, he walked over and sat down. He gazed down at his shoes and the gravel of ground white shells that had turned gray and slimy from all the rain.

"Hey, what's wrong with your boy?" Gabe whispered to Trixie.

"Better let him have a moment to take it all in," said Trixie. "I forget to do that with him sometimes."

While raindrops splattered hard against his hood, Thomas thought about the past few hours. The afternoon had been a healthy dose of weird—no spoonful of sugar to make it go down easy, either. Killers and angels, headless ones and ones with unicorn heads sticking out of their stomach. *What would Jeni say if she was still around?*

Without being able to see the supernatural world like him, it would be tough for Jeni to accept all the new developments. The only other person who Thomas could think of, the only other one who might be able to make sense of the supernatural caught up in the *supernormal*, wore a black leather jacket and gloves and had somehow managed to use magic to get Thomas to steal official documents from the Gloomsbury Sheriff's Office.

Thomas heaved a deep sigh. He sat up. Feeling a seeping chill against his ribs, he turned to find Headless Jerry sitting next to him.

"Now what are you doing?"

The ghost held out his white gloves and proceeded to perform the old moveable thumb trick as if Thomas was a toddler.

"Seriously? Are you kidding me?"

But even Thomas couldn't overlook what the ghost was trying to do.

He was trying to cheer him up.

The white gloves fanned in front of Thomas, making a *Well?* gesture. Thomas made a slow, reluctant clap. Headless Jerry bowed. It was a kind gesture, or mostly kind. As the ghost bowed forward, his severed vertebrae swung close to Thomas's face.

"Okay," said Thomas, jerking up onto his feet. He knew it was time for a speech. He hated speeches, but he'd stood in front of empty graves before with no one so much as sniffling a few kind words for the departed. He hated those kinds of silences, even if his mother liked to say that "silence is sometimes grief's only answer." Whatever that meant.

Trixie and Gabe broke off their conversation and came closer. The wind pulled at Thomas's rain slicker. Rain fogged his glasses again. It wasn't the best stage for a speech, but he knew he had to say something. It was one of those moments in life that separated the big Before and After, the same way Byron's accident that had robbed him of his eyesight was a clear line down the middle of his life. If Thomas were some great superhero like his spy movie idol Ken Darby, the next words that came from him might have sounded a little more heroic.

"Fine. You're all angels. That doesn't change the fact that there's someone here in Gloomsbury who's killing people. Korvin's not going to figure it out. So I guess it's up to us."

Trixie nodded to Gabe. Leaning over, she whispered, "See, told you he'd come around."

"I'm going to the library to try to figure out what those letters the killer is leaving on eyelids might mean. If you want to help, spread out. Trixie, you're a great blabbermouth—"

"Hey!"

"Relax. In this case it's actually a good thing. Go do what you do best: ask around, see if any other ghosts—angels, whatever—whoever will talk to you, if they've seen somebody dumping bodies in the ocean. Maybe Gabe and Jerry can help you. Jerry seems to be pretty good at slipping between walls and stuff. He might be able to get into places you guys can't."

"Fine," said Trixie. "But can we have a team name? I mean, hasn't any group who's ever done anything good for the world, didn't they like . . . you know . . . have some famous name?"

"This isn't for the world, this is for Gloomsbury," said Thomas. "But sure. Fine. What do you want to call us, Trixie?"

Trixie narrowed her painted eyebrows. She looked at Gabe, then over at Headless Jerry, and finally back to Thomas.

"Hmmm . . . how 'bout . . ." She drummed her pale fingers against her dimpled chin. "That's it! How 'bout we call ourselves the Unicornettes?" She nudged Gabe in the ribs. "You see what I did there? Cornet and unicorn? That's pretty clever, huh?"

"Aces," said Gabe, nodding and stroking his goateed chin.

"Yeah! Aces!" said Trixie. "That can be our battle cry."

Trixie held out a blue-tinged hand.

Gabe put his hand over Trixie's.

Headless Jerry followed suit, placing a gloved hand over Trixie's and Gabe's.

Last of the four—the ever-reluctant Fixer—Thomas inched over and held his hand over the others. The magnified chill coming off the pile of undead hands felt like reaching down into an ice-fishing hole.

"A-a-a-a-ces," Thomas chattered.

"ACES!" Gabe and Trixie cried in unison.

Headless Jerry shrugged his shoulders. *If only he had a mouth!*

They broke the circle and headed off. As Thomas weaved his way down the road, following the flood walls to the entrance of the Gold Coast, he could hear Gabe's deep voice over the wind and Trixie answering back.

"Unicornettes? Like Rockettes? That mean we're ladies?"

"Shut up, man."

• • •

Thomas pushed through the large revolving door and stepped into Gloomsbury Memorial Library, his home away from home.

He scoured the room, searching for the face of his friend, the brilliant and ever resourceful Ms. Katz. On the Head Librarian's desk, Thomas could see the usual pyramid of books waiting to be checked back in, but no Ms. K, smiling back at him with her wild squirrel's nest of hair and oversized tortoise shell spectacles.

Thomas tapped the toe of his sneaker nervously against the floor. He scanned the library stacks. There were a few readers milling about, but still no Ms. K. anywhere. Maybe the kooky librarian had disappeared into her office for a cup of one of her disgusting Nepalese "tongue root" teas. As Thomas's gaze focused on the teetering mound of books at checkout, he felt a pang of guilt. At the beginning of August, he'd broken the news to Ms. Katz that he wouldn't be returning in the fall to work for her as the library's Lead Page, an assistant position that not only paid decently, but gave Thomas first dibs on all new books and DVDs acquired by the library.

With his homeschooling workload and his night classes in the Preparing Room ramping up, combined with all the daily chores needed to keep the funeral home up and running, there wouldn't be much time left over for anything else. The reason Thomas had given Ms. Katz for giving up his job wasn't the full story, however. The *real* reason why Thomas was resigning his duties had to do with a certain someone.

Jeni.

Without Jeni around to share shifts with Thomas, the once magical library now felt like a favorite TV show that had gone on a season too long and had turned stale and predictable. Time had changed the actors, but not the setting. If Thomas stayed on at the library, no amount of interesting articles about new scientific or archeological discoveries Ms. K printed out for him each shift, or her horrible jokes that always had their punchlines mistimed, would cheer him up. There was no way he was going to be able to keep his mind off missing Jeni, not here in their favorite place where Thomas could forget about the funeral home, and where the two of them couldn't be called nerds by their peers. At the library, Thomas and Jeni could be the true versions of themselves: two brilliant teenagers in love with books, in a magic place where ideas and stories seemed to swirl in the very air they breathed.

Still not seeing a flutter of mauve in the stacks—Ms. K's preferred clothing color—Thomas had half a mind to walk back out the door, if it wasn't for the ghost that had spotted him.

Stepping out of the path of two young girls who'd tumbled into the room, talking a mile a minute, and ignoring Ms. K's sign that hung from the Circulation Desk—*Whisper! Books Are Sleeping!*—Thomas edged his way over to the magazine display rack, hoping the ghost's gaze would not follow him.

He was wrong.

Very wrong.

She—at least Thomas thought the ghost was a she—was hovering along the edge of a massive mobile suspended from the ceiling. The mobile was a gift from a wealthy trustee of the library. It had been installed earlier that year and depicted . . . Thomas wasn't quite sure. There were several few swooping panels someone might interpret as sails, though a few of them had giant holes bored into them so they looked more like the spots on butterfly wings that had evolved to mimic the eyes of greater predators.

"It's definitely modern," Ms. K announced the day the mobile went up. Modern or not, the mobile was truly anyone's guess.

Today the ghost hovering along the edge of the mobile appeared to be an infant. She was dressed in what was probably once a clean white gown, but had been stained by a stream of blackberry-colored liquid pooling from her mouth.

Looking down at Thomas, the infant-ghost gummed her lips together excitedly, clapping her hands together as if a puppy had bounded into the room. Unfortunately, this repetitive motion only further splattered the stream of grossness dripping from her mouth until her miniature hands were coated in ectoplasmic filth. Thomas felt his lunch start to come back up. He was thankful when he heard a familiar voice whisper-shouting down the hallway, a voice that drew him away from the horrifying scene playing out above him.

"By the tacked-up sleeve of Admiral Nelson, Flip Carson. If I've told you once, I've told you a thousand times. 'General Collection' doesn't mean books about generals. So, yes, there's a very good reason this book about traditional Mithai dishes for the Indian festival of Diwali doesn't contain battle maps or pictures of men with rapiers on horseback."

Trailing Ms. Katz, pushing a wobbly cart full of books, was Arnold Myers's best friend, Flip Carson.

He was an unnaturally tan teen—unnatural by Gloomsbury standards—a result of his love for wakeboarding far out beyond Mad Marge's reach with his older cousin, Bunny, thus named because of his prodigious overbite and disproportionally large ears. On more than one occasion, Flip, Bunny, and Arnold had landed in Sheriff Korvin's office for various stunts involving fireworks, wakeboarding, and, on rare misdemeanors, a combination of the two.

The previous summer the trio of friends had invented a new extreme watersport called "Crotch Cannon," what they believed would make them all rich and famous someday. Crotch Cannon featured two wakeboarders pulled by two opposing boats called Joust Buggies. Positioned carefully—very carefully—between the thighs of each wakeboarder was a powerful water-resistant Roman Candle, ordered direct from Captain Sparky's Firework Bonanza.

The rules were simple: the first wakeboarder to let go of the line from a direct hit by their opponent's "cannon" lost the match.

It was during one of these legendary matches that a poor elderly fisherman by the name of Mose Burgleweiss found himself caught between two opposing Buggies. The side article that appeared the following day in *The Morning Mooring* was a bit over the top with its use of alliteration—"Crotch Cannon Crossfire Cauterizes Old Clammer." The game was instantly banned from all shore points by Sheriff Korvin, while many volunteer hours raking up jellyfish slime from Town Beach were logged by Flip, Bunny, and a very disappointed Arnold Myers who believed he'd finally found his true calling as Gloomsbury's first professional Crotch Cannoneer.

Today Flip Carson was a pretty sorry sight. Thomas could tell Flip was way over his head in his new job as his replacement. He wore a wrinkled, oversized button-down shirt with the collar twisted halfway up. He looked like he'd rolled out of bed only moments before his shift, which was probably the case. Plastered up and down both sleeves were Ms. Katz's favorite brand of neon green Post-it notes. Stopping the book cart beneath the mobile, a few drops of the infant-ghost's ectoplasm splattered down over the book jackets. Even if Flip had the eyes of a Fixer, Thomas wasn't sure he would have noticed. He kept pointing back and forth from the books on the cart to the handwritten reminders pasted to his sleeves. A mortified look came over Flip's tan face, like someone being chased by a tiger into a room filled entirely with mousetraps.

"Thomas! Thank the mighty wind bag of Aeolus that blew you here. You're just in time."

Hearing yet another weird pronouncement from the mouth of Ms. Katz, even the vomiting infant-ghost seemed to crinkle her face in confusion.

Before Thomas could protest, Ms. Katz thrust a sheet of paper into his hands. Thomas turned the paper right-side up and read what was written. It was a sheet of printer paper, torn from the library's ancient printer that was always jamming up. On the page was a list of over a dozen items—books, DVDs, periodicals—all with their respective call numbers. Most had the handwritten word *CIBM* next to them, Ms. K's shorthand for "Checked In But Missing," while a few of them had *PHAN* inked next to them, short for Phantoms, Ms. K's personal term for books that seemed to have disappeared into thin air.

"It'll only take a few minutes, I promise. Please, Thomas," Ms. Katz moaned. "Can you show Flip some of your tricks? Like that memory game you and Jeni do before reshelving. What's it called again? Rack 'Em Up?"

"Stack Attack," Thomas answered weakly. Jeni was the reigning queen of Stack Attack. She held the library record. Thirty-seven books sorted in under a minute.

Thomas opened his mouth to protest. A giggle sounded above him, a giggle only Thomas could hear. A glob of ectoplasm landed on Ms. Katz's tortoise shell glasses. Seeing the desperate look on his friend's face, Thomas caved.

"Sure. Okay."

"Hot pickles!" Ms. Katz whisper-shouted (it was another one of her unique expressions).

Shaking her fists in triumph, the librarian turned away, heading for the growing line at the checkout desk. Thomas left the first-floor atrium, Flip following close behind, pushing his squeaky cart. They maneuvered their way through the library stacks until they came to the first stop indicated on Ms. Katz's sheet—the library's DVD collection.

Thomas knew people often returned DVDs in mismatched cases. While Flip looked on with his mouth open "huffing dust" as Uncle Jed would say, Thomas used his old admin password to log into one of the nearby computers.

He knew he had to work fast if he wanted to have time to get his own research done, his investigation into the mysterious letters *RN*. Making lightning taps on the keyboard, he cross-referenced the other titles checked out along with the missing DVDs. Using their call numbers, he tracked down the other items checked out by the same guests. His hypothesis was correct. The bulk of missing DVDs had been mismatched in the cases Flip had checked in but had failed to open and inspect properly.

Thomas returned to the computer and kept working down the list while Flip rattled on and on about the new wakeboard he was going to buy with his library earnings. Thomas made the mistake of nodding a few times during Flip's description of the "SliderX Zero Torque Wakerunner," making Flip think Thomas was really interested in "non-dragging, poly-fibrous skim technology." In reality, Thomas was only nodding along with the deductive reasoning going on in his brain as he tried to locate the whereabouts of the remaining PHANs and CIBMs.

"The SliderX has like zero drag, Creeper," Flip rattled on in his usual wheezy, mouth-breather voice. "You can do Potato Peelers, Butterslides . . . no problem, bro."

Thomas did his best to ignore Flip, as well as another ghost he now detected in the Reference Section about fifteen yards away: an old woman in a moss-green cloak, seated at a small reading table directly across from an old man snoring into his newspaper.

As Thomas scanned a shelf for his next sorting assignment, Flip leaned in.

"Hey, Creeper. Arnold said something about some psychos you guys ran into this summer?"

Thomas shrugged. He wasn't about to share any big secrets, not with a mouth-breather like Flip Carson.

"Arnold says you guys have kind of a gang or something? Not a gang, I mean, like a posse who solves crimes and stuff. You think . . . you think you guys could use a new member?"

"Don't you have your hands full here?" Thomas threw a glance at Flip's Post-it covered sleeves.

"Yeah, it sucks. No . . . I mean, it's great! Ms. K is nice and all. And I need money for the SliderX, but . . ."

Thomas turned his head. The cloaked old woman-ghost across the room was now staring back at him, only there was not much left of her face to stare with, only a hollowed-out crater with the skin all gross and goopy.

"Most people think I'm an idiot, you know? Whatever. I don't care. But I notice things too. Like . . . like I think someone's been stealing books from the library, Creeper."

"Stealing books?" said Thomas, not looking up. "What are you talking about?" He felt like throttling Flip. One of the missing books on his list, a book about the science of gamma rays, had been mixed up with a primer on English Grammar for budding writers called *Grammar Pays*.

Flip leaned back against the book cart and huffed a long, wheezy breath.

"Well, there's this weird thing that happened a couple weeks ago. Ms. K asked me to find this Phantom. I knew the one she was talking about 'cause I'd seen it before. It's always sort of falling out of the cases—"

"Stacks. They're called stacks."

"Yeah, yeah, stacks." Flip removed his finger from exploring the crater of his nose. "I'd even fixed the book from falling out of the ca—stacks, I mean—like more than once. Sometimes I'd see it lying on the ground. I don't know maybe the cover is all greasy or something. Doesn't feel greasy. Anyway, the cover is weird. It's got these triangles with dots all down the side. But, Creeper, you know what the weirdest part is?"

Thomas stopped fluttering his hands over the stacks. He'd been searching for a missing copy of *Red Herring, Red Dawn*, the latest thriller by Hampswich's literary celebrity Philip Masterson. Something Flip had said stuck like a twig in the spinning spokes of his brain. *Where had he seen a book with silver triangles and dots running down the spine recently?*

"Well, I checked the computer," Flip continued in an exhausted voice, as if remembering the task required every ounce of energy left inside his sun-scorched cerebellum. "It took me a couple of times to remember the login. When I finally got in, there was nothing about the book in the system. No listing. *Nada.* That's weird, right? I remembered the writer's name Korvac because it sounds like my dentist. His name is Korvell. Not like the cake people, that's Carvel. They make really good ice cream cakes. Last year, for my birthday . . . "

While Flip rattled on, something clicked in Thomas's brain.

It all made sense. *H.P. Korvac.* Thomas had picked up the same book earlier that summer. The way Flip described it, lying on the ground, the same thing had happened to Thomas. He probably would never have come across the book had he not stumbled into it walking down through the stacks. He'd left it behind in Ms. Katz's office after seeking her help about identifying the strange figures lurking about town, what had turned out to be Jacob Crowley and his Sieve minions. And it wasn't the last time Thomas had seen the book, either. Only a few days ago he'd spotted it, peeking out of the pocket of a certain black leather jacket.

"So, is that like a new mystery we can solve?" said Flip, flashing a gummy smile. "Does that mean I'm in the posse?"

Suddenly, crawling up from under the cart, pulling herself on top of the pile of books, the infant-ghost lifted her spewing mouth and smiled. Thomas grimaced.

"Trust me," said Thomas, turning away. "I don't think you want to be in this posse, Flip."

When he reached the main atrium he could see Ms. Katz cornered by a long line of visitors all holding stacks of books in their arms. The research into the mysterious letters *RN* would have to wait, Thomas realized, checking his watch. A friend needed his help, and for once it wasn't some moping spirit from beyond the grave with some unfinished agenda they need him to resolve.

Slipping behind the desk, Thomas moved the CLOSED sign off the desk and opened up a second checkout line. Straining her neck over a heap of books, Ms. Katz exchanged a look of pure gratitude before going back to stemming the tide of eager readers. Thomas set off at a rapid pace, checking out all the books, periodicals, and other media materials in front of him. As he swiped all the selections through the degaussing machine to demagnetize them, he didn't notice the titles or names of the authors on the covers.

There was only one name flashing like a billboard in his mind.

Cyril Barnes.

Why was Cyril Barnes sneaking books out of Gloomsbury Memorial Library, and of all books, one that wasn't listed anywhere in the library's system? Who was H.P. Korvac, and what had he written that was worth the risk of getting caught stealing?

Chapter Ten
Backfire / Thomas Gets a Visitor

Ms. Katz met Thomas at the door of the library before he could sneak out. He wondered whether the zany librarian—who often forgot about the rest of the world's responsibilities with her laser focus on the library—might try to ask him to stick around for the second wave of checkouts.

"Thanks again for saving the day, Thomas," Ms. Katz beamed up at Thomas (she was quite small and often referred to herself as "travel size"). Unhooking a cord with a laminated card from around her neck, Ms. Katz handed the card over to Thomas. He turned the card face-up in his hand. He recognized the logo on the front: a seagull balancing on a large spinning wheel, the logo of Gloomsbury's Shoreline Transportation System.

"Thought you might be able to use it," said Ms. Katz, smiling with purple painted lips. "Give those sneakers a break, eh? Should be good for the rest of the month, I think. I finally broke down and bought one of those new electric cars last week, Thomas. Yep, Ms. K is riding private from now on. About time, too. You know it's the third time this year someone's spilled their lunch on me on one of Mayor Plugg's new trollies? I feel like putting up a sign that announces to the world *Hey! Over here!* I'm a giant cafeteria tray. Slop your soup all over me."

Thomas was right. Being around Ms. Katz *did* make him feel better. He thanked her for the bus card. He turned to leave, but Ms. Katz gently touched his arm.

"Hold on a second. What's eating at you, Thomas? You look like you got the weight of the world on your shoulders. I hope I didn't add to it today with checkout help. If I did, I'm sorry."

"No, no, I'm—"

"It's okay. We don't have to talk about it right now. But anytime you want to vent, or need a good cup of tea to perk you up, you know my door is always open."

"Thanks, Ms. K."

Suddenly, a loud crash boomed through the foyer. Ms. Katz closed her eyes and shook her head. She didn't turn around. She didn't need to. There was only one hurricane of incompetence that touched down each week at Gloomsbury Memorial Library.

"It's Flip, isn't it?" Ms. Katz whispered out of the side of her mouth.

"Uh-huh," said Thomas.

Thomas could see Flip's cart had slammed into the water cooler by the periodical section. The big water drum lay on its side, spewing out liquid like an open fire hydrant.

"At least he's trying . . . right?" said Thomas. He watched Flip struggle to fit the water drum back on the cooler only to end up slipping on the wet tiles and falling back into the book cart.

"Trying *my patience* is more like it," grumbled Ms. Katz. Then, like a passing storm, she brightened back up. "Well, get home safe, Thomas. And come see me soon, okay? I have a feeling—"

The laser eye of the brilliant Eloïse Katz concentrated its powerful beam on Thomas.

"—our local celebrity and Lead Page *Emeritus* may be knee-deep in another mystery."

Casting Thomas a knowing smile, Ms. Katz spun on her heel and headed over to help Flip who was standing looking dejected, holding up a pile of soaked Post-it notes with the ink all bleeding away. *How on earth was he going to remember everything now?*

The last thing Thomas heard before the revolving door swung shut was Ms. Katz breaking her own "whispers only" rule at the library.

"I've got a new filing for you, Flip Carson! We're gonna file *you* under PH. Nope, that's not shorthand for power of hydrogen ions. It's for positively hopeless!"

• • •

Lucky for Thomas, one of Mayor Plugg's trollies was idling curbside at the base of the library steps. The fleet of vintage-looking trollies were part of the mayor's campaign to bring tourism back to Gloomsbury, though anyone who lived within town limits knew it was going to take a lot more than a few refurbished trollies to turn business around.

The brief disappearance of one of the trollies down a sinkhole—with customers still aboard—definitely didn't help boost faith in the mayor's tourism plans. The fact that the sinkhole debacle happened on the actual ribbon-cutting day of the campaign did not go unnoticed by Fletcher Morris, one of the mayor's sworn enemies and Editor-in-Chief at *The Morning Mooring*.

As the doors of the trolley flicked open in front of Thomas, a speaker over the door blasted out jangly carnival music.

"Welcome to a journey back in time!" the driver perched behind the steering wheel called down to Thomas. "Step right up and take in the delights of—oh, is that you, Creeper?"

The driver's prodigious overbite hadn't escaped Thomas's gaze. It was Flip Carson's cousin, Bunny, one of the three infamous inventors of Crotch Cannon.

Usually dressed in his wakeboarding attire of rash shirt, bathing suit, and flip flops, today Bunny was clad in a different uniform: a three-piece suit complete with tails that looked like it had been pulled from the bottom bin at a second-hand clothing store. A large top hat with a warped brim sat propped up on Bunny's shaggy blond head, and an earpiece microphone was hooked over one of his oversized ears, the kind telemarketers use to sell you magical self-cleaning shower curtains or miracle cures for hair loss. Boarding the trolley, Thomas did his best to hide his shock. The last time he'd seen Bunny Carson he was holding a Roman Candle between his legs and shrieking, "Look out for my fiery death ray!"

At the top step Thomas held up his card up to a small scanner and watched the light tick from red to green.

"Since it's just us right now, Creeper, you cool with me not doing the whole tour guide thing?" Bunny flipped the ear microphone away from his mouth so the rest of the passengers couldn't hear. "I've musta said the whole speech like a *hundred* times today. Mom said I woke up the whole house last night shouting in my sleep. 'And on your left, ladies and gentlemen, behold! The ruins of the Wheel of Wonder, Gloomsbury's legendary circus attraction!'" Bunny face-palmed himself and shook his crumpled top hat.

"Sure," said Thomas. "Hey, aren't you . . . you know . . . a little young to be driving this thing?"

"Had my license for about three months now," said Bunny, perking up. "Nobody wanted the job after that trolley went down over on Willow and Crescent. You heard about that, right? Korvin pulled me in the next day. Said it was time for me to give back to my community. Can you believe that? Korvin's all buddy-buddy with my supervisor Carl. Carl says all the roads have been like double and triple-checked this week. But ya know what, Creeper? I could have sworn I saw cracking points all the way down Thirty-Fifth this morning."

Thomas considered turning around, taking his chances walking home. He didn't feel like getting lost down a sinkhole with Bunny Carson behind the wheel. Before he could reconsider other transportation options, Bunny made a loud jerk on a lever and the accordion doors swung shut.

"Anyway, no biggie. The *la-dies* love the suit." Bunny flashed his giant overbite and made a loud *TH-WAP* with his suspenders. "All aboard!" Bunny slapped his forehead with hand again. "You see, Creeper? I can't help it. It's like it's programmed into me . . . like I'm some robot or somethin'. Sheesh."

Bunny let out another deep sigh and cranked the gear shift. The trolley took off, lurching over the moldy cobblestones, slickened with fresh rain.

Gripping the backs of seats for balance, Thomas found a spot near the middle of the empty trolley. He peered around. *No ghosts. At least that's good.* He tried to not think about what Bunny had said—about the cracking points running down Thirty-Fifth Street. When the jangly carnival music started up again, he was thankful Bunny elbowed the speaker and the music fizzled silent.

Crumpled on the seat next to Thomas lay a copy of the latest issue of *The Morning Mooring*. As the trolley rounded a particularly bumpy corner, the newspaper slid off the seat, landing on the toe of Thomas's sneakers. He picked up the paper. Before he could set it back down again his eyes locked on the black-and-white image of a familiar face.

It was Marylène.

She was standing on a barnacle-strewn jetty next to her father. A clipboard was clamped under one arm, and she held a fishing net in the other hand. Thomas almost didn't recognize her at first. She wore a baseball cap pulled down over her face, but her pretty smile and elf-like ears gave her way. In the background the great Marvale Lighthouse rose, distinguished by its giant rusted *M* on the front side of the tower. Thomas mouthed the article's headline:

GAUMONT FAMILY IN PURSUIT OF GREAT AQUATIC MYSTERY
IS GLOOMSBURY NEXT STOP FOR LUMINOUS WONDER OF THE DEEP?

Thomas turned the newspaper face-down on the seat. He thought back to Jeni's phone call, how she'd forgiven him for being a total jerk. He knew he shouldn't have feelings for anyone else. *But the way Marylène had hugged him back at the Sheriff's Office.* It made it pretty tough. It wasn't a switch you could flick on and off. Still, he knew he had to try.

About a half-mile from Thomas's stop at the corner of Thayer and Mt. Parnassus, a heavy-set woman carrying several plastic bags boarded the trolley.

She was bundled up in a heavy wool coat, the hood pulled down over her face. Thrashing her plastic bags around, she fought for balance inside the jostling, rollicking cabin. Waddling over to a seat near the front of the trolley, she plopped down and proceeded to curse in a shrill voice, complaining about "this dreadful weather," and her "achin' feet always swelling up like arthritic balloons." When the trolley ground to a halt at Thomas's stop, Thomas got up from his seat, thankful they were all still alive and not at the bottom of some sinkhole.

On his way to the door, he felt a sharp tug on the corner of his rain jacket, pulling him back.

He looked down. A sickly, pale face leered up at him from beneath the cowl of a dark wool hood. It was the bag lady. Her eyes were devoid of any color—or even pupils, it seemed. They were nothing but dark little wells, round and bottomless black.

"You don't want to see him," the woman hissed in a slithery voice filled with laughter. "The Purple King!"

"I-I'm sorry?" Thomas stammered.

Finger by pale finger, the woman unlatched her hand from Thomas's rain jacket.

"My purple *ring*," the woman said and her voice switched to a cheery tone. "I thought you might like to see it. It's in here somewhere, I promise. Hold on."

Bunny flashed Thomas a mystified look as the woman started clawing through her many bags.

"Th-that's okay," Thomas mumbled, backing up a few steps. Turning, nearly slipping down the trolley steps, he made it to the curb. He felt all queasy again, the anxious, churning feeling returning to his stomach. Lifting his chin, he stared up at the trolley cabin. Bunny nodded in the direction of the strange woman and shrugged his shoulders. The accordion doors swung shut. As the trolley pulled away, Thomas peered up through the dirty window at a hooded face with black eyes. Seeing Thomas watching her, the woman tilted her head towards the window . . .

. . . and grinned back at Thomas.

Thomas watched the trolley rattle down the block until it disappeared around the far end where there were no streetlamps. He felt sick and keyed-up at the same time, like whenever he stumbled upon a new ghost sighting. But the woman on the trolley wasn't a ghost. Bunny could see her, and there was no way Bunny Carson was a Fixer. *Was he losing his mind? What did the woman say before she switched her voice?* It wasn't about any ring. He was certain she'd said it.

You don't want to see him. The Purple King!

Head down, mind racing, Thomas slogged his way up the muddy flagstones towards the porch of Creeper & Sons. He didn't get far. His jaw dropped. He couldn't believe his eyes.

Buzzing in and out of the front door of the funeral home was a team of men all dressed in white lab coats and medical masks. A few held blinking devices up over their heads, calling out numerical readings to assistants who jotted down notes on metal clipboards. One member of the lab crew had appeared from the bushes and nearly knocked into Thomas as he began unrolling a thick band of red tape, blocking off any path up onto the porch. As Thomas waited for someone to say something—anything to explain what was going on—the smell of stale cigarette smoke came wafting through the soggy air.

Thomas turned to find the half-masked face of Uncle Jed staring back at him from a shadowed corner of the porch.

Flicking ash over the rotting railing and jabbing a large middle finger at one the lab coats, Jed let out a stream of X-rated curses. This creative combination of curses caused several members of the lab crew to stop taking readings and look up from their clipboards with wide, shocked eyes. While one crew member ran off, visibly shaken by Jed's reference to something involving "duct tape and twenty pounds of chili peppers," Thomas craned his neck over the side of the porch and read the sign.

He could only make out the larger type, but what he read was the icing on the cake of an absolutely insane day.

"*Closed by the Massachusetts Board of Health and Safety*," Thomas read. "Jed, what's going on?"

"Freakin' Fipps, that's what," Jed snarled back.

A few globs of rain from the gutter over Jed's head splattered down, extinguishing his cigarette. Cursing and muttering, Jed launched the soiled cigarette at the back of one of the men in the lab coats, missing by a wide margin. Jed crossed the arms of his soaked Vietnam Vet jacket covered with patches and pins.

"Old Gerry thought he'd play some chess with us," said Jed. "Only he ain't no Bobby Fischer."

Jed banged his fist against the wall of the house, which only served to shake more rain down. Thomas could see the pile of crushed beer cans behind his uncle's Army boots. The rain pouring from the gutters probably didn't register any pain to Jed, not this late in his drinking day.

"What does it mean, Jed?" Thomas asked.

The swarm of men in lab coats were starting to file out of the house. One stopped at the edge of the porch, holding up the red tape so the others could dip under.

"What does it *mean*?" Jed slipped his way to the railing of the porch and screeched at the retreating lab coats. "I'll tell ya what it means. IT MEANS THE STATE OF THE MASSACHUSETTS IS GONNA GET A LAWSUIT LIKE THEY NEVER SEEN! RIGHT AFTER I PUT MY BOOT RIGHT UP THEIR AS—"

Flailing, slipping on wet floorboards, Jed careened backwards. At the last moment, right before he fell flat on his rump, he grabbed hold of a down-spout, saving himself from a harder fall, but ripping the spout off the side of the house in the process. While Jed cursed and searched the floor for the loose bracket and screws, through a gap in the drawn maroon drapes Thomas could see his father sitting on one of the mothballed couches in the Viewing Room.

There were several levels like shades in a pH scale Thomas could measure to gauge his father's anger. The wordless, sullen stage was the most concerning. It was during this simmering, pre-explosive stage that words—horrible words that could never be taken back—began to form on Elijah Creeper the Fifth's cruel lips.

Peeking through the drapes at the mortified and defeated form of his father, Thomas finally realized what had happened. The scheme to beat the Fipps at their own game had backfired. They had hit rock bottom. The only sensible thing Thomas could do in these situations was to stay out sight. Like the hair-trigger on a land mine, the smallest movement could set off a cascade of irreparable damage.

Thomas slipped under the tape blocking the steps. Opening the door a foot, he wedged himself into the foyer. He made it to the staircase and climbed a few steps unnoticed before a soft warble sounded behind him.

"Thomas?"

Turning around, Thomas found his mother staring up at him with watery, red-rimmed eyes. A wad of crumpled tissues hung from one pocket of her threadbare sweater. One of her bony hands clasped a pink slip of paper.

"So you know, then?" said Mrs. Creeper. "Jed told you they shut us down?"

"He said Gerry or one of the Fipps must have called in a complaint to the Health Board."

Mrs. Creeper held a finger to her lips and slowly pulled the Viewing Room door shut. "We don't know if it was Gerry for sure, but I suspect Jed's threat made *someone* get creative. I knew I should have trusted my instincts. I knew this was a bad idea."

Mrs. Creeper paused and cocked her ear to the door to make sure there was no register from the Viewing Room. Nothing stirred. They were safe . . . for now.

"Gerry probably called in a favor with his cousins," Mrs. Creeper continued. "The Sneeds have their people everywhere, you know. I asked one of those lab rats running around what was going on. All they told me was that someone put in an anonymous tip, saying that the funeral home was unhygienic and breaking code. Poor ventilation, unsanitary surfaces. You know I've made sure everything is up to code. Sure, the house needs some work, but I've delivered all the forms to Town Hall myself, always on time. No outstanding bills or lapsed permits. It's maddening, Thomas. Absolutely maddening."

Staring at his mother's fear-stricken face, the idea dawned on Thomas. *He knew a Sneed. A good one.* At least he thought he was good.

"The tour guide at the Alderfer, the one I did my report with today, he's a Sneed. He's nice, Mom. He might be able to help us. He's not like the rest of them."

"At this point . . . " Mrs. Creeper nodded back at the Viewing Room door. "I'll take any help we can get. I don't know what your father will do without work, Thomas. If this lasts longer than that whole re-licensing fiasco that happened when you were in kindergarten, I really don't—"

"I'll talk to him," said Thomas. He couldn't stand to watch his mother in such a hopeless state. "The tour guide at the Alderfer. His name is Byron. I'm sure he'll help us."

Mrs. Creeper took a step back. "You don't mean Byron Sneed? The former sheriff? Byron Sneed still lives around here?"

"Yep," said Thomas. "Do you know what happened? Why he's blind now?"

"Don't know all the details, I'm afraid," said Mrs. Creeper, thumbing the ball of tissues hanging from her sweater pocket. "Morris Fletcher's father covered everything in *The Chronicle* before it became *The Mooring*. The article pretty much set the whole town against Byron. He was in a car accident with his fiancée, Caroline Bly. We all called her Carrie back then. Oh, she was beautiful, Thomas. Curls you could die for. The May Queen three years in a row! That was before they did away with Spring Fest because of sinkhole spreads. Anyway, the accident happened out by the Gold Coast. Byron was behind the wheel. The car went over the side and . . . well, somebody fished out Byron, but poor Carrie never made it. I always wondered what happened to Byron after that. I assumed he picked up and moved away."

One of the photographs on the wall. Thomas had glanced at it in Byron's study, but it didn't register until now. There was a photograph of a pretty woman with curls. She was smiling back at the camera with her arms wrapped around the shoulders of a much younger Byron.

"Well, I better fix something for your father. Take his mind off this mess," said Mrs. Creeper. "Are you hungry, sweetie?"

"No, thanks. I'm going to go translate the tape recorder interview I did with Byron—"

"Transcribe," the eternal teacher inside Adele Creeper corrected.

"Right, transcribe," said Thomas, smiling faintly. He turned back up the creaking staircase.

It wasn't until he was back inside his bedroom that Thomas realized he knew a piece of Byron Sneed's story—maybe the most important piece—the dividing line separating the big Before and After of his life.

Thomas unzipped his rain jacket and sat down on his unmade bed next to a familiar swirl of green light that only he could see.

The swirl rolled over. Out of the ectoplasmic glow a large green snout and two ears perked up in attention and gusted over to Thomas's shoulder. Thomas reached out and without looking made the customary fake scratch over Finn's head. The weird ectoplasmic light illuminated Thomas's worried face as his mother's warbly voice echoed in his ears.

Oh, she was beautiful, Thomas. Curls you could die for. The May Queen three years in a row!

• • •

The next few days slipped by in a series of misadventures as Thomas tried his best to avoid all contact with his father.

It was easy going the first day. Mr. Creeper had spent the whole morning and most of the afternoon locked in the Viewing Room, taking stock of all the caskets in the event Creeper & Sons had to sell their inventory to offset what was looking to be the worst fourth quarter of business in decades.

By the third day of tiptoeing around the funeral home, trying to make as little noise as possible, Thomas ran smack into his father.

Usually sporting a neatly-trimmed beard, that morning Mr. Creeper looked like a disheveled soldier crawling out of his foxhole to see if the world had been blown to smithereens. Clenched tight against his chest was a large cardboard box with the word "Consignment" written down one side, which Thomas almost knocked to the floor as he rounded one corner of the house, lost in his own thoughts. After muttering an awkward "Good morning," Thomas slipped past. At the doorway to his bedroom, he turned back. His heart sank. His father hadn't moved from his spot in the hallway. He stood stock-still, gripping the consignment box, staring off at nothing but empty air.

During the three days of slinking around the funeral home, Thomas hadn't let his nerves kill his drive to find at least one solution to the maze of problems converging on his world. He couldn't see any clear way out, not at first. He shifted his plan of attack.

He would stay busy.

The solution to the family's crisis would present itself in time, he told himself. And so, transcribing his interview with Byron, he typed out his report on the exhibition at the Alderfer and left it on the kitchen table for his mother to review. With the threat of a new lawsuit consuming his parents, Thomas was pretty sure his homeschooling assignments were not high on the priority list. Though Creeper & Sons had received no further indication of legal action by the Fipps family, it didn't matter. With little savings to stretch, and no new business coming in, it was only a matter of time before they'd be forced to sell everything.

As for the suspension of the funeral home's business license, Thomas's father had left three impassioned voicemails to the Health and Safety Board. Though everything had been dictated from the script written by Thomas's mother so the expletives would be limited, no reply had been received.

On the fourth day after being shut down, a clearer Thursday than Gloomsbury had seen in months, there came a sharp knock at the door of the funeral home.

Before Jed could rouse himself from his radio broadcast in the Viewing Room, Mrs. Creeper ran to the door and pulled back the rusted handle. Grinning on the front stoop, standing between the strips of tape Jed had slashed to ribbons the second the Health Board surveyors left, stood an older teenage boy with long jet-black hair. The older boy waved a gloved hand at Mrs. Creeper.

"Hello! Is Thomas home? I'm Cyril. We work together at the library."

Overhearing the conversation from the upstairs bathroom where he was brushing his teeth, Thomas almost spat out his toothpaste. *Work together at the library?* Rinsing his mouth and toweling off, he flew to the second-floor landing just in time to see his mother wave Cyril into the foyer.

"Sorry it's such a mess in here. So nice to meet one of Thomas's new friends," said Mrs. Creeper, bending down and pushing a few boxes away from the door. "Thomas? You have a visitor!"

As Thomas inched his way down the steps, he could see the silver spine of a book peeking out of Cyril's jacket pocket. It was one of the library's current Phantoms.

H.P. Korvac's Magical Emporium.

"Hey, buddy," Cyril called out, laughter glittering in his eyes.

"Hi," Thomas shot back like gunfire.

"Well, I'll leave you two to it," said Mrs. Creeper. "Nice to meet you, Cyril."

Thomas watched his mother slip back down the hallway, heading off in the direction of a perturbed voice coming from the Funeral Director's Study. Once they were alone, Cyril took a long, revolving look around the foyer piled high with whatever Thomas's father and Jed had assembled for consignment. Jed's help in the project, as expected, had been minimal.

"Nice place," said Cyril, flashing his ferret smile.

"What do you want?" spat Thomas. "Guilty conscience for stealing that?"

Cyril followed the trajectory of Thomas's finger. "Oh this? This I can explain."

Thomas blinked his eyes. He couldn't believe it. *Was the book glowing?* There was definitely a weird sparkle coming off the book's spine—

A grumbling voice sounded down the hallway. Thomas could hear his father winding up into another tirade.

A new friend? You let them in with all this mess?

Cyril glanced back at the door to the Funeral Director's Study. He made a bugged-out face that said *Yikes.* Thomas nodded to the staircase.

"Come on. We can talk in my room."

Once they were out of earshot up in Thomas's bedroom, Thomas turned to Cyril. He was ready to lay into him—the stolen book, all the lying. He opened his mouth . . . but the words died on his lips. His eyes widened to saucers. *Korvac's book was definitely glowing!* Wisps of silver light danced around Cyril's jacket pocket.

"W-why is it doing that?" Thomas whispered in a nervy voice.

"Thought you might ask. You being Mr. Big Detective and all. Hey, hey, relax. I came here to tell you that your parents are gonna get a call in a few seconds." Cyril sidled closer to Thomas. The weird cologne smell that hung about the older boy seemed heavier and more noxious than usual. "Should be any minute now." Cyril raised his arm and checked his wristwatch. "It's Martha Fipps, Gerry's wife. Gerry's too proud to do it."

"Do what?"

The question was broken by the rattle of the antique phone down in the kitchen.

Cyril put his hands back behind his neck and let out a loud, exaggerated breath.

"Apologize, of course. For everything. Apologize and promise to make things right."

Chapter Eleven
Down the Tubes

Thomas left Cyril grinning by the windowsill. Opening his bedroom door and tiptoeing out into the hallway, he paused at the second-floor landing and keened his ears.

At first, it sounded like Thomas's mother was going to rip the head off of whoever was on the other end of the phone.

You have no right! You're sabotaging our livelihood!

There was a long pause, after which Thomas heard his mother say *Yes! Yes! I'm still listening!* After a couple *uh-huhs* Thomas's mother's voice changed. Now she spoke calm and evenly without any screaming. *Martha, you sound like you caught that cough that's going around. Okay. That's better. I can hear you now.* Another pause. *Hmmm. Okay. I'll relay that to Elijah.* The conversation ended on an almost congenial note. *I appreciate you . . . reaching out, Martha. It's been a very stressful time for all of us, as you can imagine. I'll speak to Elijah. Bye.*

There was a rattle as the old phone returned to its cradle. Footsteps receded from the kitchen. Thomas heard the door to the Funeral Director's Study open and shut. A hushed conversation commenced behind the door, though it was hard to make out the details. Hearing no echo of his father's caustic voice, Thomas deduced that his mother was sharing some piece of positive news—news that had temporarily shut up Elijah Creeper the Fifth. Turning around, he tiptoed back into his room.

Closing the door behind him, he turned to find Cyril holding up the P.B.O.U.D. and looking rather insane. He was grinning wide with his black eyebrows pulling his scalp back.

The magical pill box was glowing. Streams of silver sparks—the same color as whatever had poured out of Korvac's book—shimmered in the palm of Cyril's gloved hand.

"You see, Creeper?" said Cyril, not looking up, gazing at the P.B.O.U.D. with possessed glee. "Told you they'd call. We Fixers take care of each other."

The queasy feeling returned to the pit of Thomas's stomach. He didn't like being jerked around in some supernatural game of wills. *How could he be sure Cyril hadn't used Korvac's magic book on him?*

"Why are you doing this? Helping us, I mean. And where did you get that?" Thomas's eyes narrowed. "Did you go through my stuff?"

Thomas looked past the glowing pill box to his desk drawer. A trail of silver light, like a faint after-glow, glimmered around the open drawer.

"It's Korvac's book," said Cyril, sliding the P.B.O.U.D. into his other jacket pocket. "It's incredible, Thomas. It can locate things, enchanted things. Bring them out of hiding. You can't read anything in the book if you're not a Fixer, though." Cyril pulled the slender volume out of his pocket and flipped the cover around so it faced Thomas. "I mean, you can *try*. But it'll just read like some silly story about a carnival. But if you're a Fixer . . ."

Cyril's eyes sparkled even wilder.

". . . you get an entirely different story."

Thomas squinted behind his glasses. Seeping out like ectoplasm from the pages of *H.P. Korvac's Magical Emporium* came more of the weird silvery light. Blurred words and even blurrier images swirled inside the frame of the page. It was just like when Madame Purfoy had appeared, smiling up at him from the bottom of the P.B.O.U.D..

And it got weirder.

As Cyril opened the book and held it out, Thomas could see a flickering image. The image blurred in and out until everything sharpened. A scene started to play out inside the page like an old black and white film. Thomas could make out a shadowed building in the background, surrounded by wrought-iron gates all wreathed with cobwebs. As Thomas watched, transfixed with wonder, the image zoomed in.

He gasped.

The cobwebs weren't cobwebs at all, but thousands of little gray snakes. The wriggling, slithering mass of snakes unwove from the picketed spikes and the gates flew open. The image zoomed in closer and closer, until everything came to a full stop in front of a massive copper door, bathed in moonlight. There were words etched in stone above the door, but the moonlight illuminated only one Thomas could read:

OPUS

Cyril slapped the book shut.

"Bet you wish you had your own copy, huh?" said Cyril, still grinning like a madman. Thomas didn't answer. Out of the corner of his eye, he caught a few wisps of silver light shimmering under his closet door. *Or was that just from looking at the book too long, like seeing sunspots after staring at the sun?* Thomas blinked his eyes. The traces of silver light faded away.

"So what's with the photos in your drawer, Creeper? Purple bodies? Pretty dark stuff, even for a mortician's apprentice."

Before Thomas could chew out Cyril for going through his personal things, Cyril stepped closer. Still gripping Korvac's book, Cyril held up his gloved hands in surrender.

"*I know, I know*," he cooed in a mock-pleading voice. "Shouldn't have gone through your stuff. I'm sorry, Creeper. I get a little caught up in what the book wants to show me. Sometimes I don't know when to quit."

Thomas brushed off the apology like a blood-sucking mosquito. "Well, it looks like you got the Fipps family to change their minds. How'd you manage to pull that off?"

Cyril shrugged. "That? Oh, that was easy. Child's play."

Thomas was about to inquire how brainwashing an entire family who hated the Creepers—hated them even more now after Jed's blackmail stunt with the police records—might constitute child's play. Then he remembered the incident back at Korvin's office, how Cyril's weird magic had defied the very laws of physics. Maybe a little brainwashing wasn't that big of a deal for someone like Cyril Barnes.

"Hey, by the way." Cyril's ferret smile slipped a little. "I saw your friend Trixie hanging around town last night. I was . . . on another case. Don't think she saw me, though. Seemed like she was looking for someone. She's made a few new friends, huh? There's that headless guy. You know the one I'm talking about? Follows Trixie around like her lapdog?"

"Yeah, that's Headless Jerry," said Thomas, sighing out his nostrils and trying to clear his brain from the vapors of Cyril's disgusting cologne. "Trixie thinks she's an angel because something her friend Gabe told her. Gabe's this ghost who's good at music. He plays the trumpet." Thomas shook his head. "Cornet, I mean. Anyway, Gabe thinks he's an angel too, because of this song that came to him. I haven't heard it, but apparently the song told Gabe about everything."

"Everything?"

"Why some ghosts are the way they are. I don't know. Seems crazy. Angels don't exist, right?"

Cyril stuffed Korvac's book back into his jacket pocket. "Haven't come across any in my work," he said, switching to an overly-official sounding voice. He shrugged his shoulders and turned for the door. "Not that it couldn't happen, though. Especially in a place as weird as Gloomsbury."

Reaching for the door handle with his gloved hand, he paused and turned back around.

"Listen, Creeper. About those photos."

For once, Cyril Barnes's joker persona seemed to dissolve right in front of Thomas's eyes. A troubled look passed over his face. It was a total sea change, as bewildering as watching Korvac's magic book reveal its portal of spooky images. Cyril's face suddenly contorted—a sharp strain of his pale cheeks. When he spoke again, for once he didn't sound sarcastic or pompous. He sounded scared.

"I'm not lying when I say we gotta stick together. I know you're not really *over the moon* about being a Fixer. It's not all puppy dogs and ice cream, for sure." Cyril shook his head and stared at the floorboards. "It's like . . . like you're in this movie, only it's different from the one everyone else is watching. Other people, they don't see all the death and the bad stuff we see. If they do, it's just make-believe. Some stiff in a grave with its eyes shut. Not standing next to you so cold, so cold you can . . ."

Cyril looked up. He stared at Thomas—*through* Thomas, as if Thomas was as thin as a piece of tracing paper.

". . . you can feel them under your skin."

Cyril's face contorted again. All the remaining color in his pale cheeks seemed to drain away. Thomas wondered whether Cyril was going to pass out. Then, he blinked his eyes and the impish smile returned.

"Oh, man, listen to me. I'm really losing it today, huh, buddy?"

Thumbing the glowing spine of Korvac's book, Cyril reached out for the door handle and gave it a swift turn. Thomas followed Cyril out to the second-floor landing.

"Let me know if I can help with," Cyril whispered over his shoulder as they started down the steps. "You know."

"Thanks," mumbled Thomas.

The door to the Funeral Director's Study creaked open. When Thomas and Cyril reached the bottom of the steps, they found Mrs. Creeper standing, beaming up at them, looking miraculously transformed. Her face was flushed with color, and she seemed to radiate hope, not waves of dread.

"Heading out so soon?"

"Thanks for having me," said Cyril, reaching for the door knob. "I don't know if Thomas told you, but I'm his replacement at the library. He's helping me find some missing books." Cyril chuckled and winked back at Thomas. Thomas felt like belting Cyril across the jaw, even if he *had* just saved the day with the Fipps lawsuit.

"Oh, that's my Thomas," said Mrs. Creeper. "Always thinking of others."

"I think I know who he gets it from," said Cyril, flashing another wink, this time at Thomas's mother. Now Thomas really wanted to belt Cyril. If Cyril hadn't scooted out the door with a wave of his gloved hand, Thomas would have done it.

Closing the door, Mrs. Creeper bounced her shoulders up and down in a perky, pleased motion that made Thomas want to vomit.

"You really are making some wonderful friends these days, Thomas . . . Thomas?"

The sound of his retreating footsteps was all Thomas had left to offer on the topic of Cyril Barnes.

Back in his bedroom, examining the gap underneath the closet door for any traces of the strange silver after-glows, but still finding none, Thomas wondered if he could be friends with someone like Cyril Barnes. *Could he be friends with someone who had no problem going through his stuff, lying to his mother's face one moment and then flirting with her the next? Had Cyril flirted with his mom? Gross!*

Thomas clenched and unclenched his fists. Wherever Cyril was now, Thomas felt like he could see the older boy in his mind's eye—strutting through the fog, grinning and chuckling like a madman. With a flash of Korvac's enchanted book and a wave of his germaphobe gloves, Cyril Barnes could fix any problem he came across, even if it meant lying or using magic to brainwash those who crossed his path. Perhaps for the first time in his life Thomas felt a new sensation, a new drive coursing through his veins.

The drive to be better.

No, not better.

The best.

It wasn't like the drive to surpass some family member who doubted him. Not in the way Thomas did everything in his power so he didn't end up like Uncle Jed, or his father—stooped-shouldered, belligerent, a slave to the all-encompassing god of Work. No, Thomas had to be better than one person.

Cyril Barnes.

If that meant being a better Fixer, so be it. Sure, Cyril had tricks up his sleeves. *But did Cyril have friends, friends who would stand by him in times of trouble like the Unicornettes? It was doubtful. How many real friends would stick around once they discovered Cyril's lies?*

Thomas pushed himself up from the floorboards. Whatever Cyril was snooping around for in his closet it would have to wait.

There was a bigger problem to solve, a problem that wouldn't go away until Thomas and Byron beat the killer at their game and caught them, once and for all, maybe with a little undead help from the Unicornettes.

Byron was right. They needed help. They needed *illumination.*

If magic was somehow involved in the killer's game, it was still a crime. Even the most clever criminal left a trail of evidence. Evidence was the real illumination they needed to make all the horror stop. Fortunately for them, Thomas had a pile of it, right there in his bedroom.

He crossed the room and headed over to his desk drawer. Sliding out the photos from Korvin's folder, he placed them side by side on his desk. Steadying his shaking hand, he breathed deeply and clicked on his desk lamp.

"Okay," he whispered, his heart throbbing way up in his throat. "Okay."

• • •

After ten minutes of carefully critiquing each crime scene photo, Thomas surveyed his notes.

A piece of Ströher's hard pretzel, Thomas's favorite snack of choice, dangled out the side of his mouth. He checked his official Ken Darby spy watch: almost nine o'clock.

On a notepad stamped with the words *Property of Creeper & Sons Funeral Services*—his father was both stingy and suspect of thieves—Thomas jotted down the names of the three victims, along with possible questions about their connections: Eddie Jones, Rocelia Sanchez, and an elderly man with a thin white mustache named Gunther Strasser. *Did the three victims know each other? Or were they random selections made by the killer?*

Thomas chomped the pretzel harder, eyes darting from one photo to the next. Nothing seemed random. All three corpses were dyed head to toe in purple ink, and all bore the letters *R* and *N* tattooed in purple ink on their left and right eyelids. Thomas gazed down at his handwriting, a furious scrawl of pen strokes beneath the light of his desk lamp. *Why purple? What was the meaning of the color purple? What connection did it have to the killer?*

He flew over to the old decommissioned dumbwaiter that ran from the kitchen to his bedroom. Though broken, the dumbwaiter still had a few good uses. If Thomas listened close enough he could hear conversations in the kitchen, find out what his parents were scheming, or whatever topic Thomas's father was currently sour over so Thomas knew not to bring it up. Even more useful, the dumbwaiter held the spillover from Thomas's overflowing bookshelves.

Snatching up a well-loved copy of *The House with a Clock in Its Walls* by John Bellairs, one of Thomas's favorite mysteries, Thomas thumbed his way to the page about Mrs. Zimmerman, the friendly witch who lived next door to Jonathan Barnavelt and his crime-solving nephew Lewis. Purple was Florence Zimmerman's favorite color, a color often associated with witches. Thomas's eyes brightened. *Were the purple corpses victims of some kind of witchcraft?*

He flapped blindly through the pages of the novel as if willing some other tantalizing bit of information to leap out at him. Stopping on one of the great pen and ink illustrations by Edward Gorey, he scratched his head. *If the purple corpses were the work of someone practicing black magic, could there be other signs of witchcraft on the corpses? Hexes? A newt in the throat?* Each corpse was discovered tangled up in sea-drift. Someone had thrown them into the water, that much Thomas knew for sure. If some black magic ritual had taken place high atop a cliff, or on one of the many islands out in Gloomsbury Bay, the ocean had erased any trace of such mischief.

He went back to the desk and flicked on his computer. He opened the web browser and did a quick search for associations with the color purple. Scrolling past a famous album cover by the artist Prince and the novel *The Color Purple* by Alice Walker, he stopped. He moved the cursor and clicked on an image of a figure created by dozens of small painted tiles. A mosaic. The paint was faded in places, but Thomas could see traces of a man seated on a throne holding some kind of scepter. A robe was draped over his shoulders.

A purple robe.

Feeling his pulse start to spike, Thomas read the short paragraph beneath the image. *Royal purple, often known as Tyrian purple, is a secretion produced by predatory sea snails of the* Muricidae *family known commonly as Murexes. From the robes of Phoenician and Roman kings, to the High Priests of Jerusalem, the Murex's dye has distinguished the mark of royalty and piety for centuries.*

Thomas clicked on the blue hyperlink underscoring the word Murex. A new window flashed open, revealing a textbook-style drawing of the spiny marine mollusk of the *Muricidae* family. Several sharp spikes rose from the Murex's spine, rising and enlarging around the snail's bulb-like central chamber. Underneath the image of the species was a chemical definition with numbers and dashes Thomas didn't quite understand.

6,6'-Dibromoindigo is the major pigment component of Tyrian purple. It is not only the most expensive pigment, but the oldest and perhaps first of its kind to be subjected to major industry.

Thomas backtracked through the article to find out how many Murexes it took to make one robe, but he couldn't find any immediate answers. If whoever was dumping bodies in

Gloomsbury Bay was using Murex dye, that meant they were incredibly wealthy and knew something about ancient manufacturing and probably even more about the ancient world. The only person Thomas could think of who fit that description was blind, knew gobs about Roman history, and loved to train Icelandic rats. There was no way Byron could be the killer, no way, thought Thomas. His thoughts raced instead to the bag lady on the trolley, the one who'd warned Thomas about the Purple King. He looked back at the computer screen at the mosaic. *The mosaic, the Murex dye, the bag lady's warning . . . What did it all point to? Someone like Byron at the Alderfer Museum who loved Roman things and was in earshot when Byron mentioned the name of the gladiator Fulvius Marcius Cinta?*

Thomas scooped up the crime scene photos and put them back in his desk where his parents couldn't come across them. Clicking off his lamp, he got up out of his chair and went over to his bed. Even if he was just talking to himself, he wished Finn would appear. *Where was his faithful companion now that he needed him the most?* He hadn't seen a green glimmer of him all night, nor any sign of the Unicornettes for that matter. Maybe they were doing what Thomas had asked: combing through Gloomsbury, searching for clues. He stared up at the ceiling, feeling incredibly small and alone, like a mote of dust flying around an empty coliseum. *Who would have access to 6,6'-Dibromoindigo, or at least know where to get it?* A gnawing feeling told him that it had to be someone from the Gold Coast. With wealth and connections at their disposal, they could live a life that was shuttered and unnoticed by the public eye.

Thomas drew in a few dusty breaths on his back, watching his stomach go up and down. He conjured the spiny Murex into his mind's eye. The description had said "tropical marine mollusk." He chewed the side of his lip. *That means someone is either importing the shells into Gloomsbury and making the dye, or importing dye that's already been—*

"SHELLS!"

Thomas bolted straight up in his bed and covered his mouth. A muffled voice called out from the direction of the dumbwaiter. It was his mother calling from the kitchen, asking him if he was okay.

"GOODNIGHT!" Thomas shouted back.

A faint "Goodnight!" sounded in reply. Soon silence resumed downstairs, broken here and there by the usual creaks and sighs of the old house.

Though Thomas had tried to block the thought from his brain, he knew Saturday was only hours away, spinning back to him like some deadly boomerang. Saturday meant ballroom dance class—that was the terrible part.

But it also meant Marylène, marine biologist in training.

Thomas smiled and pulled the covers up to his chin. Marylène and her father probably knew everything there was to know about shells, or if not, at least more than anybody in Gloomsbury. Even though Thomas hadn't figured out the connection between the three purple corpses—*if* there was a connection—if he could somehow find a way to confirm that the actual pigment was Tyrian purple, then he might be one step closer to find out what the letters *R* and *N* meant, whether they were someone's initials, perhaps the initials of the Purple King himself.

There was still one crucial part, one gaping hole in all the scraps of understanding he'd pieced together.

Why would someone dye three bodies in the most expensive pigment in the world and then throw them into the ocean?

Above the house a fresh rainstorm fueled by Mad Marge began its splatter-assault on Gloomsbury. Thomas listened to the heavy drops pummeling his window. Fatigue from working all the angles and unanswered questions in the case had finally set in. Sometime around midnight, after taking one last look around the room for Finn, Thomas sank into a deep sleep with the covers pulled around his ears to block out the rain and the bag lady's slithery voice echoing in his brain.

In the middle of the night he awoke to the scratch of something like sandpaper rubbing against his cheek.

Peering through the darkness without his glasses on, he spied a little pink tongue and a pair of eyes, blinking back at him from his pillow.

Usually aloof, the family's large Maine Coon cat, Moses, crawled underneath Thomas's arm and settled in. No longer alone, not completely, Thomas slipped back into the fog of sleep, a corner of smile peeking up over the top of his bedsheet.

• • •

Donning the hideous Bravado tuxedo once again the next morning—Sally at the Hygienic Hen had managed to salvage the family heirloom after all—Thomas climbed into the shotgun seat of the old Customline hearse.

He mentally prepared himself for the bumpy ride to Brindle & Marsh Ballroom Academy, declining the to-go cup of orange juice his mother had tried to hand him at the door, knowing it would only become a pulpy mess the moment they hit the first pothole.

What Thomas couldn't prepare himself for was his father, not Jed, sitting behind the steering wheel.

A tense silence reigned in the car all the way from the funeral home to the Uppercrust, Jeni's neighborhood. Passing Jeni's house, Thomas looked out the window and spied Arnold Myers standing in front of a new mailbox, a bucket and paintbrush in his hands. Waving at the Customline as it rolled past, Arnold lost control of the bucket. Bright blue paint sloshed out, spilling down the front of Arnold's shirt and pants. As the hearse sped away, in one of the side mirrors Thomas watched Arnold gnash his teeth and flex his arms like the Hulk. *Don't do it*, Thomas whispered in his mind. Arnold's arm cocked back . . .

The paint brush went aerial. Thomas shook his head and slunk back into his seat.

When they reached the state road leading out to Marvale, Thomas's father cleared his throat and made a shifty glance over at Thomas's seat. *We're almost there*, thought Thomas. *We won't even have to talk—*

"Soooooooo," Mr. Creeper began, stretching the word awkwardly until it filled the space of a whole sentence. "I hope you know, Elijah Thomas, this momentary lapse in business doesn't mean that there should be a *moratorium* on your studies, your apprenticeship."

"Sorry. I'm trying to keep up with Mom's assignments." *And a murder mystery that is WAY more important than my night class*, he wanted to add.

"Yes, yes," sniffed Mr. Creeper. "All that *effluvia* and filler your mother loves. Jane Austen and a bedtime story."

"It's not just Mom. I have to meet the requirements. It's the law."

Thomas flinched. *Wrong word.*

"Oh, yes," seethed Mr. Creeper. "The *law*. Every little corner of this god-forsaken county governed by their oversight boards with their suckling bureaucrats . . ." Mr. Creeper seemed to have more to say on the subject, but broke off into a string of muffled curses.

"Dad?"

"Yes, Elijah Thomas."

"Is Fipps really giving up the case? Mom said—"

"We'll see. Gerry Fipps is about as trustworthy as a bank teller with a gambling addiction. Ah! Here we are. As usual, I suspect you would like to shame your ancestral profession and have me park out of sight, hmmm?"

"Yes . . . please."

The Customline ground to a halt. Thomas flung open the squeaky door and clambered out onto the side of the road. He had to duck his head and maneuver his spindly body to avoid brushing a patch of poisonous scabber weed. Finding a safe place to stand, he looked back down at his father in the driver seat.

For the first time that morning he noticed the bracelet.

It was a small, ordinary rope bracelet. The last time Thomas had seen it was in the Preparing Room on his older brother David's wrist. Before Thomas could ask why his father was wearing it, Mr. Creeper jammed the hearse back into drive.

"I'll be home late tonight. I'm taking one of the Health Board commissioners out to dinner. Five-star dining just to get back to business as usual. Remember this lesson well, Elijah Thomas: it's not *what* you know, but *who* you know in this life. The bureaucrats and committees of this world control everything. Never forget that!"

And with that cheery observation the hearse rattled away, shooting sand and road scum up into Thomas's face.

Wiping himself off and sighing into his overly-starched collar, Thomas turned and made his way towards the winding gravel driveway that led to the dance studio. After dodging a few more patches of scabber weed that seemed to reach out their spiked tendrils to maim him, Thomas was soon standing inside the old slaughterhouse turned ballroom.

The paired dancers had already lined up along the wall, awaiting their instructions. Curiously, no schmaltzy waltz music blared from the overhead speakers. Thomas scoured the room. *Where was Marylène?*

Locking eyes with Daphne Muldroon, Thomas watched the girl scowl and slide farther down the wall, as if sensing another projectile vomiting attack coming on. Charlie Fipps was back in class too, right as acid rain. He sneered back at Thomas from the shadows near the poster of the leaping Mikhail Baryshnikov, the one Headless Jerry had oozed out of last class. Over the murmur of the chatting students Thomas could hear Mr. Brindle's voice coming from the open office door:

"Well, that *is* regrettable, Mr. Gaumont. You see, without Marylène we'll be an odd number today, which impacts our *flow* and *movement* quite considerably. But yes, yes, I understand. I've been following the papers along with the rest of town. Do tell us what you find out there. It all sounds rather fascinating. *À bientôt, Monsieur Gaumont. Bon courage.*"

So there it was.

Marylène wasn't coming.

Thomas tried to think fast on his feet. He hadn't been spotted yet by Mr. Brindle or Madame Marsh. He couldn't see the latter, only smell the stench of her cigarette smoke nearby. Maybe he could make it out to Marvale on foot, catch the Gaumonts before they headed out from the Alderfer Foundation. Footsteps sounded from the direction of Mr. Brindle's office. Ducking his head, Thomas scooted across the dance floor, heading for the door to the bathroom. Over his shoulder, he could hear Daphne's mopey voice:

"Told you! Barf-face can't hold it in."

Thomas slipped into the bathroom right as Mr. Brindle's voice sounded through the drafty ballroom.

"Alright, class! We're down one today, I'm afraid. Shall we do a final head count?"

Panting with his back against the bathroom door, Thomas surveyed the miserable situation. The bathroom was smaller than a janitor's closet. But there was a window. He couldn't go back to class. He wasn't going to spend another afternoon getting kneed in the groin by Daphne Muldroon or turned into a pin cushion by Charlie Fipps.

Rushing to the windowsill, he tried hoisting the window. It wouldn't budge. His eyes narrowed. The cracks were painted shut. He fell back against the small porcelain sink. He clawed at his bowtie, unhooking the clip attached to the pre-woven bow. He couldn't breathe. He felt claustrophobic, like the room was shrinking in on him. If he went back out, he'd have to find some other way to escape . . . and there was still Charlie to deal with.

"In the bathroom, you say? Loosening things up?"

"I'll check on him, Mr. Brindle."

"Oh, you're a doll. Thank you, Charlie."

Thomas's stomach lurched. He could hear footsteps, heading for the bathroom door. Accepting his grim fate, he reached out for the door knob but stopped suddenly.

Something white—white and glowing—waved back at him from inside the toilet bowl.

Thomas inched closer to inspect. It was a white glove. The luminous glove reached up from the toilet, waving back at him.

"Jerry?" Thomas whispered.

The glove flashed a thumbs up.

"What the hell are you doing down there?"

The footsteps were right outside the door. The white glove made several gripping motions.

"You want me to what . . . ?" Thomas shook his head. "I don't—"

The door handle started to turn . . .

Thomas bit his lip and closed his eyes. He reached down into the toilet bowl right as the bathroom door started to creak open.

A freezing vise of fingers clamped over Thomas's wrist, jerking him down. He felt a wild rush of particles, like a million infinitesimal stars exploding inside him all at once. Right before the gray, washed-out bathroom fell away to a tunnel of oozing light, Thomas had the sensation that he too had turned into a mass of particles, all separating and whizzing through time and space.

Chapter Twelve
Ivymount / The King Speaks

There were no words in the English language Thomas could use to explain what happened next.

The nearest he could come to describing the feeling of being sucked out the tunnel of oozing light and reassembled from a million particles was a word that didn't exist in any known dictionary:

Devaporated.

Not feeling like he had any face, only an amorphous, hovering presence of mind, Thomas watched his fingers slowly *revaporate*—first the tips, then the fingernails, then finally both hands. The process continued all the way up his body until, fully reassembled, Thomas found himself standing, staring out at panorama of gray sky with a darker band—the ocean—moving beneath it.

Thomas stared around dumbstruck. Everything looked hazy, as if all the edges had been rounded away. It got worse. He was soaked, head to toe. Raking a hand through his wet hair, he held the hand to his nose and gagged.

He was drenched in toilet water.

"Are you kidding me?" He felt around the bridge of his nose. "No! My glasses! Where are my glasses?"

Bounding out of a veil of fog came a great green blur. The green blur rushed over to Thomas's side. The blur had a face—a face and a snout—though both were equally hazed-over from Thomas's perspective. Nudging the sand at Thomas's feet, the green blur made several insistent barks, confirming Thomas's growing suspicion: it was his beloved companion Finn, making an unusual daytime appearance.

The trusty ghost-dog sat back on his hind end and let out a few more enthusiastic barks. Thomas hunkered down. There was a faint sliver of metal, curling up out of the sand. Reaching down, he grabbed hold of his missing glasses and blew any lingering specks off the lenses. Hooking the cheap plastic sides over his ears, he peered up through the gathering mist.

For a few moments he forgot about everything—the toilet tunnel, the fact he'd just defied the laws of physics, even his fervent prayer that he'd soiled Cousin Morrie's tuxedo once and for all. Smiling down at him from a sand dune swirling with fog, Thomas beheld the oddest collection of supernatural faces.

The Unicornettes.

"I told Jerry you wouldn't like being flushed out like that," Trixie said, shaking her bobbed head. "Looks like there wasn't really any other way."

"I could have slipped out the back!" snarled Thomas, ignoring Headless Jerry's pantomimes of forgiveness. The headless ghost bowed his severed vertebrae and pressed his gloved hands together in prayer. Gabe, who'd been busy polishing the valves of his cornet with a handkerchief, looked up and frowned.

"Jerry shoulda laid back. You know how fools rush in."

"C'mon, guys. Coulda, woulda, shoulda," said Trixie. "Let's stop jabbering and get on with it. Thomas, I'll fill you in on where we've been since we were all together. What's the plan? You *do* have a plan, right? I told Jerry to go find you and free you from that dance studio. What's with all that lousy classical music by the way?"

Thomas ignored Trixie. He squinted through the thick mantle of mist pouring off the ocean like dry ice. On a high bluff in the distance, he could see the Marvale Lighthouse, rising like a skeletal finger through the charcoal sky. He knew that the Alderfer Foundation where Marylène and her father were staying was located on the same grounds as the lighthouse.

"We have to get to the lighthouse," said Thomas. "If we're lucky, Marylène and her dad haven't left yet." Thomas turned and took off down the beach. It was tough going. The sand was getting deep and soggy. The tide was coming in.

"Who we lookin' for now?" Trixie called over the sound of the crashing waves as she sped up to follow Thomas.

"My friend Marylène," Thomas called over his shoulder. "Her dad is a marine biologist. I think the killer is this guy who calls himself the Purple King. He's using some kind of special purple dye that comes from seashells—"

"Don't know 'bout seashells," said Trixie, cutting Thomas off. "But we've seen him, Thomas. Well, Gabe did. Last night, down by New Harbor in Hampswich."

Thomas stopped and turned around. "Seen who?"

"Your Purple King," said Trixie without any glimmer of her fox grin.

• • •

Trixie nodded to Gabe. The ghost-musician strode over, making smooth strides, unencumbered by the weight and challenges of the living. Stuffing his polishing rag back into his jacket pocket, he relayed the story as they walked on through the mist.

"It's like this, Thomas. I used to wake up over at the blind man's house. You know, Byron? Every day. Don't know why. After a while, I started thinking: Why am I here? What am I supposed to do? Nothin'. Not a word. No big shout down from heaven. Just me talkin' to myself. Then I started remembering, little by little, and I was like *oh yeah, that's right.* Me and my buddy Earl, we used to play parties here back in the day. I guess that's why I keep waking up wearing this silly cocktail suit.

"So then I start thinkin' about this other place we used to play down in New Harbor. We called it Uppityville back then, 'cause those folks down there, oh man, Thomas. They get on your case. Like they don't even want you to catch your breath between sets. Anyway, there I am, back at Byron's house. Musta been a couple days ago. Can't say for sure, time not being straight and all, like a song that keeps getting away from you, know what I mean? I start thinkin' about Earl and the Summer Stomp they used to throw down in Uppityville. Next thing I know—*BAM!*—I'm down by the docks in Uppityville. Only everything's changed. No bandstand. No Earl or Lefty either. That's Lefty Rollins, Thomas. You gotta find his records. Man could swing a hi-hat right off its—"

"GABE!"

Trixie raised a painted eyebrow and made a wind-up motion with one hand.

"Right," said Gabe, flashing a pearly smile. "So I slide down by the docks, because that's where I remember seeing Earl the last time, and I'm hopin' he's an angel now too, like maybe he's heard the same song I've been hearing from my horn."

Gabe paused and smiled lovingly down at his cornet. Catching Trixie throwing him another exasperated look, he straightened up.

"That's when I see him. Not Earl, Thomas. Some guy on his boat, drifting along the water. Motor boat, from the sound. Couldn't see a name or number in the dark. Then the moon peeks out, and I see the dude's wearing this cloak. I can tell it's purple, and it's blowing all crazy. Nobody else on the boat. Just the guy with something wrapped up, leanin' against the side of the boat. Well, when the boat rolled past the . . . whatsit called? Buoy? The one with light out in the middle of the water."

"Channel marker," said Trixie.

Thomas flashed Trixie an incredulous look.

Trixie shrugged. "What? Told ya I know things. Go on, Gabe. Then what happened?"

"Nothing, really," said Gabe, frowning. "Guy turns around and looks at me. But he's wearing this mask."

"What-what kind of mask?" said Thomas, his voice cracking with fear.

"Metal," said Gabe, shaking his head. "Some kind of metal. Silver? Don't know. But it was bright. Bright as this horn."

Gabe held up the glowing cornet in front of Thomas's face. He shook his head. "Then he was out of the light. Gone. Just like that. The boat too. It was like they were never there at all."

They'd reached the part where the shoreline fell away to craggy boulders, each one the size of a small tank. The lighthouse was close now; Thomas could see the light coming from the lantern spinning inside the top chamber, slicing through the fog and low-lying clouds. Trixie opened her mouth to speak. Thomas held up a finger, waving her off.

"I need to think," said Thomas, scrunching up his brow.

Trixie cast a quizzical look back at the rest of the Unicornettes. Headless Jerry threw up his gloved hands. Gabe went back to gazing at his cornet. Over the sound of the surf and whipping wind came more enthusiastic barks from Finn. Thomas turned to find the ghost-dog wagging his tail at the base of a rotting wooden staircase that led through a tangle of high brush. At the foot of the staircase Thomas paused and turned back around.

"Gabe, do you remember what the mask looked like? I mean, enough to draw it?"

"I'm no artist, Thomas," said Gabe, smiling. "Music's the only thing I've figure out how to do right. If I had to guess though, I'd say it was old. Something you'd see in a history book. Or a museum. Sorry that's all I got, Thomas. Does it help?"

Thomas nodded. *Purple cloak and an old mask?* Definitely fit the killer's profile.

He climbed the first few steps of the staircase leading up through the bluffs, following the glow of Finn's tail. In a gap in the staircase in front of him where the wood had splintered away, he stopped. A tangle of tendrils filled with barbs blocked his path—more scabber weed. While he debated the right course of action—up and over, or climbing back down and trudging up another side of the bluff that might be safer—he caught Headless Jerry reaching up at him, making another gripping motion.

"No, Jerry," said Thomas, lifting his foot carefully over the tangle. "I think one toilet adventure is enough for today."

As they climbed higher and higher, Thomas could hear Trixie's voice over the whip of the wind.

"Don't take it so bad, Jerr-Bear. He always says the first thing that pops into his brain. You'd think there'd be room in that big brain for a nice word once in a while. I mean, how hard is that?"

• • •

Reaching the summit of the dunes, having successfully avoided all poisonous entrapments, Thomas gazed up at the Marvale Lighthouse, looming and swirling with mist.

"Bet whoever is on duty gets their exercise each day," Trixie whispered behind Thomas's shoulder. "How many steps you think that is?"

Thomas ignored the question. "C'mon. Maybe Marylène and her father haven't left."

Trixie threw up her and hands and looked over at Headless Jerry. "See what I'm talking about?"

Thomas passed beneath the columned shadow of the lighthouse, heading for the outline of another building obscured by floating ribbons of fog. As Thomas crunched down a pathway of ground seashells, the Unicornettes trailing silently behind him, he could make out a signpost and a sign swinging in the fog:

ALDERFER FOUNDATION FOR MARINE LIFE
Caldwell Pennycress Alderfer, Dir.

In front of a rounded metal door speckled with rust and welded in thick sheets like the hull of a submarine, the odd group of adventurers paused. In the center of the door a large bronze door knocker gleamed. The knocker was shaped like a narwhal's tusk, though as Jeni had once reminded Thomas, it wasn't a tusk at all, but a protrusion of the whale's upper canine tooth.

"What the hell is that?" asked Trixie. "Some kind of mutant dolphin?"

"It's a narwhal," said Thomas, reaching up and grabbing hold of the tusk.

"You sure?" said Trixie.

"Yep, pretty sure," said Thomas. "Our Lady of the Waves gave me a sword made out of its tooth once."

"Our Lady of the what now?"

"Forget about it," said Thomas, reaching up and giving a sharp pull on the knocker. As he suspected, the tusk was jointed. The top half of the knocker came down, clanging against the bronze catch plate. Thomas gave a few more clangs for good measure.

"Jeez, you'd think they'd have heard of a doorbell," muttered Trixie.

Before Thomas could tell Trixie to play another round of the silent game so he wouldn't be distracted, the door opened and a grizzled, sun-weathered face poked out.

"Afternoon! Can I help you?"

"Hi, yes," said Thomas, piping up. "I'm Thomas. Thomas Creeper. I'm a friend of Marylène's. Are the Gaumonts still here?"

The door swung open. In the doorway stood a thin old man with yellow sun-bleached hair. He had a face like a weathered prune sucked of all its vital fruit. He wore a ropey Irish sweater and navy corduroy pants tucked into thick black boots.

"Afraid they disembarked over an hour ago, m'boy," the man said, smiling sadly. His wrinkled eyelids opened wide. "Why, you're positively drenched. Come in, come in. The least our august institution can do is provide you with a cup of something warm until the Gaumonts return. I'll see if I can rustle up a change of clothes or at least a towel. I'm Caldwell Alderfer, by the by. But you can call me Cal. Please. Come in."

Thomas followed the Cal Alderfer's kind invitation and stepped inside. As the Unicornettes and Finn slipped in undetected behind him, Thomas examined the room.

It was a wide chamber with high ceilings that seemed to serve the dual purpose of waiting room and exhibition hall. Glowing aquarium tanks bubbled behind leather armchairs, each one filled with curious, floating creatures. In the tank closest to Thomas he could see a particularly well-fed lobster with a claw about the size of a baseball catcher's mitt. There was a handwritten sign affixed to the tank written in florid black ink:

Philby the Finger-Masher. Homarus americanus.
Found near Bretton's Shoal, Marvale.

Cal caught Thomas taking in the colossal lobster and let out a hearty chuckle.

"We call him that nasty name so children won't bother him. The sign helps divert them so the poor old boy can work on his favorite pastime . . . sleeping! He's a sweetheart, really. Don't even need to band the claws. We found him tangled up in a twenty-four pack of soda rings. Can you believe the junk people throw into our great Mother Ocean? I think old Philby is grateful for the rescue. At least, I like to think so."

Cal tapped the aquarium glass and let out another chuckle. At the sound of the tap, Philby the Finger-Masher didn't budge an inch, but exhaled a stream of bubbles, giving proof that he was indeed still alive.

Cal clapped his sun-spotted hands together. "Why don't you grab a seat over here in the Roost. That's what we call our main deck here on this landlocked vessel. I'll see if I can't rustle up some hot cocoa and dry clothes. This way!"

Headless Jerry flashed a thumbs up.

"Kind of a kook, but I like him," whispered Trixie.

"Dude's on his own trip, for sure," added Gabe, nodding his goateed chin.

Thomas followed Cal out of the aquarium waiting room to a narrow hallway. Finn bounded ahead, letting out a few barks and passing straight through Cal. The old man shivered and rubbed his hands against sweater sleeves.

"Sorry about the chill, Thomas. Modern heating still hasn't figured out how to keep out the sapping effects of Mad Marge, I'm afraid."

The hallway ran on until it came to a room that seemed composed entirely of glass.

"Holy smokes," Trixie whispered, breaking her vow of silence for the second time. "Would you get a load of that."

Thomas didn't bother to chastise Trixie. She was absolutely right. The sight was something to behold. Cal turned around, grinning, enjoying Thomas's shock. By no means a small man—he was even a few inches taller than Thomas—he looked like a child standing next to the giant glass windows that vaulted over the room. Outside the windows a half-moon shaped viewing deck could be seen through the swirling fog. There were various telescopes positioned inside cut-outs in a steep wrought-iron fence presumably designed to keep people from slipping off and falling hundreds of feet to their death.

"If the Gaumonts make it back early, this will be the spot to see them come in, my friend. Mad Marge willing, of course," said Cal. He tapped a weathered finger against the glass. "There's the dock down there. Our little Alderfer fleet."

Thomas stepped towards the window. As the mist parted, he could see a dock far below, though the boats looked like toys from such a height. There was a large empty gap between two smaller boats moored to the dock. A few figures were moving around: a dark speck wearing a hat, seated in a wheelchair, and a bundled figure who seemed to be pushing the wheelchair along.

"Aye," sighed Cal. "That's my dear father, Thaddeus. Ninety-seven and still kicking, would you believe it? He thinks someone's been stealing one of our boats for joy rides at night. He's not all there these days, I'm afraid. But that's the way of things. No one likes giving up the captain's chair as you get older. Anyway, be back in two shakes of a cephalopod's *hectocotylus*."

Cal chuckled at his extremely esoteric reference and hustled off towards a door with a faded metal placard over it reading *Mess Hall*. A few seconds later there came a rustling of drawers and a few sharp *pings* of metal. Thomas felt a damp chill hovering against his side. Peering down, he found Finn smiling up at him. Thomas made a scratch over the ghost-dog's head while Headless Jerry slowly oozed out the window closest to Thomas. Soon the ghost was standing with his gloved hands on his hips, taking in the dramatic drop.

"May I speak now, Lord Master Creeper?" said Trixie.

Thomas rolled his eyes. "Yeah. Fine. What?"

"So if your friends aren't here, what are we supposed to do now? You gonna ask Captain Kooky over there about the purple dye, if he thinks it's the same kind that comes from those special shells?"

"Haven't figured that part out yet," said Thomas.

Suddenly, from somewhere beyond the Mess Hall door, a phone rang. Thomas heard Cal's hoarse voice repeat "I see, I see" several times. Then there was the rattle of something hitting the floor as Cal exclaimed, "By the barnacled beard of Poseidon! So it *is* true! Something is pulling the *Architeuthis* magnetically towards us. A global magnetic shift, eh? Is there even a precedent for that, Monsieur Gaumont? I didn't think so. Well, be safe on the return trip. Please tell Marylène her friend Thomas is here. I'll tell him the news. *Merci, Monsieur*."

A minute or so later, Cal emerged from the Mess Hall door holding a steaming cup of hot chocolate in his wrinkled hand and passed it over to Thomas.

"Europe's finest, Thomas. The Gaumonts spoil me with tins of this glorious stuff. Don't know what I'll do when they go back to France."

Cal pulled out a bundle of clothes from under one arm.

"Julian, Marylène's brother, left these behind. Don't think he'll mind, Thomas, seeing that he's sworn off ever coming back. A little run-in with a Portuguese man o' war, I'm afraid." Cal made a nod back at the Mess Hall door. "You can change in the restroom in the Mess Hall if you like. It seems like the Gaumonts are still several klicks out, way past the old shipping lines. I wish I could be out with them. But who would be here to make hot chocolate when a soaked refugee like yourself showed up, eh?"

Thomas took a sip of the hot chocolate. Cal didn't lie. It was wondrous stuff. Rich, sweet, and absolutely warming to the core.

"There's a phone near the bathroom in the Mess Hall if you'd like to call someone to pick you up. I don't suspect the Gaumonts will be back before nightfall . . . or whatever you wish to call this daily dying away of secondhand light we get from Mad Marge. If it wasn't for the wonders of the deep that lurk around these waters, I probably would be a sunburnt snowbird in Florida by now."

"Thank you," said Thomas, taking the bundle of clothes. He stepped over the raised lip of the Mess Hall door designed to look like another pressurized seal on a submarine. Walking over to the bathroom, he glanced down at a small breakfast table.

Scattered across the table were several sheets of paper with sketches and words written in tidy, almost mathematical handwriting. Though Thomas couldn't read the writing because it was written in French, he recognized the drawing of a giant squid. He remembered Marylène's words that afternoon on the beach.

Un calamar. Un calamar géant.

Whoever had drawn the diagram had included a dozen little star-shaped squiggles around the squid's ten tentacles. *Were these the sea fireflies Marylène had mentioned? The tiny glowing shrimp following the path of the giant squid?*

After a quick "sink shower" like he used to do after track practice, Thomas tried to untangle the web of unanswered questions in his brain. He was certain of one thing: he wasn't calling his parents to pick him up. If he couldn't get to the bottom of the purple dye, at least he was going to see what Byron had come up with. *Where was Byron? Why hadn't he called the funeral home that week?*

Holding a hand up under the bathroom's single light bulb, Thomas smiled. *The number was still there.* He'd written Byron's telephone number in permanent black marker on his hand after finding it in an old Gloomsbury telephone directory sandwiched between his mother's cookbooks. He'd intended to call Byron once he'd come up with some great clue, but so far all he had to go on were Murexes and some vague Roman connection to Tyrian purple. He examined the ink on his palm. One of the numbers was smudged, but he could make it out well enough. Heading over to the phone, he plugged the numbers in and waited for the line to connect. The phone rang three times before a froggy, guttural voice answered.

"*Já? Hállo?*"

"Hi, it's Thomas. Thomas Creeper?"

There was a long pause followed by something barked in a foreign tongue.

"Um . . . hello?"

A click sounded on the other end. "Thomas! It's like we're on the same wavelength, my friend. I had Sigrún drive by your house today. Your mother said you were at some dance class?"

"I'm not." Thomas shook his head. "Not anymore, I mean. I'm at the Alderfer Foundation in Marvale right now." He cupped the phone closer to his mouth and lowered his voice. "I think I've figured out the purple dye, Byron. I think it comes from some kind of seashell. I was hoping to ask my friend here whose father is a marine biologist, but they left for a research trip. Would you mind . . . could you come and pick me up?"

"We'll be there soon," said Byron. "For my part, I believe I've figured out the connection between the victims. Thomas, I think I know who's next."

Thomas shuddered and almost dropped the phone. "You do? Who is it?

"It's someone in my family," Byron whispered into the phone. "All the victims have worked for my step-sister and step-uncle in some form or other. I think the killer is working their way from the outside in. We have to go and tell them before it's too late."

"Go where?"

"To the 'mountain of laurel and ivy' as Arthur Greaves, Gloomsbury's poet laureate, once wrote," said Byron in a theatrical voice. "Ivymount."

"I can't go up there. They won't let me in. I'm a Creeper."

"We'll be there in ten minutes."

The phone clicked off.

Thomas emerged from the Mess Hall a few moments later looking paler than normal. He had donned Marylène's brother's borrowed clothes—a scratchy blue sweater and wool pants. He felt itchy and anxious all over, but at least he was dry.

"Ah!" exclaimed Cal. "Now that looks better."

Thomas was glad Cal didn't ask about the other pair of clothes, the soaked ones he'd stashed in the large trash bin in the bathroom. *He was rid of the Bravado tuxedo forever.* Even that good feeling couldn't loosen the vise of terror he felt tightening around his chest. *Pay a visit to Ivymount?* Eugenia Sneed hated his guts. Every time they crossed paths in town Eugenia glowered at Thomas like he had the plague. *How was Byron going to convince Eugenia to let a Creeper into the Sneeds' secret fortress?*

As Thomas waited for Byron's car an elevator bell dinged on the far side of the Roost. Out of the shadows of the long hallway two figures emerged—an old man in a wheelchair wearing a round straw hat, and behind him, a woman bundled up in several coats, with frizzy hair matted down inside a thick wool cap.

"At it again, I told you," the old man mumbled, shaking a fist in the air. "Hooligans. It's the drugs, Cal. They're using my boat for drugs."

"No one is stealing your boat to traffic drugs, Pop," Cal pleaded. "If that was the case, why would they return the boat the next day with a full tank of gas? Think about that. Why wouldn't they keep it?"

The grizzled old man in the wheelchair lifted his head, side-eying Thomas like a shark.

"Maybe it was you! You and your hooligan friends!"

"Melita," said Cal in an exasperated voice. "I think we've had enough excitement for one day. Maybe it's a time for some strawberry shortcake. You love strawberry shortcake, don't you, Pop?"

The old man in the wheelchair relaxed, though his fist stayed raised in the air.

"Yes, Mr. Cal," said the woman in a thick foreign accent. She redirected the path of the wheelchair away from Thomas. "We will have the dinner now. Maybe we will have the napping after? This is best plan for everyone."

Casting one final scowl at Thomas, Thaddeus Alderfer lowered his head back to his chest. As he disappeared down the tunnel-like hallway, Thomas could hear him muttering:

"Hooligans. They think I can't see what they're up to. But I do. Ohhhhh, yes I do."

Once Cal was certain he and Thomas were alone again, he frowned and shook his head.

"Please forgive my father, Thomas. He says he sees . . . *things*. Ghosts. How unnatural is that?"

Thomas gave a little nod and looked away. If Cal only knew.

From the direction of the hallway a few distant car honks sounded, followed by a voice somewhere higher up in the building.

"We're under attack, Melita! Get my Balearic harpoon!"

Cal smiled a somber, resigned smile, and shook his head. Thomas thanked him again for the hot chocolate and dry clothes. Cal escorted Thomas back down the dark hallway towards the aquarium waiting room. Thomas sat for a few minutes while Cal asked him a few questions—how long Thomas had lived in Gloomsbury, what his parents did for work. Before Thomas could get into the gory details of living in a working funeral home, a car horn sounded outside. Smiling and telling Thomas he was welcome back anytime, Cal opened the submarine-style door and let Thomas out into the drizzling mist.

Trudging back down the path of ground seashells, Thomas found a brown luxury sedan idling in the Alderfer's driveaway.

"Okay, you guys are on your own," said Thomas out of the corner of his mouth, not pausing to glance back at the Unicornettes.

"Figured," said Trixie. She squinted down at the sedan. "We could probably squeeze in with you, but that would be one cold ride, Thomas." Trixie nodded to Byron settling into his seat in the back of the car. "You gonna be okay? You trust this guy, right?"

"He's fine," said Thomas.

Headless Jerry flashed Thomas a little wave.

"See you up at Mount Crazy," said Trixie.

"See you," said Thomas, smiling in a pained way.

Thomas reached out, opened the back door of the sedan, and slid in. He could see Sigrún's weathered face glaring back at him in the rearview mirror. Muttering something in her native tongue, she jerked the car into gear. As they sped off, Byron held onto his cane, tapping his thumbs against the worn golden pommel.

"Apologies for being out of touch this week, Thomas," said Byron. "I had to follow up on something. Well, on this, actually."

Byron reached into his coat pocket. He retrieved a small metal object and handed it over to Thomas.

"What is it?" said Thomas, rotating the curious object around in his hand. It was made out of tarnished black metal and had three legs like a small tripod. Each leg was sharp and no three legs were the same length.

"It's called a *tribulus* or *caltrop*," said Byron. "The Roman version of a land mine. Sigrún found it on our doorstep last night. I haven't seen one of these since Caspar."

"Caspar?"

"My step-brother. We were both interested in ancient history, though he was a far better student than me. He always said I was cursed with a 'hero complex'. Said I always needed someone to save. Maybe that's why I put down the books and joined law enforcement, much to my family's disgust."

Thomas scrunched up his forehead as he weighed all the new information. "You don't think—"

"That Caspar's behind all of this? Yes, I *did* think that at first. Some kind of family vendetta? The two of us haven't exactly been on speaking terms these past years. Maybe he went off his rocker, I thought. So I called my step-sister Eugenia. I don't trust the phones over there, so all I did was ask her when was the last time she spoke to Caspar. She acted like I was insane, like I was off *my* rocker. She said Caspar's in prison for some sort of financial pyramid scheme. They visited him last week to sign papers to cut him out of any lingering clauses in my step-uncle J.W.'s will."

The sedan hit another pothole. Once everything stabilized again, Thomas turned the *tribulus* over in his hand.

"If it's not Caspar, who do you think left it on your doorstep?"

"Who, indeed, Thomas, who indeed."

Thomas thought that the old man was going to elaborate, but a long, contemplative silence fell over the cabin. Still gripping the sharp *tribulus* in his palm, Thomas peered out the window. They'd reached Shellburne Road. On either side of the sedan the towering shapes of mansions began rising up out of the fog. All of a sudden, Thomas thought he saw a cloaked figure standing in the shadows between two overgrown hedgerows. Sinking back into the crinkly leather seat, he felt his courage ebb away from him as if mirroring the dying light.

"Almost there," said Byron, leaning forward on his cane. He uttered something in a foreign language. Sigrún nodded in the rearview mirror. The sedan made a sharp turn down through a gulley flanked by another set of towering hedgerows. The car bounced and jostled, though Sigrún showed no signs of easing up on the gas. Thomas looked back through the sedan's rear window. He could see traces of old cobblestones, poking up through the patches of dead, unmowed grass. He and Jeni had never ventured off this part of Shellburne before, not wanting to get chewed out by some rich person who probably wouldn't think twice about unleashing their dogs on them.

The remains of the old road continued to sink until the hedgerows fell away to marshland. Where everything had been claustrophobically tight before, now everything opened like a vast panorama. Running down the middle of the marsh was a long dock made out of hammered railroad ties. As the sedan rolled a steady click across the railroad ties, Thomas saw a gatehouse emerge out of the mist. In front of the gate's arm the sedan came to a sharp stop. Out of the door of the stooped shack a burly figure appeared and started shuffling towards the car. The figure was so huge and muscle-bound Thomas wondered how he fit inside the miniature gatehouse. Then it dawned on Thomas who it was: thick moustache, shaved head, glittering black eyes.

It was Mr. Contenescu, J.W. Sneed's all-around handyman and hired muscle.

Roving his eyes over the car and its occupants, the old Romanian former boxer paused in front of Thomas's window. For a few tense moments Thomas didn't know what would happen. Grunting and shaking his head, Mr. Contenescu turned around and hunkered back into the gatehouse. A jarring buzz split the air. The gate arm went up. As the sedan began its steep ascent up a winding gravel path bordered on either side by walls of dark ivy, Thomas gazed back through the rear window. Mr. Contenescu stood by the gate, arms crossed, watching the car intently.

As the car rose higher and higher, Thomas could see the outline of Old Town, Gloomsbury in the distance, materializing and evaporating through the fog. It was no great mystery why the Sneeds had built their mansion high up in the cliffs overlooking Gloomsbury. From their steep vantage point the lights of the town looked like little playthings, pawns on a chess board they controlled. The rising and winding, the pulling away from any safe marker below—it all came together to form a dizzying spectacle of ivy, stone, and fog.

At the top of the gravel path the sedan came to a halt in front of a staircase rising between two marble urns overflowing with more ivy. Thomas lifted his head and spotted a very distressed Eugenia Sneed storming down the flagstone path, heading straight for their car.

"Come," said Byron. "And don't worry, Thomas. I'll handle Eugenia."

"Wait!" Thomas cried before Byron reached for the car door handle. "I think I know what's all over the bodies that have washed up. It's not ink. It's some kind of dye."

Byron hesitated. As Eugenia's shrill voice grew louder and closer, he smiled and said, "Let's get Eugenia settled first. Then we'll unpack all the dreadful details. Sound like a plan?"

Thomas nodded. He opened his car door and stepped out into the damp night air, following Byron and feeling more apprehensive with each step.

Eugenia met them at the top of an elaborate stone staircase chiseled out of the very bedrock of the mountain itself. At first, Eugenia seemed oblivious to their presence. She waved her arms frantically around, screaming into a cellphone in her hand as if it were a bullhorn. She was dressed in a belted red Chinese robe decorated with a pattern of gold leaves. Her tawny-reddish hair, marked here and there by streaks of white, was drawn up in an intricate network of braids, some of which were starting to come loose from all her thrashing about. The image Eugenia cast, the one that remained fresh in Thomas's mind whenever he thought of her, hovered somewhere between the Bride of Frankenstein and a possessed version of the blues singer Bonnie Raitt who Thomas had seen on the cover of one of his mother's old records.

"YES! THE HILLSIDE'S ON FIRE! THEY'VE WRITTEN SOMETHING! SOME SORT OF . . . I DON'T KNOW . . . SOME KIND OF PYSCHOBABBLE! WHAT DO YOU MEAN THE FIRE TRUCKS ARE STUCK AT THE BOTTOM?"

Fire trucks? Thomas had noticed a burning smell when they first stepped out of the car. Now he could hear sirens, wailing from somewhere down below the mountain. He spun around.

Back down the winding path where they'd just come he could see red and blue lights flashing through the fog.

"Did you do this?" Eugenia hissed, stabbing a fingernail at Byron. "Contenescu says the fire trucks are all stuck at the bottom. He says their tires have been popped by some . . . some kind of machine part. They can't get up the road and they're blocking all other cars."

Byron held up his hands in defense. "Calm down, calm down. What do you mean machine part? Do they look like this?" Byron nodded to Thomas. "Show her the *tribulus*, Thomas."

Thomas shook his head. He wasn't about to put himself in the middle of a Sneed firing squad.

"YOU!" screeched Eugenia, fixing her eyes on Thomas. "YOU CREEPERS DID THIS!"

Slowly, feeling like he was signing his own death certificate, Thomas removed his hand from behind his back. He held the *tribulus* up under the light of the single lamp at the top of the steps.

"What the hell is that?" spat Eugenia.

"Ask your man Contenescu," said Byron. "Ask him if that's what popped the trucks' tires."

Eugenia turned away, cradling the phone against her cheek. When she turned back again her expression was caught somewhere between outrage and utter confusion.

"Now before you say anything," said Byron, jumping in, "Sigrún found the same device on our doorstep last night. It's a message, Eugenia. Don't you see? Somebody wants us all here. They want us to see."

"See?" Eugenia snarled. "They're trying to burn us down. There's your message, Byron. Come! I'll show your little protégé even if you can't see for yourself."

Eugenia stalked off towards the house. Byron followed after her, clicking his cane against the flagstones, while Thomas trailed a cautious step or two behind. As they stepped inside the Sneeds' grand estate, Thomas could see Eugenia scowling down at him from halfway up a winding staircase.

"Up here! This way!"

Thomas made it a few steps and turned back. He could hear Byron struggling for breath.

"Why are you stopping?" Byron called out, shaking his cane at Thomas. "Keep going! Don't worry about me, my friend. I know this place inside out. It was once my home too, you know."

Thomas turned around and followed the sound of Eugenia's stomping up through the higher levels of the mansion. He climbed three flights until he reached a landing where the carpet fell away to wood. Up ahead he could see a rectangle of darkness—an open attic door—flickering with orange light.

He stepped through the doorway and squinted, forcing his eyes to adjust. He didn't have to wait long; the orange light grew stronger in one corner of the room, along with the acrid stench of smoke. He could see Eugenia's backlit figure, standing by an open window. As he ran over to her, she stabbed a finger down into the searing haze.

"See, I told you. A bunch of psychobabble."

Thomas peered down. Across the backside of the mansion, on a high bluff that fell away to nothing but ocean and salt air, the grass was on fire.

And there were words.

Words of fire, writhing in the grass.

"What? What does it say?" Byron shouted from somewhere in the darkness behind Thomas.

"I . . . I can't read it!" Thomas shouted back. "There's too much smoke. No . . . Wait."

The smoke parted. Thomas's lips quivered, forming the archaic words.

"*Res Novae . . .*"

His heart quickened a few beats. It was the illumination he and Byron had been searching for. *Those were the initials. R and N. Res Novae. That was the killer's message. But what did it mean?*

Thomas staggered backwards into the attic. When he looked up again, he could see Byron's boxy, tinted glasses, etched with slivers of orange light, staring back at him.

"What does it mean, Byron?" Eugenia called from the window.

Byron licked his lips nervously and steadied himself with his cane. His voice was soft against the blare of the sirens, though Thomas could hear the words.

"It means revolution."

Part Three:
The Floating Room

Chapter Thirteen
Requiem for Solo Cornet

It was nearing nine o'clock when the helicopter from the Coastal Emergency Center in Gloucesterport broke through the smoke and cloud cover, unloading gallons of liquid relief and flame retardant down upon Ivymount's back lawn.

To anyone but Eugenia Sneed the response might have seemed excessive: the perpetual damp caused by Mad Marge limited the radius of the fire to the area around the flaming words the arsonist had somehow treated ahead of time, allowing the flames to burn strong and clear despite the miserable weather.

Not one for mincing words, Eugenia pressed the case that the fire was "Gloomsbury's greatest emergency since the Great Carnival Inferno of '28," and had the helicopter not arrived sooner, "the legacy of the Sneed family and its dedication to this ungrateful barnacle of a town would have gone up in smoke."

Sheriff Korvin arrived on foot shortly after the fire was extinguished.

Huffing from the steep climb, his horrible bedside manner and suspicious tone immediately put Eugenia on the warpath. She accused the sheriff of "biting the hand that feeds him." When Korvin cited the "well-known history of tax evasion maintained by the Sneed family," Eugenia reminded Korvin of the coming county elections. The spectacle concluded with the sheriff promising further inquiries before stomping off to assist in the bottleneck of three Gloomsbury firetrucks still stuck with popped tires at the base of the narrow causeway leading up into Ivymount.

Thomas listened to the interviews behind the safety of a locked door in a room off the mansion's main hall. He'd been whisked inside by Byron the moment Sheriff Korvin's disdainful voice sounded through the foyer. Thomas was grateful for Byron's quick thinking, leaving Thomas's name off Korvin's list of witnesses to interview. Anxious, fearing the worst, for twenty minutes Thomas watched the door, waiting for the handle to turn and Korvin to burst in, ready to accuse Thomas of having some hand in the crime. When the door handle eventually did turn, it wasn't the sheriff Thomas saw in the doorway, but the wrinkled, jovial face of Byron Atticus Courtney Sneed smiling back at him.

"We're supposed to get cozy until the firetrucks get sorted out," said Byron, closing the door behind him. "You'd think Gloomsbury's Fire Department could store at least a few extra spare tires now and then. It seems with Mad Marge growing more and more angry by the day, fire prevention isn't at the top of the list for town planning. I asked Eugenia if we might be able to get you home another way. I thought we could commandeer one of the boats from the great Sneed fleet. Even if Eugenia was feeling charitable—which she never is—a nasty squall is blowing in. We might be marooned here for the night, Thomas."

"For the night?" Thomas gazed across the room at a half-shuttered window rising over an antique billiards table. Claw-like fronds of some overgrown plant or tree batted wildly against the glass.

"Sounds that way, I'm afraid," sighed Byron.

Thomas sunk back into the couch near the door where he'd been waiting nervously before Byron came in. A large plastic dust sheet covered the couch's cushions. Every time Thomas made the slightest move, the plastic crinkled against his borrowed clothes.

"I'll have Eugenia rustle up some dinner for us," said Byron, changing the subject. "Maybe quote something from the Bible about Christian charity, perhaps?" Byron made a few probing clicks with his cane. "Now, if I'm not completely turned around, this is J.W.'s old study. I can smell that disgusting incense he liked to burn for his late wife Claudia. There should be a phone in here somewhere. Why don't you find it and break the news to your parents that you might not be coming home tonight. I'll be back as soon as I can get Eugenia to take a few deep breaths so the oxygen actually reaches her brain. Hang tight, my young detective."

And with those words Byron opened the door and slipped out into the drafty foyer still reeking of smoke and flame retardant.

Thomas listened to Byron's clicks across the marble floor. He pushed himself up from the crinkly dust sheet and stared around the room. His temples throbbed. *What would his parents say? A Creeper having a sleepover at Ivymount?*

A sleepover . . .

That's it! Thomas almost let out a whoop of triumph. They didn't have Caller ID at the funeral home. He could tell his parents he was sleeping over somewhere else. He scrunched up his face. *But where?*

As Thomas went through the short list of friends that had dwindled considerably since Jeni had left town, he peered around the room. He searched for a desk or a side table that might have a phone resting on it. Somewhere down the hallway he could hear Byron and Eugenia arguing, their pitched voices echoing across the marble.

"Fine! Why not? Why don't we feed whoever shows up at our door holding one of the weapons from the crime scene in their hands! By the way, you still haven't thanked me for not telling Korvin you were here with your little protégé."

On the other side of the room, past a large glass display case filled with framed black and white photos and gleaming trophies, Thomas discovered another chamber tucked away from the main room.

The musty smell was stronger in this part of the room. A leather sofa and a pair of leather wingback chairs sat in the center of the room facing a marble fireplace. Against another wall stood a desk with an emerald banker's lamp resting on it. A massive oil painting—a portrait towered over the desk. The portrait revealed a cheerless man, clad in a three-piece suit, with an imperious and penetrating gaze that seemed to fix on Thomas and pierce *through* him, much like the portraits of his ancestors, the Elijahs, back in the Funeral Director's Study at home.

Thomas recognized the face in the portrait. It was a younger J.W. Sneed, the man Thomas had heard his father refer to on more than one occasion as "the puppet master of Gloomsbury." As for the portrait itself, Thomas recognized it too. It was the image the Sneeds used in *The Morning Mooring* whenever they wanted the world to know about the latest estuary or marsh they were donating as a wildlife preserve, what everyone in town suspected to be yet another carefully orchestrated tax move by the penny-pinching family. Gazing up at the portrait, Thomas could see what the newspaper had cropped out: a small side table with another painting resting on it, another portrait, this one of a homely, brunette woman holding a small dog.

Thomas crept over and examined the desk. There he found the painting of the woman and her dog sitting on a green desk pad circled by several votive candles. Byron had been right about a phone: an antique rotary phone sat on the desk, next to a pad of paper with a few indecipherable scribbles and a large inkwell with a pen sticking out of it. Reaching for the phone, Thomas hesitated. Then he smiled because it was all so clear now.

Arnold.

Arnold Myers would be his alibi.

Not perfect, not "airtight" as they said in movies, but good enough.

He lifted the phone from the handset and punched in the numbers for Arnold's house. He knew the numbers by heart for he'd spent many nights in the kitchen of the funeral home, chatting with Jeni until the early hours of the morning, keeping his voice low and listening for footsteps in the hallway.

On the second ring, a strange voice—one Thomas didn't recognize—answered. It sounded like Arnold . . . if Arnold was sucking on a mouthful of grapes.

"Uh, hullo. Y-y-yes. This is Steve . . . Steve Gooberman."

"Arnold?"

"Thomas? Is that you?"

"Yeah, it's me. Who the hell is Steve Gooberman?"

"Sorry, dude. Caller ID said unlisted, so I thought it might be Captain Sparky's. They come up like that sometimes. Steve Gooberman's the name I use for all my packages. I'm not eighteen so Captain Sparky's has to . . . you know . . . verify stuff."

"You picked Steve Gooberman as your—whatever. Listen, I need a huge favor."

"*Oh*, so you need a *favor*, huh?"

Thomas could see Arnold grinning in his mind's eye, and what he saw made him want to throat-punch him.

"Just shut up and listen, will you? Something bad's happening again."

"You mean like freaky dudes in black hats bad?"

"No, no, it's not the Sieve. It's someone else. I'm up here at Ivymount—"

"Ivymount? Holy crap. It must be bad if you're up *there*, Creeper. Those guys hate your guts."

"Thanks for the reminder. I'm stuck here for the night. Not my choice. Trust me. My parents would have a heart attack if they knew I was here. So I'm gonna tell them that I'm staying over at your house. They'll never come by or anything, so don't worry. But you're gonna have to pick up the phone if anyone calls tonight. And don't answer as Steve Gooberman. Got it?"

There was a long pause. A really . . . annoying . . . pause.

"Arn—"

"Fine. But I want in, Thomas. Whatever goes down, you gotta call me in, okay? You know, for firepower."

Thomas cursed. He reached up and parted the blinds in front of his face with two fingers. The red and blue lights still pulsed in the distance. The wind howled wilder than before. Byron was right. A storm was blowing in. As if to answer Thomas's thought, a large branch snapped off a tree outside the window and clattered to the ground.

"We've been through this before, Arnold," Thomas hissed through clenched teeth. "You always screw things up."

"Screw things up? I saved our asses back in Pop's basement. Jeni told me that it was really that dirtbag Crowley pretending to be Richie. She told me everything before she left. If one of those guys is still hanging around, I want in. Got it? I've got Scorchers and Royal Rockets out the butthole right now. They're stashed under my dad's truck, the one in the shed he's never gonna fix. C'mon. *Pleeeeeeease*, Thomas. I'm *dyyyying* over here. You saw me. They made me paint the mailbox like . . . like some lame-ass Huckleberry Finn."

"You mean Tom Sawyer. Fine. Whatever. You're *in*. Now will you promise to pick up the phone if my parents call?"

"Sure. No sweat. *Chill out, professor.*"

Thomas ignored Arnold's horrible impression of Jeni.

"And Arnold?"

"Yeah?"

"Can you please stop talking to Flip Carson about all this stuff? He thinks we have some kind of posse."

"Don't we?"

"Bye, Arnold."

Click.

Thomas banged the phone against his head a couple of times. He could only hope Arnold would hold up his end of the bargain and not ruin everything.

He prepared himself for the call home to his parents. The call went pretty much how he thought it would: his mother was worried and a little annoyed at first, then, finding out that Thomas was "branching out" and "making an effort to help steer that misguided Myers boy," she softened. They were just about to sign off—Mrs. Creeper was reminding Thomas to make an extra effort to thank the Myers for their hospitality—when the phone went dead.

Thomas stared at the mouthpiece. He held the speaker back up to his ear.

"Hello? Mom?"

A creak of gears sounded behind Thomas's shoulder. Slowly, he turned around, holding the phone in front of him like a smoking gun.

He looked past the phone to the desk. He watched a pale hand the color of milk slide away from the switch hook on the antique phone's handset. He followed the hand to a body, slunk deep into a wheelchair, then upwards, to a drooping, sallow face, barely reminiscent of the man in the portrait over the desk. Only the eyes seemed to glitter with the same white-hot intensity that neither time nor illness could diminish.

"Who in God's name are you? And what are you doing in my study?"

• • •

Thomas stared down at the bowl of reheated stew slopped in front of his nose. *Were those kidney beans or actual animal kidneys?* He scooted the mystery ingredients to the edges of the bowl where he could isolate their threat to his digestion. Had he not been starving, he would have insisted on maintaining a hunger strike, for he was indeed a captive in dangerous territory.

It had taken another intercession by Byron to smooth things over—*if* things could ever be smoothed over between Sneeds and Creepers.

After hearing the explanation of why Thomas was in J.W.'s study to call his parents, the Sneeds' elderly *paterfamilias* did not relinquish his air of suspicion. Throughout the strained meal his brow remained furrowed, his bushy white eyebrows raised like post-pupa moths. More than once, he cast a knowing glance at Eugenia, as if father and daughter possessed some powerful telepathic connection, a result perhaps of the many years they'd lived together in such close proximity.

Ripping drop cloths off five of the twenty chairs positioned around a long oak table, Eugenia made sure her uninvited guests knew that the room she'd chosen for their meal was "the family's winter dining room, and wouldn't be in use for another few months." *In use by whom?* Thomas wondered, gazing around the cavernous, cloth-covered chamber. Other than the occasional housekeeper flitting around, Thomas had yet to see anyone else in the house except J.W. and Eugenia herself.

Byron was finishing bringing the Sneeds up to speed on his "inquiry"—the discovery of the three corpses dyed head to toe in purple ink, the initials *R* and *N* inscribed on their eyelids—when the light from the overhead sconces zapped out.

The dining room plunged into darkness, broken here and there by veins of lightning in the distance. It took a few minutes to gather all the candles. Once soft yellow light returned to the room, Thomas stared around the eerie space, made even more unsettling in the candlelight. Weird shapes had started to form in the swoops and curves of the draped furniture. Thomas looked down. The bowl of vegetable stew in front of him had turned even more ghastly in the muted light. The wet squiggly parts looked like brains.

"Strasser, your chauffeur, and Rocelia Sanchez, one of your housekeepers," said Byron. "You never reported either one of them missing."

"People come and go," Eugenia rejoined flatly. She dunked a teabag down into her cup for what seemed like the twentieth time. Thomas watched her. Though there was no change in her disdainful voice, her hands were shaking. Dribbles of amber tea spilled out over her saucer.

"That's hard for me to believe," said Byron, not letting the matter drop. "Strasser worked for the family back when I lived here. You didn't raise the alarm bell when someone who's worked for you for nearly four decades falls off the face of the earth?"

"Get to the point, Byron," snapped J.W., drawing a snifter of something blood-red up to his lips. He waved his other wrinkled hand in front of him as if swatting away an errant fly. "I thought you'd given all this up . . . this *sleuthing* about town."

"The point *is*," said Byron, wiping a corner of his lips and setting his napkin down on the table. "Those were early signs that something was at least off. But Strasser and Sanchez were later victims. The first victim made me doubt any connection to them at all. It took a little more *sleuthing* as you say."

Eugenia sniffed and made a contemptuous little wave. "I suppose this is where you reveal your grand theory?"

Byron ignored the slight. "His name is—*was* Eddie Jones. He worked as a line cook at Sappy's. And if I'm not mistaken, you patronize that fine establishment every Thursday, don't you, Eugenia? A certain particular sandwich made personally for you each week?"

Eugenia lifted the cup to her lips, but her hand was trembling too hard to drink. She set the cup down. "So I have a special sandwich. I don't think that's a crime, inspector general."

"Jones made that sandwich," said Byron. "Every week. Not that either of you would care to learn that fact. I had Sigrún try to order the same one this week. They told me the 'Sneed Club' was off the menu. Indefinitely."

Thomas's stomach muscles tightened. *What was Byron doing? Trying to get them thrown out on their heads?*

"Here's my grand theory, Eugenia. The killer has worked their way from the outside in, removing all your creature comforts—mobility, a tidy house, and yes, even your personal sandwich. Privileges."

Suddenly, from behind J.W.'s shoulder, a pale glow appeared.

It was a faint miasma, like wisps of fog, rustling up from the shadows behind the wheelchair where the candlelight couldn't reach.

"Uh . . ." Thomas gulped. He quickly covered his mouth. "Sorry. Too much pepper." But pepper was the least of his problems.

A face had appeared inside the swirling miasma.

The rough contours crystallized, forming a face, a woman's face, hovering parallel to J.W.'s cheek.

"It's a mild Black Forest vegetable medley for heaven's sake," said Eugenia, though Thomas barely heard her. For once, he wished his Fixer eyes were lying to him. *It was the woman from the painting! The woman with the dog!*

The eyes of the ghost-woman pierced through Thomas, searching him like tiny black mirrors that swallowed up all light instead of reflecting it. A clump of dark hair hung from her head, and as she turned slightly, Thomas could see a bloody hole where the candlelight peeked through. The ghost-woman twisted back towards J.W.'s cheek. As she leaned closer, her pale lips fluttered, whispering words that were soundless to the living. J.W. shivered and let out a phlegmy series of coughs. Setting his snifter glass back down on the table, he pulled his heavy wool sweater tighter around his frail body.

"Damn draft. I told you we should have made a fire, Eugenia."

Thomas watched the ghost-woman recede back into a covered painting behind J.W.'s wheelchair. Soon she was gone, though the memory of her hungry, black mirror eyes stayed with Thomas and wouldn't be shaken from his mind.

"Thomas?"

At the sound of Byron's voice, Thomas swiveled around.

"You seemed to have made some headway with this purple dye? You mentioned something about it in the car?"

Byron gestured to Thomas to speak. Thomas swallowed hard into his chest. He didn't know what was worse: the ghost-woman's chilling gaze or sitting in the crossfire of J.W. and Eugenia Sneed's collective wrath.

"I . . . um . . ."

A peal of thunder rattled the mansion. The thunderclap receded. Thomas straightened up in his seat and tried his best to coax an intelligent sentence out of his lips.

"I did some research online about purple dye . . ."

At the word *online* Eugenia covered her face with her hand. Thomas took a deep breath and continued his awkward report, his head turned slightly away.

". . . that's what all three bodies were covered with when they were found. I think the purple dye comes from a shell. They used the shells to make the same dye back in ancient times . . . like Roman times."

Thomas peered down at his Black Forest vegetable medley. He knew that if he caught another disparaging look from Eugenia or J.W. he was going to lose his nerve. Byron's soft voice was the only encouraging sound in the room.

"Go on, Thomas. It's alright."

"Well," Thomas continued, fiddling with his spoon. "If the killer is using these *tribulus* things, there's a pattern here. They're obviously obsessed with Roman stuff. Byron said that Caspar was into all that—"

"Caspar!" Eugenia smacked her teacup down onto her saucer. "You mean *our* Caspar? Caspar who I talked to today? From the Federal Detention Center in Boston?" Eugenia made sure the last line was enunciated clearly so everyone at the table could hear.

"Yeah," said Thomas, weakly. "But we know it's not Caspar. So it has be someone . . ."

Thomas froze. He dropped his spoon. It clattered against the bowl, making a sound like a bell ringing out. Eugenia threw up her hands.

"Byron, are you just recruiting every lost soul who's read *Sherlock Holmes*? What is this ridiculous charade?"

Thomas closed his eyes. He couldn't hear Eugenia's acerbic voice anymore, nor Byron's reply in his defense, nor even the shivering cracks of lightning outside.

He was back inside the Endless Library.

It was more powerful than any episode that had happened before. The dining table morphed inside his mind's eye, filling with stacks upon stacks of books that soared as high as skyscrapers. Loose pages fluttered around him like giant moths. *He was threading it*, threading the whole horrible mystery. He was lost in the flow of ideas and energy. It pulled him like an invisible current, flowing from a great cosmic river that stood outside of time, outside the surface game of life and death.

"What's happening, Byron? Don't tell me the boy's going to faint."

Thomas's eyes flashed open.

"That's it." He gazed around the half-lit dining table, undaunted for the first time by Eugenia and J.W.'s suspicious glares. "The letters. *Res Novae*. Don't you see?"

"I, for one, don't," muttered J.W. before sneezing into a handkerchief. "Please, Headmaster Creeper. Enlighten us."

Thomas turned and faced Eugenia. "Eugenia, you knew that you could only read the words from way up in the attic."

"Of course. It's the only point in the house that you can get a clear view of . . . of . . . my god." Eugenia collapsed back into her chair and stared blankly off into space. "Byron, your little protégé is right."

"You'd have to be that high up to read those words," Thomas yammered on, threading the mystery. "Anywhere else and they don't make sense. You'd see flames but no words. It's the attic. It has to be. There's something up there. Why would the killer want us to be standing there at that exact moment with no fireman or police getting in the way?"

For the first time that evening—perhaps for the first time in her life—Eugenia Sneed's rage was overwhelmed and compelled to silence, a thoughtful silence. The faces around the table stared back at Thomas, casting him a look he rarely received: a look of total astonishment. Only Byron didn't seem nearly as mystified or shocked. For he knew what the others were only beginning to comprehend.

There *was* something special about his little protégé.

• • •

The next stop in the investigation was clear.

J.W. elected to remain behind, retiring to his bedroom where no "detective delusions" could follow. More stone-faced and gloomy than usual, Sigrún's enthusiasm for the investigation seemed to be waning by the second. She insisted on helping one of the Sneeds' housekeepers remove and clean the dishes, something Eugenia in her complete lack of hospitality—Sigrún was still a guest in her house—did not insist against.

As they left the draped gloom of the winter dining room, Eugenia stopped Thomas at the door. She passed him a candleholder with a stubby candle, dripping hot wax.

"Careful," Eugenia whispered, grinning wickedly. "We've already had one call to the Fire Department today."

With that cheery reminder they began their ascent up the winding staircase. Eugenia led the way, talking out loud in her usual insensitive way.

So is this what it looks like in your head all the time, Byron?

Oh wow! I'd go crazy with all that darkness!

Somewhere around the fourth floor, Thomas noticed a figure slip out from the shadows cast by a suit of armor.

Thomas jerked backwards, splattering wax all over the carpet. His heart seized up; the figure inched closer, drawing towards the radius of candlelight. The tip of unicorn horn appeared out of the gloom. Thomas relaxed. It was Trixie. When he was sure he was out of earshot—Eugenia was a floor above him, Byron still a flight below, tapping his cane up the steps—Thomas leaned in and whispered:

"Well, it sure took you guys long enough to get here."

"Sorry," Trixie whispered back. "It's not like I can jump through some portal whenever I want like Jerry. I can't control it. The truth is, after you left, I started thinking about Chateau Sneed." Trixie glanced around the room. Whatever she saw apparently didn't please her much. "I went to a party here years ago. Real snob fest. The next thing I know—*BAM!*—I'm standing in the middle of some yucky marsh, looking up at this weird place. We ghosts don't travel the same way you do, Thomas."

Thomas cracked a smile. "Oh, so you're back to being a ghost now?"

"You know what I mean, bub. Ghosts, angels . . . all I'm saying is it's best not to make dinner plans with us."

Thomas grinned. He was about to tell Trixie he was glad to see her when Eugenia's voice bellowed from the top floor.

"I DON'T HAVE ALL NIGHT!"

Thomas rolled his eyes. Trixie shook her head and fox-grinned back. Turning away, Thomas crept across the landing. As he climbed the last flight of stairs he looked over the banister, down into the dark chasm between floors.

At the bottom of the staircase Thomas could see a swirling, ectoplasmic blur. A pale figure stood next to the blur, holding a sparkling object in one hand. *Finn and Gabe.* He kept climbing. Though he could never predict when or where it would happen, he mentally prepared himself for the shock of seeing Headless Jerry come oozing out of some wall—or worse—out of the middle of someone's chest. If Jerry and the rest of the Unicornettes really were angels, at least they might be able to keep the angrier evil spirits in the house at bay. That was Thomas's prayer as he crossed the threshold into the dark attic. He found Eugenia inside, gripping her candleholder and looking like her regular, peeved self.

"So where do we begin, Sherlock?"

Thomas swung the candleholder like a torch—too fast. Hot wax splattered all over the floorboards.

"Whooops. S-s-sorry," Thomas stammered.

He scooted over to the window before Eugenia could let out whatever nasty remark was already simmering on her lips. As his eyes adjusted to thc candlelight, he surveyed the scene.

The attic window where they had first seen the flaming words was shut tight. He went over and examined the windowsill. *Maybe there was a false compartment?* He'd read about false compartments in a book about Cold War spies and how they would sneak secret documents back and forth across the East-West border in Berlin. There were even cars designed with secret crawl spaces to carry people past all the checkpoints. Hunching down, Thomas held the candleholder up to the wood while Eugenia exhaled an annoyed breath behind him.

He made a few taps with his fingers against the unvarnished wood and listened. A deeper tone might suggest a hollow, hidden cavity. He did the same tapping around the sides of the recessed bay window. Both times the sound returned: short and sharp. He moved the candleholder away, carefully this time, aware of Eugenia's hawk-like gaze at his shoulder and her squawking in his ear ("The drapes! For God's sake, watch the drapes!"). He frowned and shook his head. There was no secret door, no dummy panel that sprung loose from all his tapping. He stepped back. Eugenia raised a penciled eyebrow.

"Dead end?"

Soft cane clicks coming through the door announced Byron's arrival. Out of the corner of his eye Thomas noticed an unnatural glow. Trixie, Gabe, and Finn—still no sign of Headless Jerry—had joined the search party.

"Any leads?" said Byron.

"Not yet," said Thomas, backing up and reexamining the window. "I thought maybe something was hidden . . . like a secret message we're supposed to read. But I can't find anything."

Thomas turned around and squinted at the few objects piled around the attic—boxes, a covered dresser, a stack of parcels wrapped in white tissue paper turning a mustardy yellow.

"What are those?" asked Thomas, pointing to the stack.

"Nothing special," said Eugenia. "Portraits mainly. The Fipps and Courtney families." Eugenia eyed Byron and let slip a cruel smile. "Nothing all that valuable."

Thomas winced as hot wax dribbled off the edges of his candleholder onto his fingers. He stepped back towards the window. He furrowed his brow and chewed the side of his lip. *Maybe he was looking at it wrong. Maybe it wasn't what was in the room now, but years ago. Something that was missing.*

"Has this always been an attic? I mean, did anyone ever live up here?"

Byron and Eugenia answered at the same time.

"No—"

"Yes."

Thomas caught Trixie elbowing Gabe out of the corner of his eye. *See!* Trixie whispered. *Told you he was good!*

"Have you finally gone batty, Byron?" hissed Eugenia. "It's always been an attic."

"It has," said Byron. "Since *you* were born."

Trixie flashed Thomas a knowing glance while Byron steadied his hands on his cane.

"One summer, back when Caspar and I were teenagers . . . I believe you were still getting pushed around in your stroller, Eugenia . . . Caspar said he wanted to make a hideout in the house. So we moved our beds up here. We gave the attic a new name." Byron lowered his brow and shook his wrinkled head back and forth. "What was it? Lookout Peak? Pirate's Peak? Yes, that's it. Pirate's Peak. It was our clubhouse that summer."

"But we know it's not Caspar," said Thomas, jumping in. "Are you sure there wasn't anyone else? Someone who stayed with you that summer? A friend? You know, like a sleepover?"

"You think we were allowed sleepovers?" said Eugenia. She cursed low under her breath and turned away from the light. A tense silence fell over the room. Finn ran over to Thomas's side and tried to elicit a head scratch. Thomas flagged him off.

"Eugenia's right," said Byron in a hushed voice. "We were always on our own. The only time we spent with other children our age was at—"

"Bonny Ridge."

Eugenia's cold, hard face appeared above her flickering candle. Thomas watched the skin around her jaw tighten, as if she was clamping down her teeth.

"Bonny Ridge was the Fipps family's old retreat, Thomas," said Byron. "It's across the water in Hampswich. The three families—the Fipps, the Courtneys, the Sneeds—would meet there for holidays if the families were talking and on good terms."

The uncomfortable silence returned. Thomas felt like screaming. He was sure he was getting somewhere by asking if the room had always been an attic. He could see Eugenia was back to her old self, doubting and hating him with a passion. His temporary brilliance at figuring out the attic was the only place to read *Res Novae* was just that—temporary.

"Well, Sherlock," said Eugenia. "You got us all up here. What do we do now?"

Thomas shrugged. "Search the room, I guess. In case we missed something."

Thomas and Eugenia set to work, Eugenia grumbling every step of the way, Byron tapping against objects with his cane, asking Eugenia questions that were met with exasperated answers. After searching every dusty floorboard and shadowed recess for ten minutes, their candles had all burned down to charred wicks. The search party was a total bust.

"I'm going to bed," said Eugenia, letting out an audible yawn. "Don't wake me up if you have any more revelations." Passing by Thomas, she cast one final look of disgust. "There should be a blanket on one of the chairs downstairs."

As the light from Eugenia's candleholder disappeared down the staircase, Trixie shook her head. "A real catch that one," she muttered.

"Don't worry, Thomas," said Byron, tapping his way towards the door. "A minor setback. We'll hit it again in the morning. Please don't let Eugenia's lack of faith weigh too heavy on you. She has a sapping effect on people's will. Like Mad Marge in the flesh. Goodnight, Thomas."

"Goodnight," said Thomas gloomily.

As if right on cue, the candle in front Thomas's nose sizzled out. Darkness fell over the dusty attic like a cloak. Seizing the opportunity, Finn ran to Thomas's side, wagging his tail insistently.

"Alright," sighed Thomas, "you lead way. Nothing to see here, anyway."

Thomas followed the light of his faithful ghost-dog back down the several flights to the ground floor. Finding a chair in the foyer with a wool blanket thrown over one arm, he settled down.

Finn made a few nudges with his frigid snout under Thomas's hand until Thomas gave a few obligatory scruffs.

"Don't worry, Thomas," said Trixie. "Gabe and I'll keep watch. We saw her too. The lady with the chunk out of her head. She made a grab at Gabe. Would you believe it?"

"Like she wanted to rip my head clean off," said Gabe, nodding a couple times. He tapped his cornet. "Gave her a little blast of old King Oliver. Didn't like that. Not one bit."

"Yeah," said Trixie. "Must be one of those classical types."

"Must be," said Gabe. He flashed his brilliant smile. "Don't you worry, Thomas. We got your back. Maybe . . ." Gabe's shoulders heaved up and down. He closed his eyes, forcing back ghost tears. "Maybe Jerry will show up and burst right through her. I'd love to see her try to take *his* head off."

Trixie staggered back, gripping her sides. Dark blood gurgled down the sides of her stained dress. "Oh man . . . you didn't . . . " Trixie gasped, choking back laughter. "You said take *his* head off."

Finn let out a couple enthusiastic barks.

Thomas rolled his eyes. "Goodnight."

He didn't know why he said it. There was no way he was going to sleep a wink in a house with a vengeful ghost roaming around trying to rip people's heads off.

• • •

Drowsy and jumpy, Thomas greeted the early hours of dawn. The Unicornettes had all vanished, though they'd been true to their word: Thomas was still alive, his head still firmly attached to his neck. There was still no sign of Headless Jerry, however, though that wasn't exactly a tragedy.

Thomas pushed himself up from his makeshift chair bed and walked over to the restroom off the foyer. He washed up and made sure he placed the hand towel stitched with a large *S* back exactly as he'd found it. Stepping out into the hallway, he listened.

Voices echoed from the far end of the hall. It was Eugenia and Byron going at it again. A loud slam reverberated across the marble, followed a second later by several swift cane taps, pinging their way towards Thomas. A few seconds later, Byron appeared beneath the shadowed doorway, looking disheveled and even more than a little annoyed. Thomas watched Sigrún fly past him, cursing in her guttural language as she huffed her way towards the front door.

"Thomas. Ah, there you are," said Byron. "I can hear you breathing, which is a far better sound than my step-sister's caterwauling." Byron nodded back over his shoulder. "The good news is that the road out of this god-forsaken place has been cleared. The bad news is that we must take our investigation elsewhere for it seems we've worn out our welcome, if we ever had one."

Byron tapped his way over to Thomas.

"I'm sorry," Thomas whispered.

"Sorry?" croaked Byron. "What in heaven's for?"

"We were supposed to solve everything. You said all the clues led here."

Byron reached out a wrinkled hand. He searched his way to Thomas's shoulder.

"And they *do* lead here. I'm sure of it. We just have to approach things from a different angle, that's all. We're like an old siege engine, my friend. They've taken away the level ground. We'll plan our second attack. Onward!"

Byron gave Thomas a few taps on the shoulder and headed for the door. Thomas followed. Outside they found Sigrún revving up the sedan. The car sped off, leaving a silhouetted Eugenia scowling from an upstairs window.

"Let's get you fed, Thomas," said Byron once they had passed through the gatehouse. "We can't do any good thinking without proper sustenance. And I don't mean Black Forest vegetable medley. Sound good?"

"Yep," said Thomas, smiling faintly.

At the gatehouse they were greeted by Mr. Contenescu. He hit the buzzer on the gate, allowing the car to pass. Through the rear window Thomas watched the old Romanian bodyguard and former boxer follow the sedan's path all the way until it disappeared on the other side of the long marsh plankway of railroad ties billowing with fresh fog.

On the way back through the Gold Coast, Thomas spied Trixie, Gabe, and Finn. They were gathered together beneath the shadow of the old Feinhurst mansion. Trixie and Gabe were laughing and talking and Finn was bounding and circling around them. Thomas waved to them from his seat. Catching Sigrún's face in the rearview mirror, he quickly lowered his hand and went back to surveying the scenery. When they reached Byron's house, Sigrún pulled the car around the side. As they piled out, Thomas ran up the path to the house's side entrance. Though he shouldn't have been shocked because Trixie had already explained that ghosts didn't travel like humans, he was still a little surprised to find Trixie and Gabe already standing by the door.

"Yeah, that's not good," said Trixie, shaking her head and pointing.

There was a fist-sized hole in one of the glass panes.

And the door was ajar.

Noticing the door, Sigrún let a stream of guttural curses. Thomas felt a freezing hand on his shoulder.

"Better wait here, bub," said Trixie.

Trixie nodded to Gabe. The two ghosts passed through the doorway. Sigrún barked something over her shoulder to Byron. Snatching a walking stick from the door, she barreled into the house. Thomas lingered in the doorway as Byron hobbled up behind him.

"What? What is it? What's going on?"

"I think somebody's broken in," said Thomas.

Byron tapped his cane through the doorway. "Don't move. And don't come inside until I say everything is clear."

Thomas did as he was told and stayed put. He felt fear tighten around his throat like a noose. *Should he call the police?* The nearest phone was in the house. *What was Byron going to do completely blind if the trespasser was still in the house and Sigrún couldn't handle them?* Before he could consider these consequences Trixie was back.

"They're gone. But one of the rats . . ." Trixie lowered her eyes and let out a deep shudder. "Oh, it's awful, Thomas."

From inside the house came a terrible moan. Thomas rushed inside. He followed the moaning to the study where he found Byron collapsed into Sigrún's arms, sobbing like a child.

"Why, Sigrún?" Byron rasped. "Why would they do that to such a sweet creature?"

Thomas searched the room. "What's going on? What happened?"

Sigrún pointed a gnarled finger at one of the striped couches. Thomas followed the direction of the finger. Maneuvering his long legs around a pile of rat tubes blocking his path, he took a few steps towards the couch before coming to a dead stop.

His eyes filled with horror.

A series of spikes, like thin white teeth, poked up through the fabric. A furry shape was caught on one spike, dangling in the air, its legs stiff. Thomas felt his heart sink as he inched closer. It was Facto, the larger brown rat, the one who'd won the cheese in the maze game. Thomas squinted his eyes. The spikes weren't made out of metal or the teeth of some animal. He knew the shape. *They were shells.*

Murex shells.

Over his shoulder, Thomas heard Gabe strike up a somber melody on his cornet, a slow dirge-like march. Looking down, he could see drops of dark liquid splattered all over couch. *Not blood. Blood was red.* These splotches were purple.

A telephone rattled in the corner of the room.

Gabe stopped playing. Sigrún looked down helplessly. There was no way she was going to get Byron to unlock his arms from around her waist. Making a little jerk with her chin, she nodded to Thomas. Thomas crossed the room and found the phone resting next to Byron's illegal police radio. Slowly, he lifted the phone off the handset.

"H-hello?"

"I know who's doing it," a ragged voice hissed on the other end of the line. "I wasn't sure until I checked the letter. She sent it the day after I had Contenescu take her away. She was never supposed to come back.

"That was our deal . . ."

Chapter Fourteen
A Shot in the Dark

In a smooth patch off the side of the house, unspoiled by scabber weed, they buried Facto.

Thomas offered to take over digging when it seemed even Sigrún was too overwhelmed with grief. The smile Sigrún had let slip the day before while ladling out food for the two rats had been merely a glimpse of the wellspring of love and emotion buried deep within the craggy woman. It caught Thomas by surprise. As he shoveled the black wet dirt, he watched Sigrún and Byron out of the corner of his eye. Sigrún was stooped over, pressing her forehead against Byron's. Choking back tears, Byron clung to his old friend and companion as if she were a life raft in the middle of the ocean.

Breaking away from Sigrún's embrace, Byron tapped his way across the rainswept yard. As Thomas stopped to catch his breath from shoveling, he turned to find Byron shaking and holding an old toolbox. Thomas took the toolbox from Byron and flipped open the rusted latches. Inside he found no tools, only a small package, delicately wrapped in soft powder-blue fabric.

"I don't want any pests getting to my dear boy," whispered Byron.

Thomas nodded grimly and lowered the toolbox down into the dark hole. As he began filling the dirt back in, once more he heard Gabe's cornet strike up over the whipping wind, this time accompanied by a sweet voice, one Thomas had never heard before.

It was Trixie.

The song and the lyrics were so moving Thomas had to stop shoveling and listen. And though he felt a deep sorrow for Facto, and for Byron and Sigrún's loss, it was only then, listening to Trixie's beautiful song that Thomas felt tears stinging the corners of his own eyes.

Goin' down the road
A million miles to go
Searching for that River of Love
To carry me home

The city rubs me raw
Treats me like a dog
But the River of Love
River of Love
It could wash my soul

One foot in, that ain't enough
I need to go all the way
River of Love, River of Love
Take me home today

Later, after the burial, when Thomas thought it appropriate, he spoke up and shared the revelation from the phone call in Byron's study.

Sigrún had prepared a small brunch of toast and eggs, though Byron seemed unable to manage a single bite. On the third time after asking Thomas to repeat J.W.'s exact words, Byron's gnarled hands clenched and unclenched several times. He removed his boxy, tinted glasses and set them down on the table.

"Of course," he whispered through the cracks in his fingers covering his face. "That summer. In Pirate's Peak."

"What do you mean?" asked Thomas.

Byron removed his hand. For the first time Thomas saw the deep pink scars around the old man's missing eye. The right eye was still intact, though it was pale and milky looking.

"I suppose I lied to you, Thomas, when I told you that I can visualize nearly everything I've seen from before the accident," said Byron, running a thumb over the side of his glasses. "The main scenes I still remember. Smells and sounds can help bring back some of the missing pieces. But there are . . ." He shook his head. "Gaps . . . like spaces between the stars you don't think about because you're fixed on the light. And people . . ." Byron trailed off. But Thomas could guess who he was thinking of.

Curls you could die for. The May Queen three years in a row.

"I don't know why it didn't come flooding back to me last night. But I'm certain of it now. It's the reason she wanted us all up there in the attic. It's where I saw her . . . that last time." Byron fit the glasses back onto the bridge of his pitted nose. "Forgive me, Thomas. I must look like some frightening cyclops to you."

"No, it's fine," said Thomas. He'd seen way more frightening wounds on the cooling board at Creeper & Sons. "Who do you mean? Who did you see from the window that summer?"

Byron reached down and retrieved a half-finished glass of wine from the table. He took a long, deep sip.

"Her name is Lorelei. She's Caspar's twin. They sent her away because she had . . ."

Byron set the glass down on the table, but his hand never stopped trembling.

". . . difficulties. I never believed my step-uncle's claim that she was insane, that they had to keep her away for the family's sake. She wasn't insane, Thomas. She was brilliant. Too brilliant to function in a closed world like Ivymount. You see, this was a time when children were expected to be seen not heard. And Lorelei was no shrinking violet. She could be difficult. Even violent. Because of her outbursts, she was often alone. More than any of us. She was an auto-didact, Thomas. She taught herself from her own private library in her room, the same library Caspar and I inherited when Lorelei was sent away to that hellhole, that school for troubled youth up north. I must have buried the memory of seeing her that summer because I felt guilty for doing nothing to stop them taking her away. After the second time she broke out of the school, J.W. had her committed to a psychiatric facility. We weren't even given a name or an address. Oh god, Thomas . . ."

Hearing Byron's ragged cry, Sigrún appeared in the doorway. Byron held a wrinkled hand up, flagging her off. Sigrún ignored the gesture. Flying from the door, she wrapped her strong arms around Byron's shoulders.

"Why? Why is she doing this? Why doesn't she come for me instead? She saw me in the window that night . . . and I . . . oh, Thomas, I just stood there while they chased her . . . chased her through the woods like some wild animal."

Sigrún leaned down and whispered gentle words into Byron's ear. Reaching into his jacket pocket Byron retrieved a handkerchief and blew his nose several times. Thomas watched Byron's fist return to the table, the knuckles whitening as he clenched and unclenched the handkerchief.

"We must stop her, Thomas. There has to be some inkling of a person left inside who will listen to reason. But she would be older now, Thomas, and so many people would recognize her. She made national news ten years ago when she tried to take J.W. to court for cutting her out of the family trusts, citing psychological damages. She must still have some secret roots here in Gloomsbury where she can live without causing too much attention."

Byron pushed himself to his feet.

"Give me a few hours. I'll call J.W. and do some digging. In the meantime, we need to get you home. I can only imagine the lies you must have spun to your parents to get you through the past twenty-four hours."

"I told them I was staying over at a friend's house," said Thomas. "I think they bought it."

"Well," said Byron, "we'll drop you within a good distance of the house, just to be safe. How does that sound, my young detective?"

Thomas nodded. They left the house and piled into the old sedan. As they headed back down the steep gravel driveway, Thomas looked back through the rear window.

He could see Finn's green ectoplasmic blur hovering near the gravesite where they'd laid Facto to rest. He remembered something his mother always said about how animals "know things about life and death us humans don't have a clue about."

Staring back at the glimmering ghost-dog, Thomas wondered what undead animals knew, whether it was something really frightening, or even worth knowing at all.

• • •

Sigrún and Byron deposited Thomas two blocks down from the funeral home where he'd be safely out of sight.

As Thomas unlatched the rotting gate to Creeper & Sons, he could see Jed up ahead through the yard. His incorrigible uncle was holding the world's rustiest pair of garden shears and seemed to be battling the hedges bursting up around the house. Catching sight of Thomas trudging up the flagstones, Jed turned and roved his eyes over his nephew, grinning his half-masked grin and scattering ash from a cigarette stuck out of the crook of his mouth

"You look like hell, Tommy Boy. What'd you guys get into last night? Stay up to catch the sunrise?"

Thomas ignored his uncle's throaty, smoker's cackle. "Did they get it all worked out with the Health Board? I mean, are we—"

"Back in business?"

Jed blew a breath out of his nose. Reaching down with his rusted garden shears, he snapped the head off what may have once been an unopened peony bud, but from all the rot and damp looked more like a goopy, oversized eyeball.

"We better be, Tommy Boy. Or else it's gonna be a healthy diet of roadkill from here on in."

Jed let out another throaty cackle. Thomas left his uncle's charming company and made his way up the steps to the foyer. Inside he found his parents standing outside the Funeral Director's Study, doing what they did best—arguing.

"I don't have time to go wade through the line at Town Hall, Elijah," Mrs. Creeper warbled, waving a large manila envelope over her head. "I have a conference with the School Board in ten minutes."

"Ah! There it is," Mr. Creeper snapped back. "Always short-sighted, Adele. You never see the big picture, do you? If we don't get the new permits filed today, we'll all be reading Jane Austen in the homeless shelter."

"Um? Guys?"

The two seething faces of Thomas's parents turned in tandem, fixing their gaze on their only living son.

"I can go," said Thomas, shrugging his shoulders. "It's no big deal."

"Oh, would you? Thank you, sweetie," gushed Mrs. Creeper. "I'm tied up today, and your father has Orem Chester coming by any minute now. Orem's doing us a favor and purchasing a few Thermolux Repositors for Chester Funeral Home." Mrs. Creeper handed the envelope to Thomas. "If you could drop this off with Candace Baker at Town Hall, she'll know where to file everything. Don't go to—"

"Patty Korvin, I know," said Thomas.

"Or Langley Sneed," said Mr. Creeper.

"And better stay away from Harlan Fipps's office just in case," added Mrs. Creeper.

"Yeah, guys. I got it," said Thomas.

"Oh, you're a life-saver." Mrs. Creeper leaned in and planted a kiss on Thomas's cheek.

"Gross, Mom," Thomas moaned, wiping his cheek and retreating backwards.

"Do you need money for the bus, Elijah Thomas?" Mr. Creeper asked, though the offer sounded pained like anything involving money around the funeral home.

"Nope," Thomas called back, already halfway out the door. "Ms. Katz got a new car and gave me her old bus pass. Bye! See you later!"

He left his parents in the shadows of the foyer. Before the door clicked shut Thomas heard them switch to a new argument—how much to inflate the price of the Thermolux

Repositors because the Chesters were obviously doing very well, having recently opened a second funeral home in nearby Wolchester.

Thomas headed down the porch steps. He found his uncle muttering and cursing next to a rotting handrail. His half-mask was pushed back on his head, and the garden shears were jammed into a bush exploding with purple pokeberry and poison ivy.

"Care to fill me in on whatever's going?" wheezed Jed out of the corner of his mouth while he tried—unsuccessfully—to relight his soaked cigarette. "You got that look again, Tommy Boy. I know that look."

"What look?"

Jed side-eyed Thomas and smiled so wide Thomas could see his missing back molars.

"Fine, don't squeal. You're a natural born hustler like me. Trust me. I can spot a hustler a mile away."

Looking at the red wavy scars around his uncle's face, a light bulb went off in Thomas's brain.

"That's it! Jed, I owe you a million bucks!"

Thomas flew down the muddy, moss-strewn flagstones while Jed called out, tossing his cigarette to the ground.

"Well, cut me a check sometime then, will ya?"

As Thomas sprinted down the cobblestones, he started to fit the pieces together. *Byron said Lorelei would be recognizable to most people from being on the news. If she was still living around Gloomsbury, pretending to be other people, she'd need some way of hiding her identity. She couldn't wear masks like Jed without getting noticed. She'd need a disguise, maybe several.*

Rounding the corner at Mt. Parnassus and Thayer, heading for the bus stop in Jeni's neighborhood, the Uppercrust, Thomas stopped a few feet short of a minivan that came careening through the intersection. But even the driver's horn couldn't break his concentration. *Lorelei would need wigs and other accessories to hide her appearance. There was one place in town that sold exactly what she needed.*

Thomas smiled and leapt over a puddle caused by one of the street's overflowing gutters. About a half-block down from Jeni's house, he spied one of Mayor Plugg's trollies chugging along the street. *Bingo!* For once the Universe had decided to throw him a bone.

Ignoring the lactic acid burn building up in his spindly limbs, he sprinted on, following the jangly carnival music blasting from the trolley's loudspeaker. As the trolley slowed to let a large moving truck nose its way out of an alley, Thomas seized his opportunity. Calling on the muscle memory of his short career as a cross-country star at school, he threw his whole body into overdrive. He was just a few yards away. He could hear the trolley switching gears, accelerating with a choke of exhaust—

Out from a rotten cleft in the trunk of an old oak tree, a glowing specter emerged. The specter had hands. And white gloves.

Headless Jerry.

Pantomiming a runner in full sprint, pinstriped arms pounding like pistons, Headless Jerry zoomed alongside Thomas.

"Not now, Jerry!" Thomas shouted through clenched teeth.

Something hard—hard and green—went up in front of Thomas like a barricade.

"Yeeeeee-OWWWWWWWW!"

He hit the dumpster and bounced off like a pigeon striking a windshield. Crumpling to the wet ground, he rubbed his bruised arm. Stars of white-hot pain exploded before his eyes. He stood up and looked around blearily. The yellow envelope at his feet was slowly turning brown in the gutter.

"Damn it, Jerry! Look what you made me do!"

Snatching the envelope, Thomas shook it violently before it could get soaked any further. Headless Jerry made a praying gesture with his gloves. Then he started waving his hands wildly around in the air.

"I told you. I don't have time for stupid charades."

Headless Jerry jumped out into the street. Cars flew past—*and through*—him. He pressed his gloves together like joining the two halves of an egg. Then he made another gesture that looked like the letter *P*.

"Whatever it is, it can wait," said Thomas. "C'mon."

At the next stoplight two streets down Thomas finally caught up with the trolley. Through the foggy glass he could see Bunny Carson perched behind the wheel wearing his ridiculous antique suit. The accordion doors flapped open. A blast of jangly circus music assaulted Thomas's ears.

"Oh, hey, Creeper. Need a lift?"

Thomas leapt on board. He swiped Ms. Katz's key card through the scanner. The scanner pinged green. The doors closed, the trolley lurched forward—

Too fast.

"Stupid clutch," cried Bunny while everyone whiplashed forward. "Sorry, folks!"

Thomas fell into a portly man with a giant beard who looked like the portrait of the poet Walt Whitman he'd seen in the back of a book at school. Apologizing profusely for using the man's beard as a handhold, he made his way down through the cabin until he found an open spot.

The trolley hadn't gone more than a few bumpy feet when Headless Jerry oozed up from the seat next to Thomas.

"Can you," Thomas began in a breathless voice, "*try* not to do anything weird until we get there? Please?"

Headless Jerry twiddled his thumbs.

"Seriously, Jerry. You can't keep popping up like that. We need a warning system or something."

The trolley lurched and began bumping its way down through Old Town, Gloomsbury. In an exasperated voice, Bunny relayed for the fifth time that afternoon all the landmarks he was required to point out: Gloomsbury Treats, formerly the Sneed Shark Cannery where the largest great white shark ever discovered in Massachusetts was turned into shark fin soup during the Great Depression, not to feed the starving masses, but attendees at the Sneeds' summer gala; the Ethel Greaves Building, struck by lightning seven times during a single evening in 1896, and whose twisted weathervane still bore witness to seven successive blasts; and, lastly, right next to the post office, currently serving double duty as Town Hall after the former site was destroyed by sinkholes, the Elgin Winterborn Wax Figurine Museum that sadly lost half its inventory to flames like so many other shops and buildings during the Great Carnival Inferno of 1928.

The trolley came to a rolling stop in front of the post office. Once everything and everyone found the right side of gravity again, Bunny cranked open the accordion doors. Rattled, but still in one piece, Thomas made his way carefully towards the door. Before he could make his first step down Bunny reached out and grabbed his shoulder.

"Hey, Creeper, I wanted to say that even though Arnold and I told everybody at school you were sick with this flesh-eating virus, which is why you had to get homeschooled—"

"You guys said what?"

"Look, it doesn't matter now. What I'm saying is Arnold told me about all the bad stuff going down around town. I just want you to know I got your back, bro. Flip, Arnold, me. We're all on your side."

Bunny stopped and waved to the portly man who Thomas had given a beard yank to earlier. The old man glared at Bunny and grumbled down off the steps. Bunny lowered his voice and leaned closer to Thomas.

"And we're all packing in case things go down. Check it!"

When Bunny was sure no one was looking, he fanned open his suit jacket. Thomas could see the heads of two 5-Ball Roman Candles poking up from Bunny's jacket pocket.

"You guys are nuts," sighed Thomas. He made his way down to the curb while the annoying circus music struck up again.

"Say the word, bro!" Bunny shouted over the music. "The Crotch Cannoneers are standing by!"

Headless Jerry, who'd been following the conversation word for word, appeared next to Thomas on the curb. He held his gloved hands up in the air as if to inquire about the strange exchange on the trolley deck.

"Don't worry about it," muttered Thomas.

With a shrug of his pinstriped shoulders the headless ghost followed Thomas into the old post office.

• • •

It had taken over twenty minutes waiting in line but Thomas managed to get the new permits filed for the funeral home. An even greater coup was that the pages weren't completely soaked after all. He had no idea what kind of tongue-lashing would be waiting for him from his father if he returned home with soppy, ink-bled pages.

On the way out of the post office Thomas heard a heavily-accented voice shouting through some kind of bullhorn that kept fizzling in and out.

"DONATE YOUR MONIES TODAY—*ZZZSSSSST*—TO THE ALDERFER FOUNDATION AND JOIN OUR RAFFLE OPPORTUNITY—*ZZZSSSSST*—TO ENJOY FRONT-ROWING SEATS TO SEE THE GREAT WHITE PHANTOM!"

Thomas's mouth flapped open.

It was Marylène. She was dressed in a fuzzy squid suit, complete with a squid head that opened to reveal her pretty face. She held a large red bullhorn in one hand that kept fizzling and popping with static. A poster board display rose behind her. A giant question mark was drawn in magic marker in the center of the posterboard with several dollar bills pinned to it. Smoothing back his squirrel's nest of black hair, Thomas walked over and caught up to Marylène right as she raised her arm to dash the bullhorn to the ground.

"*Salut,* Thomas."

Seeing Thomas, Marylène's annoyance and frustration with the bullhorn seemed to lessen. She smiled back at him from the shadows of the squid hat.

"What in all worlds are you doing here?"

"Had to drop something off for my parents," said Thomas. He looked side to side, making sure Headless Jerry was at a good distance and wasn't about to burst through Marylène's sternum.

"I too am helping my father," said Marylène. She pointed up at the poster with the giant question mark. "The Great Phantom is getting close, Thomas. The satellites are showing the path of the magic shrimp. It is any day now they will be arriving."

"Coooool," said Thomas, trying his best to ignore Headless Jerry wiggling his shoulders around and pretending to make out with the air. "Hey, look," he continued, stepping closer to Marylène. "I wanted to tell you at dance class, but they said you were helping your dad. It's about what we found down by Town Beach."

Marylène made a little nod with her squid head but said nothing.

"Well, I think I found out who's doing it. I know it's kind of crazy, but I feel like maybe I can stop them before Korvin gets involved."

"This Korvin," said Marylène. "He is a very bad man, Thomas."

"Yeah, total nightmare."

While Marylène worked out the translation, nodding as the parts came together, out of the corner of his eye Thomas watched Headless Jerry make several points at his wristwatch.

"Anyway," said Thomas. "I could use your help. If you're up for it, I mean. I don't want to get you in trouble or anything. It's totally fine if you don't—"

"Yes," said Marylène, raising a fist in the air. "I will be your comrade in this mystery, Thomas. We will show Korvin he is like a dog's gift to sidewalks."

That's one way of saying it, thought Thomas. Scowling one last time at the faulty bullhorn in her hand, Marylène tossed it over into a trash can. Then, reaching up, she started unpinning the dollar bills from the posterboard one by one. Pulling off her squid head, she threw the dollar bills inside while Thomas raised an eyebrow.

"I will ask for the pockets next time," said Marylène, grinning. Thomas grinned back.

Walking over to the only bike wedged into the Post Office's rusted bike rack, Marylène stuffed the squid head down into a milk crate attached to the bike's back bumper. When she came back, she flashed Thomas her Wonder Woman pose, elbows making triangles with her hips.

"I am ready for the kick-assing, Thomas."

"Don't you want to . . . you know . . . change?"

Marylène shook her head. "This is not possible. I don't have the changing clothes. It would be a great embarrassment to take this costume off."

"Right," said Thomas. An image flashed in his mind, but he quickly banished it.

As they headed down the street, Thomas did his best to summarize what had happened over the past few days: his research into the purple dye, the letters found on the eyelids that meant *Res Novae*, the fire and the sleepover at Ivymount. Finally—and most importantly—he shared the news of Lorelei's reappearance. Marylène listened to everything with an expression of wonder mixed with terror.

"So she changes her faces? All the time?"

"That's what we're thinking," said Thomas, shrugging. "There's a shop in town that sells wigs. I thought that because Lorelei wears all these disguises maybe there'd be something there, like a receipt or an address if she had anything shipped. I don't know. It's a shot in the dark. Okay, we're here."

A slanted brick rowhouse rose in front of them. Fog wafted over the crumbly and stained bricks. Over the door, a mess of vines partially covered a sign hanging from a broken hinge, though the smaller type was still readable.

Wigs and Beautifying Accessories!

Headless Jerry stepped up to the display window. Reaching up, he held his gloved hands in front of his missing eyes like binoculars, before proceeding to pantomime taking a look around.

Thomas did the same, albeit with living eyes. In the window were several mannequins modeling various products and accessories. One of the male mannequins was dressed in a tan suit called a seersucker with a red flower pinned to his lapel. Catching sight of the suit, Headless Jerry flashed a thumbs up. *He approved!*

Thomas turned to Marylène.

"Okay. Do you think you can distract them? I'm gonna ask if I can use the bathroom. All you need to do is make up some story . . . like maybe you're in a play. Yeah! A play. And you need a wig for your part. Something like that?"

"Yes," said Marylène. Her eyebrows narrowed and her voice went very low and serious. "You can bet your bottom's dollar I can do the distracting."

"Great," said Thomas. "Here we go."

He walked over to the door and turned the cold brass knob. Behind him he could hear Marylène preparing some speech in broken English. They stepped into the shop.

They hadn't been standing for more than a few seconds when the smell of stale cigarette smoke mixed with noxious perfume invaded their nostrils. As the bell on the door died away, a stout, elderly woman with bright blue eyeshadow wearing a strawberry-blonde wig appeared from behind the counter. Thomas and Marylène exchanged a knowing glance. *It was Madame Marsh! Their enthusiastic yet pungent dance instructor!*

"Well, you've found me at the home of my second passion," the old dance instructor croaked. "And what brings my two young pupils to Marsh's Menagerie?"

"I am researching a wig for *ma mère* . . . my mother," said Marylène, her eyes darting around as she translated the lie. "We have an insect in France and . . . and it is eating the heads off people . . . *non, non* . . . their hairs I am meaning to say."

"Sounds quite painful," said Madame Marsh. "I had a case of elephant chiggers in Madagascar. Must have been '58. No, no, no." She fluttered her sausage-like fingers against her chin. "Or was it '63? I'm sure it was—"

"Sorry, Madame Marsh," Thomas interjected. "Can I use your bathroom?"

"Of course," said Madame Marsh. "Straight down the hall on the right. I apologize for all the Smooth Knee Kits I haven't unpacked yet, Thomas. You wouldn't believe how a smooth decoy knee can accent a well-toned thigh."

While Madame Marsh proceeded to show Marylène her decoy knees, Thomas nodded to Headless Jerry who up until that point had been busy mimicking the pose of the mannequin next to him, a woman making a dramatic gesture with her hands above her head like a flamenco dancer. Thomas walked around the checkout counter, following Madame Marsh's directions, Headless Jerry trailing close behind. They traversed a short, slanting hallway covered with pictures of Madame Marsh in full dance attire until they came to a small office opposite a bathroom.

"Okay," Thomas whispered to Headless Jerry. "You keep watch. I know you can't speak, so let's figure out some kind of signal."

Headless Jerry threw his arms up and did a wild wiggle reminiscent of the time Gabe played his cornet for him.

"That'll do."

Thomas left Headless Jerry in the doorway to stand watch. Covering his nose with his forearm, he waded into the windowless, unvented room swirling with a sea of unappetizing smells.

The room itself was a total disaster. There were boxes stacked floor to ceiling around a small desk cluttered with reams of loose paper. *How in the world was he going to find anything important or secret about the shop's customers in this dump?*

Creeping over to the desk chair, he pushed the chair aside, knocking off a pink feather boa draped over the chair's back. Hunching down, gathering the feather boa in his hands, he spied a box in the shadows at the back of the desk. It was a small shoebox. *LOST AND FOUND* was stenciled down one side. Carefully, Thomas slid the box out and removed the lid.

Inside he found the usual items forgotten in public places: sunglasses and oversized reading glasses, "cheaters" as Ms. Katz liked to call them; a key fob with a few keys attached to the ring; a sweat-stained baseball hat for the Tauton Trollers, a local minor league baseball team whose mascot was a large green troll holding a bat and a fishing net.

A chill wafted over Thomas's exposed neck. He twisted his head and looked up.

Headless Jerry was standing next to him, wiggling his hips like a go-go dancer who'd just slammed ten espressos.

Heart pounding, Thomas fished around the shoebox one last time until his fingers grasped the cool plastic of a card attached to a small lanyard. Over his shoulder he could hear Madame Marsh coming down the hallway.

". . . checking to see if he found it. It's a disaster zone back there."

Thomas covered the shoebox and scooted it back under the desk. Standing up, he examined the card. On the front was a grainy black and white photo showing an unsmiling woman with a mop of curly hair. A name was handwritten underneath the photo: *MELITA FORTUNA*. The footsteps in the hallway came closer. Thomas thumbed the laminated plastic on the card that had started to peel around the edges. He pulled the plastic back further. *There was a second photo underneath the first!* The bottom photo revealed a grizzled man with sunken eyes and a walrus-style moustache. The man's name wasn't written by hand, but printed by a computer: *Corbin Cartwright, Supervisor. The Alderfer Foundation.*

Thomas flipped the card around. A piece of masking tape was stuck to the back side. And there was writing. *Left on the counter. Nice foreign lady who ordered a few Curly Suzannes.* He stuffed the key card into his back pocket right as the Madame Marsh appeared in the doorway. She flashed Thomas a flabbergasted look.

"There was a . . ." He turned away, doing his best to hide his non-existent poker face. He spun back around and snapped his fingers. "A mouse. It ran right . . . right out of the bathroom and behind those boxes."

"That's the third one this week," Madame Marsh fumed, shaking her wigged head. "They love the new line of toners made with repurposed sunflower oil. Go after 'em like candy. Don't worry, Thomas. I'll have Edgemont set a few more traps. We'll get 'em before they can ruin the next batch."

Madame Marsh turned and straightened one of the photographs on the hallway wall.

"Ah, there I am, Thomas. So young. So naïve. Dressed in my little Balmoral tartan. It was the fifth round at the Larchmont Invitational. Imogene LaFronde had pulled off a perfect arabesque—"

"I'm sorry, Madame Marsh," said Thomas, hurrying past. "I just remembered we're supposed to pick up a prescription for . . . um . . . Marylène's mother. For her . . . insect bites."

Thomas met Marylène at the checkout counter.

"C'mon," he whispered out of the side of his mouth. "I got it."

"The mouse?" said Marylène.

"No," said Thomas, flashing a smile. "The key. The key to everything."

• • •

While Marylène pedaled furiously down the potholed road Thomas did his best to keep up. Cars flew past in the damp mist. A few drivers even slowed down to take in the sight of Marylène in her partial squid suit.

"I am not believing it, Thomas, but I must, I must!" Marylène called back over her shoulder as she peddled on. "All this time she was disguising herself at the Alderfer. She's always been so kind to Julian and myself, and she never let angry words fly around the room with Monsieur Cal or Monsieur Thaddeus who is a very angry and frustrating man."

Marylène jerked her bike to a stop, scattering wet sand everywhere. Thomas paused alongside her, panting and staring at a blank patch of air in front of his nose while all the jumbled pieces came together in his brain.

"I bet that's why the boat's been missing," he said. "Cal's father kept saying that someone was stealing the Alderfer's boats. Lorelei must be waiting until everyone is asleep and using the boats to move up and down the shore to dump the bodies."

Back down the road Thomas could see Headless Jerry. The ghost was sprinting through the wet haze, arms pumping like pistons. Stopping and making an exaggerated pantomime of catching his breath, bent over, clutching his ribs, he straightened up and waved a gloved hand at Thomas.

"I hate Korvin," said Marylène. "But do you think, Thomas, that we should—"

"No," said Thomas, though he was thinking the same thing. They were in over their heads, *way* over. "I'll call Byron at the

Alderfer while you track down Melita—Lorelei, I mean." Thomas placed his hand on Marylène's fuzzy squid shoulder. "Don't let her see you, okay? Find out where she is and then stay out of sight. When Byron and Sigrún get there, we'll try to corner her. Sigrún is pretty scary. Even if Lorelei is some crazy psychopath, I'm pretty sure Sigrún can take her. Lorelei has to be pretty old. That's what doesn't make sense to me. The lady I saw pushing Cal's father around didn't look that old. But maybe that's part of her disguise? Anyway, let's go."

They took off again. After fifteen minutes of pedaling and sprinting down the state road, they made it to the crushed seashell driveway of the Alderfer Foundation.

Marylène grabbed Thomas's hand.

"This way."

She pulled him around the side of the building until they were standing in the shadow of the great Marvale lighthouse.

"*Attention*, Thomas," said Marylène. "It is slipperish around here on the stones, but there is another way. Follow me."

Footing their way along the "slipperish" path that circled the lighthouse, they came to a steep overlook of boulders stained almost as white as the lighthouse from years of seagull droppings. Letting go of Thomas's hand, using both arms to balance, Marylène led the way up and over one boulder to a deck coming out the Alderfer's side. Sidling up to an unshuttered window, Marylène peered inside.

"*Formidable*," she whispered. "I see no one, Thomas. Come. The lock is broken always."

Marylène pushed open the window and slipped inside. Thomas followed. Pulling the window shut behind him, he turned around to find himself standing in a room full of piled nets and buoys. The air was thick with the smell of salt and rotting rope. Marylène tiptoed over to a door and cracked it open a few inches.

She flagged Thomas over to the door and held a finger up to her lips.

"See. There she is."

Thomas could see a woman, the one calling herself Melita, pushing Thaddeus Alderfer down the hall in his wheelchair. A shiver rippled up Thomas's spine. Even though he couldn't stand Korvin, for a second he hesitated at the door, wishing for the first time in his life that the sheriff was there. He hadn't thought the plan through. *What was the plan exactly?* He'd done exactly what his father always criticized—flying into a serious situation that called for serious decision-making without doing any real planning or consideration of the consequences. *Marylène.* His heart sunk. *Marylène was one of those consequences.*

"Thomas?"

Marylène's voice jolted him back to reality.

They did have a plan. It wasn't fool-proof. Not by a long shot. But it was all they had.

"I know where the phone is," said Thomas. "You follow them. But stay out of sight, okay? I'll call Byron. I'll meet you back here in five minutes."

"Five minutes?"

"Yep."

Marylène smiled. "*Bonne chance*, Thomas. This means good luck."

"You too. *Bonne chance*."

Marylène slipped through the door. Thomas waited for her to make her way down the hallway. Once she was out of sight, he opened the door and tiptoed out over the cool stone floor.

Sneaking past the bubbling aquariums he found the tunnel-like hallway off the main waiting room that led to the Roost. As Thomas tiptoed along, he worked out the lie in his head in case he was caught. *He'd stopped by to return Marylène's brother's clothes.* The only problem was that he didn't exactly have the clothes in hand. He'd tell whoever caught him that he stashed the clothes somewhere in another room and was going to use the phone to call his ride. It wasn't a perfect lie, not air-tight, but it would have to do.

Stepping into the Roost, he could hear Cal's father's voice echoing from another room:

"Don't leave me here, Melita. Bring me my Balearic harpoon."

Thomas turned and headed over to the submarine-style door of the Mess Hall and hooked his head through the door. He smiled. *Nobody inside.* He ran to the phone. The Sharpie marker on his hand with Byron's phone number hadn't worn off completely. He punched the numbers and waited.

"Hello? Sigrún? It's Thomas. No, I can't speak any louder. Can you get Byron? I'm at the Alderfer Foundation. I've found Lorelei. She's been here all along—"

Something small—small and sharp like a wasp's stinger—went through the back of Thomas's jeans.

He spasmed and grabbed the back of his thigh. The thigh went instantly limp. He collapsed, writhing on the linoleum floor. The phone clattered from his fingers.

Hello? Thomas? Thomas are you there?

"Been here all along, has she?" a throaty voice whispered above Thomas's quivering body. "And nobody seemed to mind as long as she bathed and cleaned the rich man counting his little ships and crying out for his lost harpoon . . ."

Thomas felt his throat constrict. He gasped for breath. Everything from his waist down had turned to immovable stone. He flailed his arms around the floor. He tried to scream Marylène's name. The surge of numbness flooded up under the surface of his skin, prickling through the veins of his face. His tongue and lips lost all feeling. Terrified, he arched his eyelids and watched as a shadow rose above him, blocking out all light from the flickering overhead bulb.

A woman with frizzy hair stood smiling down at him, her white teeth gleaming stark against the shadows of her face. With a scarred hand full of deep, wavy burns, she removed a pair of pearl-white dentures and set them down on the table. Then, crouching low, she smiled at Thomas with a mouth full of rotten, twisted teeth. Her merciless eyes bore into his soul, as deep and as harrowing as any ghost Thomas had ever seen.

"But did you do all your work, my young friend? Do you really know who I am?" The woman let out a snicker, her shoulders bouncing with glee. "Let's try a different approach. How does this sound?"

The woman leaned closer. As Thomas writhed and shrieked on the floor, the voice above him started to change.

"Pardon me! Pardon me! Would you be able to direct me to the death mask of Ful . . . Ful . . ."

The room flipped over on itself. Thomas felt sharp nails jerk his head up. As his eyelids started to close, the woman cradled his chin, brushing a thumb over his numb lips.

"Fulvius Marcius Cinta? Is that right?"

Chapter Fifteen
The Posse Cometh

He can't be mad at me. He can't. He'll never find it . . .

Arnold Myers lay on his bed, staring up at a glow-in-the-dark poster of Jessica Steamwick, the hottest wakeboarder in the world. He knew he wouldn't be able to see anything in the poster for hours, not until it was completely dark, but he was willing to wait.

In the background death-metal blared from the Krypts, Arnold's favorite band. Distorted guitars screeched like buzzsaws. Crumpled in a ball next to Arnold's head was the list of chores his parents had given him after the whole exploding mailbox incident. Not surprisingly, only the first of a dozen tasks—paint the new mailbox—had been checked off the list. Like most young people who banked on parental ADD, Arnold Myers was banking on his parents forgetting about the list.

A sharp knock on his locked bedroom door begged to differ.

"Arnie? I know you're in there. Jeni's chicken coops aren't going to clean themselves. You got five minutes, bud."

Arnold shot upright in his bed. He was going to tell his mom off, even if it meant more chores added to his list, when the window over his desk jerked open.

Crouching like Spiderman on the side of the Empire State Building was a shadowy figure wearing a top hat.

The sight of the hat made Arnold recoil back against the headboard of his bed. Images of Jacob Crowley, the Sieve's wicked ringleader, flashed in his mind. Then he saw the goofy smile. He relaxed against his pillow. The light shifted. Bunny Carson was leaning on the windowsill dressed in his top hat and vintage suit from his trolley job.

"I PLANTED IT!" Bunny cried over the sound of dueling buzzsaw guitars. "JUST LIKE YOU SAID!"

Arnold leapt off his bed and yanked the volume knob on his stereo. The musical mayhem ceased.

"What?"

"I said I planted it. You know, that little tracking device thing you blew your money on? I put it right under Creeper's collar. Stopped him on the trolley on his way out. Dude has no clue, bro. No clue."

Arnold threw up his hands and flashed a pair of heavy metal horns at Bunny. Bunny returned the gesture before proceeding to noodle on an imaginary guitar.

"I'd like to see him try to keep us from the action now," said Arnold, grinning ear to ear. "I installed the app last night. Let's see if it works."

Bunny climbed into the room. With a garbled cry he fell down into Arnold's dirty laundry hamper. As Bunny wedged his way out, Arnold flew over to a side table next to his bed stacked with dust-streaked copies of *Fireworks Enthusiast* and *Wakeboard World*. Jerking open a drawer in the side table, he dug around until he found the phone, the one he'd stolen from Jeni's room the moment she left for Germany. He swiped the lock screen and scrolled through a few pages until he came to the tracking app called *TransPonderous*.

More knocks came from the door.

"C'mon, c'mon," Arnold whispered, shaking the phone.

"Arnie! I'm counting to ten . . ."

Arnold slapped his forehead. *Duh! He'd forgotten to swipe on Wi-Fi.* He turned the local network on. The app finished booting. Possessed with joy, Arnold and Bunny watched as the app's GPS tracking system went from high above the continent of North America, zooming and zooming in until it magnified the Massachusetts shoreline, and finally, Gloomsbury.

Off the shoreline, in a small series of dark splotches in the middle of the ocean, there was a flashing red dot.

"We got a ping," said Arnold. "BUNNYMAN! WE GOT A PING!"

"Duuuuude, we're like freakin' *Mission: Impossible.*"

More knocks at the door.

"Arnold Engelbert Myers, this is the last time . . ."

Bunny twisted up his freckled face. "Wait. Hold up. Your middle name's Engelbert?"

"Shut up, man."

Arnold looked at Bunny. Bunny looked at Arnold. It was all so clear now. *The emergency skiff.* The one they'd stashed down by Miller's Pond.

"The skiff!" they both said in unison.

"You still got the stash in your trunk?" asked Arnold, helping Bunny up and over the windowsill.

Bunny sucked in a deep, wheezy breath. "Who do you think you're dealing with? Of course, Engelbert. I'm always rollin' heavy."

Halfway out the window, Arnold turned back and looked at his room. His dad would be taking the door off its hinges at any moment. It was going to be hell to pay when he got back, but it was still better than being bored to death. He blew a kiss up at Jessica Steamwick. There was a twelve-year difference between them, but that wasn't huge. *And girls like bad boys.* At least that's what Bunny's older sister Martha told Arnold last Christmas.

When they reached the rusted hand-me-down Buick idling by the curb, Bunny opened the door and leaned in and flicked the earlobe of his brother Flip slouched behind the wheel. Flip crab-crawled over the stick shift to the passenger seat.

Arnold had been waiting to scream the words the moment he slid into the car.

"FLOOR IT!"

The old Buick took off, fish-tailing like a brown whale. They were halfway down the block when Flip leaned over from the front seat and grinned back at Arnold with his new braces full of bright purple bands.

"CROTCH CANNONEERS UNITE!"

"UNITE!" Arnold and Bunny shouted back, pumping their fists.

They were unstoppable.

The posse was on its way.

Chapter Sixteen
The Floating Room

Thomas awoke to the sound of classical music crackling with static.

Something cold and wet covered his eyes. He could feel the numbness from earlier starting to lift, breath by breath, though everything around him was a sea of impenetrable blackness.

He moved his legs a few inches. *They were untied!* His arms, however, were twisted behind him. Something sharp and tight bound both wrists. He panicked. *Had he given himself away that he was awake?*

The classical music kept playing. He felt the pressure of something pushing up against his back, something hard, butting against the chair. The music swelled, the scratchy, syncopated digging of the strings grew louder and louder. Behind him, over the music, he heard a voice:

"That's called *ponticello*. The bow cuts right over the bridge. Do you hear those high harmonics?"

Thomas kept his mouth shut. He tried not to move a finger.

"I said do you hear it?"

With a wild screech of gears, Thomas lurched forward. The gears went silent. The chair locked somewhere in the open air. Thomas's neck tendons strained as gravity vied to pull him over the abyss he couldn't see but could feel from the cold wind rushing up over him. A hand ripped the cloth from his eyes. For a second all he could see were lights—lights dancing all around him, stinging his corneas. He lowered his gaze. Below him, in the gaping chasm beneath his feet, he saw a chandelier, ringed with dozens of flickering candles. His heartbeat quickened. *It was just like the video of the screaming man.* Through the gaps in the chandelier he could see a body squirming below. It was a man in a wheelchair turned on its side. The man was struggling and kicking his feet in a mound of white shells. At that moment, he looked up. Thomas recognized the sallow, terrified face.

J.W. Sneed.

The gears screeched again. Thomas's chair flew back. When everything settled, he looked down. The legs of the chair were attached to some sort of mechanism, a conveyor belt. Behind Thomas came a scratch of old vinyl. The classical music went silent.

A rotten mouth, ringed with wavy scars, appeared next to his ear.

"The antidote should be doing its trick, so I'm going to let you in on a little secret. You are going to choose how we send J.W. into the Great Beyond. Part of me thinks we're doing him a favor. Doesn't have much left in the tank. You know I can still remember when I thought he was a giant. A god. Now look at him."

Sharp nails dug into Thomas's chin, forcing his face down.

"Do you see, Thomas? Do you see how small he is? A little dung beetle, squirming around in the dirt."

Thomas clenched his eyes tight. His heart beat like a cornered bird, thrashing against the cage of his ribs.

"You're not like them, Thomas. You adore details, don't you? I knew you were going to be a great addition to my kingdom.

That's why I strung you along. I had to test your *virtue*, you see. Now look at me, Thomas."

A pause. Broken by muffled whimpers from below.

"I SAID LOOK AT ME!"

Thomas opened his eyes. The woman from the kitchen at the Alderfer smiled back at him with her mouth full of ravaged teeth. The frizzy wig was gone. Her head was bare and shaved, dotted with fine black hairs, and there were places where the wavy scars bubbled over the skin and the hair wouldn't grow. Her eyebrows were missing and unpainted. A purple shroud hung about her thin but wiry frame, the edges of the fabric clinging in tattered wisps. In the holes in the purple shroud Thomas could see gold—a golden breastplate—shimmering and reflecting the light from the candle clenched tightly in the woman's scarred hand.

"Y-y-you're not her," Thomas chattered. "You're not Lorelei. You're too young."

"Aren't you a sharp little tack," the woman whispered back. "No, no I'm not. But she's here with us, Thomas."

Dragging a nail across the table butting against Thomas's chair, the woman moved away. Thomas jerked his head as far back around as his neck would allow. He could see masks, masks all piled around the table—glimmering bronze and silver ones and ones with strange eyeholes and spiked studs like the masks worn by gladiators Thomas had seen in movies. And there were wigs—wigs and skin-colored molds hanging from metal hooks that stretched them so they almost look like real faces. Thomas looked past the masks and the disguises to the shadow of a slumped figure, seated at the table.

"Mother, we have a guest."

What was left on the other side of the table was nothing but a skeleton. The skull was bowed forward as if staring down into the plate of ashes in front of it. A few clumps of blonde hair hung from the scalp. Resting on a table behind the skeleton was a giant mirror with an intricate golden frame festooned with cobwebs. There were words streaked in dust across the mirror's glass. Thomas tried to read them, but the candle jerked away, lowering down instead to light the skeleton's vacant eye sockets.

"She told me where to find her, her final resting place. But it isn't in this world. She lives on in the kingdom of souls where I will send you tonight, Thomas, where you and the others will await me as subjects in the afterlife. They all thought she'd died in that hellhole where J.W. sent her after she struck that cop outside the courthouse. Of course, J.W. had the trial rigged. Paid off all the judges, you see. No, my mother was a fighter."

"Your mother," Thomas mouthed numbly.

"The day her heart finally gave out she willed me her strength, her strength to survive against all odds. She came to me in a dream. She showed me the way. Together we set fire to that joke of a treatment center they tried to seal me in like a bug in a jar. Old buildings burn funny, Thomas. I didn't see the beam come down. And then I awoke in the flames, flames rising . . . rising all around me . . ."

The woman reached up and stroked her scarred face.

"And do you know who I saw, Thomas? My mother. Beckoning me through the flames. She named me, the name they never told me all those lonely years going from house to house, from one self-righteous family to the next. If you did your work properly you would have figured it out. It was all there. In J.W.'s papers. That's how Lorelei found out where they hid me so I wouldn't be a threat to the Sneeds. She made one last trip to Ivymount. She must have known she was dying. She mailed the book to me, the one she stole from her old library the night she broke in. She put a note inside the book. She told me my true name. Her daughter. Her vengeance on earth."

The woman closed her eyes and inhaled a deep breath.

"Aurelia! The Golden One! Her name for me, her redeemer. I found her resting place and recovered her bones. I vowed to help her, help her in a way the Sneeds never could. I vowed to raise her to the heights she deserved, in my kingdom beyond this world."

A muffled groan sounded from the chasm below.

Aurelia leaned over the side. Gnashing her rotten teeth, she screamed down into the hole, flecks of saliva flying from her lips.

"*I'M* TALKING NOW! YOU COULD HAVE SAVED HER! WITH A SINGLE PHONE CALL, WITH A SINGLE WAVE OF YOUR BENEVOLENT HAND YOU COULD HAVE SAVED HER! BUT NO! YOU AND YOUR BROTHER, THAT STERILE SLUG, HASTINGS, HE COULDN'T ACCEPT THAT LORELEI AND CASPAR WERE NOT HIS REAL CHILDREN, THAT HE'D BEEN MADE A FOOL! AND YOU LOCKED HER AWAY! LIKE SOME LAB RAT TO HIDE THE FAMILY'S SHAME!"

"That's why you wanted us up there," Thomas whispered after the echoes of the screams died away. "In the attic. That's what you wanted us to see."

"Yes," said Aurelia. "I wanted you all to *see*."

Aurelia's shoulders quivered. The muscles in her face spasmed and contorted. Stretching her neck and making a clicking sound with her tongue, she relaxed. The cracked-tooth smile returned. Swooping back to the mirror, she set the candle down and dug through an open drawer. The candle was closer now. In its light Thomas could read writing on the mirror.

CALL THE BOY'S HOUSE TODAY, MY DARLING
5 SHARP
THESE ARE YOUR WORDS

There were several other lines, but they disappeared outside the candle's radius. Thomas's mind reeled. The call to the funeral home came around five o'clock. *Just like Cyril said it would.*

Aurelia spun back. The letters on the mirror fell back into shadow. She set the candle down on the table and bowed her forehead. Her voice was a venomous hiss.

"*Damnatio memoriae.* That is what the Sneeds have done to us. They've blotted out any trace my mother and I ever existed. But I am my mother's vengeance and redeemer. I will take away everything the Sneeds have ever loved. And then I will burn Ivymount until it flakes away in the wind. For you see, Thomas, it's not only men who must struggle to preserve the *dignitas* of their family. I learned that from my mother's book. Lorelei was a master historian. She knew that for every Caesar there is a Pompeia, a cast-off wife, struggling to kill suspicion . . . before it kills her!"

Aurelia reached over and slid a newspaper in front of Thomas's seat. It was the article from *The Morning Mooring*, the one showing Thomas and Jeni dragging the skeletons across Town Beach.

"Thanks to you and your special goggles, I can see her again before I leave this earth. What mysteries you have enfolded at such a tender age. Pity the road has led you here."

Aurelia tapped a jagged fingernail at the spot on the photograph where the Ocu-Occus hung from Thomas's belt, the magic goggles given to him by Mulvaney's Raiders that allowed the wearer to observe the spirit world.

"Lorelei told me she would bring them to me. And she did. She placed them in our little Floating Room, the gateway to the kingdom of souls."

Though every nerve in Thomas's body felt paralyzed by fear, his mind radiated with a Fixer's drive for truth. *The phone call by*

Marjorie Fipps. The writing on the mirror. It was so obvious, but only to him. Cyril had stolen the goggles from his closet. The visit to the funeral home was one big setup.

"That's not your mother talking to you!" cried Thomas. "He's using you, don't you see? It's Cyril! He's—"

"SILENCE!"

The backhand cut across Thomas's jaw. Pain bloomed across his cheek like a hot iron pressed against his skin. Spasming and stretching her neck, Aurelia made the strange clicking sound again with her tongue. She drew the purple shroud tight around her shoulders. When the clicking stopped, she whispered into Thomas's ear:

"You don't get to alter destiny, Thomas Creeper. You had your chance, and you squandered it."

"I-I'm telling you the truth! He's setting you up!"

A drawer jerked open. Thomas heard the fiddle and scrape of metal pieces.

"Enough! I'm going to show you my Floating Room now. You'll appreciate all the faces there. They gather when they're summoned."

There were a few quick slashes on the straps binding Thomas the chair, though the straps around his hands remained unsevered.

"Get up."

As Thomas staggered to his feet, Aurelia gave a prick of the dagger. Thomas cried out.

"Have no illusions. There is nowhere to go. We are quite far from the shore." Aurelia held the knife blade flat against her nose. Her shoulders quivered. A throaty laughter rumbled up, echoing through the damp chamber. "Yes, quite far from the shore in so many ways." She made another click with her tongue. The demented smile vanished. "You'll drown if you try to run. And that's not fair, my friend. You deserve a glimpse of the end . . .

and the beginning! I want to hold your hand right up to that glorious moment. Would you let me do that, Thomas? Would you let me close your eyes as you cross over?"

Aurelia pursed her scarred mouth and raked her hand through Thomas's hair. Thomas's body trembled; the nails dug into his scalp. Aurelia jerked his head up. She was so close now he could smell the salt and sweat on her. Tears stung his eyes. He watched Aurelia's rotten teeth and wavy scars blur in and out.

"That body, the one you found on the beach? It's a shell, don't you see? I ennoble them, Thomas. I give them *dignitas* and peace from a life of endless servitude. I paint their bodies in the everlasting garments of kings and queens and I send them to paradise."

"You murder them!"

"What? You!" Aurelia's whole body shook. "You still cling to that false reality? Of all people, I thought you would understand what's going on behind this masquerade of life and death. Ah!" Aurelia raised the knife. "Maybe it's because I've taken away your magic goggles. You've lost sight of all the shared passageways, all the overlapping streams. Come. Let me open your eyes."

A cold, surprisingly strong hand jerked Thomas forward. He could feel the jab once more of the rusted blade against his ribs.

"You saw them in their transitional shells. Glorified by my hand, yes, but shells nonetheless. Let me show you them . . . in ascension!"

Aurelia pushed Thomas deeper into the darkness. Images flooded through his brain like a film reeling too fast. *Jeni. Marylène. His parents.* He'd stared into the eyes of death a hundred times before, but never his own, never like this in the echoing dark with a moth-eaten shroud fluttering against the back of his ankles.

"It's a little further," Aurelia whispered into his ear, pushing him forward. "I'm glad it's you. Really, I am. You alone will appreciate this fork in the story you thought you were following. I'll see you blotted out like spilled ink before the writing of a beautiful new chapter. And then I'll watch you float, Thomas.

"Oh, how you'll float along with them!"

• • •

The emergency skiff raced over the white-capped sea. Bunny cranked the craft's horsepower to the max while Arnold sat next to him. Arnold cradled the phone under his nose, following the steady pings, calling out directions to Bunny whenever the skiff veered off course. Of the three Crotch Cannoneers, it was Flip Carson who held the most important job: he had to keep the payload of last summer's purchases from Captain Sparky's safe and dry from the sea-spray flying at them from every angle.

Any indication of land had long disappeared. They were out in open water now, at the mercy of Mad Marge's game of fog and shadow. They almost didn't see the large fishing troller appear out of the mist until it was too late.

Bunny cut the gas, jerking the skiff parallel to the other boat before it rammed right into the letters *S. S. Alderfer.* Though thrown from his seat to floor of the skiff, ever true to his task, Flip cradled the payload between his arms and legs, not letting a single drop of salt water touch the bag stuffed with the collective potency of military-grade dynamite.

The only casualty was the phone.

The moment Bunny spun the skiff to avoid ramming the other boat the phone jerked out of Arnold's hand. Their one link to Thomas's location somersaulted through air for a second before disappearing down into the black water.

"NOOOOOOOOOOO!"

Gripping the side of the skiff and gnashing his teeth, Arnold felt like exploding right through his clothes, like Bruce Banner morphing into the Hulk. Gazing up at the starboard deck on the fishing ship, he locked eyes with an old man wearing a pair of boxy, tinted glasses. A black rat was perched on the old man's shoulder, and on either side of him were two other figures—a giant woman with a sour-looking face and a pretty girl in a sweatshirt with elf-like ears.

"Ahoy there!" the old man called down.

"Ahoy yourself! Do you know what you made me do, bro? We were tracking our friend Thomas and—"

"Then we have the same goal!" the old man called back, cutting Arnold off. "The only point on this bearing from shore is a place called the Anchorage, a retired weather station and old fishing lodge. Marylène . . ." There was a hushed conversation between the old man and the girl with elf-like ears. The old man nodded. "We'll tow you behind us. It's a blessing in disguise. The captain says the sea wall around the Anchorage has collapsed in places making landing a bit tricky with this big girl. We'll need your ship. Your timing is impeccable!"

"Impec . . . what?" Arnold stammered. "Listen . . . we . . ." He was furious. They weren't being hijacked by some old fruitcake with a rodent on his shoulder. "How do we know you don't have Thomas hostage in there?"

"Yeah," said Bunny, raising a freckled fist. "How do we know you're not like double-crossing us, bro-migo?"

"Enough!" cried Marylène. "You are all idiots! Thomas is my friend as well. Now shut your faces and take this rope I am throwing at your hands."

"Whoa," Bunny whispered, elbowing Arnold. "She's dope."

A large knotty rope was thrown over the side of the *S.S. Alderfer*. Still suspecting foul-play—after all, Jacob Crowley of the Sieve had pretended to be their friend—Arnold took the rope and he and Bunny secured it around a cleat on the skiff's bow.

"Hold on!" Marylène shouted.

There was a sputter of black exhaust. The troller took off, dragging the skiff and its three Crotch Cannoneers along with it.

"Yo, Flip," Arnold called over his shoulder as they bounced over the white-caps. "Pass me a Royal Rocket."

Arnold's eyes narrowed.

"Just in case."

• • •

Thomas crept across the slippery flood wall that circled the abandoned lighthouse and weather station. To the right of the lighthouse, what Thomas took to be their destination, stood the ruins of an old stone building, no more than a pile of moss-strewn blocks with half its roof exposed to the elements.

The wind howled in Thomas's ears, throwing him off balance. Unable to use his hands to steady himself, he had to lower his body to find his center of gravity so he didn't tumble over the edge. He paused and looked back over his shoulder. Aurelia leered at him, her face spasming in and out, her purple shroud billowing around her golden breastplate. She jabbed the knife at him, forcing him forward. He made the mistake of looking down: thirty feet of cliff face falling away to nothing, nothing but waves crashing against barnacled rocks.

"I HAVE TO STOP!" Thomas screamed over the shriek of the wind. "I'M GOING TO FALL!"

Aurelia made a few more jabs with the knife. "NO! IT DOESN'T END HERE! MOVE!"

Thomas made a few uncertain steps forward. A gust of wind smacked into him. He crumpled to one knee and threw his bound hands around a broken segment of sea wall. Salt-spray and tears stung his eyes. He forced himself back up. Clenching his teeth, he staggered forward into the shadow of the ruins. Panting with his back against a wall trickling with rain, he tried to catch his breath. Aurelia snagged him by the elbow and pushed him farther into the darkness.

Thomas hunched through the passageway until it widened to a central chamber. As his eyes adjusted, Thomas could see a large stone slab in the center of the room, rising like a makeshift altar. Above the altar, where a ceiling should have been, there was nothing but a gaping hole through which the darkness gave way to the lighter gray of the sky. Puddles lay all around, and a few gaping holes shone through the walls as if someone had gone crazy with a wrecking ball. Through one of the holes Thomas could see the horizon in the distance, and beneath it, the darker ink-wash of the ocean.

"Stay here," said Aurelia. "Don't even think about moving."

Keeping the knife trained on Thomas, Aurelia struck a match against her breastplate. As the match flared to life, she walked over to the altar and lit three candles bobbing inside three waterlogged glass hurricanes. In the glow cast by the candles Thomas caught a flash of green ectoplasmic glass. *The Ocu-Occu Goggles!* The enchanted goggles sat on the edge of the altar. Setting down the knife, Aurelia snatched the Ocu-Occus from the altar and fit the straps over her ears. She raised her arms high above her head. The purple shroud fluttered all around her as her voice pierced the wind:

"COME OUT, MOTHER! YOUR GOLDEN CHILD IS HERE!"

Seeping out from the damp rock walls, the faces came.

Thomas watched them—spectral forms, oozing out from the weathered stone as easily as water through a sponge. Other, less definite beings appeared too; these were more weepy and fluid, with only the faintest indication of heads and bodies. Two ghosts with definite features hovered above the altar—a woman with braided blonde hair and a man in a three-piece suit who looked like a thinner, much younger version of J.W. Sneed. Thomas watched Aurelia reach up and grasp the hand of the hovering ghost-woman. His eyes flitted back to the altar. *The knife was close, only a few steps away . . .*

Before Thomas lunged for the blade, he spied a few familiar glowing faces who appeared in the shadows: a headless ghost in a pinstripe suit, standing next to a pale woman with a unicorn head bursting out of her dress; and, next to her, another ghost in a cocktail suit and porkpie hat, smiling and holding a gleaming cornet. Thomas wasn't the only one to notice the arrival of the others.

"What are you doing here?" Aurelia screeched, backing up, knocking into one of the hurricanes and sending it crashing to the ground.

"You were right, Thomas," said Trixie. "He's no Fixer. We followed him here. Look out, Thomas! He's over there behind that wall!"

Thomas wheeled around. He scoured the darkness. The ghosts hovering around the room stopped moving. They were all pointing—pointing at a shadow, leaning against the far corner where the candlelight couldn't reach. Over the hiss of the wind coming through the holes in the ruins, Thomas heard it:

A muffled clapping.

Black leather gloves raised in the air, Cyril Barnes stepped out from the shadows. His eyes were bright and frenzied, his mouth twisted up in his usual ferret sneer. But it wasn't his voice that came from his lips. It was a lower, deeper voice, and as he spoke Thomas watched all of the ghosts cower in fear.

"Brilliant. All of you. Played your parts to the hilt."

"Who are you?" cried Aurelia. "You can't be here! You have no right to stop the ritual."

"I told you," said Thomas. "He's the one who set you up. That wasn't your mother writing on the mirror. It was him."

"Bravo, again," cackled the shell of Cyril Barnes. "I've really loved being him, though. He was a Fixer like you. That part is true. Only he came too close to his prize years ago. Shall I show you how close he came?"

Reaching up with a few gloved fingers, the shell of Cyril Barnes pulled down his turtleneck. In the candlelight a crimson gash shone like an open red mouth, stretching end to end across the pale neck.

"He was a wonderful playmate. It's been so long since I've been inside a body. Walking these streets, seeing everything through his eyes. And you, Aurelia, I felt like I'd found a pen pal with that mirror. You were so convinced, so devoted. I was moved, Aurelia. Truly. Your conviction inspires me."

"No . . . no . . ." Aurelia stumbled back a few steps. "She told me . . . she said we would be joined forever."

"And you will. All of you. You and your purple sacrifices, Aurelia, along with Thomas and all his loved ones. The Sneeds, of course. Can't leave them out. You will all rise and float through town when the carnival returns. All of Gloomsbury shall spin inside the Wheel and despair!"

Aurelia snatched the knife. She lunged forward, slashing wildly.

"DECEIVER!"

A slithery chant sounded through the room. Thomas felt the words wriggle and unravel in the air like invisible snakes. The leather jacket became illuminated with an unnatural silver light. Aurelia's slashes went through the jacket as if it was no more than an empty hologram.

"Such fighting spirit, my dear. I give you that much."

Rubbing a gloved thumb over the spine of the book hanging from his jacket pocket, the shell of Cyril Barnes started to chant, louder and wilder than ever before. Thomas covered his face as the room filled with more unseen snakes made out of wind, slithering and circling through the air. When Thomas opened his eyes again he watched the candles jerk up from the hurricanes and hover in the air, flames sputtering and popping like sparklers. Then, with a wave of the black leather gloves, the candles inverted and flew straight at Aurelia's face.

"You should have died in that fire!"

As the candles flew forward, their flames grew and grew until they exploded into a fireball, enveloping Aurelia and her purple shroud. Shrieking, she dropped the knife. Flailing out wildly, she knocked off the Ocu-Occus and collapsed on the ground, writhing in a ball of flames.

"Now, Thomas!" cried Trixie. "Grab the knife! We'll distract him!"

Thomas dashed forward. He lunged for the knife . . . but stopped when a voice cried out in his brain.

It was a woman's voice.

Listening to the mysterious voice, Thomas felt the tempo and terror in the room slow to a crawl. The woman's voice rippled through him like a soothing, sinuous music echoing across water.

Do you swear it, Thomas Creeper? Would you forfeit your life if you were to veer to the path of evil?

Thomas watched Aurelia's hand reach up through the flames, grasping for help. He knew what he needed to do, and he sure it was on the list of Most Stupid Decisions Ever Made in History.

As he ran to the altar everything in the room sped back up. Gabe's horn blared off to his left; the chants from the shell of Cyril Barnes slithered through the air. Awkwardly, Thomas bear-hugged two waterlogged hurricanes with his bound hands. He turned around just in time to hear Trixie's voice shouting above the tumult:

"WHAT ARE YOU DOING? GRAB THE KNIFE!"

Dodging a block of something deadly that flew over his head, Thomas crouched and hobbled over to Aurelia and doused the water from the hurricanes all over her. The soothing woman's voice sounded in Thomas's brain again. The falling water surged, magnifying into a wide stream.

For the suffering who give no peace, chanted the voice in Thomas's brain, *be granted peace to end thy suffering.*

The flames around Aurelia's face and body smoked out. Her wailing died to a miserable moan.

"What the hell was that, Thomas?" Trixie called from across the melee. Still gripping the hurricanes, Thomas turned around. He searched the ground. The knife was too far away. He'd made his choice. But he was a Fixer.

And for a Fixer there was always another way.

He dropped the glass hurricanes to the floor. Crouching down, he pulled a shard from the wreckage. He could see Aurelia's terrified face staring up at him. Her eyes blinked a few times. *She's not dead.* Thomas sawed at the bindings around his wrist as a sneering voice rose behind him.

"So this is your final move? Save the life of a murderer before your own?"

"The Sneeds made her it that way," Thomas called back. *That's right. Keep him distracted.* "They threw her out like her mother. Like she was nothing more than trash." The first binding frayed and came apart. *Okay, good. Two more to go.*

"So pure, so selfless, Thomas Creeper. You must think the world is a beautiful place. If that were true, tell me, why am I, Herodain Pius Korvac, allowed a second lease on life?"

Thomas stopped sawing. As he turned around he felt a snake-like whip of wind surround him and jerk the shard from his fingers.

"You wrote that book?" said Thomas. "You're H.P. Korvac?"

"Top marks again. Now that I think of it, I'm going to save you for a later date. You're too much fun to play this game of life and death chess with. Come here. I've trapped others inside it before."

In the center of the black leather glove Thomas could see it:

A small porcelain box.

The P.B.O.U.D..

Tapping twice and sliding back the pill box's lid, Korvac moved closer. Shards of glass and clouds of sand flew towards him, but he didn't flinch. He no longer felt pain. Not earthly pain, at least.

"It's cold in there. You'll sleep soundly, though. A deep frost, Thomas. I promise you won't feel a th—"

Bounding out of a wall came a swirl of bright green ectoplasm.

Letting out a fearsome growl, Finn the Faithful leapt for Korvac. There was a burst of light, followed by a sizzle. The P.B.O.U.D. clattered to the floor. Korvac cursed and rubbed his arm. Thomas could see traces of green ectoplasmic light lingering in teeth-sized holes in the jacket. *He isn't invincible. Ghosts can still harm him.*

"You're Cranby's little show dog, aren't you?" Korvac seethed. "The one he changed with his magic . . . magic he could never quite understand!"

Finn growled and lunged again. Korvac whispered his slithery dark words and thumbed the spine of his book. He waved his gloved hand. Finn flew back, reeling through the air as if hit by a wall of wind.

"NOOOOOO!" Thomas screamed.

The ghost-dog let out a few whimpers and disappeared through a wall.

"Where is it? Where is it?" Korvac ranted, searching the floor. Thomas tried to steady his brain and pulse. *Think, you idiot. You can't hurt him with any physical object. His magic is too powerful. Aurelia's knife went right through him. The only way to hurt him is magic.*

As Korvac turned his back, Thomas seized his opportunity.

Headless Jerry, who'd been thrown back through the wall along with Finn, now oozed up through the stones in front of Korvac.

"You headless bastard! I'll pull the rest of you apart!"

Before Korvac could reach for his book, Thomas's fingers were already on it.

He jerked the book out of the jacket pocket. He ran over to the magic flames still lapping against the wall next to Aurelia's body. *The only way to hurt him is to destroy his only link to this life. The book must be the link.*

"GIVE ME THAT, YOU WORM! DON'T YOU DARE—"

Thomas dropped the book into the flames and watched the pages curl and blacken.

"AHHHHHHHHHH!"

Sizzling and wailing, Korvac rushed forward. With every step the reanimated skin belonging once to Cyril Barnes fell away. By the time Korvac reached Thomas, he was nothing more than a skeleton in a red turtleneck and black jacket, clawing at Thomas with leather gloves.

"LET THE SPIDER CRABS FEAST ON YOUR EYEBALLS!"

With the last gasp of his wicked spirit, Korvac pushed Thomas through the gap in the wall.

Thomas flew backwards, flailing out into the empty air. Any scream from his lips was choked off by sheer terror. The sea wall and ruins rose above him, while the dark opening in the side of the ruins, like a tiny black door, grew smaller and smaller.

Chapter Seventeen
Au Revoir, Thomas

Thomas exploded head-first into the freezing, dark water.

Kicking his feet and pounding with his bound wrists, he tried to right himself. But it was useless. Deeper and deeper he sank into the darkness while the gray glimmer of the topside world receded above him. He couldn't turn himself around. He pinched his mouth and blew bubbles out his nose. He could feel his lungs tightening. The embrace of deep water rippled over his limbs as he sunk towards the silty benthic zone, the bottom of the ocean. His tears mixed with salt water becoming an indistinguishable stream as he finally succumbed.

His jaws unclamped.

The ocean rushed in.

• • •

A constellation of a million tiny stars.

Flash. Flash. Flash—

The last bubbles rippled up from Thomas's mouth as his body settled against the freezing ocean floor. The swarm of sea fireflies—bioluminescent shrimp—danced and dazzled in furious concert like a fluid, underwater version of the Milky Way. Parting the bioluminescent wave, a great and glowing creature swooped down, hovering over Thomas's expired body.

The Great White Phantom.

A king of the *Architeuthis.*

A giant among giant squid.

Curling a massive tentacle around Thomas's waist, the Great White Phantom pulled Thomas upwards, farther and farther towards the diminished light of the world above.

The tentacle rose through the water, lifting Thomas up and placing him on a crag strewn with barnacles and dead crabs.

"THERE HE IS! HOLD ON, THOMAS! WE'RE COMING!"

Arnold Myers dangled over the side of the sea wall, flanked by the faces of Bunny and Flip Carson.

"Dude, did you see that?" Bunny wheezed. "Down there in the water? Some kind of monster, bro."

"Forget it," said Arnold. "Go look for a way down."

While Arnold, Bunny, and Flip searched for a way down, Trixie took matters into her own hands. It all made sense to her, the whole reason why the spirit of H.P. Korvac could touch things—and people.

The gloves.

There was something enchanted about the gloves and Trixie knew it. Reaching down, standing over Cyril's smoking skeleton, she touched the gloves and smiled. *She could feel real leather!* She pulled the gloves off the skeletal fingers and fit them over her own. Running over, she snatched the P.B.O.U.D. from where she'd seen it clatter down behind the altar. She turned to Headless Jerry.

"Quick! Can you get me down? You know, that special trick you do?"

Headless Jerry nodded his segment of neck bone. He reached out his gloved hand. White and black gloves joined together. In a flash of particles Trixie and Headless Jerry flew through space, *devaporating* a second later on top of a barnacled crag, standing right over Thomas's body.

"Aces!" cried Trixie.

Headless Jerry flashed two thumbs up.

Trixie reached down and opened Thomas's lifeless mouth.

"Come on, Thomas," she whispered, tapping the P.B.O.U.D.'s lid twice like she'd seen Korvac do. The lid opened. Thomas's body started to lift from the ground. "Okay, not that much." She gripped hard with the black leather gloves. And though the force was tremendous, the wild turquoise light swirling all around, she limited the opening. "That's better. Just need to get the water out."

Thomas's blue lips fluttered. Drop by drop, the water from Thomas's lungs sucked into the air. Soon it was a steady stream, pouring out of his mouth and sucking back into the magic pill box. Once all the water was out of Thomas's lungs, Trixie closed the lid and set the magic pillbox down. She made a fist with one glove and started pumping Thomas's heart.

"Come on, bub. Come on."

Sputtering and retching cold salt water, Thomas sat up. Trixie hooted. Headless Jerry jumped up and down. The sound of a cornet in the distance let out a celebratory blast. Thomas felt around for his face. *It was there. Everything was there. He was alive.*

"How . . . ?" he mumbled, shaking his head and staring up at Trixie.

"Told you, Thomas. You need a Fixer's assistant," said Trixie, grinning her fox grin. She held out her hand. Thomas blinked, recognizing Cyril's gloves.

"You—"

"Yep, I put two and two together," said Trixie. "Figured there must be some reason why that maniac could touch things. It's really weird, Thomas." She let go of Thomas's hand and held the glove up to her glowing face. "I can't remember the last time I felt well . . . anything."

Trixie paused and looked at the gloves. Before Thomas could say a word, Trixie stepped forward and wrapped her arms around him, gripping him in a tight bear hug. And though it felt like being stuck inside a block of ice, Thomas didn't care. He felt tears running down the sides of his cheeks. Tears were warmth.

Tears were *life*.

"Trixie, I—"

"Yeah, yeah," said Trixie, feeling freezing tears flood her own eyes. "I love you too, bub."

"What? That's not what I was going to say—"

"THOMAS!"

Struggling and slipping up the backside of the crag came Arnold Myers.

Trixie let go of Thomas. Reaching down, she snatched the P.B.O.U.D. off the ground and flung it over to Thomas.

"Arnold!" Thomas called out while he stuffed the pill box into his pocket. "How did you . . . What are you guys doing here?"

"We bugged you, Creeper," said Bunny, who appeared next to Arnold, flashing a goofy smile. "Sorry about that, bro. But you know how it is. A posse's got to stick together, right? Hey? What's going on with those gloves over there?"

A pair of black gloves were hovering in the air by Thomas's shoulder. Thomas nodded to Trixie. Trixie grabbed hold of Headless Jerry. They instantly *devaporated.*

"You losing it, man?" said Arnold, turning to Bunny.

Bunny held his top hat in his hand and scratched his head. "Nah, man. Could have sworn I saw some gloves. They were like . . . levitating. Real spooky, bro."

Hearing barking on the cliff above him, Thomas looked up. He couldn't believe it. Finn was bouncing up and down, stamping his paws inside one of the collapsed gaps in the Anchorage's stone wall. *Korvac hadn't killed him! Or was that even the right word? Could ghosts hurt other ghosts?* There was so much he didn't understand about the spirit world, if that was even the right name for it.

"Um . . . Creeper . . . what the hell is that?"

Thomas walked over to where Flip was standing at the edge of the crag, pointing out at the water. Thomas followed the direction of Flip's trembling finger. A pathway of underwater light was speeding away from the Anchorage. Suddenly, the pale head of something massive—massive and glowing—breached the surface, wriggling its giant tentacles before slipping back beneath the waves.

"Told you it was some kind of sea monster," wheezed Bunny.

A stone's throw from where Thomas was standing, invisible to everyone except Thomas, a beautiful woman in a sparkling green cloak lifted halfway out of the water.

It was Our Lady of the Waves, the ocean goddess who'd come to Thomas's aid in the fight against the Sieve. A diadem of seashells circled her braided hair. She raised one hand out of the water and waved back at Thomas.

You kept your promise, Thomas Creeper, a soft, soothing voice whispered in Thomas's brain. *You always do. And because of that, I will always be here for you.*

Slipping beneath a passing wave, she disappeared. Thomas stood for some time thinking about everything, about dying, about being saved by Trixie and Our Lady of the Waves. He wanted to cry. But then Bunny burped and let everyone know he was starving and "could eat a horse." The smell of Bunny's burp—Cool Ranch Doritos, Bunny proudly announced—combined with the image of him actually eating a horse, held back tears from Thomas's eyes. It was good to have friends—living, dead, and in between. A goddess on your side was definitely a bonus.

It was even better when they didn't burp in your face.

• • •

They found the rusted metal door at the bottom of the lighthouse and helped J.W. out into the waning light. Through all the cursing and groaning Thomas could detect at least one line of gratitude. J.W. promised to tell the newspapers that they'd arrived "just in time before that insane witch sent him to an early grave."

They made the call to the Coast Guard from the control deck of the *S.S. Alderfer.* Eternally suspicious, Sigrún opted to stay behind, blocking the doorway into the ruins of the Anchorage so that Aurelia—even in her compromised, miserable state—couldn't escape. On the deck of the *Alderfer*, Arnold harassed Thomas about every detail of what happened while Marylène handed Thomas a towel to dry off.

"Smells like smoke up there. Did you use Cherry Bombs or Blast Cones?"

"Did you really fall out of the building? That's gotta be like fifty feet, bro."

"*Arrêtes, Arnold.* Stand backwards. Let him find the breathing room."

Byron was wrapping up the call to the Coast Guard. Thomas could hear the old man's raspy voice, echoing from inside the control deck.

"What do you mean you didn't know the Anchorage is still out here? It's on every nautical map. What? What do you mean you have to update your GPS?"

Though he was still raw, and more than a little shaken up from almost dying, Thomas's brain wouldn't stop buzzing with ideas. He had a great idea.

"Hey, Arnold," said Thomas. "I know you're bummed out you didn't get here in time to help out."

"That's my bad, Creeper," said Bunny. "Forgot I drained the gas on the emergency skiff last summer. We had to steal some from this dude's dock. He's probably hella pissed now. That's why we were late."

"Well," said Thomas, smiling. "I bet the Coast Guard could use a little help . . . you know . . . like how they shoot up a flare in movies when someone needs to be rescued?"

Arnold jumped to his feet. He unhooked his lifejacket and fanned it open. "Screw flares, man. Check out these babies."

"Yep," sighed Thomas. "Thought you'd be packing."

A dozen different rockets were duct-taped to the inside of Arnold's lifejacket. He pulled the rockets off and handed them out. When everyone was ready he brandished his trusty Zippo lighter.

"FUSE TRAIN!" Arnold screamed.

"FUSE TRAIN!" Flip and Bunny screamed back.

Marylène raised a fine, dark eyebrow. "What does this mean, Thomas?"

Thomas slouched back against a buoy. "Just watch. It's about to be Fourth of July all over again."

While the captain of the *S.S. Alderfer*, a squat, bearded man named Corbin who Thomas recognized from Aurelia's stolen key card, passed out bottles of water, Arnold lit the combined fuses of fifteen rockets Bunny and Flip had helped tie together. Thomas and Marylène watched the clouds above the ship erupt in a fury of multicolored lights and dazzling confetti bursts. Bunny held his hand out and placed it on Arnold's shoulder.

"Beautiful, dude," Bunny wheezed, a few tears wetting his eyes. "You thinkin' what I'm thinkin'?"

"Yep," said Arnold, choking up a little. "The parking lot. After football games. We're gonna be legends. I can see it now."

Hearing the explosions over the ship, Byron appeared in the doorway to the control room.

"What's happening? Who's shooting at us?"

"No one's shooting," said Thomas, grinning. "Arnold's putting us back on the map."

"Well," said Byron, resting his gnarled hands over the hilt of his cane. "That's certainly one way to do it."

Leaping from Byron's shoulder, Ipso, the small but brilliant black rat, jumped down into Thomas's lap.

"Who is *zis*?" asked Marylène.

Thomas lifted Ipso up while the second Fuse Train burst overhead.

"A friend," said Thomas, helping the rat balance in the middle of his palm. He could see the fireworks' explosions reflected in the rat's wet and curious eyes. Thomas peered around the ship. Gabe, Trixie, Finn, and Headless Jerry were all watching the fireworks.

"I guess . . . " Thomas's voice cracked a little. "I guess I didn't know I had so many."

• • •

The second call—the call home to Thomas's parents—was less than pleasant. Thomas expected to see his father, stewing at the edge of the dock the moment they arrived back at the Alderfer Foundation with their Coast Guard escort. Instead, as the *S.S. Alderfer* sighted the Foundation's dock through the mist, they found a teeming crowd waiting for them. Someone had intercepted the conversation between the *S.S. Alderfer* and the Coast Guard and quickly alerted Fletcher Morris at *The Morning Mooring.*

"That's enough, Fletcher," a caustic voice broke through the clamor of journalists as the *Alderfer* came to rest against the dock. Thomas could see his father pushing through crowd, coming towards the ship. "Thomas will *not* be taking questions. Not until he answers all of mine first."

Arnold, however, was more than willing to share his side of the story.

"I didn't see it, not all of it," he told the eager journalists. "It got pretty intense back there. They're lucky we showed up when we did."

Not looking up from his notebook, Fletcher Morris continued his flurry of notes. "So did Thomas Creeper single handedly catch the Purple Killer?"

"I wouldn't say that," said Arnold. "He had help for sure. You see, we've got this posse . . ."

Grabbing Thomas's arm, Marylène showed Thomas and his father a secret elevator away from the rabid crowd. While Thomas's father punched the number for the funeral home into his ancient, oversized flip phone, Marylène leaned in and whispered in Thomas's ear:

"My father and I, we're going to follow the shrimps, Thomas. We are departing tomorrow."

The "oh" that came from Thomas's lips was followed by an unexpected pang in his heart. Marylène slipped her cold hand into Thomas's while Mr. Creeper repeated his last line into the phone for the third time. The reception in the elevator was quite horrible, which only made Mr. Creeper more frustrated and distracted—("And they call this the great Technological Age. Bah! What a joke!")—so at least Thomas and Marylène's conversation went unheard.

"I am not saying I will miss you, Thomas Creeper," said Marylène. "I am not saying it because I know I will see each other again . . . in future times."

When Marylène was sure Mr. Creeper wasn't looking, she arched up and kissed one of Thomas's cheeks and then the other.

"*Au revoir*, Thomas. It does not mean goodbye. It means we will see each other again."

Thomas nodded. He couldn't tell if his face was completely red. It was probably still blue from the freezing water. It didn't matter. A beautiful, exotic girl had just kissed his cheek. Both of them, actually. He felt alive. And he felt something even rarer in Gloomsbury.

He felt joy.

As the elevator door opened onto the viewing deck of the Roost, nothing dead, not even the living hell Thomas knew was waiting for him back at the funeral home could bother him. He'd stopped Aurelia. He'd beaten Cyril Barnes, even if it was H.P. Korvac's spirit pulling all the strings like a demonic puppeteer. And he hadn't done it alone. Even with all their power and manipulation, Thomas had something neither Aurelia or Korvac had.

Friends.

"Now what are they doing?" snapped Mr. Creeper, peering out through one of the giant paneled windows in the Roost. Outside, in the foggy air, the clouds erupted with more dazzling bursts and fizzles.

Thomas smiled. He gave one last tug on Marylène's hand. Even though it was time to leave, he stood for a few moments in silence, watching the silhouette of his father, framed by the light of his friends.

Epilogue
"Opus"

It was nearing the end of Thanksgiving dinner. The damp and dew that beaded down the windows of Creeper & Sons Funeral Home had crystallized with the sinking temperature. All across Gloomsbury a chilling apparition surfaced, one that would haunt the town for months to come:

Frost.

Jed had been tasked with resurrecting the old furnace in the basement. For once, Thomas's uncle succeeded in fixing something in the house without breaking something else in the process.

Trumpets of steam, rising up through the old radiators, warmed the dining room at the back of the house, a room Thomas's family used sparingly, if at all. A second cause for celebration was the meal itself. To everyone's dismay, the Thanksgiving feast prepared by Mrs. Creeper bore no lingering flavors from her past experiments like shellfish pie, or "Hoof n' Quack," a revolting soufflé made of puréed duck and calf liver.

Thomas was particularly proud of his mother that night. Only a few times did her eyes stray to the empty table setting prepared for David, and not once did tears challenge the warmth of her smile that appeared so rarely in the bleak house.

Jed was finishing up telling Thomas's father about the trifecta he hit today through his partner in financial scheming, the notorious Mr. Green. Mr. Creeper was doing his best not to strangle his glass of wine as Jed detailed how exactly he was going to pay Thomas's father back in weekly installments. Mr. Creeper nodded as he listened to his brother's proposal, and though he was allergic to the "padding" of the liberal arts, he could do math. Jed's installments, if ever completed, would stretch on for the next seven years.

While Thomas scooped up perfect pieces of pecan pie, drenched in soupy vanilla ice cream, he and his mother discussed Thomas's recent paper on *Wuthering Heights*. Thomas was more than happy to dive into school matters. Having been grounded for the entire month of October after his "second celebrity stunt for *The Morning Mooring*" (his father's words), he'd had a lot of time to catch up on schoolwork . . . and work in the Preparing Room.

The funeral home's license had been officially restored after more "wining and dining" with members of the Massachusetts Health Board, a bunch of "bloated human ticks, sucking dry the blood, sweat, and tears of the working man" (–Elijah Creeper the Fifth).

The corpses returned to the cooling board. Thomas's discovery of Aurelia's hideout where she'd taken J.W. Sneed hostage had a permanent and lasting effect on the funeral home: all lawsuits leveled at Creeper & Sons by the Fipps or Sneed families were dropped. Though Thomas's father would never fully comprehend how Thomas's "celebrity stunt" had saved the family business, Thomas didn't mind. Parents were slow, children were swift, and time marched on regardless of this perennial imbalance between young and old.

Later, helping his mother clear the plates, Thomas heard what sounded like a few sharp knocks at the door. It was hard to hear over Jed's loud recounting of his latest betting scheme, a raunchy story involving two frisky greyhounds named Cecil and Bronson. The two dogs had given up their race shortly after the gun went off, electing to pursue more personal relations with each other. Leaning back in his chair, Jed threw up his hands, giving a visual description of the two greyhounds' intimate actions, but managed to knock his mask off into a bowl of cranberry jelly.

"Oh! C'mon! Not the jelly!"

Thomas ignored his father's shout. His ears perked up again. He was certain of it now:

Someone was knocking at the front door.

Slipping through a side passage, he left the scene at the dinner table and headed for the foyer. A few steps from the door, he paused.

There was a shadow, hovering behind the frosted glass.

Just to be safe, Thomas grabbed hold of the cane near the coatrack his father had used a few years back after his knee replacement surgery. Holding the cane firmly in one hand, ready to strike, Thomas turned the rusty doorknob and . . .

The figure on the doorstep was all bundled up, their back turned away, facing the yard. At the sound of the door opening, they spun around. Thomas locked eyes with a face: freckled cheeks, strawberry-blonde hair, soft lips.

"Oh, wow, professor. So you're using a cane now? You sore from lifting all those books at Smarty-Pants University?"

"JENI!"

Thomas flung the cane down. Rushing out the door, he threw his arms around Jeni Myers.

"Easy! Easy! You're gonna squeeze all the turkey out of me."

When he was certain he wasn't dreaming, Thomas let go. He shook his head in wonder as flecks of frost whipped around in the lamplight. "But . . . you . . . you said . . ."

Right on cure, Jeni let out a perfect, *devil-may-care* Jeni Myers laugh.

"They gave us a surprise break for a week. I gotta tell you, Thomas, I think I've kicked like a *bajillion* soccer balls. My legs look like they belong to those weird body-builders, you know the ones with the ridiculous spray-on tans?"

"Yeah." Thomas covered his mouth, trying to contain his laughter.

Jeni's blonde eyebrows narrowed. "What?"

"Nothing," said Thomas, leading Jeni into the house. "It's just not what I pictured us talking about when you came home."

"What did you think we were going to talk about? The food over there? Ugh! It's horrible, Thomas. It's all like . . ." Jeni scrunched up her face and stuck out her tongue. "Stewed tomatoes . . . and sausages. Yeah, every meal has sausage sneaked into it, except they call it something clever like 'Bangers and Mash.' Chocolate's the only thing's that edible over there. It's all Cadbury this and Cadbury that, but it blows Hershey's right out of the water." Jeni frowned. "Kind of explains all the dental problems those English people have, though. Oh, man, Thomas. I probably could have sold my old retainer and headgear for the Queen's jewels . . ."

• • •

They found the least moth-eaten sofa in the Viewing Room and sat down. Chatting in hushed tones so no one else in the house might hear, Jeni shared some of the highlights from the past months: how she got revenge on a girl from Ohio named Chelsea Flack, who Jeni had affectionately renamed "Chelsea Buttcrack," she moved to the more important topics that didn't involve slipping extra-strength Robitussin PM into her enemies' coffee or drawing embarrassing shapes on their faces with permanent marker while they slept. Switching from her usual sarcastic tone to her serious, friend voice, Jeni reached over and put her hand on Thomas's.

"Arnold said he wasn't there for the really bad part. "I'm sorry I wasn't there . . . you know . . . to back you up."

"It's okay," said Thomas, staring down at Jeni's moon ring. *She was still wearing it!* The moonstone in the center of the ring gleamed softly against Jeni's pale finger. "I wasn't exactly the nicest guy to you before you left. And, anyway, I did have help."

As if on cue, through a section of wall weeping with wet plaster from a leak Jed had yet to locate, a glowing specter in pinstripes and white gloves suddenly appeared.

Jeni scrunched up her face. "What is it?"

Thomas exhaled a deep sigh. "It's this ghost. We call him Headless Jerry."

"Is he," Jeni whispered, searching the room. "Here with us, like, right now?"

"Yep," said Thomas gloomily.

"What's he doing?"

"He's doing this stupid little . . ." Thomas shook his head. "I don't know. He's been doing it for weeks, trying to get my attention. He makes these shapes with his hands like one of those weirdo mime people."

Jeni furrowed her brow. The laser-eyed look of intense focus Thomas hadn't seen in months returned to Jeni's face. "It's got to mean something, right? I mean, you're this brilliant detective and all. Don't you want to know what he's trying to say?"

Thomas exhaled a huffy breath through his nose. "Fine." He stood up and waved his arms around like an orchestra conductor with ants in his pants. "I was hoping to have a little peace and quiet, but why doesn't Thomas Creeper solve another great puzzle?"

"Okay, Elijah Creeper the Fifth," Jeni snickered.

"Shut up."

Thomas cocked his head and cast Headless Jerry a nasty scowl.

"So," said Jeni, sitting back on the sofa. "What shape is he making now?"

Headless Jerry pressed his gloves together like two halves of an egg.

"I don't know," said Thomas. "I think it's an O." He squinted. "Yeah, it's an O."

"Okay," said Jeni. "What next?"

Headless Jerry made his left hand flat like a karate chop. Placing his right hand up against the chop, he made a backwards C shape with the other hand.

"I think that's a P," said Thomas. "Now he's making—alright, that's definitely a U."

"O-P-U," Jeni spelled out.

Thomas raised his hands in the air. "Jerry, what are you doing now?"

Headless Jerry slithered around.

"You're a snake?"

Headless Jerry shook his shoulders.

"It's one word?"

Headless Jerry shook his shoulders again.

"One letter?"

Headless Jerry jumped up and down and started slithering again.

"The first letter of the word snake?"

The ghost jumped up and down, this time even more excited than before.

Thomas stared off into space. But he was certain of the word now—*dead* certain.

"Opus," said Thomas. "That's what you've been trying to say all this time?"

Headless Jerry got down on his knees and shook his fists in the air.

"What does it mean, Thomas?" Jeni called from the sofa.

Before Thomas could answer Headless Jerry started beckoning them out of the Viewing Room.

"Not sure," said Thomas. "But I think he wants us to follow him."

Jeni shrugged and pushed herself off of the sofa. "Home for a few hours and already I'm on another mystery with you, professor."

"Jeni, we don't have to—"

Jeni grabbed Thomas's elbow and yanked him through the door.

"Trust me, professor." She flashed another fearless Jeni Myers smile. "Right now I'd pay to do anything that doesn't involve a soccer ball. But if your headless buddy is leading us to Gloomsbury High for a pick-up game, then you can find yourself a new best friend, Thomas Creeper."

Thomas grabbed his winter coat from the coatrack. He fit his arms through the wooly sleeves and shouted something down the hallway to his parents about walking Jeni home. A semi-intelligible reply sounded back. Thomas took it as consent.

They weren't more than a few feet off the porch, following Headless Jerry's glowing form into the darkness, when Thomas realized he was smiling. It was the words Jeni had used. *Best friend.* Headless Jerry could lead them into a nest of blood-thirsty spiders for all he cared. It still wouldn't change the fact he was someone's best friend.

Headless Jerry flagged them up Thirty-Fifth to the intersection with Oakwood, the road leading to St. Mary's by the Sea and Gloomsbury Memorial Cemetery. When their supernatural guide didn't stop to turn into the grounds of the church, the destination seemed pretty clear.

"Really? The cemetery?" moaned Jeni.

"Yep," said Thomas. He forced a fake chuckle. "Glad to be home yet?"

"I'd rather get pelted with penalty kicks after eating a pile of overcooked sausages. But, c'mon. Might as well see what your buddy is all up in arms about."

The entrance to the cemetery was padlocked as it always was at night. Headless Jerry oozed through the fence as easily as a knife through butter. Thomas and Jeni weren't so lucky. After searching the grounds for any gaps, they found an opening in a few missing pickets. Jeni reminded Thomas of the dangers of tetanus ("You could end up chomping on your own tongue!"). Carefully, making sure they didn't touch any rusty, sharp parts in the fence, they slipped into the cemetery grounds.

Once inside, Thomas did his best to ignore all the ghosts propping up around them. It was like a receiving line at a wedding . . . if the guests were all ghastly, undead spirits.

"Are there lots of them?" Jeni whispered, huddling closer to Thomas.

"Yeah, but you're fine," Thomas whispered back. "Some pirate looking guy back there took a lunge at you, but I think your moonstone ring scared him off."

"Really?" said Jeni. Her eyes flashed bright in the moonlight. She gritted her teeth. Making a fist with her ring hand, she held the fist out like a gun, aiming it at all the headstones as they passed. "KA-POW, YA DEAD JERKS! SUCK ON SOME MOONSTONE!"

"Yeah, maybe don't do that so much."

Thomas's eyes widened. More ghosts were spilling down the hillside towards them, oozing up out of the ground from the walls of their moss-covered mausoleums.

Jeni lowered her fist, but the intense look on her face stayed. "Just got to let them know they can't pull any funny stuff."

At the top of a hill Thomas and Jeni found Headless Jerry standing in front of a giant mausoleum surrounded by a picketed fence wreathed with cobwebs. All the ghosts that had followed their footsteps seemed to retreat back into the shadows as they approached the mausoleum.

"I don't get it," said Thomas, shaking his head.

"Get what?"

"None of the ghosts want to come near the fence. They're all staying back. I don't think it's because of Headless Jerry."

Headless Jerry bent over and shook his undead rump at all the retreating ghosts. One of the ghosts—a child with a sunken face and a missing arm—pointed up at the mausoleum as he fled, disappearing behind a large, slanted headstone with a bowing angel.

"Well, the gate's open," said Jeni, slipping from Thomas's side and making a few steps towards the fence. "That's probably not good, huh?"

Thomas crept forward. In the keyhole of the lock was a broken key. Not knowing what he was doing, feeling caught in a trance, he reached out.

"Ouch!"

He rubbed his finger. A few drops of blood dotted the tip.

"Hope you're up to date on your shots," said Jeni.

"Wait a minute," said Thomas, examining the key. *The metal was broken away just like* . . . He flashed Jeni a wild, possessed look.

"Okay, psycho. What's up?"

"Do you still have the photo I sent you of those weird metal pieces that fell out of that pill box I told you about?"

"Yeah. Why?" Jeni's mouth dropped open. "So you think . . . Oh, I get it. Hold on." She dug though her jacket until she found her phone. Swiping through her photo library, she came to the picture Thomas had sent her. She held the phone up to his face. Thomas glanced back at the broken key, tracing his finger in the air. He was right. It was the same shape. If he had the pieces glued together, he was sure they would fit perfectly with the other half of the key handle.

"So that guy Cyril," said Jeni. "I mean Korvac *working through* Cyril, he must have—"

"Had a key to this place," said Thomas. "Doesn't explain why a piece of it was in the P.B.O.U.D. unless—"

"Unless that was a trap Korvac set to get you here?" Jeni shook her head. "I don't know, Thomas. Seems iffy."

"We don't have to go in," said Thomas. "Let's see what Headless Jerry won't stop bothering me about. Come on."

Hearing his name, Headless Jerry raised a gloved finger and bolted through the overgrown yard outside the mausoleum. Thomas and Jeni followed with cautious steps. Off to the left, something skittered through the thick, unmowed grass. They kept moving until they reached a large copper door where Headless Jerry was jumping up and down like a madman.

"Alright, you got us here," said Thomas. "So what's the big deal?"

Headless Jerry pointed a gloved finger at the sign over the doorway. The clouds shifted overhead, allowing a little moonlight to stream down. Thomas's mouth felt dry. *It was just like the vision from Korvac's book. One word, bathed in moonlight.*

OPUS.

The vision had only shown Thomas the one word. Now, looking up at the mausoleum, he could see three other words, chiseled into the marble above the door. One of the words was a Roman name, a name Thomas recognized. Reading the words, he felt his skin prickle to gooseflesh.

HADRIAN CROKE OPUS

Headless Jerry made a praying gesture with his gloves. Before Thomas could say anything, Headless Jerry waved and disappeared down through the frost-tipped grass.

"WAIT!" cried Thomas. "WHAT ARE WE SUPPOSED TO DO?"

He wheeled around. But there was no Headless Jerry, just the frightened faces of dozens of other ghosts, peeking out from their hiding places in the shadows.

"He's gone?" said Jeni flatly. "What do you think that's all about?"

"No clue," said Thomas. He looked back at the words over the mausoleum door. "Who the hell is Hadrian Croke Opus? The guy who cut off Jerry's head? I mean, it could be anybody."

"Maybe," said Jeni. "Maybe . . ." Her eyes focused on some indiscriminate spot in the air.

"That's all you have to offer? Maybe?"

Jeni flashed Thomas a dirty look. She went back to her phone and started thumbing through several screens. "What if it's not a real person?"

Now it was Thomas's turn to flash Jeni a dirty look.

"No, idiot," sighed Jeni. "Not a ghost or anything like that. I mean what if the name isn't the *real* name. What if it's a word scramble?"

Thomas stepped back. Jeni ignored his dismay. She had grown accustomed to people underestimating her, even those who should know better.

"Ah! Here it is," she said, holding the phone up to Thomas's face. "It's a pretty sweet app. I use it when I can't get to sleep. It has all these word games and puzzles. There's a word generator where you can plug letters in and scramble them to get other words. It's like Scrabble but on steroids."

Jeni plugged Hadrian Croke Opus into the word generator. There came another rustle in the grass. Thomas turned around. He squinted his eyes. *Nothing.*

"That's weird," said Jeni. "It's not coming up with anything. Oh! Duh. Forgot to change the preferences to include names and stuff. Hold on. There."

"Uh . . . Jen . . ." whispered Thomas.

"Just give me a second."

"Jen, we need to get out of here. NOW!"

It was the shout of *NOW* that made Jeni look up and see the snakes gathering all around them.

One particularly wet and irate snake, the color of tarnished silver, slithered out of a hole in the mausoleum's wall and was flashing its fangs right over Jeni's head.

They took off sprinting. As they flew through the grass, dozens of snakes whipped out, hissing and slithering towards them. Thomas leapt over one snake as thick as his thigh as he made for the opening in the gate.

"Soccer legs, Jen!" he shouted over his shoulder. "Use your soccer legs!"

They slipped through the gate while a snake dug its fangs into Jeni's jacket. She ripped off the jacket and threw it behind her.

"You okay?" Thomas shouted once they were clear of the shadow of the mausoleum.

"I'm fine!" Jeni shouted back. "It didn't get me. I hate that jacket anyway. I left it in our chicken coop. It smells like chicken butt. Not my favorite fragrance."

They booked it down through the mist until they reached the cemetery gates. Thomas peered back through the darkness, broken here and there by moonlight. He heaved a sigh of relief. *No snakes.*

He helped Jeni through the gap in the pickets and climbed through after her. They turned and stared back at the frightening backdrop of the cemetery veiled with fog. Suddenly, there came a sharp ping from Jeni's phone.

"Uh, Thomas?" said Jeni. "It came up with a scramble."

Thomas leaned in. "What does it say?"

In the light of the cellphone Jeni's freckled face was drained of all color. "Two of the words are highlighted in green. Green means *archaic*, you know, *ye olde English*. Or Latinate."

"Latinate?" said Thomas. "Who's the professor now?"

"Shut up, nerd-turd." Jeni passed the phone over to Thomas. "Here. See for yourself."

Thomas took the phone and held the screen up to his face. A dry taste filled his mouth. His stomach roiled. Jeni was right. It *was* a word scramble, perhaps the most clever scramble ever, hidden right there in plain sight.

Jeni covered her mouth.

"That's not his—"

"Yep," said Thomas. "C'mon. Let's get out of here."

They left the cemetery gate and headed down through the shadows cast by the old oak trees. When they got to the church, Jeni stopped and clamped her hand on Thomas's shoulder again.

"Swear to me, Thomas. Swear to me you won't go back there again. At least not while I'm gone."

Thomas felt a sharp pinch through his coat sleeve. "Fine! Okay! I swear."

"Don't lie to me, Thomas Creeper," Jeni waved her fist, her moonstone ring sparkling against his pale skin. "Remember, even ghosts are scared of me. Think of what this ring could do to the living."

Lowering her fist, Jeni flashed Thomas her trademark smile. She pulled him by the elbow and they continued on through the fog and mist. As they walked on, Thomas listened to Jeni going on about more incidents involving snotty girls at her soccer program in Germany, but he wasn't listening . . . not really.

He was thinking about the mausoleum.

In his ear he could almost hear the low, rumbling voice of Herodain Pius Korvac—or Hadrian Croke Opus—as he had scrambled his name, hiding his tomb in plain sight in Gloomsbury Memorial Cemetery.

Thomas rubbed his chest. Like a wound that was still tender, he could almost feel the gloved fingers of Cyril Barnes' skeleton as he pushed him through the hole in the Anchorage, out into empty air. Thomas had dreamt the scene more than once since that horrible day in September. His homeschooling coursework and all the miserable tasks around the funeral home had provided welcomed distractions from the image that replayed in his brain whenever his mind strayed back to that day, the day he died and was brought back. A sizzling, screaming skeleton, rushing towards him . . .

He'd made a promise to Jeni. Whatever they were, best friends, or something even greater than that, he had to keep his word. That was what honorable people did. And Jeni was right: ghosts *were* probably scared of her. Jeni Myers was a force to be reckoned with, like tropical hurricanes or freak hail storms in the middle of July. She was exactly the kind of person you wanted by your side when the terrible turned terrifying.

They walked back through the cobblestoned streets to Jeni's home in the Uppercrust. Neither one of them said much. It felt good to walk with someone whose connection went beyond words. At Jeni's doorstep, she turned back.

"Not really how I planned my first night back," she said, rubbing her shoulders and exhaling a few frosty breaths in the light of the porch lamps. "But I guess that's a normal day for Thomas Creeper."

"I guess," said Thomas, laughing a little. "Hey, you didn't say how long you were—"

The kiss on Thomas's lips was warm, perhaps the only warm thing in the whole frosty night.

"Happy Thanksgiving, Thomas Creeper."

Jeni smiled and turned for the door. Before she grabbed the handle she looked back.

"Sal's tomorrow?"

Two words had never sounded so wonderful.

"Yeah!" Thomas called back. "That would be awesome."

Jeni smiled again before slipping back into the house.

Thomas walked the four blocks home feeling ten feet tall. Even the bloodthirsty snakes that had tried to kill them only minutes ago seemed far away. He tiptoed back into his own house—no way he was going to answer questions from his mother about the night—and padded up the steps to his bedroom. He sat back down on his bed and shook his head. He couldn't stop smiling. *When was the last time that had happened?*

Looking up, he caught a faint glow across the room. Trixie and Gabe were standing by his closet.

And there was someone else—*something* else.

A gleaming rat sat on Trixie's shoulder. Thomas's heart leapt.

"Yep," said Trixie, turning her head and smiling. "Facto's been waiting for you. You sure do have a lot of friends, Thomas."

The ghost-rat jumped off Trixie's shoulder and skittered across the room. Blinking its wet, curious eyes, it cocked its head and gazed up at Thomas before settling on his shoe. A chill went through his sneaker all the way to his toes, but Thomas was happy. Whether Byron believed in ghosts or not, he was sure the old man would be happy to know his friend still lived on in some mysterious way.

"Listen," said Trixie. "I know you don't believe in the whole angel business, but Gabe and I figured it all out. Why we're still here, I mean. It's because of this song. I know the words now. They came to me tonight. And I realized something. It wasn't

Jefferson, my fiancé, I was looking for. It was you, Thomas. I'm supposed to share the song with you."

Gabe gave a short blow on the cornet and nodded his goatee. He was ready.

"Go grab a pen and paper," said Trixie. "You need to write this down. It's like the order of things here in Gloomsbury. You're gonna need to know it going forward."

"Going forward?" said Thomas. "What do you mean, I don't—"

"Just get a pen," said Trixie, narrowing her fine, dark eyebrows. "Trust me."

Thomas got off the bed and went over to his desk. He rifled through a drawer until he found a pen and a pad of paper. When he looked up again, Facto was sitting on the desk, blinking up at him.

"I meant what I said," said Trixie. "I love you, bub, even if you don't deserve it with all your moping around and treating me like cra—"

"Hey, I don't—"

"Let me finish. I don't know what's going to happen next." Gabe reached out an placed an arm on Trixie's shoulder. "But I think I've seen it, Thomas. The next place. It's like waking up every day on the first day of summer like you're still a little kid, and you know there's nothing, nothing ahead of you but time to do whatever you want." Tears started rolling down Trixie's pale cheeks, but she didn't stop. "I don't know what it means, or if it lasts like . . . you know . . . forever. I guess I'll have to see for myself. Now write these words down I'm gonna sing to you. Gabe calls it 'Messenger Blues'."

"That's right," said Gabe, stroking his goatee. "It's all there, Thomas. I swear."

"Okay, Gabe." Trixie closed her eyes and fluttered her fingers against the sides of her hips. "Hit it, man."

Sweet, swinging notes poured from Gabe's cornet. Thomas held the pen between his trembling fingers, all the while keeping one eye fixed on Trixie. As her beautiful voice filled the room, she began to fade like glimmers of a dream and Gabe along with her. The music drifted away, but Thomas caught every last word. By the end of the song, all that was left of the two ghosts was a faint silver transparency, softly burning out. Only Facto remained behind, watching the strange scene with curious, thoughtful eyes.

Thomas stood up from his desk. He ran over to Trixie. He reached out his hand . . . his fingers passed through Trixie's. The nerve-numbing chill was gone. *He could feel her.* For a moment she was there and warm again, like an errant summer breeze that passes with the grace that moves and warms others, but is never quite understood.

Messenger Blues

Dictated to Thomas Creeper by
Patricia "Trixie" Wheelwright

Hey, Horn Man
Blow on high!
Play that tune
Of Love gone by!

This wounded world
This dead old town
This paradise spoiled
Hellfire come down

It's a dream between
The living, the dead
A secret scene
In the Fixer's head

Now comes Death
All before us
But angels' breath
Shall ring the Chorus:

You messenger
You mover
You heart of gold!
You angel
You devil
You spirit bold!

Perry Peripheral
The Sideman
Only see him at a glance
Shifters and Oozers
Slippin' at every chance

But for the Strayback
The Standback!
The Delayer at the Door!
Even the Horn Man trembles
His next notes ain't so sure

What a town!
What a world!
What a mixed up dream!
But don't the kill the messenger, baby—
They're just things I've seen

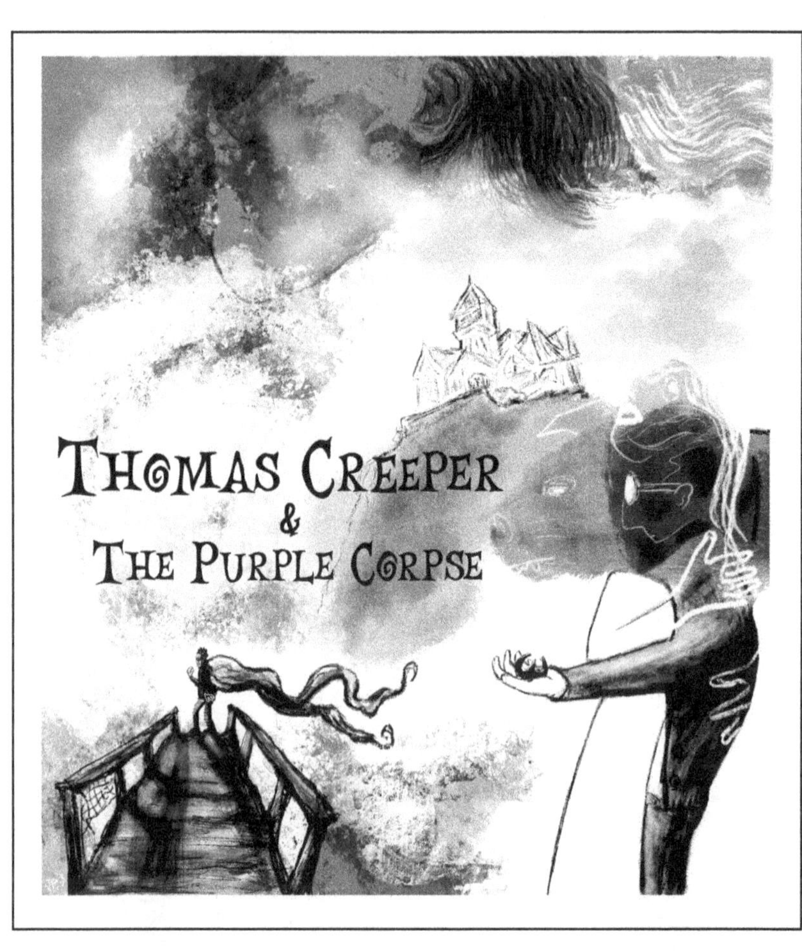
THOMAS CREEPER
&
THE PURPLE CORPSE

Preview

Thomas Creeper and The Funicular Fiasco

It's springtime in Gloomsbury: moldy, wet, and miserable. Breaking up the monotonous calendar of homeschool assignments and work in the Preparing Room is the announcement by Thomas's father that Thomas will be joining him for the 200th assembly of the UCFP, the United Coalition of Funerary Professionals. The site chosen for the momentous anniversary is the same as the Coalition's first meeting two centuries ago—a remote hunting lodge turned resort in the Alps, accessible only by funicular transport.

When a blood clot is discovered during Mr. Creeper's annual physical, he's quickly ruled out for travel. An unlikely and potentially dangerous chaperone steps in: Thomas's uncle Jed. Warily, with the greatest misgivings, Thomas's father accepts Jed's offer. After almost missing their flight due to Jed's carousing in the airport bar, Thomas and Jed arrive at the resort only to suffer horrible altitude sickness.

While recovering, Thomas learns from two ghosts—twins—that all is not well at the resort. On a trip down to the base of the mountain, Thomas looks across at the opposite funicular and spies a strange figure leering back at him. Dressed in antique clothes and wearing a silver "replacement nose" worn by victims of disease in the 18th and 19th centuries, the figure reaches out their hand . . . Thomas's throat constricts. The hand pulls back. The stranger vanishes.

The next morning a few members of the Coalition go missing, their belongings left in their rooms. Other members start to go mad, tormented by a figure matching the description of Thomas's stranger with the silver replacement nose. Soon Thomas is embroiled in a new mystery, one that will test him to the limit, and take him to the edge of precipices both illusory and as real as the hazardous alpine peaks that surround him.

Classroom Discussion: *Spot* Check

In *Thomas Creeper and the Purple Corpse*, several Latin words appear, some in *italics*, others interspersed more seamlessly throughout the text, so seamlessly you might not even notice them.

And that's because we use them every day.

It's estimated that anywhere from forty to sixty percent of the words we use today come from Latin. Whether you know it or not, words like "bonus," "extra," "intro," and "impromptu" are all ripped directly from the language of Cicero, Caesar, and Augustus, that devious master of propaganda. Language is a curious thing. An army can conquer a capital, replace a flag with their own, but after all the fighting and booms and busts of fortune, words are the true soldiers that live on. The French king Louis XIV once had the Latin phrase *Ultimo Ratio Regum*—"the last argument of kings"—chiseled into his cannons. But even rich Louie didn't know that all his cannons would never outlive the power of language and ideas to circulate, and keep circulating, with or without the permission of kings.

Can you spot-check all the Latin words and phrases that appear in this book? Both the *italicized* ones and the more seamlessly interspersed ones?

Here's a short list to get you started: *moratorium, emeritus, opus, per se, effluvia, tribulus, res novae, damnatio memoriae* . . .

Ms. Katz's Reading Nook ("Shhhhhh! Books Are Sleeping!")

SALUTATIONS, BOOKWORMS!

I had the great pleasure of catching up with J.R. Potter this week at Gloomsbury Memorial Library. Mad Marge must have got up on the wrong side of the heavenly bed, because we lost power and had to break out the candles. Oh, wonderful Gloomsbury living. Said no one ever!

I, for one, have been clamoring for someone to record Thomas's exploits for ages. I'm so glad Mr. Potter has finally taken notice. So, fellow bookworms, feast your digestive juices on these tantalizing tomes that will be great secondary reading after *Thomas Creeper and the Purple Corpse*. And remember: a book is a passport to a new world. Floods, pandemics, and the occasional onslaught of giant ants (SEE Book Three, passages 102 to 105 in Herodotus's *Histories*) will never stop the mind from roaming where the heart wishes to follow. Keep reading and keep dreaming. Your dreams are the fuel of the future, my friends.

Hot pickles,

Ms. K

Post-script from the author: *Thank you, Ms. K, for such a lovely time at the library. Again, I'd like to stress that it was a new canker sore that kept me from trying your delicious tea. How the tea makers were able to reproduce the smell of old brussels sprouts mixed with oysters is truly a feat worthy of a Michelin star. Warmest regards, JRP*

Here's a short bibliography I drew up to whet the appetites of you ravenous bookworms out there!—Cheers, Ms. K

A History of the Roman People by Allen M. Ward, Fritz M. Heichelheim, and Cedric A. Yeo, Routledge, 7th edition, 2019.

Catiline's War, the Jugurthine War, Histories by Sallust, Penguin Books, 2008.

Rubicon: The Last Years of the Roman Republic by Tom Holland, Anchor Books, 2003.

Selected Works by Cicero, Penguin Books, 1977.

The Norton Book of Classical Literature edited by Bernard Knox, W.W. Norton & Company, 1993.

The Last Generation of the Roman Republic by Erich S. Gruen, University of California Press, 1974.

The Twelve Caesars by Suetonius, Dover Publications, 2018.

Emperors of Rome a great—and free!—podcast on Roman History currently on Apple Music and Spotify featuring the brilliant Dr. Rhiannon Evans from La Trobe University in Australia. If the history of Rome is dominated by egotistical men, this podcast goes beyond this well-known trope to bring to light stories of powerful women like Livia Drusilla, first empress of Rome, and Agrippina the Younger, mother of the invidious emperor and wannabe rock star, Nero.

Acknowledgements

A book is not something created by a monk in a cell. Not anymore, at least. It's the magical by-product of many laboring souls who come together across vast distances to believe in a story and will it a home in the world.

There were a lot of pitfalls in the journey of Thomas Creeper's second adventure and some very dark days indeed. But, like a rare sun sighting in Gloomsbury, joy won out in the end. Thank you to my family and my loving partner, Amy, for sticking by me through changing contracts and changing morale. *Kudos* must be heaped upon the brilliant Jessica Fassler, who went beyond her task as first proofreader to offer criticism and feedback that helped shape the novel in its primordial stage, a stage when writers so often lose hope (and face). To my fellow Krakens, Jude Atwood and Marcie Roman, brilliant beta readers who caught many errors and made crucial edit suggestions, I am eternally grateful, especially to Marcie's plea about a certain bumbling rat. Thank you, Roxana Coumans, for providing excellent final proofreading at the eleventh hour.

If Dickinson said "hope is the thing with feathers – that perches in the soul," then a book is a hopeful thing with pages that perches on a shelf. I'm so grateful to the steadfast and supportive community of Thomas Creeper readers around the globe; the amazing Slater family for their incredible support and for hosting Thomas's first big book release at their magical vineyard Slater Run in my hometown of Upperville; my first Thomas Creeper reviewer and long-time friend from Canada, ukemaster Diane Woolfenden; parents who read to their children like Kim Piersig; indefatigable and dynamic teachers like Nicole Jorge and Carla Meyrink at the Community for Learning in Santo Domingo; and Sarah Buxton, Jennifer Young-Beccaris, and Nora Griffin-Snipes at Newtown Friends School in Pennsylvania; wonder-curating librarians across the world; kind and supportive booksellers like Jamie McCauley at RJ Julia Booksellers who took a chance on Thomas Creeper right from the start. You've all helped me set this adventurous book up to roost. May it sing its bewildering song for many years to come.

About the Author

Photo credit: Alyona Vogelmann

J.R. Potter is the award-winning author and illustrator of the Thomas Creeper series about a reluctant mortician's apprentice turned detective for the dead. *Thomas Creeper and the Gloomsbury Secret*, Potter's debut novel, won the 2019 Kraken Prize for Middle Grade Fiction and is now featured in libraries from San Francisco to Saudi Arabia and included in two teaching curricula in the United States and the Dominican Republic. His graphic novel work has been published by Image Comics, and his short fiction has appeared in *The Portland Review* and various fiction anthologies. When not working on the next *Thomas Creeper* mystery, Potter writes and illustrates teen fiction for educational publishers Pioneer Valley Books and Heinemann Publishing, helping to boost literacy, empathy, and wonder in schools across the world.

Note from the Author

Word-of-mouth is crucial for any author to succeed. If you enjoyed *Thomas Creeper and the Purple Corpse*, please leave a review online—anywhere you are able. Even if it's just a sentence or two. It would make all the difference and would be very much appreciated.

All heart,
J.R. Potter

Printed in the USA
CPSIA information can be obtained
at www.ICGtesting.com
JSHW022334161023
50254JS00001B/8

9 781685 132132